When Love Becomes Fantasy . . .
When Secrets Become
Dangerous . . .

Romance, Inc.

CAROLINE SHAW—Even in the turmoil and poverty of her childhood, she had a vision of the glittering life of the very rich through her visits to The Breakers. But when she married, it was for love, not money—a love so idyllic, the gods must have become jealous, and so destroyed it. Heart-broken, impoverished, and despised by her husband's family, Caroline—as beautiful as a tragic princess—decided to fight her way to success with a dream called Romance, Inc. . . .

JAMES GODDARD—He wasn't born with a silver spoon in his mouth—in the Goddard family, the spoons were solid gold. Brought up in privilege, surrounded by wealth, this generous, blond Adonis was ready to walk away from it all to be a simple craftsman in Maine . . . and to be with the girl he loved with all his young, doomed heart. . . .

CHARLES GODDARD—Head of the Goddard dynasty, his ruthlessness was eclipsed only by his ambition. Nothing escaped his control, or his wrath—not his icily perfect wife, the reckless son-in-law whose murder he arranged, or his only son James's pretty widow, Caroline, whose child would become the prize he had to possess at any cost. . . .

COUNTESS TAMARA BRANDT—A mysterious, glamorous, and brilliant businesswoman, she made her boutique, L'Elegance, into one of the poshest stores on Palm Beach's Worth Avenue. But her biggest challenge was to take the gawky, overweight young Caroline Shaw and turn her into a stylish beauty . . . and give her what money couldn't buy. A friend . . .

JEAN-CLAUDE FONTAINE—A tall, breathtakingly handsome celebrity chef and bestselling cookbook author, his ego was enormous, his personality fiery, and his appeal to women notorious. But it was his French sensuality that would thaw Caroline's frozen heart and let her feel the pleasures of loving and being loved again. . . .

CLIFFORD HAMLIN—The dark prince of Wall Street, he was a gambler who loved to take risks and reap the rewards. His own life was a rags-to-riches story, and Caroline Shaw attracted his interest as no other woman ever had. But now he was working for Charles Goddard, who was out to destroy the very woman he wanted to protect. . . .

BRETT HAAS—The baseball superstar was everything Caroline hated in a man—crude, womanizing, full of himself—as well as good-hearted, fearless, funny, and dazzlingly handsome. She consented to see him only because her small son, Jack, idolized the recently retired ballplayer. But Haas didn't play fair, broke the rules, and intended to win . . . her body and her heart. . . .

JOCELYN RAINES

POCKET BOOKS
New York London Toronto Sydney Tokyo Singapore

An *Original* Publication of POCKET BOOKS

POCKET BOOKS, a division of Simon & Schuster Inc.
1230 Avenue of the Americas, New York, NY 10020

ISBN: 0-671-89953-8

First Pocket Books printing February 1996

10 9 8 7 6 5 4 3 2 1

Cover design by James A. Lebbad

Printed in the U.S.A.

To the two Michaels

Prologue

Lake Worth, Florida

At just after eleven on the second Sunday morning of March, Caroline Shaw tiptoed out of the house that had never felt like a home. She moved stealthily, almost furtively, knowing from experience just which creaking floorboards to avoid, and she opened the front door quietly. Her mother had already left for church, and she was careful not to rouse her father. Saturday night was Al Shaw's binge night, Caroline knew, and Sunday was the day to get out of the house and stay out of his way.

"Your father needs his rest on Sundays," Caroline's mother always said, forever trying to explain away her husband's escapes into the bottle. "He works hard and gets very tired."

He drinks hard and gets very drunk, Caroline would think to herself, amazed at her mother's capacity for self-delusion. Ever since the accident that had robbed him of the use of his right hand, her father worked only sporadically. He had become desperately bitter and self-pitying, and his black moods terrorized his wife and daughter. But no matter how violent Al Shaw became, no matter how abusive, how distant, Mary Shaw maintained that he was merely temporarily down on his luck—a basically good man whose only problem was time. In time, Mary said, he'd feel better about himself. In time he'd find a well-paying job. In time he'd transform himself back into the man she'd married.

"You didn't know him the way he was, the way he used to be," Mary Shaw told her daughter. "Al Shaw was the handsomest man in town. Swept me right off my feet. And sweet? He never raised a hand to me. Not then."

"But he raises a hand to you *now,"* Caroline would point out, not meaning to be cruel to her mother. Just hoping to make Mary Shaw face reality, as *she* had, ever since she was a little girl. But while Caroline was wise and knowing well beyond her fifteen years, her mother continued to live in a fantasy world, a world where she was still young and pretty and Al Shaw didn't raise a hand to anyone.

"What happens between your father and me is private, Caroline," Mary would say. "Between married couples. I don't interfere in your life at school. You mustn't interfere in my life with your father."

Caroline *wanted* her mother to interfere in her life at school, yearned for the attention. But Mary Shaw was so busy with her job, so consumed with trying to appease her demanding husband, that sometimes the kids half wondered if Caroline even had a mother.

"Private?" said Caroline. "You think what he does to you is private? I can hear him hitting you. I can hear you crying."

"He doesn't mean it," Mary insisted.

"Then why does he do it?"

"Because he's frustrated that he can't do his woodworking. Things have been difficult for him ever since the accident."

The accident. Always the accident. It was Al Shaw's Big Excuse.

Children often find creative ways to escape a troubled family life, and Caroline Shaw was no exception. As a lonely, unpopular teenager, who was shunned by her schoolmates because of her chubbiness, her awkwardness, her unfashionable clothes, and her antisocial parents, she found refuge not in television shows or movies or books but in good grades and hard work—and on Sundays. For on Sundays she fled to The Breakers, the grand, legendary hotel where her mother worked as a bookkeeper.

Ever since the day she'd first visited Mary Shaw at work, she'd been mesmerized by the magic of The Breakers and began making Sunday pilgrimages to the Palm Beach landmark, with its soaring, frescoed ceilings, its priceless antiques, and its well-dressed guests. To her the hotel was a fairy land, and the people in it characters from a fairy tale. Caroline had never seen such good manners, such easy smiles, such self-assurance.

No one—except her mother—knew of her secret trips there. Not her father, who sneered at her dreams and accused her of "putting on airs." Not Evelyn Addams, who owned Evelyn's Nicknacks, the gift shop where Caroline worked after school. And not her schoolmates, who already thought her weird and never hesitated to tell her so.

Sometimes Caroline stayed in the lobby, sitting in one of the ornate chairs, trying to imagine a life without loud curses, frightening threats, relentless criticism. Other times she wandered down to the beach and gazed at the people sunning and swimming and sipping cool drinks in frosted glasses. She listened to them as they spoke to each other in quiet tones, talking about last night's party, today's tennis game, tomorrow's shopping expedition to Worth Avenue. *What would it be like to be one of them?* she asked herself. What would it be like to be treated nicely? To have a sense of security and peace and well-being? To know that you belonged and weren't considered peculiar and didn't have to be afraid?

What would it be like? Caroline wondered. She held back the tears that pricked behind her eyes as she witnessed the enormous gulf between their lives and hers.

Caroline got off the bus that sparkling March morning and walked the rest of the way to The Breakers. With each step, she put Patterson Avenue farther behind her. Yet as she made her way down the hotel's long, palm tree-lined driveway, she looked around her, glancing from right to left, from left to right, feeling a catch of apprehension in her throat. She didn't belong and she knew it. Anyone looking at her in her cheap, poorly fitting clothes and worn shoes would know it, too. She was an intruder at The Breakers, out of place and out of her league. What if someone notices me, she asked herself, and doesn't believe me when I say that my mother works here? What if someone sends me away?

She entered the lobby and began her ritual. She stood up very straight and pretended that she was an orphaned heiress. Then she began to circle the vast space. She admired the rich furnishings, the impressive tapestries, the handsome rugs. She wondered if the teardrops that hung from the glittering chandeliers might even be diamonds because of the way they caught the light and threw it back in a magic array of colors. She was reaching out to touch one of the polished tables when a voice startled her.

"Did you know that it took twelve hundred workers to build The Breakers?"

Caroline turned around to find a young woman looking down at her. She was blond and dressed in a chic, light cornflower blue linen suit that matched the color of her eyes. Caroline caught the scent of a delicate, refined perfume. The woman was only seven or eight years older than Caroline but seemed light-years older in terms of confidence and style and experience.

"I wasn't harming the table, really I wasn't," Caroline managed, sure that she was about to be put out.

Instead of scolding and shaming her, the woman smiled.

"I could see that you weren't," she said. "I only wanted to give you some background on the hotel since you seem to enjoy coming here. I've seen you here before."

Caroline turned hot and scarlet, ashamed of herself, ashamed of her dreams, the dreams her father ridiculed as "uppity" and "stupid." Her secret wasn't secret any longer.

"My name is Francesca Palen," the woman told Caroline, introducing herself. "I'm an assistant in the hotel's public relations department."

Caroline didn't know what a public relations department was, but it didn't matter. It seemed official and important, and she liked the sound of it. "My name is Caroline Shaw. My mom works here."

"Really? What's her name?"

"Mary. Mary Shaw. She's worked in the business office for over five years," Caroline said proudly. "She says it's okay to come here on Sundays when she's not here, as long as I don't disturb anyone."

Francesca smiled again. She knew Mary Shaw all too well. She had heard some of the staff make fun of the dour woman who wore cheap, heavy jewelry and kept to herself.

So this young girl was Mary Shaw's daughter, she thought, and felt an immediate wave of tenderness toward Caroline.

"You're not disturbing anyone. We like to have well-mannered young people here," Francesca Palen said. There was something about the girl—her obvious sadness and the sense of isolation that she projected along with her evident appreciation of beauty and admiration of her surroundings—that intrigued Francesca. "Has your mom told you very much about The Breakers?"

"No, she hasn't," said Caroline. All her mother had ever said was that The Breakers was very expensive and that people like the Shaws didn't belong there.

"Did you know that it's absolutely unique?" Caroline shook her head and Francesca continued. "There's no other hotel like it in the whole world. Its design is based on two famous buildings: the Villa Medici in Rome and a magnificent palazzo in Genoa."

Caroline's eyes opened wide. A villa! A palazzo! She wasn't exactly sure what the words meant but they spoke of another world, one in which people were happy and didn't hurt each other.

"Would you like the official tour?" Francesca Palen asked.

"Would I!" Caroline exclaimed. Her mother had never offered to show her around the hotel.

Francesca took Caroline by the hand and showed her the hotel's boutiques with their luxurious merchandise; the Florentine and Circle dining rooms with their stiff linen, gleaming silver, and sparkling crystal; the tennis club across the street; the clubhouse overlooking the golf course; even one of the large, oceanfront suites.

"Presidents have stayed here. So have kings and queens," said Francesca, walking Caroline down one of the opulently appointed corridors.

"It's just like a fairy tale," said Caroline.

"It's hard to believe this hotel burned down, isn't it?" Francesca asked as they walked to the elevator.

"Burned down?" replied Caroline, shocked. Everything was so perfect. And everything looked as if it had been there forever.

Francesca nodded. "The whole building burned to the

ground—twice, as a matter of fact. First in 1903. Then again in 1925."

Caroline listened carefully as Francesca spoke of the terrible flames and utter destruction. She imagined the fire, the smoke, the ashes, and rubble and thought how the buildings looked strong and indestructible today, as if they'd always been that way.

"As you can see, the entire structure's been completely rebuilt, restored, and fireproofed," Francesca said, offering to show Caroline her office. "It was a lot of work, but it was worth it, wasn't it?"

Caroline didn't answer. She didn't have to. Her response shone in the wonderment in her eyes and the delighted glow on her face.

They took the elevator to the mezzanine and Francesca showed Caroline into an outer office that served as the reception area for the three more spacious offices around the corner. One of them, the smallest, was Francesca's.

"The slave quarters," Francesca said with a wry smile.

Caroline's eyes widened. Francesca's office, what she called the slave quarters, was twice the size of her bedroom! Caroline looked around at the orderly desk, the comfortable chairs, and newly upholstered leather sofa. She thought that she could happily move in and live there forever.

"What are all these?" Caroline asked, pointing to the array of products on the desk, each monogrammed "The Breakers" in elegant gold lettering. There were soaps, shampoos, bottles of toilet water, lacy hand towels, silk scarves, and an ashtray in the shape of a shell.

"They're samples of special merchandise for VIPs," said Francesca. "We like to pamper our guests. We want them to keep coming back."

How intelligent, Caroline thought. *Make the guests feel pampered and they'll keep coming back.* It made perfect sense. She gently fingered the monogrammed scarf on the desk and couldn't recall ever touching anything so smooth, so silky.

"Take it," said Francesca.

Caroline pulled her hand away from the scarf.

"Take it?" she asked. Rarely had anyone given her anything.

"Sure. As a souvenir. Come on, it's yours, Caroline."

Francesca draped the scarf around her neck and carefully arranged the folds to show the green and gold pattern on a white background. When she was finished, she stood back and admired the effect and then showed Caroline how she looked in a mirror on the back of the office door. "You're going to be a knockout in a few years, you know that?"

Caroline shrugged and looked down at the floor. No one had ever said anything like that to her. She knew what she looked like: that she was awkward and overweight and badly dressed, and that the home permanents her mother gave her dried her hair and caused it to frizz. Her bitten fingernails made her so self-conscious about her hands that she tried to keep them hidden. She also knew that the way she looked reflected the way she felt: ragged and sad inside, and sometimes very angry, too, feelings that had nothing to do with being a knockout or even halfway presentable.

"You may not think so now, but wait until you grow into yourself," said Francesca, who could see that Caroline had beautiful features; that someday, when she lost a few pounds and did something about her hair and developed a sense of style, she would, indeed, turn heads. "The boys will be lining up," she added with a smile.

Caroline shook her head. The only time boys noticed her was when they wanted to borrow her homework.

"Oh, gee," said Francesca suddenly, as she looked at her watch. "I've got to get downstairs. Charles Goddard is checking in this afternoon. I've got to make sure everything goes smoothly."

"Who's Charles Goddard?" Caroline asked.

"He owns Goddard-Stevens," Francesca said, obviously impressed.

Caroline looked blank.

"It's one of the top stock brokerage firms in the country," Francesca explained. "Their executives are having a meeting here, so Mr. Goddard is staying overnight, even though he owns a very grand estate just around the corner."

Caroline nodded, even though she had never heard of

Charles Goddard. She grew sad suddenly, realizing that her visit with Francesca Palen was coming to an end.

"We'll see each other again." Francesca smiled, as if reading Caroline's mind. "Next time let me know when you're coming ahead of time. That way, I can order us some tea."

"I'd like that," said Caroline shyly. "Are you sure I can keep the scarf?" She tightened her grip on the square of silk in her hand. "You said the merchandise with The Breakers on it is for VIPs, like Mr. Goddard."

"It is," said Francesca as she winked at Caroline. "You're what I would call a VIP-in-training."

Caroline wasn't precisely sure what the young woman meant, but she sensed that it was a compliment. And, as she hadn't had many compliments in her fifteen years, she savored it. All the way back to Lake Worth.

Al Shaw was awake when Caroline let herself into the small house on Patterson Avenue. There was a beer can in his left hand, a cigarette smoldering in an ashtray, and a wrestling match blaring on the television.

"Where the hell have you been?" he asked.

"I was over at Sally Cunningham's," Caroline lied, quickly stuffing the silk scarf into her purse to protect it from him. "We were planning our science project."

"What did you do? Split the atom?" Al Shaw's bloodshot eyes mocked her, and Caroline wondered what it would be like to have a father who didn't drink or chain-smoke, a father who smelled of soap and shampoo, a father who wanted to know about her science project and might even offer to help her with it.

"Mom home?" she asked.

"In the kitchen, making dinner."

"I'll go and help her," said Caroline, "as soon as I drop my purse upstairs." She went up to her room, retrieved the scarf from her purse, rested it on the bed, and smoothed it out. Then she folded it carefully and laid it gently in her top dresser drawer. It was the nicest thing she had ever owned, and she would never let anything happen to it.

"Hurry it up, would'ja, Mary? I'm hungry," Al Shaw shouted, his voice carrying up to Caroline's bedroom.

Please, no. Don't let anything happen, prayed Caroline, crossing her fingers. She could never predict what her father would do. Sometimes he would yell at her mother and then, the next minute, quietly help set the table. Other times he would mutter to himself, have another beer, pass out on the living room sofa, and leave Caroline and her mother to eat alone, careful not to talk, careful not to wake him up. Still other times he would curse and threaten and ignore his wife's pleas for him to stop. *Just let him be nice this time,* Caroline thought. *Please.*

"For Christ's sake, Mary! We eating or not? I'm starved," Al Shaw shouted again. Caroline could hear kitchen noises: the rustle of a cellophane bag, the clatter of a frying pan, the sound of the refrigerator door opening and closing.

"Dinner'll be ready in a jiffy," Caroline heard her mother say. "I'm making your favorite, Al. Chicken-fried steak and french fries."

"Chicken-fried steak? Again?" Al yelled.

Caroline was still upstairs when she heard the kitchen door bang, then a smash, followed by a tinkle of glass. Her father had thrown something. There was a moment of silence, then an anguished voice.

"Please, Al. Don't," Caroline heard her mother wail.

Then she heard her father start to shout, yelling at her mother that she was useless and lazy. It was so unfair, Caroline thought. Her mother was the one with the steady job. What right did he have to call her useless and lazy?

Caroline ran to the top of the stairs and debated with herself about what to do. Her mother had forbidden her to interfere in these fights. But how could she stand by while her father was hitting her mother? As Caroline hesitated, trying to decide whether or not to disobey, she heard her father's voice again. This time louder and angrier.

"You've fed me chicken-fried steak three nights in a row," Al bellowed at his wife.

"But that's what you said you wanted," Mary Shaw said.

"I did not! And don't talk back to me!"

Caroline heard a slap, then the sound of a scuffle and a crash as something—probably a kitchen chair—fell over.

"Al, don't!" she heard her mother scream.

There was the sound of metal crashing against something with a dull, sickening *thud.* Caroline's stomach lurched inside her. She had heard that sound before, and she knew what it meant.

Caroline ran down the stairs, through the tiny front hall, and across the small, shabby living room. She stopped at the kitchen door and peeked in. Her mother was backing away from her father, her hands held up in front of her bleeding face, trying to ward off his blows as he brought the heavy, cast-iron frying pan down over her head a second time.

"No! Please, Al!" her mother screamed as blood streamed down from her hairline and into her face. The screams, the threats, the blood seemed to mean nothing to Al Shaw. He brought his arm up, about to strike his wife again. *He's going to kill her,* Caroline thought. *This time he's going to kill her!*

"Stop it!" Caroline screamed, shoving her father from behind and causing him to lose his balance just long enough for her mother to edge around him and escape into the living room.

Leaving her father staggering in the kitchen, Caroline raced to the telephone on the table in the small entrance-way, picked up the receiver, and dialed the police.

"Please come quickly," she whispered into the phone.

"What the fuck is that?" she heard her father yell just as the police dispatcher was asking her to speak up.

"Thirty-nine Patterson Avenue," Caroline said quickly to the operator as Al Shaw stormed into the hallway, grabbed the phone out of Caroline's trembling hand, and threw it against the wall.

"You little bitch," he shouted, then slapped her hard across the mouth. Her lip split and she could taste blood. "You called the cops, didn't you? Didn't you?"

He slapped her again. Harder this time. He was coming toward her, his arm raised to strike again.

Caroline looked wildly around the tiny room. She had to protect herself and her mother, had to find a weapon. She backed into the living room and pushed her mother into the bathroom and shut the door behind her so that she would be safe. At least for the time being.

Her father followed Caroline, his fists raised against her. He stumbled drunkenly over the coffee table, and magazines, the ashtray, a flashlight, a vase of plastic flowers flew to the carpet. He cursed and righted himself, then threw a punch at Caroline. She jumped back, picked up the ashtray, and heaved it at her father, who ducked just in time. The ashtray landed on the floor, scattering sparks from his cigarette onto the carpet. Al ignored them and lunged across the room, grabbing the heavy metal flashlight. He came toward Caroline, the flashlight in his upraised hand, his face red, his mouth agape. She could smell the alcohol and the cigarettes as he came toward her. Then he suddenly stumbled again, almost fell, and dropped the flashlight. Caroline dove for it, wrestling with her father, fighting for the weapon, struggling for her very life. Suddenly, hands tore at her and knocked the flashlight out of her grasp. It was Mary Shaw, and she was sobbing.

"Stop! Both of you!" she cried, pulling first at Al, then at Caroline. She could no longer deny that her husband was out of control; that her daughter was in grave danger; and that if she continued to pretend that all was well at 39 Patterson Avenue, somebody might get badly hurt. "Al, please try to calm down."

"Get out of my way," he growled, enraged by her feeble attempts at peacemaking. He raised his fist in his wife's direction. Mary Shaw saw the threat and hesitated for a moment. Just then, Caroline smelled smoke. She looked beyond her father's snarling face and saw that the shag carpet had caught fire—right where she had thrown the ashtray. Sparks glowed in the strands of shag, and here and there, patches of flame dotted the living room floor.

"Get some water!" Caroline ordered her mother as she took a pillow from the sofa and began to smother the spreading flames.

As Mary Shaw ran to the kitchen, Caroline's father reared back and landed a stinging slap with the back of his hand to Caroline's already swelling cheek.

"Let the fucker burn!" he shouted, knocking her over and kicking the pillow away. "It's your fault! You started it!"

As the flames began to spread and acrid smoke enveloped the small living room, the police arrived.

Al Shaw was not in a conciliatory mood. He fought the two police officers as ferociously as he'd fought his family, but policemen, trained and armed, were different from two frightened women, and Al Shaw soon found himself handcuffed and under arrest.

The officers radioed for the fire department, called an ambulance for Caroline and her mother, and ordered the women out of the now-blazing house.

"Wait!" Caroline said as one of the officers attempted to escort her out the door. Covering her mouth with a damp dishrag, she ran upstairs to her bedroom, opened the top drawer of her dresser, and grabbed the silk scarf Francesca Palen had given her. She stuffed it into her pocket, fled down the stairs and, choking from the smell of her burning home, joined the others outside on the tiny patch of scrabbly front lawn.

As the policemen ushered Al Shaw into the patrol car, he turned toward Caroline and pointed a crooked finger at her: "It's your fault, you little bitch! Your fault!"

The Lake Worth Fire Department did its best, but the shabby dwelling at 39 Patterson Avenue burned down. Only a few charred metal pots and pans testified to a house of violent fights and bitter memories.

Al Shaw spent a couple of nights in jail, then skipped town. He left no address, no phone number, not even a note, and Caroline and her mother, with no roof over their heads, moved into a tiny room at Selma Johannas's boardinghouse on Everglades Road.

Life went on. Mary Shaw blamed Caroline for the fire that had robbed them of a home—and for the telephone call that had triggered Al's desertion—and Caroline escaped her bleak circumstances by thinking of The Breakers, her special place. When she was sure her mother had fallen asleep, she retrieved the carefully folded silk scarf from her bureau drawer and cradled it in her arms as she fell asleep.

That scarf represented what life could be. Now, more than ever, Caroline Shaw felt an almost magical connection to the hotel, a link forged in fire. The Breakers was the tangible, visible reality of what, until then, had been only a dream—a gossamer fantasy she had spun out of thin air. Francesca had told her that The Breakers had been destroyed by fire and then rebuilt—better and more beautiful than ever—and Caroline could not forget those words. They became her beacon of hope, and she clung to them in the days and weeks that followed. If structures could be rebuilt, why not lives? If buildings could be made whole again, why not hearts?

Caroline knew that something inside her had not been destroyed and that that something, that tiny, flickering pulse of life, just might be her most important possession.

PART ONE

~

Love Story Three Years Later

1

Dreams, Caroline had learned long ago, were her friends. They softened the jagged edges of a difficult life, and because her dreams were hers, she could create them and mold them as she wished, changing and perfecting them as she went along, letting her picture not the way things were but the way they could be. Real friends were not nearly as easy to come by, she found, as toward the end of her senior year of high school, she watched her classmates make their plans to move on to college or vacation or marriage, without so much as a backward glance at Caroline or even a question about her future.

Afraid to reach out to others, afraid of being rejected, Caroline lost herself in her dreams—and in her work. She worked at her studies and worked at her after-school job and worked at trying to win her mother's forgiveness for making the call that drove her father out of the house. She was quiet and obedient and gave her mother the salary she earned at Evelyn's Nicknacks for her share of the expenses.

"You're a good daughter," Mary would concede after accepting Caroline's hard-earned money each week. Mary Shaw spoke from between tight lips, but there were times when she let down her guard in front of her daughter and turned to Caroline for comfort.

"I should have left him a long time ago," she'd confide as she wept.

"Then why didn't you?" Caroline would ask, unable to comprehend her mother's unrealistic view of her marriage. She had been very young when the accident happened. She didn't remember it. She didn't remember her father the way her mother said he had once been: handsome and hard-working, a good husband and a good father.

"Because I loved him," said Mary, who *did* remember. "I

still love him. The accident wasn't his fault. It could have happened to anyone. One day he'll be his old self again. I know he will."

Caroline didn't think so, but she didn't say anything. She knew her mother was deluding herself. She also knew that when she was old enough to fall in love, she wouldn't make the same mistake her mother had; she would find a man who treated her with respect, a man who made her happy.

On the last Thursday of May, just as Caroline was about to graduate from high school, two things happened to set her already fragile world reeling. The first occurred when she reported to work one Thursday after school. Her boss, Evelyn Addams, looked pale, gray, and on the verge of crying as she called Caroline into the small stockroom. She must be having one of her headaches, Caroline thought. Evelyn's migraines were so severe that she often had to lie down in a dark room for an entire day, sometimes two.

"I've just come back from the doctor," Evelyn began, fighting back tears. "He told me that my blood pressure's dangerously high and that if I don't change my lifestyle, I could have a stroke."

"Oh, no!" Caroline said. "I would hate it if anything happened to you."

Evelyn patted Caroline's arm and tried in vain to smile. "I'll be fine," she said unconvincingly. "But there's something else I have to tell you. It's about the new lease. The landlord told me that he has another tenant, one who'll pay what he's asking. I have no choice. I'm going to have to close the store."

"Close Evelyn's Nicknacks? When?" asked Caroline, feeling her throat close and her heart start to pound.

"At the end of the month. I'm sorry, Caroline," Evelyn said. "I was hoping things might change. I kept thinking I'd feel better. I thought I'd be able to negotiate a better lease. I guess I was just fooling myself."

Caroline swallowed hard. She had been planning to ask Evelyn if she could work full time as soon as she graduated from high school. She wanted to use the extra money to go to night school. The tuition at the local community college was pretty reasonable, Caroline knew, but now even "pretty reasonable" was out of reach. And what would happen when she told her mother that she no longer had a job—or the money for her share of the rent?

"Where will I find another job?" Caroline asked, suddenly bereft. "I've been working here since I was fourteen."

Evelyn patted her shoulder encouragingly.

"There's Joe Daniels over at the hardware store," she told Caroline. "He mentioned that he was looking for someone. And Arlene Kaslo said something about needing help at the Stitch and Sew. You tell them to ask me about you. I'll give you a glowing reference. Don't you worry."

But Caroline did worry. She worried about whether Evelyn would be all right. She worried about finding another job. She dreaded telling her mother that she was out of work. As she walked home from the store, she rehearsed what she would say and how she would say it. As she approached the small lime green boardinghouse with its aluminum siding and asphalt roof, she noticed that Selma Johannas was standing outside. Her hands were on her ample hips, and there a sour expression on her sun-wrinkled face as Caroline greeted her.

"He's back." Selma scowled in reply.

"Who?" said Caroline.

"Your father, that's who. He's inside with your mother, Lord help her." Selma crossed herself.

Caroline's face fell and her stomach lurched. First her job. Now this.

Caroline hadn't seen her father in almost a year, hadn't spoken to him in almost as long, but she already knew what was going to happen. He would smile, say a few conciliatory words, offer some promises, ask for forgiveness, say that everything would be fine, that this time things would be different. Then, as soon as he was forgiven, his promises would be forgotten, his good intentions would dissolve. She and her mother would be prisoners of his temper and his fists, his moods and his vicious words. The thought crushed her, and she was tempted to turn around and leave and never come back. But where would she go? Where would she live? How could she support herself?

Caroline blinked back the tears that threatened to flow, and she stared at the boardinghouse for a moment.

"He's waiting to see you," said Selma.

"I don't want to see him," said Caroline.

"He was smiling," said Selma.

"He always is," said Caroline. "In the beginning."

Swallowing hard, she crossed the stoop, opened the front door of the boardinghouse, and went upstairs.

"Glad to see me?" Al Shaw asked as Caroline entered the tiny room she shared with her mother. Broken capillaries sprinkled his cheeks and nose, and long brown hair fell over his forehead only half hiding his bloodshot brown eyes—eyes that looked out at the world with a combination of hostility and wariness. He wore a Miami Dolphins T-shirt and lumpy denim work pants. The sight of his gnarled right hand with its useless thumb and missing digits flooded Caroline's mind with visions of beatings and brawls.

"Hi, Dad," she managed.

"Your father's found work," Mary Shaw said cheerfully, smiling for the first time in months. "A steady job at a parking lot in Port St. Lucie."

Caroline nodded. It was difficult to speak. The very smell of her father made her physically sick. The cigarettes, that ashtray, the carpet, the fire. Their house had burned. They had lost everything. According to her parents, it was all her fault, her doing. They had been reduced to nothing. Because of her.

"He's taken a place over there," her mother continued. "We're going to make a new start, aren't we, Al?" she asked, turning to her husband and looking at him with the shining eyes of a bride. Then she looked at Caroline, wanting approval.

"So you're going back to him? Again?" Caroline asked. "After what he did to you the last time?"

"Things will be different this time," said Mary. "Won't they, Al?"

"You've got that right, honey. I'm a new man," he said.

The last time Al Shaw had been a "new man" had been five months ago. He'd come back one afternoon, while Caroline was at work and made vows and promises that Mary Shaw was all too happy to believe. She'd left with him, and three weeks later, she'd called Caroline from the small motel where she and Al had been staying just north of Fort Pierce. Caroline arrived to find her mother's eyes swollen and black, her torso a mass of bruises and bloody welts. Caroline took her to the emergency room, where Mary Shaw said that she had fallen; and the doctor, a woman, had looked at her and asked three times if anyone had hit her. Each time Mary Shaw shook her head and denied it. She just kept repeating that she had fallen.

Now Al Shaw had returned and here she was again, talking about taking him back.

"What about your job?" Caroline asked. "The last time you went off with him, The Breakers nearly fired you."

"I'll give two weeks' notice. Then I'll find something else, something in Port St. Lucie or maybe in Stuart," Mary replied.

"But what if you can't?" Caroline asked, thinking of her own job, the one that didn't exist any more. She hadn't even had a chance to tell her mother.

Mary Shaw shook her head.

"I'll find another job. There's nothing to worry about," she insisted. Then she smiled again. "Your father said you can move in with us."

Caroline said nothing. Neither did her father.

"Isn't that right, Al?" Mary looked at her husband with a bright, encouraging glance, prompting him to reply.

Al nodded.

"Yeah, I said that. I sure did."

Move in? Caroline thought bitterly. *Move in with* him? *After the way he treated my mother? The way he treated me? The way he never said he loved me? Except when he was drunk and sentimental and needed to be dragged upstairs to bed?*

"No. No, thank you. Not this time," Caroline said suddenly, not knowing where the words had come from.

Never mind that she didn't have a job. Never mind that she didn't know where she would live and how she would eat. Never mind any of that. She couldn't do it again, couldn't go along with the charade, had to draw the line. If she couldn't save her mother's life, she at least had to save her own. She spoke with the steely-eyed determination, not of an eighteen-year-old girl but a wary, chastened adult: "You two go to Port St. Lucie. I'll stay right here at Selma's."

"But how will you get along?" Mary Shaw asked her daughter.

Caroline had no idea.

"I'll be fine," she said, touching her mother on the arm. "I'll be just fine."

Her mother had at least asked how she'd manage. Her father, she noticed, didn't even bother to ask *that*, much less to try to get her to change her mind.

Later that night, after her mother had packed her belongings and gone off to Port St. Lucie with Al Shaw, Caroline contemplated her future. Her mother had said that she would send money each month, now that her husband had a paycheck. That would help pay Caroline's room and board, of course. But there was more to life than room and board. What about college? What about her future? What about her dreams? Her dreams of being someone? Her dreams of being admired and respected? Even her dreams of happiness?

There was only one answer, she knew, only one possibility: work. What other people were given, she would earn. The next morning Caroline began knocking on doors. She called on Joe Daniels, whose hardware store was down the block from Evelyn's Nicknacks.

"Sorry, hon," he said. "I've got work but not for a girl. Need me a big, strong guy to help load my pickup for deliveries."

Caroline thanked him and walked two more blocks to Arlene Kaslo's Stitch and Sew.

"Just hired someone two weeks ago," she told Caroline. "And I'll probably have to let her go. Business is pretty slow these days. Don't quite know how I'm going to make it, in fact. Discount stores like Kmart and Penney are taking my customers."

Caroline spent the hot Florida summer trying to find work, work that would pay a decent salary, work that might lead somewhere, somewhere out of Lake Worth and unhappiness and discouragement. She read the want ads and applied for those jobs that seemed possible; she inquired about the Help Wanted signs in store windows and found that no one wanted her. She was too young, too inexperienced, had nothing to offer.

She made ends meet with a minimum-wage job at Roy Rogers. She knew she was lucky to have a job, any job, and she was grateful for her mother's checks, but she also knew from experience that her father's income could evaporate at any moment, and that as soon as it did, the checks would stop coming. If only someone would hire her. If only someone would take a chance on her.

In late August, on the Sunday just before Labor Day, Caroline was in her sweltering hot room in the boardinghouse, imagining how cool it would be at the beach, when she suddenly thought of Francesca Palen. She hadn't been to The Breakers all summer long; her mother didn't work there anymore, and she hadn't been able to afford the bus fare. Perhaps Francesca would remember her. . . .

Francesca's office, sunny and neat, was just as pleasant as Caroline remembered. Francesca motioned her to the comfortable sofa and, as a waiter wheeled in a room service cart, she told Caroline that she was so happy she had called and how glad she was to see her again. She also told her that she had checked with the personnel department to see if there might be a job at The Breakers.

"Unfortunately, there aren't any openings right now. Not for someone who doesn't have hotel experience," said Francesca.

Caroline's face fell but before she could even thank Francesca for inquiring, Francesca had a question: "You've got sales experience, isn't that what you told me?"

Caroline nodded, pleased that Francesca remembered.

"My mother has a friend who's opening a shop here in Palm Beach," said Francesca.

Caroline brightened—she had loved working at Evelyn's Nicknacks, had loved selling.

"Now I'm not making any promises," Francesca cautioned. "But perhaps this woman—don't laugh, her name's Countess Tamara Brandt—might need some help."

"A real countess?" Caroline asked, impressed.

"By marriage," Francesca said with an amused smile. "Tamara married a count, and when they got divorced, she decided to keep the title. Titles come in handy in Palm Beach." She laughed. "In any case, I've asked my mother to call her and see if she's hiring."

"Oh, thank you!" said Caroline. "I've been looking all summer, and I haven't been able to find anything . . ."

Francesca nodded sympathetically and smiled.

"Well, let's see what the countess has to say."

The next morning Francesca called.

"Guess who you're going to see this afternoon?" she asked as soon as Caroline picked up the telephone.

"The countess?" Caroline guessed, crossing her fingers and cautioning herself not to get her hopes up too high.

"Bingo."

"She has a job?"

"She told my mother she needs a stock girl," said Francesca. "Put on your best dress and go over to 225 Worth Avenue at four o'clock."

Worth Avenue? Caroline thought. She knew that Palm Beach's Worth Avenue was one of the richest, most famous shopping streets in the world. Exclusive designer boutiques like Tiffany, Cartier, Armani, and Chanel showcased their wares behind glittering plate-glass windows that sparkled like diamonds, beckoning customers who emerged from chauffeured Rolls-Royces to shop in lush, elegant surroundings—surroundings in which she was sure she did not belong.

"The name of the shop is L'Elegance," Francesca continued. "Countess Tamara will be expecting you."

"Oh, Francesca. I don't know how to thank you. *Or* your mother," Caroline said.

"You don't have to. It's a pleasure to help," said Francesca. "But a word of warning—my mother has known Tamara for years. She says the countess is quite a handful."

Caroline smiled ruefully.

"I'm used to handfuls," she told Francesca, thinking of her father. "In fact, I'm an expert."

Francesca laughed.

"From what my mother says, you'll need all the expertise you can get."

Caroline wore the scarf that Francesca had given her to her interview—for luck. She knew that the fine silk made her cheap polyester outfit look even shabbier. Still, the scarf was by far the nicest thing she owned, and she draped it carefully around her neck just the way Francesca had, arranging the folds to show the pattern and the high quality of the silk. The scarf would mean more than just luck. It would be a sign to the world that although she was poor, she had taste and style and class.

Caroline arrived at the shop at 225 Worth Avenue at five minutes before four o'clock. Peering into the display window, she saw a magnificent strapless, wide-skirted evening gown of jonquil-colored silk taffeta with matching high-heeled slippers, arrayed on ivory-colored velvet, along with a tiny, rhinestone-studded evening bag. She opened the heavy gilt front door, entered L'Elegance for the first time, and found herself alone. The interior of the shop was hushed and muted, lusciously perfumed and deliciously cool. A gold clock ticked calmly on an ornately carved coffee table. The thick carpet was the color of heavy cream, and delicate gilt chairs were upholstered with tufted silk in the same fragile color. Everything looked brand-new and immaculately clean.

Floor-to-ceiling shelves painted ecru and decorated with gold leaf held a ransom of silk, satin, velvet, and lace. On the left, there was a vast selection of lingerie—nightgowns and their matching peignoirs, slips and camisoles, bras and panties, all fashioned of the most exquisite fabrics and shades, shades ranging from white to ivory to champagne as well as hues of peach, blush, and very, very pale blue. On the right, in extra-long hanging cases, were sumptuous evening gowns of chiffon, taffeta, silk mousseline, and peau de soie. Their designs covered a wide range, and there were styles for every kind of gala event—from a festive cocktail party to a grand masked ball. In the center of the shop, arranged on a table whose ecru moiré cloth fell to the carpet, was a selection of long white kid gloves, fabulously expensive costume jewelry, and glittering, elaborately jeweled evening bags that Caroline would soon learn were called minaudières.

"Countess? Is Countess Tamara here?" Caroline called out, unsure of how else to make her presence known. She was alone in the store, and except for the ticking of the clock, there wasn't a sound. She looked around, feeling like an interloper; then she straightened her shoulders and reminded herself that she hadn't come to gawk; she'd come to apply for a job.

What she didn't know was that, as she had opened the front door, a discreet buzzer had announced her entrance. She also didn't know that, from behind a valuable Japanese screen at the rear of the shop, she had been carefully examined and immediately found wanting. She stood uncertainly for a moment in the hushed, intimidating silence and looked around. Suddenly, the most glamorous and exotic creature she had ever seen swept into the room from behind an ivory velvet curtain.

Her hair was almost blue-black, and she wore it combed back into a tight chignon. Her eyes were almost black, too, and they were heavily shadowed and mascaraed. She wore a turquoise blue caftan and lots of colorful jewelry and held a black cigarette holder in her long, thin fingers, the nails of which were painted a dark blood red. Caroline couldn't take her eyes off her.

"I suppose you're here about the job," she said in a vaguely foreign accent Caroline couldn't place.

"Yes, I'm Caroline Shaw. And you're Countess Tamara?"

The woman nodded wordlessly. Caroline extended her

hand, but Countess Tamara did not take it. Caroline let her hand drop awkwardly to her side. Maybe countesses didn't shake hands.

"Mrs. Palen spoke to you about me. About the job as a stock girl?" Caroline said, plunging ahead.

"You have experience?" said the countess, not referring to the mention of Mrs. Palen's name.

"Yes, I worked at Evelyn's Nicknacks for four years," Caroline said.

Countess Tamara gave her a withering look.

"What and where on earth is Evelyn's Nicknacks?" she asked.

"It's a gift shop. In Lake Worth."

The countess rolled her eyes.

"And what did you do there?"

"I waited on customers—"

The countess cut Caroline off in midsentence. "I don't need help waiting on customers, as you call them. Here at L'Elegance, we have clients. What I need is a stock girl."

"That's what Francesca said—" began Caroline.

The countess cut her off again.

"Do you know what a stock girl at a shop like L'Elegance does?" Tamara asked.

Caroline shook her head.

"Not exactly," she admitted, sure that she had lost the job before she'd even had a chance to explain how hard she would work and how willing she was to learn.

"I didn't think so," sighed the countess. Sounding like a professor with a slightly backward class to educate, she explained, "A stock girl unpacks boxes as the new garments come in, unfolds them, steams and hangs the merchandise before it's put out on display. Then after the items have been tried on, she resteams and spot-cleans them if necessary, then hangs them and returns them to the display cabinets. And, of course, she cleans, polishes, vacuums, and straightens up the store."

"I did some of those things for Evelyn. I did some gift-wrapping, too," said Caroline, anxious for the countess to know how helpful she could be.

The countess sniffed.

"I hardly think Evelyn's Nicknacks is in the same league as L'Elegance."

"Perhaps not, but if you'll show me how you like things done, I'd be happy to oblige."

The countess narrowed her eyes and assessed Caroline. Good God, she thought. The hair was dry and frizzy, home-permed to death. The dress was strictly Salvation Army. The nails had been bitten to their quicks. And that body! Blubber and baby fat. Still, there was the expensive-looking scarf, beautifully tied and arranged. And the clear complexion and flawless ivory skin. The hazel eyes fringed by long lashes. The chiseled nose, the full, lush lips. The girl had possibilities, Tamara thought, feeling a catch in her throat, recalling her own awkwardness as a teenager, remembering how gawky and uncomfortable with her own body she'd been. But that had been years ago, another life, another existence. Would this girl standing before her be able to metamorphose herself into the essence of chic, as she had?

The countess doubted it. Not without her help, anyway. It wouldn't take much really. Just a few pounds here and a makeup lesson there. And several conditioning treatments for that Brillo hair! But did Tamara Brandt need a "project"? At this stage of her life with a rotten marriage barely behind her and a brand-new shop to get off the ground? Hardly! She needed a stock girl! Someone she could rely on. Someone who would fade efficiently into the background and allow her to concentrate her full efforts on designing and selling. Still—

"You're awfully young, you know," she said, shaking her head. "And you've most certainly never worked in a shop like L'Elegance."

"I'll be nineteen soon. And even though I've never worked in a shop like L'Elegance, I'm a very quick study," Caroline said.

The countess bit back a smile, recalling that she had used the very same expression to describe herself at her first job interview.

"You have references, I suppose?"

"Oh, yes. From my teachers at school. From Evelyn, the woman I used to work for. And I could probably get—"

The countess cut her off. "Audrey Palen's daughter has already vouched for you. One can never rely totally on someone else's word, of course, but Audrey is as reliable as people around here are capable of being."

It was Caroline's turn to squelch a smile. This countess obviously didn't mince words.

"So, when can you start?" Tamara Brandt asked suddenly.

"Right now," replied Caroline instantly.

The countess admired the girl's eagerness and again was reminded of her own youth, before she had become jaded and tough, before every new day ceased to be an adventure.

"Tomorrow will do," she said. "Can you be here at nine o'clock sharp? Monday through Saturday?"

Caroline nodded.

"I'm very prompt," she said. "As you already know, I was early for our four o'clock appointment."

The countess looked at her for a moment. Touché, she thought, rather enjoying being spoken up to.

"I guess you'll do," she finally said, giving Caroline a final, top to toe once-over and wondering what on earth she was getting herself into. "Although you'll have to do something about that hair."

Caroline brought her hand up to her hair.

"For a start, you'll tie it back," said the countess. "I won't have hairs all over my beautiful things. What's more, I won't abide an employee who looks like a mall rat with a perm gone wrong. My stock girl must look like she belongs on Worth Avenue."

Caroline gulped and tried to take the insults in stride.

"You'll let the hair grow out," the countess commanded. "No more permanents, you understand?"

"That won't be a problem," Caroline said politely.

"Very well. Then I'll see you tomorrow. Nine o'clock. Sharp. That'll be all." The countess flicked her wrist in a gesture of dismissal.

Caroline didn't budge.

"We haven't discussed my salary," she said.

The countess fluttered her lashes.

"No, I don't suppose we have," she said. "I'll pay you the minimum wage."

The minimum wage? That's what I earn flipping hamburgers, Caroline thought.

"I'm earning the minimum wage right now," Caroline said. "I thought that on Worth Avenue I could expect a salary more in keeping with the expenses of living."

"You thought wrong," said the countess. "Now, do you want the job or don't you?"

Caroline thought for a moment. If she went to work for the countess, she wouldn't be moving out of the boardinghouse any time soon, that was evident. Nor would she be able to afford night classes at the community college. But at least the countess was paying her, she told herself. And the job as stock girl at L'Elegance was a step up from Roy Rogers. A big step up. It wasn't just any job—it was a job on Worth Avenue, a job that, if she handled herself well, might even lead to something else.

Caroline nodded.

"The minimum wage is acceptable, although if I do well, I'd expect a raise," she told the countess, adding that Evelyn Addams had given her yearly increases.

"I'm not Evelyn Addams," said the countess with obvious disdain.

Caroline managed a smile and swallowed the comment that popped into her head.

"I'm very grateful for the opportunity, Countess. I'm looking forward to working here," she said.

"I would think so," the countess said, and walked back into the rear of the shop, disappearing behind the Japanese screen and the ivory curtain.

Caroline sighed as she left the store. Francesca had been right. Countess Tamara Brandt was going to be a handful, that she knew. What she didn't know, couldn't have known, was that the countess was a brilliant businesswoman who would teach her more than any college or department store executive training program—and that in Tamara's chic little shop on Palm Beach's famed Worth Avenue, Caroline would meet a man who would bring her dreams to life as she never believed anyone could.

James Huntington Goddard was not born with a silver spoon in his mouth. In the Goddard family, the spoons were solid gold. At least, that was the way the Goddards presented themselves to the high society circles in which they moved. The story behind the glittering facade was, in fact, even more interesting than the myth the family spent two generations and millions of dollars to create and then to burnish.

James's grandfather on his father's side, Carl Goddard, was a handsome, broad-shouldered man with a wicked smile and a fierce ambition. He had been brought up on a dairy farm near the Finger Lakes but had decided while still in his teens that milking cows at four A.M. was no way to make a living—not when there was a better way a little bit farther north, just across the border. After a few months under the watchful eye of a bootlegger named Itchy Mallone, Carl went out on his own. He loaded his father's big milk delivery truck with cases of imported wine and liquor and drove his precious cargo south from Canada, through New York State, all the way down to Manhattan. His competitors were among the toughest rumrunners on the East Coast, and more than once, Carl had had to use his fists to keep his routes, his suppliers, and his clients. Some said that Carl had even used a gun now and then, and all agreed that Carl Goddard was not a man to be crossed.

Carl's clients included nightclubs on Harlem's 125th Street, restaurants on Manhattan's fashionable Upper East

Side, high-class call girl operations on Sutton Place, and a number of families in the Jewish and Italian mafias. They also included a number of rich Wall Streeters, and his good looks, pleasant manner, and elegant clothes made him quickly noticed. He was prompt with his deliveries, charged fair prices, and was known to be both honest and discreet. The real money, Carl quickly saw, was made not in the jazz joints or whorehouses where easy come, easy go was the order of the day, or in the underworld where a man could too easily get shot, arrested, or fitted for cement shoes. The real money, he saw, was made on Wall Street. It was safe, it was legal, and it was practically foolproof. Stocks did only one thing: they went up. Carl put his money away, planning to make his move into Wall Street when, to his shock—and that of the rest of the world—the market crashed. Brokers were jumping out of windows, the value of shares plummeted, black headlines announced that the financial markets were in crisis—and Carl Goddard knew that the biggest opportunity of his life had arrived.

He approached one of his best clients, Wendell Stevens, a partner at a suddenly bankrupt Broad Street stock brokerage, with a proposition: Carl would put up the money for a new brokerage firm if Wendell would contribute the know-how and the contacts. It was an offer Wendell Stevens couldn't refuse, and in a kind of shotgun marriage, Goddard-Stevens was born in the depths of the Depression. Shares in the best companies in the United States could be bought for ten cents on the dollar, and by the time Carl retired in 1954 and installed his son Robert as the "Goddard" in Goddard-Stevens, the firm was one of the premier stock brokerages in the country.

As for Wendell Stevens, in 1964 he retired to the golf courses of Scotland and Palm Springs, and his son Austin replaced him. Five years later, Robert Goddard, a man who had never smoked, was diagnosed with lung cancer. He was given eighteen months, most of which he spent at the office, offering his son, Charles, an accelerated course in management, finance, and administration. When Robert died in 1972, Charles Goddard, at the tender age of thirty-one, replaced his father and became the "Goddard" in Goddard-

Stevens. He had a natural instinct for the business, had paid very close attention to Robert's lessons, and his father had passed away with a tranquil mind, knowing that the firm would be in good hands.

And Goddard-Stevens was in good hands. Austin Stevens, now forty-seven, was a mature man with vast experience in the financial markets, there to guide Charles in the present and to help provide continuity into the next generations. Goddard-Stevens seemed poised to prosper and grow even greater and richer.

In 1975, thinking that it might be a good time to take the company public, but wanting to get an independent analysis first, Charles Goddard employed an outside auditor to prepare the figures for a potential offering prospectus. What he learned when the reports were ready was that Goddard-Stevens was not a company on the verge of a new spurt of growth but a firm in serious trouble. His partner, the man his father had trusted, had had not one but two hands in the till. Up to the elbows.

When Charles confronted him, Austin was outraged, infuriated that Charles had gone to outsiders without consulting him first. When Charles, indifferent to his fury, gave him a choice of either leaving the firm or of being reported to the SEC, Austin refused to budge. He informed Charles that if the SEC was brought in, he would have a few unsavory tales to tell about Carl Goddard and his bootlegging days, tales that would destroy everything the Goddards had built and achieved over three generations.

Charles thought over Austin's threat and wondered how his grandfather, who had told him many rough-and-ready stories of his early days running booze over the Canadian border, would have handled the situation. As he turned his partner's threat and his grandfather's tales over in his mind, it occurred to him that Itchy Mallone, Carl Goddard's original mentor, was still alive. He was eighty-four years old, in perfect health, and living with his fifth wife on a horse farm in North Carolina. Charles tracked Itchy down and sent his grandfather's pal a gift he was sure would be appreciated.

Itchy remembered Carl perfectly, thanked Charles effusively for his gift of a case of single-malt scotch, and told him how much he missed the good old days of cops and rumrunners. When Charles told Itchy that he had a problem, the old man gave Charles a name: Sid Shine.

"What exactly does Mr. Shine do?" Charles asked Itchy.

The old man chortled.

"Sid?" said Itchy. "He solves problems. Discreetly but definitely. You'll never have to worry again."

"A tragedy," Charles said when it was time for him to speak at Austin's funeral, "for a man to be taken at the prime of life by a hit-and-run driver. A terrible, terrible tragedy."

In Austin's memory, Charles went on to announce, Goddard-Stevens was contributing a half a million dollars to a program to teach safe driving in high schools.

"It is only fitting," Charles said, concluding his eulogy, "that the program be named after Austin."

Charles then spent the next ten years of his life rebuilding the firm that had almost perished. He was determined that the firm—his security, his reputation, his past, his future and that of his heirs—would never be put at risk again. There would be no outside partners, only family. The name Stevens would be retained because explaining its absence would be too complicated, but from now on, Goddards and only Goddards would run the firm.

"I don't want you to inherit the mess that I did," Charles told his son James many, many times as the boy was growing up. "I want you to be able to devote your time and energy to expanding Goddard-Stevens, not to rescuing it."

James's mother, Dina von Halter of Park Avenue, Locust Valley, and Palm Beach, had been born Diane Haltz of Hoboken, New Jersey. Her father had been a dreamer, a failed sculptor who had supported his family by teaching art at a public high school. Her mother was a housewife with no interests beyond sparkling floors and her husband's inability to earn more money. At the age of eight Diane vowed to get out of Hoboken. At the age of fifteen she modeled at a local department store; at seventeen she got pregnant by a Princeton junior; and at eighteen, using the payoff money the boy's family had given her, she settled in New York where she began looking for a rich husband. By twenty-one she had dropped a few vowels from her name, added a few others, diddled with the consonants, and decorated her new name with the "von" just for class. At twenty-two she met Charles Goddard, and at twenty-three she married him.

She was a tall, blond beauty in the Grace Kelly mode with intelligent but cool blue eyes, a quick wit, and an uncanny knack for getting what she wanted. Her talent as a hostess was legendary, and her ability to make each of her guests, however toadlike, feel dazzling, sophisticated, and witty had been crucial in helping her husband build Goddard-Stevens to its formidable size and power. She had two children, first a son, James, then two years later, a daughter, Emily. After bearing her babies, she promptly moved into a bedroom of her own.

"Two children are appropriate. More would be vulgar," she informed her husband, having no intention of ruining her body with further pregnancies. She understood that Charles required heirs, but enough was enough. She felt she had done her share.

James spent his childhood shuttling between his family's fourteen-room Park Avenue apartment, a Locust Valley mansion built for a semiliterate press lord in the heady days of the twenties, and an oceanfront estate on Palm Beach's north end, just down the road from the Kennedys. James attended Choate, his father's alma mater, and the University of Pennsylvania, whose library had been donated by and named after his grandfather. He grew up knowing what was expected of him—that he would go to work at Goddard-Stevens upon his graduation from college, that he would be named a vice president before he was thirty, that he would marry well, that he would produce heirs, and that he would carry on in the carefully constructed tradition of the Goddard men before him.

He should never have met Caroline Shaw—and almost didn't.

From the day she opened L'Elegance, Countess Tamara had one goal in mind: to compete with Celeste, Palm Beach's long-established purveyor of exclusive and elegant gowns. Tamara spent all day and many sleepless nights thinking of ways to outdo her mortal enemy, the brazen hussy who had run off with her husband. From the decor of L'Elegance to the selection of expensive and exclusive merchandise, from the alterations policies to the antique chauffeured Rolls-Royce that the countess used for deliveries, she was determined to be the best—and to put that peroxided slut, Celeste, out of business. When that happened, the count, that two-bit Transylvanian gigolo, would drop Celeste like a hot potato and, if the past was predictor of the future, find some other rich woman to sponge off!

In the ten months since she had opened L'Elegance, the countess had achieved a remarkable success. She had poached several of Celeste's best clients, and a satisfying number of Palm Beach's most prominent socialites shopped there for gowns, trousseaux, and accessories to wear to the dinner parties, charity balls, weddings, and elaborate soirées that formed the resort's very active social life. The countess was a shrewd businesswoman who had taken her small boutique from out of nowhere to become a formidable rival to Celeste.

For Caroline, those first months at L'Elegance were dizzying, exhausting, exciting, and exasperating. On her first day at work, she spent the morning sweeping, cleaning, and scrubbing until the small shop glistened. Her glamorous job on Worth Avenue was turning out to be a janitor's position! At noon, when she paused to eat the lunch she had brought from home, Countess Tamara snatched the sandwich away from her. Holding Caroline's hands tightly, she examined the bitten nails and chapped skin and curled up her nose at the sight.

"Completely unacceptable! I can't have you touching my precious merchandise with those ragged paws," she said, shaking her head in distress. She then instructed Caroline to see Carmilla, the manicurist across the street at the Georgette Klinger salon. "Immediately! And make sure you choose the palest pink polish they have. I will not have you in dragon lady red," she commanded, imperiously waving her own carmine, straight-out-of-the-jungle talons.

"But my lunch—" said Caroline, who was starved.

"Lunch? You need to lose some weight and you know it. Besides, who can think about food when it's obvious you desperately need a manicure?" said the countess.

"But I can't afford a manicure. I—" Caroline began. She could barely afford her peanut butter sandwich. Not on the countess's minimum wage. A manicure at Georgette Klinger's would certainly be out of reach.

"Tell Carmilla to charge it to my account," the countess interrupted, blithely dismissing Caroline's objections.

"I don't know when I'll be able to pay you back," Caroline said.

"Who said anything about paying me back?" said the countess. "It's my treat."

Stunned by Tamara Brandt's unexpected largesse, Caroline crossed Worth Avenue and let herself into the elegant, hushed beauty salon. That half hour at the manicurist's table was the most soothing, relaxing half hour of her life. Never, ever, had she felt so cared for as her cuticles were neatly cut, her hands massaged with a fragrant, pink lotion, and finally, her nails carefully buffed, shaped and polished.

My, my, she thought as she walked back to L'Elegance. So this is how it feels to be pampered. So this is how it feels to be at your best. She felt so good about herself that she forgot all about her sandwich and barely even noticed that she was hungry.

Caroline quickly learned that her nails weren't the only aspect of her appearance that displeased the countess.

"Those clothes will have to go," Tamara said of the polyester outfits that were too tight, too shiny, too bright. "They're cheap and they make *you* look cheap. Not to mention what they do to L'Elegance's image!"

She stood back and studied Caroline as if she were a cattleman assessing a prize heifer. Celeste's stock girl, she knew, wore white pants with a matching tunic and, in the countess's opinion, looked like a dental hygienist. There would be no such nonsense at L'Elegance! Thinking for a moment, the countess made her pronouncement:

"From now on, you'll wear silk," she told Caroline, squinting her eyes in order to bring her vision more clearly into focus. "I see you in a cream silk blouse, matching skirt and hair ribbon, and a thin gold belt."

"It sounds beautiful, but where would I be able to buy that kind of outfit?" Caroline asked. "You know that I can't begin to afford clothes like that."

"Buy? I'm going to have it made for you," said the countess, surprising Caroline once again. "At my own atelier."

Caroline had never heard of an atelier, but it sounded more expensive than a mere store. Far too expensive for her meager salary.

"Relax," said Tamara, sensing Caroline's discomfort. "I'm not going to make you pay for it. It'll be a business expense. Totally deductible."

Now Caroline was totally confused. "You mean I don't have to— You mean you'll—"

"I'll give you the outfit, but only to wear in my shop," said the countess. "You'll be responsible for having it cleaned and pressed."

With that, the countess disappeared into the stock room and returned with a measuring tape. She took measurements of Caroline's bust, waist, and hips, placed a phone call, and barked a few orders. Four hours later, the blouse and skirt were brought to the shop by a seamstress.

"Here," the countess said as she handed Caroline the garments. "Try these on in the dressing room. Then come out and show me."

Caroline carried the blouse, skirt, ribbon, and belt into one of L'Elegance's three spacious, opulently appointed dressing rooms, removed her polyester outfit, and slipped into her silky new "uniform." She fastened the belt around her waist and tied her hair back with the cream silk ribbon.

She couldn't get over how smooth and luxurious the fabrics felt against her skin and hair. She didn't look beautiful, that she knew, but she suddenly looked different, not quite so lumpy, a bit more graceful, almost as if she belonged on Worth Avenue.

She emerged from the dressing room, head high, shoulders back, eyes bright, and showed the countess how she looked.

"Turn around," said Tamara.

Caroline turned slowly.

"I think you've lost a little weight," said the countess approvingly.

Caroline's heart soared.

"I think so, too," she said shyly.

"It's not eating lunch," declared the countess who kept Caroline busy nonstop all day long. "Tell me, what do you eat for dinner?"

"Selma's wonderful, but she's not a very good cook," Caroline said, referring to her landlady and friend. "She opens a can of something and a bag of potato chips."

"Then buy yourself some fresh greens and a bit of chicken," ordered the countess. "You can charge it to my account at C'est Si Bon."

"That's so generous of you!" said Caroline excitedly.

"Don't gush. It's not chic," said the countess, handing Caroline a roll of paper towels and a bottle of Windex. "Now, enough talk! I want this shop to shine!"

For the next ten months Caroline Shaw didn't just make L'Elegance shine—she made it glisten. Countess Tamara insisted that the shop always look bandbox neat and that it was Caroline's job to make it so. The gowns had to be hung with precisely five inches between each padded hanger. The accessories—the gloves, jewelry, evening shoes, and slippers—were to be carefully organized and displayed. The trousseau-quality lingerie was to be perfectly folded and put away in the rolling display drawers lined with scented paper. The countess inspected the shop with a ruler to check on Caroline's work, and her eagle eye missed nothing.

"Clients walk right out of a dirty, messy store," she said.

Caroline sensed that the countess was correct, and she tried hard not to resent all the scrubbing, vacuuming, and polishing she was made to do. She especially tried not to resent the fact that it was often the countess's own cigarette ashes that were making the messes she was endlessly cleaning up.

Countess Tamara also demanded that the merchandise always look fresh and appealing. She stood over Caroline, showing her how to use a piece of cardboard as a guide in order to refold the delicate silks and laces after a client had handled them. She personally demonstrated to Caroline how to spot-clean, steam, and rehang a gown so that no one could ever tell that it had been tried on by someone else.

"A client must believe she is the only one who has ever touched the garment," she said, supervising as Caroline returned the unpurchased garments from the dressing rooms to the immaculate display cases.

"The client is queen—or king," the countess explained, telling Caroline that another part of her job was to offer every client something to drink—coffee, tea, mineral water, champagne (Dom Perignon, no less, because, according to the countess, that cheapskate Celeste only offered Mumm's)—along with an appropriate nibble. Thin currant-studded mini-scones with coffee, crisp lemon wafers with tea, crunchy salted nuts with Evian or Perrier, and flaky cayenne-spiked cheese sticks with Dom Perignon.

"Only the very best for my clients," the countess maintained. "It puts them in a good mood. And when they're in a good mood, they buy more. Besides, it's deductible. A legitimate business expense."

Caroline listened and learned—quickly. She learned that it was important to make a store and its merchandise look fresh and appealing at all times; that it was crucial to have a continuous supply of brand-new styles and designs; that it was essential to smile and be polite, no matter how difficult or demanding clients could be; and that when clients felt pampered and catered to, they bought more—and came back to buy even more the next time.

That's what Francesca Palen had said, Caroline recalled, thinking back to their conversation years before at The

Breakers. If you pamper them, they'll come back, her friend had said. The business of business was beginning to make sense to Caroline, and the longer she worked at L'Elegance the more interested in business she became. The dreams that had once been inchoate now began to possess a form and a direction. *A store,* thought Caroline, in the most private of her private thoughts. Perhaps, one day, she might own a store of her own.

The seasons rushed past as Caroline, working harder than she ever had in her life, cleaned, polished, vacuumed, folded, refolded, gift-wrapped, served beverages and snacks, and ran between the shop and the atelier, which turned out to be nothing but a sweatbox of a workroom on the wrong side of town from which Countess Tamara's exclusive and wildly expensive designs emerged.

As hard as Caroline worked, though, there were rewards that went beyond money. She had finally lost all her excess weight and discovered that beneath the lumps and bumps were hips, a waist, a bust. And that once the perm had grown out, her chestnut hair had a glossy sheen to it. It was lustrous now, feminine, soft. It was beautiful—even the countess admitted that. And while Caroline didn't quite believe that she was beautiful, even she couldn't deny that she had blossomed, grown into herself, begun to feel comfortable inside her own skin. As she moved about the shop in her newly altered cream silk "uniform," she felt graceful, light, free, as if she'd shed not just pounds but burdens. She was flattered when a man from Beverly Hills asked her for her phone number.

"He must have been at least fifty!" She giggled when she told the countess the story and explained why she'd discouraged the man's advances and refused to give him her number.

"He wasn't a day over forty. And he's probably worth a bundle, besides," Tamara corrected her. "Who are you waiting for, Caroline, anyway? Prince Charming?"

Caroline smiled.

"Yes," she replied. "As a matter of fact, I am."

* * *

While Caroline waited, she worked—and watched. Always a good student, she observed the countess carefully, studied her methods, tried to imitate her techniques. Tamara Brandt left no possibility unexplored as she maneuvered and manipulated and cajoled her way to a sale.

"Have you lost weight? Or is it my palazzo pants?" she would ask a client whose figure was far from model-thin.

"My dress makes you look like a debutante," she'd tell an old dowager well known for her penchant for younger men.

Tamara had a knack that seemed almost a sixth sense for knowing exactly what the client wanted and needed. And what she didn't know, she researched.

"*The Shiny Sheet* is my bible. I read it first thing every day with my coffee," she told Caroline, referring to the *Palm Beach Daily News.* The paper was printed on glossy stock and faithfully covered in words and photographs the comings and goings of the resort's social set. "That way, I know who went to which party and what they wore. You want to learn about Palm Beach? Read *The Shiny Sheet.*"

And Caroline did want to learn. Almost as if she were an anthropologist studying an unfamiliar tribe, she began to read *The Shiny Sheet* every day. She got to know the names that counted, and by looking at the party photographs, she began to find out what kind of dresses and gowns the Palm Beach social set preferred. She also paid attention to the bylines that topped the articles and became accustomed to the names of the reporters who wrote the stories and took the photographs. She studied the countess's clients and their needs and made a point of remembering their names and even the names of their little dogs, the miniature poodles and bichons frisés that accompanied their mistresses on their shopping trips. And when she didn't know something, she asked.

"What's a minaudière?" she asked the countess. She had never heard the word before she had set foot in L'Elegance.

"It's a small jeweled case that a woman carries in her hand in place of a purse when she's formally dressed. The word is French, and the best-known designer is Judith

Leiber," the countess replied promptly, as always, a walking encyclopedia of the habits of the rich and social.

"What's a *thé dansant?"* Caroline wanted to know after hearing a Palm Beach dowager argue with her debutante daughter about whether or not to have one.

"It's a tea dance," said the countess. "In the old days they were quite popular, and they seem to be making a comeback."

In January, after Caroline had worked for the countess for almost seven months, she went to her boss and asked for a raise. She had worked very hard, she reminded the countess. Surely, she had proven herself worthy of more than just the minimum wage.

"The clients know me now. Some of them even ask for me especially," Caroline pointed out. It was the same thing that had happened at Evelyn's Nicknacks.

"I don't care if you're Coco Chanel herself," replied the countess, unimpressed. "There's a recession going on, in case you didn't know it. You're lucky to have this job, and if the salary doesn't suit you, you can leave."

The countess had her moments of generosity and kindness, but when it came to money, she was all business. Caroline knew what "recession" meant; she'd been reading about it in the newspaper. But as far as she could see, the recession certainly didn't apply to L'Elegance.

In February, after an extremely busy Valentine's Day during which the countess had no choice but to allow Caroline to wait on clients (the unimportant ones), Caroline brought up the subject of a raise once more.

"Almost every one of my sales was a multiple," Caroline pointed out. She had learned from her boss that the real money in retailing came from repeat clients, as well as from clients who made multiple purchases. When Caroline sold a gown, she always made a point of showing the appropriate accessories and undergarments, too.

"So?" replied the countess, not bothering to look up from the stock quotes in the *Wall Street Journal.*

"I'm still only earning the minimum wage," Caroline reminded the countess.

"That's all a stock girl is worth," said Tamara, continuing to immerse herself in the stock tables.

Caroline didn't want to give up. She knew that her responsibilities extended far beyond those of Celeste's stock girl, and she knew that the sales she made added to the countess's profits.

"If you won't consider a raise, would you at least give me a commission?" she asked. Caroline had learned from the other girls who worked at the designer boutiques along Worth Avenue that some of the shops paid commissions to their sales personnel.

"Commission?" replied the countess, finally looking up from her newspaper and recoiling as if Caroline had driven a stake through her heart. "There are no commissions here at L'Elegance and there never will be! I'm running a business, not a charity. Let me remind you, young lady, that you're getting a free education, not to mention free manicures, a free outfit, and free groceries. You should pay me."

The countess was right about the free education and the other perks, but she was also being extremely unfair and astoundingly cheap. Caroline decided to visit the personnel department at Saks and to fill out employment applications at Gucci, Cartier, and Armani.

Unfortunately, the countess knew what she was talking about: there *was* a recession. Saks wasn't hiring. Neither were any of the other shops where Caroline continued to make inquiries, continued to be turned down, continued to try again.

March is the height of the season in Palm Beach—the social and tourist season. Rolls-Royces, Ferraris, and top-of-the-line Mercedes glide along Worth Avenue, the reservation books at elegant restaurants are full, and shops and boutiques are crammed with customers adding to their wardrobes. The third Tuesday of that month was especially busy at L'Elegance. By three-thirty in the afternoon, the refrigerator in the stock room was out of mineral water, iced tea, and scones, and Countess Tamara instructed Caroline to fetch more.

"Can you manage here alone?" Caroline asked her, thinking of the clients who might be left unattended if she left to go to C'est Si Bon.

"Of course I can manage," the countess snapped. "Just hurry."

It took Caroline almost a half hour to buy the groceries, and as soon as she reappeared in the selling area, the countess, seeing that the shop was quiet momentarily, ducked into her private office. To call her stockbroker, Caroline guessed, one of the most important people in her life. No matter how busy L'Elegance was, the countess telephoned Clifford Hamlin often, sometimes two or three times a day, to check on her investments. And she often spoke about Clifford, telling Caroline that she had known him for a very long time and that he was a financial genius. Caroline had a mental image of a boring white-haired man who smoked a fat cigar, played golf in plaid pants, and rambled on endlessly about stocks, bonds, and pork belly futures. But it was no concern of hers. Clifford Hamlin was Tamara's concern.

As Caroline stood in the back of the empty shop, the front door opened and a man walked in. Because the light from Worth Avenue illuminated him from behind, she couldn't quite make out his features. She could see that his hair was thick and blond and that he was tall and carried himself with the grace and strength of an athlete. He was dressed casually in the style Caroline had come to associate with the Palm Beach rich: a short-sleeved polo shirt, freshly laundered khaki pants, and rubber-soled boating shoes. He was lean, but strong and muscular, just about six feet tall, with broad shoulders that tapered in an inverted triangle to a slim waist and hips.

"Is there something I can help you with, sir?" she asked, the way the countess had taught her.

Caroline still couldn't see the man's face as her question hung in the air. His head was down as he searched the display case. He seemed hesitant, unsure of what he wanted.

"I'm looking for a gift," he said finally in a voice that sounded like molten gold. His accent, Caroline knew, now that she had been working on Worth Avenue, was a product of the best nannies, the best schools, and the best clubs. He was clearly from one of Palm Beach's richest, most socially prominent families. "For someone special," he added.

And then he looked up.

James Goddard was, without doubt and with no close second, the handsomest man Caroline had ever laid eyes on. He seemed like someone from out of a storybook or out of one of her more improbable dreams. She blinked and opened her eyes wide to focus on him, to assure herself that she hadn't somehow conjured him up. But, no, she hadn't. He was real. And he was smiling at her.

His features were classically carved and symmetrically placed, his forehead broad, his eyes wide-set, his nose straight and perfectly formed, his lips full and sensuous. His blond hair, falling rakishly over his forehead, was streaked by the sun, his skin was lightly tanned, and his teeth, revealed by a slow, mischievous, wildly seductive smile, were so white they nearly blinded her. His eyes, a deep, clear bluer-than-blue, were framed by dark lashes, and they twinkled as they gazed at her. Caroline guessed he wasn't much older than she was.

Someone special, he had said. Caroline didn't doubt it for a moment. *Special* meaning young, rich, and beautiful. And, of course, very, very spoiled. He was obviously shopping for the woman in his life.

"Something special for someone special?" asked Caroline.

He didn't reply. Instead, he cocked his head and, taking his time about it, took her in—all of her. The glossy chestnut hair, held back with a silk ribbon; the skin, radiant and healthy; the lithe, long-limbed figure. Caroline tried to pretend that she didn't notice that he was staring.

"We have some very chic evening bags and some jewelry that's just come in from Paris," she said, flushing under his gaze.

"I don't think so," he said as he continued to look at her.

"Perhaps you're thinking of some lingerie," she said, uncomfortably aware of his assessing eyes and trying desperately to remain calm, unflustered.

At the mention of the word "lingerie," his face brightened, and his smile—a wicked, dashing smile—broadened.

"You've nailed it," he nodded, his eyes glued to her, seemingly magnetized to her body. "Yes, right at this moment, I am *definitely* thinking of lingerie."

Caroline willed herself not to blush.

"In that case—" she said.

She reached into the display counter and retrieved a sexy black teddy, low-cut on top, high-cut on the bottom, the laciest, raciest item in the shop. A scanty piece of luxurious frippery meant to be slipped on and then off, for an X-rated night of unbridled passion.

"Is this the sort of thing you had in mind?" she asked.

James whistled appreciatively.

"It's exactly the kind of thing I had in mind," he said, looking directly at her. "What else could you show me?" His eyes made it clear that the double entendre was definitely intended.

"We have quite a large selection," Caroline said, unsure of how to proceed. Other male clients had flirted with her, but this man was different. This man made her heart race. This man made her knees weak. All she could do was take cover in the countess's script. "I'd be glad to show you anything you like."

"Anything?" he said with an outrageous grin, continuing the flirtation and causing Caroline to turn scarlet.

Just then Countess Tamara appeared from behind the ivory curtain. She bustled over like a windjammer under full sail, her armful of bracelets clanking, her cigarette held at full mast.

"Mr. Goddard!" she purred, lapping him up with her eyes, a cat with cream. His appeal, Caroline realized, was age-proof. Usually, the only thing that turned the countess on were the receipts at the end of the day. "How good to see you. Have you been offered something to drink? Some Perrier? Some Dom Perignon?"

James shook his head. "How about a cold Bud?"

The countess looked confused.

"Bud?" she repeated. "You mean Budweiser *beer*—?"

"Exactly," James cut her off. "Nothing like a cold brew when you're working up a thirst on Worth Avenue." He winked at Caroline, who couldn't help but giggle. The countess, irritated, silenced Caroline with a sharp, annoyed glance.

"Certainly, Mr. Goddard, whatever you'd like," the countess said obsequiously. "We don't have any Budweiser here in the shop, but I'd be more than happy to send my girl out to buy—"

"Thanks. It's okay," James said, his eyes still on Caroline. "I was only joking, Countess. Champagne would be fine."

"Caroline, get Mr. Goddard a glass of Dom Perignon," the countess ordered, clapping her hands.

Goddard, she thought, as she lifted an ice-cold bottle of Dom Perignon out of the refrigerator with mysteriously shaking hands. The simple movements were difficult, almost impossible. Her pulse was racing, her hands suddenly, unaccountably, trembling. The way James Goddard had looked at her with his extraordinary blue eyes, the way they had traded suggestive remarks, the way they had laughed together over the small, shared joke—

Nothing like this had ever happened to her. It was like nothing she had ever dreamed. She took a deep breath and tried to control the flight of her heart. The moment the countess said his name, she knew exactly who he was: James Huntington Goddard, son of Dina Goddard, the beautiful socialite whose every party was adoringly written up in *The Shiny Sheet,* and of Charles Goddard, the prominent financial titan who was one of the most powerful men on Wall Street. Her hands shook and her heart fluttered as she poured the golden bubbling liquid into a tall fluted glass and set it and a starched white linen napkin on a silver tray lined with a lacy doily. Then she placed a half-dozen cheese sticks on a white porcelain plate decorated with the countess's coat of arms (Tamara contended that she had gotten that in the divorce, too) and carried the tray and its contents back to the front of the shop.

"Your Dom Perignon, Mr. Goddard," she said with a polite smile that hid her beating heart as she handed James the champagne.

"James," he said, in that voice of liquid gold. "My name is James, Caroline."

As he reached for the glass, their fingertips grazed briefly, and Caroline felt an electric current shoot through her. The tiny hairs on the back of her neck shot up, and she flinched from the exciting contact, pulling her hand back and nearly spilling the champagne in the process. She immediately straightened the glass, and their fingers touched once again, this time for just a bit longer. As she glanced up at him, their eyes locked. She flushed and looked away as the countess began to speak.

"Now, Mr. Goddard," said the countess, practically twittering with excitement. "Tell me how I can help you."

"You can help me lure Emily to Kendall Lawson's birthday party," he said. Even though he was speaking to the countess, his eyes were still on Caroline.

"Don't tell me Emily doesn't want to go to Kendall Lawson's birthday party!" the countess exclaimed, as if such a thing were beyond mortal belief. Lawson was a name Caroline had often seen in *The Shiny Sheet.* The Lawsons were not only filthy rich, they were disgustingly rich and, on top of that, exceedingly social, at the very tip-top of the high society league in which the countess most adored to play.

"She says she's still too depressed to go out," he explained.

"Poor thing," said the countess, shaking her head in sympathy, her tones drenched in compassion. "It was a terrible tragedy, but she does have to get over it. Life does go on, doesn't it?"

James Goddard nodded, then said, "Emily hinted that a bribe might change her mind about the party. Say, in a size six. Something so enticing she'll just *have* to leave the house to show it off."

Tragedy, thought Caroline. *What tragedy? And what was all that about a bribe?* It all sounded so glamorous, so exciting, so incredibly foreign to Caroline's own drab existence.

"You're a very wise young man," the countess beamed, complimenting James on his cleverness and ecstatic at the prospect of having one of her gowns at such an exclusive affair. "With Emily's coloring, I would suggest something pale, a soft blue or a creamy yellow. But if you think she might want a real conversation-stopper, a more vivid hue would be in order—violet, perhaps, or even azure."

Uncertain, James Goddard shrugged and turned to Caroline, who had learned not to interfere when the countess had a client on the hook. Caroline remained silent, not sure that she could speak anyway since her heart seemed to be somewhere in her throat. Tamara, accustomed to waiting on men who didn't know silk from satin, much less charmeuse from chiffon, took over.

"Caroline, please bring Mr. Goddard 'Jasmine' and 'Oleander,' " she ordered.

The countess always gave each of her original designs a name. "The French designers name their creations," she had explained to Caroline. "It makes them seem more glamorous, more desirable. It gives them a certain cachet."

And, incidentally, the countess had added, naming her creations enabled her to charge astronomical prices for them.

Caroline went to the boiserie door, behind which the shop's most exclusive and expensive models were hidden. "Jasmine" was a sleeveless tunic of pale lemon-colored silk, embroidered with matching lustrous paillettes and coordinated with a full organza skirt. "Oleander" was a chiffon ensemble in brilliant Caribbean blue that consisted of wide palazzo pants and a top whose deep collar was formed of chiffon pleated into layer upon layer of delicate petals. Each outfit hung from a padded satin hanger, and neither had a price tag. At that level, the countess had confided, talk of money was simply vulgar. Besides, it spoiled the mood.

As the countess had taught her, Caroline displayed each ensemble over one of the two French chairs near the counter. She carefully fanned out the folds of the fabric so the gown's design and workmanship could be seen to its best advantage.

James Goddard looked from one garment to the other with a blank expression. Then he shrugged once more and turned to Caroline.

"If I were bribing you to do something you didn't particularly want to do, which dress would make you change your mind?" he asked in those honeyed tones of his.

"They're both absolutely exquisite. It would depend on Emily's particular taste in clothes—" Caroline began diplomatically, aware of the countess's beady eyes on her.

"I mean it. Tell me. Be honest," urged James.

Caroline glanced at the countess, who forced a smile.

"Come, now, Caroline, which one would you prefer? Be truthful. Mr. Goddard wants to know," she said.

"The truth? All right," Caroline said, deciding to take the plunge and worry about the consequences later. After all, the countess herself had insisted. "Since the dress is meant as a bribe, I would prefer the yellow one; it's much more expensive—"

James laughed.

The countess scowled.

"If you're having trouble deciding between these two, there's a third possibility," interjected Tamara, furious at Caroline's reference to price—a major no-no at L'Elegance. "I've designed a brand-new creation—'Violette.' It's just come from the atelier. Caroline, please go get . . ."

As the countess stabbed her cigarette toward Caroline, a shower of sparks flew to the floor.

"Countess, the carpet," Caroline said quietly, discreetly trying to warn her employer.

"Caroline, please, not now!" Tamara silenced her, waving her away, impatient, as always, with anything that threatened to interfere with a potential sale. "Go into my office and bring out the garment bag. Perhaps Mr. Goddard will—"

Sparks were now glowing on the pale carpet and a few clung to the hem of the countess's caftan.

"Countess, watch out!" said James, pointing to the hem

of her caftan. The countess looked down. A few cinders glowed orange along its edge.

"My God! I'm burning!" Tamara shrieked, then turned to Caroline. "Get some water!"

Caroline, usually so efficient, was frozen. She remained where she stood staring at the sparks on the carpet that were beginning to turn to flame, mesmerized by the sight of fire. Even James Goddard and the strange effect he had on her left her mind. Instead, a memory of fire seared her consciousness. A fire that had burned her house down and scorched her childhood. A fire that had cost her her home, her possessions, and even her pathetic charade of a family. She stared at the carpet, unable to move, unable to breathe, paralyzed by a living nightmare she had thought forgotten.

"Don't just stand there! You work here! Do something!" the countess shouted at Caroline. She began to flap the hem of the caftan, her effort only causing the sparks to burn more brightly.

James Goddard looked at Caroline, saw the strange, haunted look in her hazel eyes. He turned to the countess and ordered her to shut up.

"What's the matter with you?" he snapped. "Can't you see she's petrified?"

With that, he ran back into the stockroom, grabbed the silver ice bucket next to the refrigerator, filled it with water, and carried it back to where the countess stood. Upending the ice bucket, he doused the carpet and the caftan's hemline, extinguishing the glowing sparks and soaking the countess's shoes and caftan in the process.

"There," he said. "Fire's out. You're fine."

"Mr. Goddard. You saved my life!" the countess gushed, lifting the caftan above her knees in a feeble attempt to dry it out. "What a wonderful, heroic man you are. I simply cannot thank you enough."

She paused, then glared at Caroline.

"You!" she exclaimed. "After all I've done for you, you make jokes about me to my clients right in front of my face! You bungle my sale! And now this! You stand there and watch my dress catch fire and you do nothing to help me!

I've never seen such ingratitude! You're fired! I want you out of my shop this instant!"

"But, Countess . . ." Caroline began, stunned by the verbal onslaught.

"Out! You heard me. Now!" said the countess, pointing toward the rear

Caroline was overwhelmed—by the sudden eruption of yet another fire she couldn't control; by the stunning appearance of James Goddard, who set her heart racing but belonged to another, by the countess's harsh words and unfair dismissal.

Her eyes filled with tears, and without a word, she turned away and walked silently to the back of the store. She could hear James Goddard saying something to the countess, but she couldn't quite catch the words. What difference did it make anyway? It didn't matter now what he thought of her, what anyone thought of her. Her emotions teetering between rage and humiliation, she grabbed her purse and stepped toward the rear exit of the shop.

She was nearly out the door when she felt a hand on her arm.

"You're not using the servant's entrance," said James Huntington Goddard in that platinum-plated accent of his. "You're walking out the front door. With me."

4

As James swept Caroline out the front door of L'Elegance onto Worth Avenue, the countess trailed after them, her charred and soaked caftan flapping around her ankles.

"Mr. Goddard!" she called out. "Caroline!" Passersby stared and pointed and whispered, but the countess persisted. "Mr. Goddard! Caroline! Come back!"

James continued walking and completely ignored

Tamara, but Caroline paused. It sounded as if the countess was having second thoughts about firing her. Perhaps she was embarrassed by her outburst. If she returned to the shop, Caroline thought, the countess might apologize and offer her her job back. She began to turn around and head back toward L'Elegance.

But James held her arm and wouldn't let go.

"Don't pay any attention to her," he said. "Keep walking."

"Caroline!" the countess called again.

Caroline struggled against his fingers, trying to free herself. She wanted to go back, wanted to smooth things over, but James Goddard only tightened his grasp and shook his head.

"Don't pay any attention to her," he said as he guided her along the avenue, forcing her to walk quickly with a kind of assurance she didn't feel. The countess, seeing what she interpreted as determination in Caroline's stride, finally gave up and went back into L'Elegance.

Caroline realized that her one chance to get her job back had just evaporated. She felt a surge of panic at the thought of what she had lost, and she suddenly stopped in midstride. Taking James Goddard by surprise, she abruptly wrested her arm from his grasp.

"*You* can ignore her. *I* can't," she said, her hazel eyes blazing. "She's my boss."

"*Was* your boss," he pointed out.

"Could be my boss again," Caroline countered, "*if* I go back and work it out with her. Right now. Right this very instant."

"Work it out with her?" James laughed out loud. "You talk about Tamara Brandt as if she's a reasonable human being. You know what she's going to do, don't you?" It was a rhetorical question, and he didn't wait for an answer before he continued. "She's going to apologize and say that she's sorry and that she didn't really mean it. Not because she regrets the way she treated you but because she realizes that she needs you. Then, when she softens you up, she's going to offer to hire you back."

"Which is exactly what I *want* to happen," interjected Caroline.

"No, you don't, because the next time you do something she doesn't like or the next time she gets up on the wrong side of the bed, she's going to fire you again," said James Goddard flatly. He sounded, Caroline thought, extremely sure of himself.

Then she considered his words and found herself thinking of Estrella Sanchez, one of the countess's seamstresses. Tamara had fired her last December for taking a day off to accompany her daughter to a health clinic. But the important holiday season was in full swing, and orders for gowns were flooding into L'Elegance. There was custom work to be done as well as the first-class alterations the countess insisted upon. She quickly realized that without Estrella's skilled hands, she'd disappoint clients and lose business. She telephoned the seamstress and apologized, explained that she'd lost her temper, and begged for forgiveness, then rehired her. In January, when business tapered off, the countess fired Estrella again, this time for good.

Perhaps, thought Caroline, James Goddard had a point when he told her not to go back the instant the countess called. Still, she needed the job, needed the money, and, in a completely unanticipated way, had become extremely fond of the erratic, volatile, demanding yet wonderfully generous countess. James Goddard couldn't possibly understand. He was rich, oblivious to the problems of working people. *And* he was a complete stranger, someone she barely knew. He had no business interfering, no right to—

"Trust me on this, Caroline. I know what I'm talking about," he said, interrupting her thoughts, almost as if he were reading her mind.

"I don't think you understand the problem," insisted Caroline. "I need a job because I need money. Not to bribe people with expensive gowns but so that I can eat. E-A-T."

James grinned.

"And E-A-T you shall," he said as he linked Caroline's arm through his and guided them once again up Worth Avenue. She went with him reluctantly, still frozen inside, emotionally catapulted by the fire back to that dreadful

Sunday at 39 Patterson Avenue, still stunned from the countess's sudden outburst and shocking dismissal, trying to decide what to do and whom to trust. James glanced at her. He saw the conflict and confusion on her face.

"Look," he said kindly, stopping for a moment and turning to face her. "People like Tamara Brandt have their good sides and their not-so-good sides, but basically, when it comes to business and their own interests, they're manipulators. They blow off and lose it, then they realize they've made a mistake. So they apologize and swear that they're sorry and didn't really mean it and will never do it again—until they get what they want. On their terms."

His words were persuasive. So was his logic. He had described Tamara perfectly. He had also, Caroline realized, described Al Shaw, a manipulator if ever there was one, a man who lost his temper, then swore he was sorry and promised to change—until he got what he wanted, on his terms.

"You sound as if you know people like the countess," Caroline said tentatively.

"I do," said James. "My father."

She glanced at him but said nothing. She was startled that, despite their dramatically different backgrounds, she and James Goddard apparently had something in common: fathers who manipulated. She sensed that James had just obliquely confided in her, and she took his arm again. For the time being, she decided, she would listen to what else he had to say. For right now she would take the biggest risk she had ever taken in her life and trust him.

"I have no intention of keeping you from getting your job back," James said as they walked along the inviting, boutique-lined street that, by now, Caroline knew almost as well as her room in Selma Johannas's boardinghouse. "Quite the contrary. In fact, if you want, I'll help you get rehired at L'Elegance. But I'm not going to let you run back there and grovel. One thing I've learned—never give in to a bully. You'll get no respect. None."

Caroline suddenly thought of her parents. Of the endlessly soothing tone her mother used when she spoke to her father. Of the constant placating and agreeing, of the way her mother had relentlessly savaged her own personality and denied her own needs to please a man who could not and would not be pleased. She had been about to do the same thing: to run back to Tamara, to placate, to give in, to apologize, to soothe.

"You're right about that," she said, suddenly grateful that he had prevented her from automatically doing what she had seen her mother do month after month, year after year. "Thank you for saving me from my own worse impulses."

He smiled at her. "My pleasure," he said and looked as if he meant it.

"The problem is that I *need* the job."

"There's a better way to get it back than just caving in."

"Such as?"

"Such as getting the countess to beg you to come back."

"Beg me?" Caroline scoffed. "You said you knew people like the countess. If that's true, then you know perfectly well that they don't *beg* people, especially people like me, to do anything."

"They do if you have leverage."

"Leverage?"

"Come, I'll explain."

They had arrived at the trellised and flower-bedecked passageway that led to Café Pavillion, Worth Avenue's jewel box of a pâtisserie. Although Caroline knew that the Café Pavillion was the place where Worth Avenue shoppers paused to gossip, catch up on local social doings, and refuel for the next bout of serious spending, she had never been inside. For one thing, she couldn't begin to afford the prices—or the calories. For another, she was intimidated by its reputation. Café Pavillion was another place where, she had grown up learning, *she* didn't belong.

"Shall we?" James smiled, placing his hand on the small of Caroline's back and escorting her inside.

"*Bon jour,* Monsieur Goddard. What a pleasure to see you," said the smiling, well-groomed Frenchman who greeted James as they entered the restaurant. He was tall and white-haired and, with a brigadier's mustache, had the erect posture of a military man. His eyes were bright blue, observant, and intelligent, and his bold nose and square chin hinted of a strong, determined character.

"Pierre!" said James, reaching out to shake his hand. "How nice to see you! How've you been?"

"Pas mal," replied Pierre Fontaine. He was the proprietor of the Café Pavillion and, James quickly told Caroline, ran it with the help of his wife, Chantal. Pierre then turned to Caroline with a slight bow and said, "And welcome, mademoiselle."

"Pierre, this is Caroline—" James began. He looked at Caroline and realized that he didn't know her last name.

"Shaw," she filled in, and returned Pierre's smile.

"Mademoiselle Shaw," he said. "It's a delight to have you."

"Where's madame, Pierre?" James asked, looking around. "I don't see Chantal today."

"She's not feeling so well lately," he said, suddenly looking unhappy.

"I'm sorry to hear that," said James.

Pierre Fontaine nodded acknowledgment of James's concern but quickly went on to another subject.

"But we had a postcard from Jean-Claude yesterday and he has nothing but good news, thank heavens."

"Caroline, Pierre's son Jean-Claude is studying to be a chef," said James. "In Cap d'Antibes, right, Pierre?"

Pierre nodded.

"At the *Auberge de Lune,"* he said proudly. "They've just gotten their third star."

Caroline had no idea what or where Cap d'Antibes was, much less the *Auberge de Lune,* but she liked the way James and Pierre Fontaine included her in the conversation, as if she belonged, as if she were worthy of their attention.

"And how is Emily?" Pierre asked James. "I haven't seen her this season."

Caroline felt her heart sink. She had practically forgotten about Emily, forgotten that James Goddard, no matter how attentive and interested he seemed, wasn't available. Emily had experienced a tragedy, Caroline recalled, and had been so affected by it that she had not wanted to leave the house, not even for a glamorous birthday party. Or even, she now realized, to shop along Worth Avenue and stop into the Café Pavillion for lunch or tea. She wondered what had happened to cause Emily so much distress.

"It's been difficult for her, but she's coming along, thanks," James said somberly. "I'm doing everything I can to get her out. It's time she began to enjoy life again."

"Tell her that I'm looking forward to seeing her soon," said Pierre.

"I certainly will," James said. "I'll tell her at dinner tonight."

Dinner tonight, Caroline thought. He had said it as if dinner with Emily were almost an everyday occurrence. She supposed that Emily and James were going steady. Then she wondered if they were engaged. Probably, she thought. Men did not spend a fortune on gowns for girls they merely dated. Even very rich men. The relationship was obviously much more serious.

"Which table would you like?" Pierre asked.

"Over there," said James, pointing to one of the tables set around an immense white filigreed bird cage in the center of the café. The birdcage, a Victorian folly, was the height and size of a small room and contained several brilliantly colored tropical birds perched on dramatically shaped trees entwined with blooming orchids. Around it grew a lush, green jungle punctuated by white jasmine and scarlet hibiscus.

"Bien sûr," said Pierre Fontaine, as he led them to the best table in the terrace café.

"Mademoiselle Shaw?" Pierre held out one of the white wicker chairs at the table.

Caroline nodded and sank into the chair's plump down cushion, which was covered in a green-and-white bamboo printed fabric that blended perfectly with the decor of the café.

"Pierre, bring us some cappuccino and a selection of pastry, would you?" said James.

Pierre Fontaine was a master pâtissier whose classic

specialties included delicious fondant-iced *petit fours,* almond-flavored rectangular *financiers,* crisp, sugary *palmiers,* and ravishing *tartelettes aux pommes.* He disappeared into the kitchen and returned several moments later with the steaming cappuccinos, frothy with milk and topped with cinnamon, and a silver tray filled with pastries arranged as exquisitely as if they were the most precious of jewels. They looked almost too good to eat.

No sooner had Pierre finished serving them and withdrawn than James touched Caroline's hand and said, "Before we get caught up in these delicious pastries and the ins and outs of leverage, there's something I'd really like to know."

"Which is?" she asked, stiffening slightly, automatically defensive.

"What happened to you back there at L'Elegance? When the countess's dress caught fire?" he asked. "You seemed to freeze."

Caroline lowered her eyes. She was humiliated by the episode and the memories it had evoked. Even though his voice held a kind note, she didn't want to tell him about it. She never discussed her childhood with anyone, not even Selma, much less people like Francesca or the countess. It was her own painful secret, something that she, alone, had to bear and overcome. And yet, suddenly something in her was grateful for James Goddard's question, and she had an impulse that was almost a yearning to unburden herself, to tell him about her father and mother, the fighting, the violence, the rejection, the blame, the fire that had destroyed their home, the fire they said *she* had started. But now was not the time. It was too soon. There was too much she didn't know. But, perhaps, one day if she ever got to know James Goddard better—

"Rather not talk about it?" he guessed.

Still silent, she nodded.

"Fine, then we won't. Not yet."

Not yet, he'd said. Did that mean there would be another time? Or was he just being diplomatic the way the countess was when she was trying to sell something? Caroline didn't know, wasn't sure, had been brought up to fear people, had been taught to be afraid to open up, to tell the truth, to trust. She looked up at his extraordinarily handsome face and he smiled at her. She returned the smile. She couldn't help herself, he *was* irresistible. And then, when he unexpectedly reached out and squeezed her hand, she exhaled in a breath that turned into a near sigh, and she almost melted into her chair.

"James! Darling!"

Caroline cut off her reverie and looked up. A tall, slender brunette with startling amethyst eyes and a flawless ivory complexion was standing over them. She was wearing a suit that Caroline recognized from Armani's window, and a quilted Chanel bag hung from a gold chain on her shoulder. A cloud of her luscious, expensive perfume wafted across the table.

James let go of Caroline's hand and rose to greet the woman.

"Hello, Miranda," he said as she kissed him on both sides of his face in the Continental style that Palm Beach socialites had adopted as their own.

"You've been very naughty! Why haven't I heard from you? Don't tell me you're still seeing Helene Vreeland!" she chided. Then, eyeing Caroline, she added, "And who is this?"

"Miranda, this is Caroline Shaw," said James. "Caroline, Miranda Eliot."

Caroline extended her hand, and with a brief nod, Miranda quickly shook it and then dropped it. She turned back to James Goddard.

"Now, James," Miranda said, almost cooing. "I've missed you terribly. Why don't you stop by the club this afternoon? We'll catch up."

James shook his head.

"As you can see, Miranda, I'm busy this afternoon," he said, smiling at Caroline.

"What about tomorrow?" Miranda Eliot tried again.

"I'm busy tomorrow, too. Sorry," he said, keeping his gaze on Caroline.

Miranda raised her eyebrows as she looked at Caroline with the first glimmer of interest. "Shaw . . . Shaw," she mused. "Of the Philadelphia Shaws? The Shaw Department Store Shaws?"

Caroline burst out laughing in spite of herself.

"Caroline is one of the retailing Shaws, yes," interjected James, keeping a straight face. "Now, if you don't mind, Miranda, we've got some business to discuss."

"Of course. Nice to meet you, Caroline," said Miranda, making an obvious effort not to look disappointed. "Bye-bye, you two."

She waved and went off to join her friends at another table.

"A friend of yours?" Caroline asked James. "Someone special?"

"A friend. A former someone special," he answered, with a twinkle in his eye. "Now taste the *tartelette,"* James prompted, interrupting Caroline's thoughts. "Pierre will be hurt if you don't."

Caroline shook her head. Ever since she'd been following the countess's prescription of chicken and greens and had lost weight, she'd avoided sweets and other fattening foods. She looked and felt good, healthy, better than she ever had. Yet she didn't want to turn into a Puritan. She could allow herself an indulgence, couldn't she?

She accepted the pastry James placed on the white porcelain plate in front of her and took a bite. "You brought me here to talk about leverage," she reminded him as she ate.

"So I did. Well, here's the story on leverage," he began, leaning across the table and talking to Caroline in a low, almost conspiratorial, voice as Miranda and her friends watched and whispered. "I'll bet the countess has been paying you the minimum wage. And I'll bet she's had you working like a demon for it—cleaning, vacuuming, selling, you name it. Am I right?"

Caroline nodded, amazed at how much he seemed to know.

"You want to go back to that?" he asked.

"Not want to, have to," she said. "It's the only job I could get in this recession. Believe me, I've been looking. Besides, I was learning a lot."

"All right then," he said. "But you'll need leverage if you want to go back to the countess and not be treated like a slave. Bargaining power. Something *you* have that *she* wants. Once you've got that, she'll hire you back on your terms."

"My terms?" Caroline asked, thinking that he might as well have been speaking Swahili. Not once in her life had anything happened on her terms. The terms had always been dictated by others: by her father, by her mother, by the countess; by her own lack of power, money, position; by her lack of confidence and experience. Leverage was something people like James Goddard were born with. Leverage was something people like Caroline Shaw had never heard of and had no realistic hope of even aspiring to.

"You heard me. Your terms," said James. "In the business world it's essential to get people to do things on your terms."

"You're a businessman?" she asked in surprise, thinking about his youth and the calluses she had noticed on his graceful, well-groomed hands.

"Hardly." He laughed. "I'm a senior at Penn. My family lives in New York, but we have a place in Palm Beach." He paused, thinking how glad he was that he had happened into the countess's shop on Worth Avenue—and found Caroline Shaw. "My father wants me to go into the business after I graduate in June," he continued, answering Caroline's question.

"You don't want to?" she asked, reacting to the tone in his voice, eager to know why, given the chance, James Goddard wouldn't want to follow in his father's successful footsteps. It was a fantastic opportunity, one most people would have done almost anything to grasp.

He shook his head.

"Dad expects me to start in the Wall Street branch in June. But I keep trying to tell him that I'm not fitted for high finance," he said. Caroline noticed that he seemed uneasy, as if he were in conflict about the words even as he uttered them.

"Then what *are* you fitted for?" she asked, temporarily forgetting about her own problems. She was intrigued by this man and his background, so alien from hers, and she was surprised to realize that, even with tremendous wealth and privilege, people who had been born on the right side of the tracks still had problems.

"Not much, according to Dad. He and my mother say I take after her father," he explained. "He was a schoolteacher."

"And they don't approve of that?" asked Caroline.

"He was also a sculptor. Not a successful one, either."

"So you're a sculptor, too?" Caroline asked.

James shook his head.

"Only of sorts," he said. "I make boat models. Model boat making has a long tradition, and many of the best ones are crafted in Maine." His eyes lit up as he launched into his subject, and he began to speak with enthusiasm. "There's a man in Camden—his name is Caleb Jones—whose models are considered among the best in the world. I'd like to go there and apprentice with him this summer, then eventually set up my own studio."

He paused and sipped his cappuccino.

"My family is appalled," he continued. "The last thing my mother wants is a son who reminds her of her father. My father insists that the whole idea is ridiculous and that I'm only going through a stage. They want me to carry on as the Goddard men have before me. Tradition is everything to them, and they expect me to become a financial wizard like my father and his father."

"Obviously, you don't want to do that."

"Not particularly," he said, shaking his head as their eyes met. "Boats are my passion. Ever since I was a kid, my dream has been to become a master craftsman, to make models that will bring people as much pleasure as I have creating them."

Caroline was silent for a moment. So this rich, handsome, charming man had dreams, too. Dreams his family did not understand; dreams his family apparently ridiculed. She thought of Al Shaw and his accusations. *Snob. Uppity.* Just because she wanted something different than he wanted. For the second time it occurred to Caroline that she and James Goddard might actually have something in common.

"Now," he said, clearing his throat, "let's get back to you and your job situation. We have to figure out a way to get the countess all fired up about hiring you back. You need some leverage. For example, what could you do that would impress her?"

Marry you. The thought, startling and unanticipated, went unbidden through Caroline's mind and, as quickly as it had appeared, she brushed it aside, ashamed of her own involuntary wish.

"I could get a job at Saks," she said. "Or Gucci. Or, best of all, Celeste's. The countess absolutely despises Celeste. Going to work for her would probably get Tamara's competitive juices flowing, and she'd be cornered into offering me my job back. The problem is that I've applied for other jobs, and there just aren't any."

"Is there anything else you could do to get a rise out of her?" he asked, encouraging her to approach the problem again.

Caroline thought for a moment. Nothing came to mind. There was nothing she had that the countess cared about. Not money. Not family. Not social position. Not even a bright future.

"Come on," James prompted. "Be wild. Let your imagination go."

Caroline blinked. As she was about to say that she wasn't the wild type, a nutty, totally outlandish notion came to her—an idea that seemed more of a joke than a solution to her problem.

"I can think of something that would definitely get a rise out of the countess," she began, laughing as she spoke. "As you probably know, she's quite a social climber. Money and status are practically all that matter to her. If she saw a photograph of me in her beloved *Shiny Sheet,* at some high-powered party wearing a fabulous designer dress that didn't come from L'Elegance, she'd have an absolute fit. *Then* she might hire me back—on my terms."

James listened quietly.

"Perfect," he said with a straight face. "Consider it done. I knew we'd come up with something."

"We?"

"Okay. You."

"What did I come up with?" Caroline sat there, with a puzzled expression on her face, completely clueless.

"A plan to get your job back—with leverage."

"But I was only jok—"

"Be my date for Kendall's party on Saturday night," he said.

"You already have a date."

"So I'll have two."

"But what about Emily?"

"She won't mind."

Caroline's jaw dropped. She couldn't believe what she was hearing. Just when she was starting to like him and even to sympathize with him, to believe he wasn't just a spoiled playboy, he was inviting her to the same party he was bribing Emily to attend! Was this how he treated women? Caroline sat up ramrod straight and glared at him.

"Just who do you think I am? One of those society girls who fall at your feet?" she asked.

"What? Of course not," said James, wondering why she was getting so upset all of a sudden.

"Then how can you even think of asking me to the party when you've already invited your girlfriend?"

"What girlfriend?" He looked completely bewildered.

"You know very well 'what girlfriend.' Emily! Or have you forgotten about her already?" she asked sarcastically, daring him to come up with an explanation.

James looked at her, registered the expression on her face, and began to laugh out loud. Softly at first; then with increasing volume. People at nearby tables turned to look at him as he guffawed and his shoulders shook with laughter.

"What's so funny?" demanded Caroline.

"Emily's my sister," he said, barely able to get the words out between peals of laughter.

Caroline was hardly amused. His sister? Did he really

expect her to believe *that?* What kind of idiot did he take her for anyway?

"I'm not one of your Palm Beach debutantes whose IQ is the same as her dress size!" Caroline said.

"Who said you were?" replied James. He had finally stopped laughing.

"If Emily is your sister, then why didn't I recognize the name when you and the countess were talking about her?" Caroline asked. "If Emily Goddard were a client at L'Elegance, I'd certainly know her."

"Not Emily Goddard. Emily *Pringle,"* James said. "My sister was married. Her husband's name was Pringle."

Caroline turned scarlet, feeling more than a bit abashed. She knew exactly who Emily Pringle was: a pale, elegant blond with chiseled features and a cool, almost haughty, manner. So that woman was James Goddard's sister! "I'm sorry," she managed contritely. "Forgive me."

"On one condition," he said.

"What's the condition?" she asked.

"That you'll be my date for Kendall's party," he said, leaning over and taking her hand across the table.

"Thanks for the invitation," she said, withdrawing her hand. "But I'm sorry, I can't."

"Why not?" asked James. *"The Shiny Sheet* will be there. It's just the kind of party that rag covers. You'll get your article and your photograph—and your job back."

"Look, I was only joking about all that," said Caroline. "I can't go to Kendall Lawson's party. I don't own a fabulous designer dress from Celeste's or anywhere else for that matter."

"Minor detail," said James airily.

"—and certainly nothing that *The Shiny Sheet* would want to photograph," Caroline concluded.

"Well, then we'd better get cracking," James said as he looked at his watch. "Celeste's probably closes at five-thirty."

James Goddard signaled for the check, paid the bill, and escorted Caroline back through the passageway and out onto Worth Avenue as Miranda Eliot and her friends looked on.

5

To Charles and Dina Goddard, their son James was more than just an enigma. He was a riddle wrapped inside a mystery. His affinity for making model boats seemed almost bizarre to them, a complete and utter waste of time. Dina had spent her whole life getting as far away as she could from a man who had worked with his hands. Charles had spent his building a company to leave to his son, a firm of such prestige and power that it ranked among the most formidable in the country. How, then, had they managed to produce someone so unlike them, so out of touch with them and their aspirations?

Their daughter, Emily, on the other hand, reaffirmed to the Goddards the validity of their own goals and values. She enjoyed the station that was hers and reveled in the privileges to which she had been born, and she was anxious to preserve and enhance the Goddard traditions in any way she could. Her parents knew that she would marry young, raise an attractive family, serve on important charitable committees, wear clothes well, and carry on her mother's talent for the sophisticated and strategically conceived entertaining that would enhance her husband's career.

Charles and Dina were ecstatic with their daughter, proud and pleased to have brought her into the world. And why not? Emily had inherited her mother's blond, patrician beauty and her father's concealed but steely determination. Like her parents, what Emily wanted, Emily got. And to Charles and Dina Goddard's delight, what Emily wanted was invariably what they wanted, too.

As Emily was about to graduate from Farmington, what she and her parents wanted was for her to marry Kyle Pringle, the only son of Audra and Leighton Pringle, a couple the Goddards had known for almost two decades.

Leighton was a scholar and well-known horticulturist who traveled to the rain forests of Borneo and the Amazon to help publicize their ecological plight and guarantee their preservation. Audra was a presence on several museum boards and known for her interest in cultural matters. They were both from wealthy Virginia families, and if Leighton had ever worked, it had been so long ago that no one recalled what he did or when he had done it. They lived, like many wealthy people, on the income from family trusts, trusts that had become severely depleted over the years. Consequently, the Pringles had plenty of class but very little cash, an inconvenient fact that they carefully concealed and that Charles was not to discover until months after Emily and Kyle had said their "I do's."

Kyle Pringle not only seemed to possess the ideal credentials, he presented the proper image. He was dark and handsome, the perfect foil for Emily's blond beauty. He was charming and athletic, an eight-goal polo player, well-known on the Southampton–Palm Beach polo circuit. He had a talent for enjoying himself wherever he went, and he especially enjoyed the prospect of becoming Charles Goddard's son-in-law. Not only would marriage to Emily guarantee him a beautiful wife, it would guarantee him a place at the very top of Goddard-Stevens.

With one eye on romance and the other on the bottom line, Kyle did more than just court Emily, he campaigned for her. He lavished her with flowers, perfume, hand-written love notes, and on her eighteenth birthday, a Tiffany's box containing a six-carat emerald-cut diamond ring.

The engagement was properly announced, and in the months before the wedding, Charles Goddard held a number of conversations with his future son-in-law and arranged for Kyle to join Goddard-Stevens. Charles assumed that Kyle would bring certain valuable connections to the firm, and since he and James were about the same age, Charles also felt secure that there was a second member of the younger generation in place to guarantee the firm's continuing growth.

"You'll start at the bottom just like the Goddard men have, but if you perform well, there'll be a place for you next to James. You're a member of the family now," he told Kyle.

"Thank you, sir," said Kyle. "I'll do everything I can to merit your confidence."

Emily and Kyle were married during the Memorial Day weekend at the Episcopal Church in Locust Valley. The champagne reception was held at the Piping Rock Club, attended by five hundred of the two families' nearest and dearest. Charles Goddard gifted the newlyweds with valuable stock in Goddard-Stevens and a $25,000 check to cover the expenses of a lavish honeymoon in the four-star hotels of Paris, London, and Rome. When they returned to New York, Emily and Kyle moved into a spacious but rundown apartment on Park Avenue and Ninety-first Street.

"I know it's a dump, but it's been in my family since the 1920s," Kyle told his bride. "Why don't you hire a decorator and fix it up? I hear that Cissy McMillan is very good."

"And very expensive," added Emily. Cissy McMillan, with her unerring eye and no-nonsense manner, had long been a favorite of top-drawer East Coast society. She knew just how to make the homes of the nouveaux riches look simply riche and how to give a bit of desperately needed pizzazz to the residences of the old-line moneyed.

"But worth it," said Kyle, giving Emily carte blanche to decorate their new home. He had just started working at Goddard-Stevens and knew that pretty soon he'd have plenty of money at his disposal.

Emily busied herself with paint chips and fabric swatches while Kyle went to work every day in the Wall Street offices of Goddard-Stevens. Charles Goddard turned over a number of the firm's smaller and less important accounts to Kyle, and as Charles had hoped, Kyle brought with him a number of new and reasonably sizable accounts. Some were from friends, some were from family, some were from members of the polo team on which Kyle played.

Charles was pleased with the new business and, at least in the beginning, pleased with his new son-in-law.

* * *

Within six months, Emily had transformed the apartment on Ninety-first Street into a series of bright, cheerful rooms ideal for entertaining, and Kyle passed his brokerage test on the first try. They began looking for a place in Southampton for the summer, and Emily began trying to conceive. On his own, Kyle made several acquisitions: for himself, two new polo ponies, and for Emily, a Jaguar in British racing green.

"Perfection!" she told him as Kyle handed her the keys to the car.

"Nothing is too good for you," said Kyle, pleased to be the dispenser of such largesse. They were young, they were rich, they were ideally matched. It seemed both to Emily and to Kyle and to everyone who knew them that theirs was a perfect marriage. Everyone, that is, except Charles Goddard.

He was seeing more and more of his new son-in-law, and he increasingly didn't like what he saw.

"Too many trades," Charles told Kyle one day that post-honeymoon winter. Charles had been reviewing the portfolios Kyle handled before the monthly statements were to be sent out, and he noticed that stock positions were being opened and closed rapidly. Stock would be bought, held for a day or two, then sold, and the process repeated all over again. "We're not speculators here at Goddard-Stevens. We're investors."

Kyle was unrepentant.

"Almost every one of these positions has made money," he said.

Charles was unimpressed.

"You're talking peanuts. A few hundred here. A few hundred there. You've made more in commissions than your clients have in profits," he said, quickly adding up the amounts. "I want to remind you that Goddard-Stevens is an investment firm. Not a trough. I expect you to configure your portfolios from the firm's approved securities list and stop this reckless buying and selling."

Charles then dismissed Kyle, considering him fairly warned.

But Kyle didn't stop his reckless trading, and the second time Charles Goddard called him into the office, he was openly angry. He had struggled for almost a decade to bring Goddard-Stevens back from the verge of bankruptcy and, in doing so, had prevented even a breath of scandal from touching the firm or anyone who had ever worked there. He was not about to sacrifice ten years of blood, sweat, and tears so that his new son-in-law could make a few extra dollars here and there. He had been extremely generous with Kyle Pringle, and he was not about to be taken advantage of or to have the firm's clients be taken advantage of.

He shut the door firmly and addressed Kyle in a no-nonsense tone.

"You're churning these accounts. And what you're doing isn't just reckless, it's illegal. Your clients have every right to sue," he told Kyle, his face red.

"My clients expect me to invest aggressively," replied Kyle calmly, apparently completely unfazed by his father-in-law's words or his tone of voice.

"Aggressive and reckless are two different matters. So are aggressive and illegal," said Charles. "These portfolios all show substantial losses. I expect you to replace the money personally, and I expect you to do so immediately. We do not—I repeat, not—lose money for our clients. And we do not—and I mean, never—churn accounts, do you understand me?"

Kyle said that he did and left the office, apparently chastened and promising to turn over a new leaf.

Nevertheless, the portfolios Kyle handled continued to show heavy activity, and when the firm's internal auditors discovered shortfalls in five of the accounts Kyle handled, Charles Goddard had had enough. He said nothing to his wife, nothing to his daughter, and nothing to Kyle, since speaking to him was obviously a waste of time and breath. Instead, Charles Goddard thought of his grandfather, Carl, and of his own father, Robert, and even of the now-departed Itchy Mallone and the mysterious Mr. Shine and how they had once helped Charles protect the firm and its reputation. Feeling linked to the past, knowing that his forebears would approve of the difficult choice with which he was faced, Charles Goddard acted swiftly and decisively.

He replaced the missing money in the accounts himself so that the company's clients would never know what had happened. He also left the office early one afternoon and made a discreet visit to a stable in Long Island where he met with a man named Ray Lyons, who had worked around horses his entire life and who had a serious gambling problem. A very serious gambling problem. Charles took Ray aside, extracted his checkbook from his briefcase, and offered to solve Ray's problem for him.

"No questions asked," he told the bandy-legged groom with the gnarled hands, asking him to name his figure. "But I want a favor in return for the money. I want you to take a little trip down to Florida. To the Palm Beach Polo and Country Club, where my son-in-law is playing a match next weekend. And then I want you to disappear. Am I making myself clear?"

Ray Lyons nodded.

"Crystal clear, Mr. Goddard," he replied and then listened as Charles laid out the details of the errand he wanted performed.

As Charles Goddard drove back to his office after his meeting with Ray Lyons, he pondered the action he had just taken. He had done what his father and grandfather would have done: he had acted to protect his family, his firm, and the Goddard reputation. His only real concern was for Emily. In the short run, of course, she would be devastated. In the long run, Charles had no doubt, she would recover. She was still very young, and the saying that time healed all wounds was true.

He had, Charles thought, no real choice. There had never been a divorce in the Goddard family and there wouldn't be one. Not now. Not ever. Personal instability would be interpreted by the firm's clients as professional instability, no matter how much they denied it or how tangled their own lives were. They wanted the people who handled their money to seem solid, reliable, responsible, respectable.

Moreover, Kyle Pringle was more than just inconvenient, more than just a small-time chiseler. He was a weak link, someone who could destroy everything the Goddards had built since the 1920s. And Charles also knew that it was up to him to take the responsibility for what his son-in-law had done—and the blame. After all, it had been he who had brought Kyle Pringle into the firm and into the family, he who had given Kyle stock and status and position. It was only right that he be the one to correct his error. He made his decision quickly and with only a trace of guilt.

Polo is not a game for sissies. It is fast, hard, and dangerous. The ponies are bred for stamina and speed and charge up and down a polo field at reckless speed. The men who ride them swing long mallets at full force in an attempt to hit a rattan ball. Accidents are not uncommon, riders have ended up paralyzed, and the accident that ended Kyle Pringle's life was shocking but not unheard of. A polo field could also be a killing field.

Emily took the news hard, but in public, she held her emotions in check. In private, however, she was devastated by the loss of her husband and spent hours weeping in her bedroom. Her parents hovered protectively over her, concerned with the degree of her depression and with how long it seemed to linger. They were, therefore, particularly pleased when James turned down an invitation to a classmate's house in Bermuda in order to join his own family in Palm Beach at spring break.

"To help cheer up Emily," he told them in the thoughtful, considerate way that had been his since childhood. James worried about his sister's frame of mind. She seemed listless and distraught, had no appetite either for food or for life. She said that she couldn't sleep at night and in the afternoons, exhausted, she retreated into her bedroom. Gentle but determined, James did not give up on his plan to help ease her out of her mourning and back into the everyday world.

"You are not going to turn down Kendall Lawson's birthday party," he said when the invitation came in the mail. "She's been one of your best friends since the first grade. You have to start going out again, and Kendall's party is a good place to make your reappearance."

Emily demurred. She said that she didn't want people to feel sorry for her. That she didn't want to be the only widow in a roomful of young and carefree people. That she was afraid she'd start crying if anyone mentioned Kyle's name. That she didn't have a dress for the party and didn't have the energy to go out and shop for one.

"I didn't come all the way to Palm Beach to watch you sit in the house," James said. "I'm going to convince you to go to that party, even if I have to bribe you."

"Bribe?" Emily perked up slightly. "What kind of bribe?"

"That's my secret," said James mysteriously. He hadn't thought that far ahead. Still, he knew he had her intrigued, and that was the first step in getting her out and back into the social swim that had always meant so much to her. Now all he needed was an idea.

The thought of a new dress came to him as he walked along Worth Avenue and passed L'Elegance's opulent window. Like his mother, James's sister had never met an expensive dress she didn't like, and besides, one of Emily's complaints had been that she had nothing to wear to Kendall's party. He went into the countess's shop intending to buy Emily one of Tamara's extravagant, exclusive creations. Instead, he met Caroline Shaw, and as it turned out, Emily's bribe was purchased not at L'Elegance as James had originally intended but at Celeste's.

"Your bribe," James said, bowing with a low flourish as he presented a large rectangular box to his sister.

"Oh, James! You're the nicest brother anyone ever had!" said Emily, opening the box and holding up the tiny-waisted, full-skirted dress of the palest apricot-colored mousseline de soie over-embroidered with crystals in a delicate floral pattern. It glittered and sparkled, the length was perfect, and the portrait neckline set off Emily's creamy shoulders and serene beauty. She admired herself in the mirror and smiled for the first time in a long time, thinking that whoever won her brother would be lucky indeed. James might be a bit impractical, but he was so sensitive and loving and he always knew just what to say and what to do to make people feel good. No wonder women fell for him wherever he went.

"Good? Great? Wonderful?" she asked, meeting his eyes in the large, gilt mirror that hung in the foyer and asking for his opinion of how she looked.

"Nothing less than exquisite," he said.

She could hardly disagree.

"Then I guess you've won," she said.

"So you'll go to Kendall's?"

She nodded.

"I'll go," she said. "If you'll be my date."

"I will, but you'll have to share me," he said.

"I should have known that! Who exactly will I have to share you with?"

"Caroline Shaw."

"Of the Philadelphia Department Store Shaws?" Emily asked.

"Of the Lake Worth Shaws," he smiled, thinking of Miranda Eliot's comment.

"I've never heard of them," said Emily. "Is she your latest love?"

James didn't answer his sister. He didn't know exactly what Caroline Shaw was to him. All he knew was that he couldn't wait until Saturday. Couldn't wait to see her again.

Couldn't wait, couldn't wait, couldn't wait . . .

Caroline glanced at the clock, then at her reflection in the mirror behind the closet door. James Goddard wasn't due for twenty minutes but she was already dressed. The gown, Celeste had said, had been inspired by Madame Vionnet, the great French couturier of the 1930s. It was fashioned of heavy silk crepe, ecru in color and cut on the bias, skimming the body yet at the same time defining its curves and planes. The effect was to make an imperfect body perfect; a perfect body impossible to forget.

It was so expensive that Caroline had forbidden James to buy it for her. He had insisted, saying that he had no doubt that she would pay him back.

"This isn't just a dress," he had told her. "It's an investment. It's going to be crucial in getting your job back."

Caroline had thought that she would feel uncomfortable in it, as if she were an impostor dressed in someone else's clothing. Instead, the simple yet dramatic column of silk fit as if it had been made for her. Caroline glanced at her reflection once more. Was she really taller? Or did she just feel that way? Was she really that slim? Or was it just an illusion? Had she become—as Francesca had once predicted—a knockout? Or was she seeing things? Had James Goddard really invited her to Kendall Lawson's birthday party? Or had she just imagined it?

"Caroline! Mr. Goddard's here," called Selma.

Caroline swallowed and wiped the palms of her hands on a tissue. Then she picked up the minaudière James had helped her select to go with the dress and made her way down the stairs. The floorboards creaked, the wallpaper was stained and torn, the carpet shabby. Now he would see where she lived, realize how really poor she was, understand how dramatically different their backgrounds were.

And leave.

But he didn't.

He stood on Selma's front porch wearing a white dinner jacket, a character from a movie suddenly appearing in real, not reel, life. His blond hair gleamed, his skin was lightly tanned, his blue eyes vivacious. He seemed freshly minted, newly created for the sole purpose of giving Caroline a kind of pleasure she'd never before experienced. He held a single long-stemmed red rose in his graceful, callused hands, and his eyes held her in a velvet caress as he assessed her from head to toe. Caroline felt that no one had ever looked at her so deeply and so intensely, seeing her, seeing into her, and she yearned to return the intangible, unspoken, yet very real caress.

"You look the way you were meant to look," he said in a husky voice, acknowledging her, her dress, her hair, her makeup, her very being.

"Thanks to you," she said, feeling embraced by his glance as a blaze of warm sensation traveled along her body. Without him, she wouldn't have the dress—or the brand-new sense of confidence.

"An artist is only as good as his material," he said, gallantly returning the compliment. "To mark our first date," he told her, handing her the rose. Not only was this Caroline's first date, it was the first time anyone had ever given her a flower.

"Thank you," she said, accepting the deep red bud. "No one's ever given me a rose before."

"An obvious miscarriage of justice," he replied, his amazing blue eyes looking her over again—all of her.

The warm sensation that had flowed through Caroline's body turned hot and she felt herself flush.

"You know," he said, still taking her in, still marveling at how delicious she looked in that gown, "I have a confession to make. Suddenly I don't feel like going to Kendall Lawson's birthday party."

Caroline nodded, struck mute by unexpected emotion that washed through her, silenced by the realization that she, too, wanted to be alone with him.

"Still, duty calls," said James, bringing them both back down to earth.

So does the rent bill, Caroline thought to herself, remembering the job she no longer had. She handed the rose to Selma, who exclaimed over it and disappeared into the kitchen to put it in water.

"You're trembling," James said, as he took Caroline's hand and walked her to his sporty little Austin Healey, vintage '67, the last year in which they were made.

"I hoped you hadn't noticed," she said, finally finding words and glancing at him.

He smiled.

"There's nothing to be nervous about. All you have to do

is flash a big smile when Roz Garelick snaps your picture," he said.

"Roz Garelick?" Caroline asked. She recalled having seen the name in print. "Isn't she one of the reporters on *The Shiny Sheet?*"

James nodded.

"You do your homework," he said, impressed. "I spoke to Kendall this morning to make sure that Roz will be covering the party. Just remember, this is your plan we're putting into action." He opened the door of the low-slung convertible and helped her in.

He drove quickly and well, Caroline noticed, and never mentioned the run-down boardinghouse or Selma's housedress and ratty slippers. He didn't ask any embarrassing questions about why she lived alone or where her parents were. Instead, he talked to her about his sister as they made their way toward Palm Beach.

"The bribe did the trick! Emily agreed to go to the party. I've already dropped her off," he said happily.

"Why on earth did you have to bribe your sister to go to a party?" Caroline wanted to know. She had never heard of such a thing.

"She's been very depressed," said James. "Ever since her husband died she's been—"

"Died?" Caroline asked, shocked. "But he must have been very young—"

"He was. Only in his mid-twenties," affirmed James.

Caroline took in a sharp gasp of air. Kyle Pringle had been only a very few years older than James when he had died. The thought of such a young person's life ending affected Caroline like a sudden bleak, cold wind, and a shiver ran involuntarily through her body. "What happened?"

"Kyle was in a polo accident this fall," he said. "Polo's a fast, dangerous game. It's for the same crowd that goes in for heli-skiing, skydiving, and race car driving. Emily was always frightened by it, but Kyle loved it. She begged him not to play so recklessly, but he refused. He used to like to talk about 'pushing the envelope.'"

"How terrible! No wonder she's depressed," said Caroline, thinking about how awful it would be to lose a husband at such a young age. She couldn't imagine how she would feel if a tragedy like that ever happened to her.

James Goddard braked to a stop in front of the fashionable Pelican Club and helped Caroline out of the automobile. As the valet drove it away toward the parking area, Caroline could hear the festive music from inside; and as they stepped in the front door, she saw a crowd of Palm Beach's most sophisticated young set dancing and sipping champagne. Instinctively, she shrank, reverting to the feelings of rejection and inadequacy that had plagued her since childhood, feeling she had no place at such a party, no right to be in the same room with the Goddards and Lawsons of the world, let alone mingle with them. She was Caroline Shaw of Lake Worth. A nobody from nowhere. What did she know of Palm Beach society?

Sensing her discomfort, James put his arm around her and pulled her close to him for a moment.

She looked up at him, anxiety obvious on her face.

"I'm not sure I belong here," she said. "Dress or no dress."

"You look beautiful, and you're just as good as anyone else here," he reassured her. "I'm proud to be your escort. They're just people, no better no worse than the rest of the world."

He took her hand and, winking at her, led her inside.

"Just remember," he said as they entered the room, "when you see Roz Garelick, smile. And when the countess calls you tomorrow, don't answer the telephone."

On Sunday morning, Countess Tamara Brandt rose early, as was her custom. She stepped outside her front door to retrieve the Sunday edition of *The Shiny Sheet,* brought it inside, and made coffee. She poured herself a cup, carried it and the newspaper out to her glass-enclosed sunroom and settled onto the comfortable cushions of her favorite chair. Bon Bon, her purebred Maltese, jumped up onto her lap.

Ummm, she thought as she sipped the hot liquid and felt

the caffeine jolt her awake. *What would I do without my cup of java in the* A.M.?

She opened the paper to the juicy pictorial spreads that covered the parties and galas of the previous evening. How such photos tantalized the countess. She loved searching them to see how many of Palm Beach's wealthiest and most socially prominent women were wearing her exclusive designs. It was a game to her, although an extremely serious one, a way of keeping score and a way, ever since Celeste had run off with her husband, of getting revenge.

She began to scan the left side of the spread when one of the photos almost leapt off the page. Her mouth formed into a shocked O and she stared at the photograph in front of her. There it was, there *she* was in full color! The countess threw down the paper and screamed. Bon Bon jumped up from her lap and cowered in the corner.

"Oh, my God!" she shrieked out loud, even though she was completely alone except for the poor, quivering Bon Bon. "I don't believe it! I just don't believe it!"

She rubbed her eyes and, picking up the newspaper, looked again just to make absolutely sure that she wasn't seeing things. It was too outrageous! Too incredible! Caroline Shaw, her former stock girl, the girl she had just fired, had attended Kendall Lawson's birthday party with James Goddard, scion of the Goddard-Stevens brokerage fortune! He was standing by her side, his arm around her. And she was wearing an exclusive gown that came from Celeste! One that Celeste, that two-bit husband-stealing slut, had obviously knocked off from Madeleine Vionnet!

It was an insult! A betrayal of the lowest kind! A slap in the face! She'd been outflanked and outmaneuvered. She'd been double-crossed!

The countess threw down the paper a second time and, marching past the terrified Bon Bon, rushed to the telephone. She didn't give a damn what time it was or whom she might wake up. How dare Caroline Shaw show off Celeste's second-rate rag at one of Palm Beach's most exclusive parties! The girl should have been in one of her designs! "Oleander." Or, perhaps, "Jasmine."

The countess shook with fury as the telephone began to ring. She knew just what she was going to say. She'd be sweet and reasonable and she'd explain that she'd been upset, that she hadn't meant a syllable of what she said; and, of course, she'd do her best to make Caroline feel guilty for not even deigning to turn around and speak to her after James Goddard had swept her out of L'Elegance. She would tell Caroline that her old job was still there, waiting for her return. At the same terms, of course.

The girl would be delighted to come back. Heaven knew she needed the job. And, after all, the two of them had developed quite a bond over the months, hadn't they?

Piece of cake.

James Goddard spent all night thinking of Caroline Shaw and the way she felt in his arms. Slender, yet supple. Graceful but also somehow strong and substantial. He recalled the way her glossy chestnut hair smelled of shampoo, how her teeth glistened as she smiled, how her intelligent hazel eyes shone. He remembered the way she spoke to people, friendly but not pushy, and the way other people reacted to her, some of them recognizing her from L'Elegance. She was sympathetic to Emily but not maudlin; sincere in her birthday wishes to Kendall; genuinely pleased to see Francesca Palen, whom she obviously knew; polite and confidently casual with Miranda Eliot. James's men friends had looked at her, admired her, and asked him about her, wanting to know her name, where she was from, and where he had met her. They lined up to dance with her and get to know her better. She was nice to all of them, but with a glance and a smile, she always made it clear who her date was.

He remembered leaving the party at one o'clock in the morning and driving her back across the empty, moonlit causeway to Lake Worth. The top of his convertible was down, and the warm tropical air stirred the ends of her hair. He had gotten out of the Healey and crossed to the other side to open the door for her. He walked her to the porch of the shabby boardinghouse where she lived, and the moment he had been waiting for all evening had finally come.

He looked at her, murmured her name, and took her into his arms . . .

Electrified by a mysterious new energy, Caroline lay awake thinking of James Goddard and the way he caused her to feel. Each and every thing he did and didn't do helped to form the mental picture she now had of him. The competence of his driving made her feel that she was safe with him. The way he had decided to spend his vacation in Palm Beach in order to help comfort his sister indicated an unusual kindness and concern for others. The fact that he hadn't questioned her about the exact circumstances of her family caused her to feel that he was willing to wait until she was comfortable enough to confide in him. He had introduced her to his friends as if he were proud of her, and he had teased Roz Garelick about charging for Caroline's photograph because she was not only the most beautiful woman in the room but the best dressed.

He had brought her champagne and filled her plate from the buffet with the delicacies he said were the ones she'd most like. He'd danced with her but made sure that she'd had other partners as well. He'd watched her, he said, because he didn't want her to dance off with someone else now that he'd met her. He'd told her more about his boat models, the plans he had of trying one day to make a business out of them, and his role as the only son in a powerful, socially prominent family. As he'd driven her back to the boardinghouse, Caroline had felt a bit like Cinderella after the ball, bereft and forlorn, afraid that the magic was about to be over and that her prince would disappear into thin air.

Instead, the magic began as he walked her up the sidewalk to the porch, looked at her, murmured her name, and took her into his arms . . .

"You're not getting rid of me so fast," he said, tilting her chin up with a forefinger and forcing her to look directly into his eyes.

"I wasn't planning to," she heard herself respond in a tone of voice, husky and low, that she had never heard before and that didn't quite sound like her own.

"This is only the beginning," he said, bending down slightly and covering her lips gently with his own. His arms reached around her, pressing her body to his. One of his hands drifted down to her waist and the other found its way to the warm, silky hair at the nape of her neck. His kiss was soft at first and she instinctively trusted it, leaning into him, allowing her lips to curve to his, finding a custom fit. As he became confident of her response, he increased the pressure of the kiss and slightly parted his lips, wordlessly encouraging the same response from her. Intoxicated by unfamiliar sensations, her mouth opened to receive his, and she felt, as if in a dream, the soft brush of his tongue across her parted mouth and then, so very tenderly, its exploration of the moist inside of her lips. With a soft moan of involuntary surrender, she leaned even further into his body. His hips, hard and demanding, molded to hers. He tasted of salt and sweetness as, without her consciously having willed it, her tongue began, at first tentatively and then avidly, to seek the interior of his mouth. Drugged by sensation, she lazily opened her eyes halfway and studied, up close, the dark fringe of his lashes and a violet vein that pulsed in the lid. Then, in the same, slow-motion movement, she closed her eyes again and gave herself up to a kiss that had no beginning, no end.

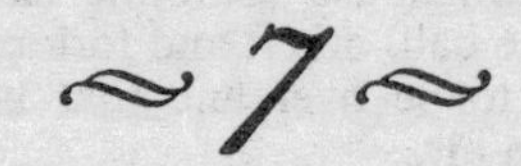

7

On Sunday morning at precisely 10:30, the doorbell at Selma Johannas's boardinghouse rang. Awake and dressed since six-thirty, Caroline hurried downstairs to answer the door and found James Goddard standing on the porch with a copy of *The Shiny Sheet* under his arm and two red roses in his hand. In the daylight, with the sun streaming down on him, surrounding him like a halo, he seemed even more handsome than she remembered. The sight of him filled her with a kind of warmth she had never experienced. *So last night wasn't a dream,* she thought. James Goddard was real, and he was here for her—at least for this moment.

"I'm early," he said, acknowledging that he and Caroline hadn't planned to see each other until noon. "But I couldn't wait another hour and a half. Not in my condition."

Caroline smiled. She knew instantly what he meant. She was in the very same condition: dizzy with exquisitely heightened sensations, drunk with the newness of the feeling, overwhelmed by the power of the very beginnings of first love. She looked up at him.

"I wasn't sure that what happened last night really happened," she said shyly. "I wasn't even sure that you were real."

"Oh, it happened all right," said James, as he leaned over and kissed her gently on the mouth. Then he admitted that, despite his words, he, too, had spent the night unsure whether she truly existed or if, in a fevered state, he had somehow conjured her up out of his imagination. Yet here she was: fresh and lovely, her shiny hair framing her beautiful face, her casual Sunday morning outfit of white shirt and shorts setting off her innate physical elegance. "I kept thinking that I had made you up," he said.

Caroline flushed and reached out to touch his hand.

"I'm real," she whispered with a sudden catch to her voice.

"I'm real, too," he said. "*We're* real."

He handed the two rosebuds to her. "For you. To commemorate our second date."

She thanked him with a kiss, the first she had ever initiated. His lips lingered on hers, their warmth spreading throughout her body, the slight touch causing her to melt and to yearn for something that she couldn't quite put into words.

"Your paper," he said, finally pulling himself away from her and handing her *The Shiny Sheet.* He watched eagerly as she flipped through the pages and saw her photograph.

"Wow! Is that really me?" she exclaimed, laughing and trying to connect the glamorous creature in the newspaper with the self that looked back at her from the mirror every day.

"Yes," said James, tracing her cheekbone with his forefinger. "It's definitely you. Now tell me, did the countess call?"

"Did she ever! She didn't even wait until nine."

"And did you speak to her?"

"Nope. I told Selma to take the call, just like you said."

"Did she call back?"

"She sure did. Fifteen minutes later—and every fifteen minutes since then." Caroline giggled. Her face lit with excitement and pleasure and James couldn't resist. Not for another moment. He took her into his arms and, in the broad light of morning, kissed her, holding her close to him, pressing the planes of his body into the yielding curves of hers.

"Looks like our little plan is working," he said finally, forcing his mouth far enough away to be able to speak. "We'll let Tamara dangle for a while. Then you'll cut a deal with her. You'll tell her you want a raise and a commission on everything you sell."

"She'll have a heart attack."

"She has a heart?"

Caroline laughed. "Good point."

"And here's something else: you're going to tell her that you won't come back to work for another two weeks."

"Two weeks? Why?"

"Because two weeks is what's left of my spring break," said James as he drew Caroline to him again. "While I'm in Palm Beach, I don't intend to share you with anyone—certainly not the countess."

The next two weeks were a blur of excitement as Caroline entered a brand-new world of pleasure and caring. There were daylight sails and moonlit walks, outdoor picnics and dinners in lavish restaurants, drives in James's Austin Healey, dancing at trendy discos, and games of tennis and croquet that ended in giggles and embraces. They walked on the beach and, hand in hand, window-shopped along Worth Avenue and stopped for coffee and pastry at Café Pavillion, where Pierre now treated Caroline as an honored client, always placing her and James at the best table, always offering them the most exquisite of the day's offerings.

Every day they grew closer, more intimate. Caroline told James about her childhood, about the fire and her guilt about it, about her parents and her tormented, conflicted feelings about them. James confided in Caroline about his respectful but uneasy relationship with his own parents. He was trying to get them to accept the fact that he wanted to apprentice with Caleb Jones in Maine, and they were doing their best to talk him out of it. He and Caroline spoke of their pasts and shared each other's hurts and offered words of support and compassion. In those two weeks they became friends and confidants.

And on the next to last Saturday of James's spring break, they became lovers.

They spent the day on his sailboat, *Salt Spray,* and when dusk began to fall, James docked the boat and led Caroline back to his Austin Healey.

"Dinner?" he said.

"Only if it can be a picnic," Caroline said, the idea suddenly coming to her, inspired, no doubt, by the round of lighthearted and affectionate activities he had been suggesting all week long. His romantic approach toward life, Caroline suddenly realized, was catching!

He drove toward Sunset Avenue and parked in front of C'est Si Bon. He roamed the elegant gourmet boutique, confident that whatever he wanted, he could have, chosing without thought of price. Into their shopping basket went imported cheeses, a variety of pâtés, a loaf of French bread, several different prepared salads, a selection of pastries, and a bottle of red wine.

"We can't live on love alone," he said, nuzzling her ear as they stood in the checkout line.

Caroline turned scarlet when she realized that the blue-haired dowager in diamonds and pearls standing behind them had heard and was staring at them.

"Don't let him get away," she suddenly advised Caroline.

James turned to the woman.

"Don't worry. She couldn't get rid of me if she tried," he said, escorting Caroline out of the shop.

The world seemed to be on their side, the stars their friend, and the moon their ally as James turned into an unmarked driveway and parked his small auto in a grove of palm trees. He spread their dinner picnic on a blanket he took from the trunk of the car. Caroline could hear the sound of the surf in the distance and smell the slight tang of salt water.

"Where are we?" she asked.

"On my parents' property," he said.

"But I can't see a house," said Caroline, looking around.

"It's hidden in its own landscaping," he said.

Caroline shook her head. "We're from such different worlds," she said wistfully, realizing once again how rich the Goddards must be.

"Does that mean you think we can't bridge them?" he said, sensing her unspoken thoughts.

"It means that it might be difficult," she said thoughtfully. "You still barely know me."

"I know you better than I knew you yesterday, and tomorrow I'll know you better than I know you today," he said, as if something important between them had already been agreed upon.

"There'll be a tomorrow?" she asked, aware that only one week remained of James's vacation.

"There'll be a thousand tomorrows," he said, taking her hand and looking into her eyes. "This is only the beginning."

The simple words triggered a torrent of feelings he had been trying desperately to restrain. Caroline Shaw was different from the women he had always known. She was a source of healing and warmth for which, in a childhood of privilege and luxury, he had often been starved. Moving closer to her, he put his arms around her and gathered her close to him. He tilted her head back and fixed her eyes with his, and just when she thought she would drown in their blueness, he touched her lips with his, gently at first and then with increasing passion.

"Only the beginning," he murmured. "Only the beginning."

"I'm nervous," she said. She was speaking of the thundering of her heart and the ecstatic, overpowering feelings that flooded her with his every word, every touch.

"There's nothing to be nervous about," he whispered, opening her mouth with his tongue and probing tenderly, then deeply. The taste of him washed her fears away, and she felt imbued with an almost magical sensation of being alight and aglow. Being with him had transformed her, caused her to feel winsome and witty, loving and lovable. Her personality seemed to have expanded in the days that she had spent with him, and the fears that had always inhibited her seemed to have disappeared. As she drifted into a bliss of pure sensation, she wondered for a moment if what was happening to her had ever happened to anyone else. Then a wave of heat flooded her, and her ability to think or even to form words deserted her. She shaped herself to him, pulling him closer to her so that he could feel her breasts against his chest, the length of her legs along his.

Her hips began to move, and with great effort he pulled away slightly. She was innocent, he knew, and he didn't want to rush her.

"Slowly," he said, moving his hands to the nape of her neck and burying his fingers in the silkiness of her hair. "I want to savor every moment."

Then he touched his lips to hers and continued the kiss, moving his tongue lightly along her lips and then, as her mouth willingly parted, he began to explore, first tentatively, then more deeply, the moist interior of her mouth.

"Sweet," he murmured. "You taste so sweet."

She felt a yearning she had never before experienced, and with a movement that was pure instinct, she began to return the kiss, doing to him as he had done to her. She moved the tip of her tongue along his lips, gently tracing their contour. There was a low moan in his throat as his mouth softened, then opened to her questing tongue. The velvety feeling of her tongue on his caused the kiss to deepen and she felt, rather than heard, him gasp as his hand moved along her throat and down to her breast. He cupped it with his palm and then began to move his thumb back and forth over her nipple, turning it into a tight, hard bud of almost unbearably pleasurable sensation, the sudden center of her being focused in that one, tiny point.

She drew a long, shuddering breath and moved her hands to the back of his head, pulling him even closer to her. Propped on his elbows, his eyes shut, he sank back to the blanket, one arm tightly around her, and she followed his movement, conforming her body to the length of his. As if of their own volition, her hands moved down the back of his head, lingered on the thick golden hair, caressed his shoulder, and traced a path under his shirt to the curly, blond hair of his chest. Her mouth followed where her fingers led and, unbuttoning the shirt, she circled his nipple with a finger, causing it to harden. He groaned and an irresistible wave of lust took over, threatening to sweep aside the restraint he had counseled.

"You knew how I felt from the beginning, didn't you? You can see how much I've wanted you, can't you?" he asked in a husky voice, his mouth close to her, both his hands now cupping her breasts, breasts that seemed filled with exquisite sensation that radiated throughout her entire body, turning it into a cathedral of arousal.

She saw it. In the sizzling fire of his eyes. And she felt it. In the hardness of his chest, the demands of his hands and mouth, in the length of the erection that pressed against her leg. He shifted out of his trousers and took her hand and moved it away from his nipple, across his navel and down into the wiry hair of his groin. He curved her fingers around him, and she gasped at his size and width and at the feeling of the silky skin that encased his steely strength.

"I never—" she began, trying to speak from a voice that was newly low, newly husky.

"I know," he whispered, reaching up and helping her out of her clothing.

With a moan that seemed to come from the center of his

being, he put his arms around her and turned them over. He was on top of her now, his eyes on hers, his hands on her breasts, his rigid erection throbbing against her naked skin. Their mouths met and opened. Their tongues intertwined and they held each other close. She felt a drop of moisture on her thigh, and she felt the movement as he held himself over her.

"Open your eyes," he said.

Without a will of her own, she obeyed and found herself looking into his eyes as he shifted over her, and she felt the tip of his finger brush her opening, hesitate, and then move inside her. Her body was on fire as she became a prisoner, helpless yet all powerful, of the sensations that blazed inside her. She moaned and moved and he probed further inside her. She was tight and wet and held his probing finger like a satin glove. One and then two fingers entered her, withdrew slightly, teased her, bringing her to a higher level of desire. Emboldened by the sensations that engulfed her, she reached down to caress him, moving her hand gently at first and then with increasing force. As they brought each other to a further pitch of fever, her hips began to move in a rhythm that coincided with his, her heart pounded violently, and she trailed her fingertips across his face as she opened her mouth wider, wanting to engulf him and to be engulfed by him. His tongue plunged into her and then retreated, and as she moaned out loud, she felt his erection brush her thigh, then her curly hair down below, and finally she felt its tip at her opening. It sought its home, tentatively, gently, as his tongue had explored her mouth. He probed, retreated, pierced her again, with each movement gaining further entrance into her. She lifted her hips higher and higher, almost sick with need for him.

"Please," she begged in a husky voice, opening her legs wider as he slipped a condom over himself. He wanted to protect her and safeguard their newfound love.

"Look at me," he commanded, and she opened her eyes again. In the moonlight she could see the changes that passion had caused in him. He reached around her and pulled her close to him so that her skin, newly sensitized, could feel his heat and his hunger. His eyes were so close to hers that she felt in danger of drowning in him as he kissed her and then, for a shattering, painful instant, moved away. She arched her back to stay close to him, curved her body to fit his, moved so that he could enter her all the way, and the restraint that he had barely been able to cling to evaporated in a roaring tide of desire.

"Now!" he said, and thrust deeply into her.

So lost was she in the sensations he had skillfully evoked in her that the moment of sharp pain dissolved immediately into ecstasy as her body merged with his. He groaned at the almost unbearable bliss he felt as her body expanded to take him in, her wet warmth holding him, embracing him. He moved further into her, and then, fighting to control the orgasm that pounded at him, threatening to cause him to lose every last vestige of control, he moved slightly out of her. His absence, however slight, was unendurable and she groaned and held him tighter to her, with her arms, with her legs. Having regained the slightest bit of control over himself, unable and unwilling to be parted from her for even an instant, he moved back into her, deeper and deeper, seeking her very core, reveling at the way her arms went tightly around him and the way her hips moved with him, welcoming him, encouraging him, loving him.

Holding her mouth in a hot, deep kiss, he thrust into her, carrying her with him into a faster and harder dance of passion, dimly aware of her nails raking his back and her shuddering moans as she moved helplessly beneath him. Cupping her buttocks with his hands, he moved her hips higher and higher, thrusting faster and faster, deeper and deeper. For what seemed like an eternity, they merged with each other, lost in a frenzy of passion, until at the same moment, gasping and breathless, they exploded into a mutual orgasm that left them wet and limp, drained and empty. They lingered in each other's arms, and then, at first gently and then with increasing hunger, he brought them to a second climax that electrified their nerve endings and shook their entire bodies. They lost themselves in her desire and his, her satisfaction and his.

In a state of almost liquid ecstasy, he collapsed on top of her and, still joined with her, shifted to his side. Breathless, their hearts pounding, they looked at each other, bereft of words, captives of overwhelming feeling. As her racing heart subsided and her breath returned, Caroline opened her eyes languorously.

"Has this ever happened to anyone else?" she murmured, feeling him still inside her.

"No," he said, acutely aware of the fragility of the moment and its infinite preciousness. "This was special. Just for us. You're part of my heart now," he whispered, holding her to him.

As James drove Caroline back to Lake Worth, Dina Goddard and her husband were rehashing the dinner party they'd given that evening. Dina asked her husband about the interruption that had occurred during the salad course. The butler had announced that a Ray Lyons was at the door and that he wanted to speak to Charles. Charles, who had a rule about not being disturbed at meals, had left the party briefly and then returned.

"What was that all about?" Dina asked.

"A problem at a branch office," Charles said, concealing his fury that Ray Lyons had dared show up at his home.

"Anything serious?"

Charles shook his head.

"A computer glitch. It's all resolved," said Charles, not wanting to tell his wife that Ray had gotten into more trouble with his gambling and that he had demanded more money in a crude attempt at blackmail, an attempt that Charles had quashed.

Then they began to speak about Caroline Shaw. They had, of course, seen her photograph in *The Shiny Sheet* that morning. They hadn't yet met her but Emily, it turned out, knew her from L'Elegance and had spoken to her at Kendall's party.

"She's quite attractive, perhaps even beautiful. And, according to Emily, pleasant enough. You don't think James has anything serious in mind, do you?" Charles asked.

"How could he? They've just met," said Dina.

"No money, I suppose," said Charles, shaking his head and thinking once again about James's impracticality and the way he tended to take up with anyone and anybody.

"No money. No family background to speak of either. In fact, quite the opposite. I spoke to James this evening before he went out. I asked about the parents. The father's a parking lot attendant and the mother's a bookkeeper," said Dina.

"Good God!" groaned Charles.

"Well, it will blow over. James is going back to college in a week, and you know how fickle young men are at that age. He'll forget all about her," predicted Dina.

"No doubt it's just another of his brief interludes," agreed Charles, feeling a sudden rush of affection for his own youthful passions and his days as quite the ladies' man. *Like father, like son,* he mused, pouring himself a brandy. Just a small one to sleep on. Between James's latest crush and the visit from Ray Lyons, he needed one.

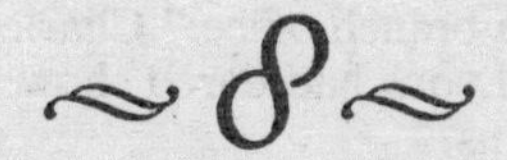

In the hours after their dinner picnic, in the moments before they would see each other again, Caroline and James each experienced the same violent, dizzying shifts in mood. One minute there was exhilaration—a wild, unabashed joy at having found each other and at having shared such an exquisitely intimate evening. The next minute ecstasy was replaced by anxiety and apprehension—a dark, nagging concern that perhaps their passion was evanescent, a kind of midnight delirium that would evaporate in the light of day. When James arrived at the boardinghouse, he and Caroline approached each other tentatively.

"How do you feel?" he asked shyly. What he meant was: Do you still feel the same way toward me?

Caroline answered the real question, the one that he hadn't dared ask.

"I didn't want to leave you last night," she said. Then she expressed her own doubts. "I was worried that you might not come back."

"You don't have to worry about that," he said, folding her in his arms and holding her close to him. "I love you."

He paused, a little overwhelmed by the enormity of his words, words he had never said to any woman, not even in the heat of lovemaking.

"I was afraid to say it last night," he continued. "Afraid it might be too much, too soon, too . . . more than you wanted to hear."

Now that he had expressed his deepest feelings, James waited for Caroline's response. Would she shy away? Would she doubt him or mock him? She was still and so quiet. He couldn't read her thoughts. Then she looked up at him.

"I love you, too," she said softly, looking directly into his eyes. "But I never imagined that you felt the same way. It just seemed impossible."

"It's not impossible," said James tenderly, his hands on her shoulders, his eyes on the face that was now the most precious on earth to him. "It's the truth. I love you. Don't ask me how I know, I just do."

"You've changed my life, do you know that?" she said, warm and safe in his embrace.

"Now I do, yes. And you've changed mine," he replied. He moved to kiss her, and they dissolved into each other's arms and then into each other's bodies, as if their union had somehow been predestined.

By the middle of the week, they had eased into a relationship that felt to both of them as if they'd been together all their lives. They began to talk about a shared future and a summer spent together in Maine. Caroline discussed her parents without inhibition and told him of the scarring events that had led to her living alone at Selma's. James, in turn, reiterated his ongoing conflict with his parents over whether or not he would go to work at Goddard-Stevens.

"I tell them I don't want to go into the firm, and they tell me that I'm being silly, that there's a family tradition to uphold," he said. "I don't want to disappoint them. But why should I abandon my own dream to make *them* happy? Why can't I be a Goddard and still make model boats?"

Caroline shook her head. She had no answer, no solution to his dilemma. Having a family tradition seemed precious to her. Her own family, such as it was, had none except broken promises and bitter accusations. She also knew about the importance of dreams—and the necessity of being practical about seeing that they came true. She thought that he would be foolish to burn bridges. What if his parents were right and his passion for boat models was only a transient phase? What if his true talent really turned out to be for business? They were only questions and neither of them had any answers.

Toward the end of the week, Caroline finally accepted Tamara's telephone call and her apology.

"She's agreed to a raise, but she said no to a commission," Caroline told James after her first conversation with her former employer.

"Let her stew a little more," he advised.

"What if she doesn't come around?" asked Caroline, the old insecurities always so close to the surface were quick to return.

"We'll go have a chat with Celeste. Recession or no recession, she might be happy to steal her competitor's secret weapon," James said.

Caroline laughed.

"Well, she stole Tamara's husband. Maybe I should let her steal me," she said.

"Good thinking!" said James, who told her to set up an interview with Celeste and to stand her ground with the countess, to remember that she had leverage now. For good measure, he had made sure to walk her past L'Elegance on their way to the Café Pavillion for afternoon tea. In the end, the countess capitulated and rehired Caroline—on Caroline's terms.

"With a raise and a commission on everything I sell!" she told James excitedly. "And you wouldn't believe how nice she was to me. She took me to lunch at Ta-boo and told me that I could be a real asset to L'Elegance. She even said that I had a talent for retailing."

While Caroline was learning how to use leverage to get what she wanted, James accelerated his discussions with Caleb Jones, the model boat maker in Camden, Maine. He discussed the terms of an apprenticeship and the financial realities of such a business. He was also deciding how to handle the important conversation he knew was looming with his father.

"He's not going to approve," James told Caroline.

She didn't envy him his upcoming talk with Charles Goddard. She hadn't met the powerful financier but he certainly sounded formidable.

The conversation with his father took place on the last day of James's spring break in the Goddard library at sunset. Golden-pink rays shone into the comfortable room, imbuing it with a roseate glow. The gold lettering on the spines of the leather-bound books shimmered, but the beauty and opulence of their surroundings went unnoticed by the two men. Each was determined to get his own way.

"Building model boats instead of taking your place at Goddard-Stevens?" Charles said in a disbelieving voice. "The firm is your heritage. It's in your blood."

James shook his head.

"High finance isn't for me, Dad," he said. "I'm planning to go to Camden this summer to start my apprenticeship. I've already made the arrangements."

"And give up a chance to be the chairman of a financial empire in order to make toys!" said Charles, a flush beginning to stain his complexion.

"Model boats aren't toys. Some people even say they're works of art," replied James.

"Ridiculous!" said Charles, thinking of Arnold Haltz and the unsold "art" that cluttered his father-in-law's Hoboken garage. Charles loved his son, but he was under no illusions that he had fathered a Picasso. "I suppose the girl has something to do with this crazy idea."

"The idea isn't crazy and 'the girl' has a name, Dad. It's

Caroline. Caroline Shaw. She's going to come to Camden with me."

"Whatever." Charles Goddard didn't want to hear about *that,* either.

"Caroline has nothing to do with my idea. In fact, she agrees with you more than she does with me. She's not so sure I'm doing the right thing," James said.

Charles Goddard didn't reply. He regarded his son silently. James was obviously serious. As he always did when confronted with a difficult problem, Charles considered the alternatives. He could become furious and cut James off. He knew fathers who had done precisely that when faced with disobedient children. He could reason with James and try to make him understand the impracticality of his plan. He could point out to James that he had grown up with every luxury and that, despite his trust fund from his Goddard grandmother, if he went off to make model boats, he'd have to scrimp along. The change in lifestyle would be quite a comedown. Another alternative was that he could try to buy James off—with money, a trip to Europe, or a new sailboat built to his specifications. Except, of course, that James was not particularly materialistic and never had been.

After thinking through the possibilities, Charles Goddard rejected them all. He decided to take a different approach, one that would, no doubt, surprise James. Charles smiled at his son as if their contentious exchange had not taken place.

"When are you leaving for Philadelphia?" he asked pleasantly, changing the subject.

"Tomorrow. First thing," said James.

"It's important for you to enjoy your last days in college," Charles said warmly, even affectionately. "It's a special time in life that you'll never experience again. But while you're enjoying yourself, I want you to think over your plans. I won't pressure you. I want you to make up your own mind. I promise not to try to force you to do anything you don't want to do—including work for Goddard-Stevens. I mean it when I say that all I want for you is your happiness."

"Thanks. Thanks very much. I appreciate that, Dad,"

said James, slightly taken aback. Expressions of concern and affection from his father were rare.

"By all means, spend the summer in Maine if that's what you really want," Charles went on. "Go with your Caroline and work on your boats, and while you're there, consider your future. Then, in the fall, we'll discuss the situation again. I don't want you to walk away from an opportunity that very few young men will ever have without carefully considering all the consequences to you, to whomever you choose to marry, and to the children you will father. Is that a deal?"

Charles held his son's eyes with his, and understanding the seriousness—and the fairness—of his father's proposal, James nodded. Caroline had made some of the same points that his father had, and his father, he realized, was being unusually conciliatory.

"You'll like Caroline once you get to know her," James said.

"We'll see," said Charles, who doubted it. It was hard for him to imagine any girl, let alone one from a poor family, who wouldn't have dollar signs in her eyes at the prospect of marriage or even a brief liaison with a Goddard.

"I'll keep an open mind about working at Goddard-Stevens, but I want you to keep an open mind about Caroline," James said.

"Are you negotiating with me?" asked Charles with a faint smile.

"Yes," said James. "Caroline's important to me. I want you to get to know her."

Charles nodded. "I like the way you stand up to me. It's one of the reasons you'd be so good at the firm."

"So it's a deal?" James asked.

"It's a deal," said Charles. "As long as you agree not to make any big decisions until we have a chance to speak again in the fall."

The two men shook hands, then briefly embraced. Whatever his father's failings might be, he was a man of honor, James thought. Even more important, his father had finally heard his side of things and agreed to let him pursue his own dreams—at least for the summer. And perhaps for the rest of his life, if that's how it turned out. Maybe, James mused, as he and his father shared a companionable glass of sherry as the sun went down, things would turn out just fine.

"James and I had a good talk," Charles told his wife later. "He'll come to his senses. Sooner or later. He may be somewhat impractical, but he's not stupid."

"He can be stubborn, though, once he gets an idea in his head," Dina pointed out.

Charles nodded.

"That's true," he said. "But he's still very young and for now, I'm giving him plenty of rope."

"And what about the girl?" asked Dina, who now knew that Caroline Shaw was a salesgirl who lived in a run-down boardinghouse in Lake Worth, and that James had spent almost every moment of his spring vacation with her.

"Hormones," replied Charles with a snort. "He's only twenty, an age when it's easy to confuse love with roses and moonbeams. Let him go to Camden. He'll get over the boats. And he'll get over the girl, too."

Caroline and James spent their last night together on the *Salt Spray*. The air was unseasonably chilly, but as they sat in the cockpit bundled in sweaters, holding each other and gazing up at the starlit Florida sky, they felt warm and snug and so very happy.

"I'm going to miss you," James said as he caressed her.

"Promise?" she asked, her tone half teasing, but her thoughts quite serious. He was returning to college. To his studies, to graduation, to the beautiful girls Caroline knew would surround him. What if he forgot all about her when he got back to Philadelphia?

He held her closer. "Promise," he vowed, looking into her eyes, his expression intense. "It's going to seem like forever until I see you again, though. I hate to even think about it."

"Then let's not," Caroline proposed, tracing the outline of his lips with her fingertips. "Let's concentrate on all the exciting things we'll do when you come back."

"Good idea." He kissed her. "You start."

"Okay. We'll go sailing. And have pastries at the Café Pavillion . . ."

". . . and drive down to the Keys . . ."

". . . and take a trip to the Everglades . . ."

"And let's not forget Maine," said James. "What a terrific time we'll have this summer. You'll love Camden."

They had been talking about spending the summer together, but the prospect seemed more fantasy than reality to Caroline. Inside her was still the girl who had grown up on Patterson Avenue, a street where summers in Maine were the stuff of storybooks, not reality.

"We're really going to Camden?" she asked.

"Absolutely," said James tenderly, taking her hand and holding it to his lips. "I've already begun to look for a place for us to live . . ."

Everything was turning out so perfectly, she thought, barely able to believe her sudden good fortune, not yet trusting it fully. First, she had met James, which seemed a miracle all in itself. Then she had gotten fired—which, in retrospect, had turned out to be the best thing that had ever happened to her. As a result, she had won a promotion, a raise, and a share of the profits she brought into L'Elegance. In addition, she had forged a new alliance with the countess, who had confided during their lunch date that she planned to close the shop during the slow summer months. Tamara would go to Europe; Caroline would be free to go to Maine with James. She would spend the summer with him and live with him as his lover. And who could even imagine what wonderful things might follow after that?

"We're lucky, aren't we?" he said, stroking her hair.

She nodded. She had never thought of herself as lucky. Hardly. But things had changed. She had changed. She had become more confident, more assertive, and she had learned to love and be loved. And all because of the man whose arms encircled her.

"Make love to me?" she said. "One last time before you go?"

Without waiting for a reply, Caroline pulled away from James, offered him her hand, and led him out of the cockpit, down the hatch into the cozy and gently rocking cabin. She wanted one last time to remember him by. Two months was a long time when you loved someone, she knew, and she was determined to make every moment count.

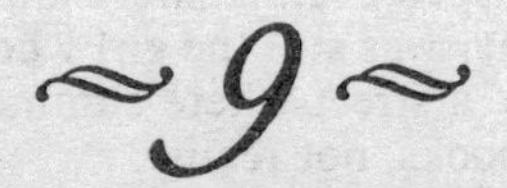

By late March, just as the winter season of charity balls was winding down, the spring season of debutante parties and weddings was gearing up. The countess, responding to the shifting needs of her clientele, refreshed her merchandise and aimed it at the spate of festive events that marked late spring and the end of the Palm Beach season. Bridal gowns replaced ball gowns. Debutante dresses in tulle replaced dinner gowns in crêpe. The racks of L'Elegance were filled with bridesmaid gowns, mother-of-the-bride ensembles, and party dresses for the mothers, sisters, and aunts of that season's crop of debs.

"Winter is for the Old Guard," the countess told Caroline. "Spring is for the young."

Caroline made good use of the experience she had gained working for the countess that winter and observing her in action. Now that she would be earning a commission, she thought of ways to expand her own client list. She began by contacting all her current clients, the ones the countess had turned over to her. She mailed them notes on L'Elegance's engraved stationery letting them know about the beautiful new gowns and accessories that were in stock. She also contacted the people she had met at Kendall Lawsons's birthday party, and whenever a new face appeared at L'Elegance, Caroline made a point of learning her name and suggesting designs that would be most flattering.

"You've become quite the merchandiser," the countess said, sounding pleased as she looked over the week's receipts and noticed that whenever Caroline sold a dress, she also sold a wrap, an evening bag, and accessories for the hair. She had displayed an instinctive knack for coordinating the elements of an outfit as well as a swiftly developing sense of knowing when to persuade a hesitant client into a sale and when to pull back and let the client make her own decision.

"And I see that your clients keep coming back to you, too," Tamara added, observing that the same names appeared over and over on Caroline's sales slips.

But the countess wasn't all sweetness and light.

"You're making a lot of money," she grumbled, handing Caroline a substantial commission check at the end of April.

"I've worked hard and I've earned it, Countess," replied Caroline, remembering what James had said about people like the countess respecting firmness, and refusing to be put on the defensive.

The countess responded with advice.

"I hope you're investing at least part of it," she told Caroline, offering to introduce her to her own broker, Clifford Hamlin.

"As soon as I have enough money in the bank, I plan to. I've learned *that* watching you," replied Caroline. She knew just how much Clifford Hamlin had helped the countess, and she thanked her for the offer. "But first of all, I have to repay my debts."

The countess didn't ask what her debts were and Caroline didn't proffer an explanation, but every Friday after she got paid, Caroline religiously went to the bank and deposited her commission check into a special account. She had always managed to live on her salary, and with the raise, it became even easier. But the commission money was different. She was accumulating it in order to repay James for the dress that had helped her get her job back—on her terms.

The telephone in Selma's boardinghouse rang every night at eight. It was always for Caroline. It was always James. To tell her about his day, to ask her about hers, and, most of all, to tell her that he loved her.

"That man is supporting the telephone company!" said

Selma one Tuesday evening in early May. They had just finished serving supper to the other boarders and were in the kitchen doing the dishes. The clock on the wall said that it was quarter to eight.

"I've told him he doesn't have to call so often," said Caroline. "But he doesn't pay any attention to me."

At five to eight the dishes were dried and back in the cupboards. The leftovers had been put into plastic containers and set in the refrigerator, and the dish towels were hung on racks to dry. By eight o'clock Caroline and Selma were alone in the living room. Selma was settling down with Judith McNaught's newest novel, and Caroline switched on the television set and waited for the telephone to ring.

"You could set your clock by James Goddard," said Selma, glancing at her watch.

Caroline smiled. It was true. But tonight, eight o'clock came and went. So did quarter past and half past. Caroline's first thought was that James had finally forgotten her; that he had gotten bored with his nightly ritual; that he had changed his mind about her, about them; that he had met someone else. But then she scolded herself for allowing her old insecurities to push their way back into her thoughts. She was different now. More confident of herself, more confident of James's feelings for her. No, James was not a fickle man, she knew. Nor was he insincere. He had said he loved her, and everything he said and did proved it. There had to be another reason why he hadn't called at eight o'clock as he always did. Perhaps something had happened to him. Perhaps he hadn't called because he couldn't.

Suddenly, visions of an automobile accident flashed through Caroline's mind. Then images of a mugging near his fraternity house. There's no safe place anymore, she thought, as she recalled how every evening's newscast began with reports of violence and murder. And Philadelphia, James had told her, was no better than south Florida when it came to crime. Dear God, she prayed silently. Don't let anything happen to him now. Not when we've only just found each other.

At nine-thirty, Caroline couldn't sit still for another minute. She went to the phone and tried to call James.

When a man's voice answered, she was momentarily relieved. Then she realized it wasn't James on the other end but his friend and fraternity brother, Phil Bradley.

"The last time I saw him was at lunch," said Phil, who had heard all about Caroline and was looking forward to meeting her.

"And he was all right when you saw him?" Caroline asked.

"Right as rain," said Phil, who had a friendly, easygoing voice that calmed Caroline slightly. "He had an economics lecture this afternoon, but after that I don't know what he was up to."

"Would you ask him to call me as soon as he gets in?" asked Caroline.

Phil Bradley said he would, no problem, and hung up.

By eleven o'clock, Caroline still hadn't heard from James, and she was nearly frantic. The worries she had dismissed as bogeymen of the mind now began to seem ominous with every tick of the clock.

"I wonder if I should call the Philadelphia police," she said to Selma. "Or maybe the area hospitals."

"It might be a good idea," said Selma, looking up from her book, a concerned expression on her features. "James is always so reliable. It's not like him not to call."

At eleven-thirty, Caroline dialed Philadelphia information and asked for the number of the local police and campus police as well as of hospitals and emergency rooms in the university area. She was making notes of the numbers on the pad by the telephone when the doorbell rang. Her dislocated heart stopped beating, and for a moment, she froze. She stared at the front door, afraid to open it, suddenly terrified of what bad news she might be letting in.

"Want me to get it?" Selma asked.

"No, I'll go," Caroline said, clearing her throat. She moved to the front door, wanting to stop time, wanting yesterday to be the day she lived in forever. Yesterday the phone had rung at eight. Yesterday James had told her he had finalized his arrangements with Caleb Jones and found them a charming place—a "carriage house," he had called it—that they could rent for the summer. Yesterday he had told her he loved her and spoken of the future they would share. Yesterday he had been alive.

She opened the front door, preparing herself for whoever or whatever was on the other side.

"Hello, you."

Caroline's hand flew to her mouth in disbelief and she gasped. It was James! He was unhurt! Smiling his rakish smile and holding a ransom of roses in his arms. A dozen, two dozen, or more. Caroline couldn't even begin to count as a feeling of relief and anger flooded through her. For a moment, she stood there facing him, not knowing whether to scold him or kiss him.

He looked slightly windblown and a bit tired but even more handsome than she remembered. He bowed slightly and presented the enormous bouquet of roses wrapped in green paper.

"Did you buy out the florist?" Caroline asked, flushing with pleasure as she accepted the extravagant gesture.

"It's only three dozen," he said with a grin. "To commemorate the three-month anniversary of the day we met."

Caroline took the flowers and buried her face in them, inhaling their fresh, sweet scent.

"Thank you! Thank you! It's the best thing that ever happened to me! The most. The nicest . . ." she said, running out of words.

He smiled.

"It's the least," he corrected. "The least I could do for someone who's changed my life."

Finally able to let go of the huge bouquet, Caroline handed it to Selma, who disappeared into the kitchen to find a vase and to leave the two young lovers alone.

"Aren't you going to invite me in?" James said, feigning a pout.

Caroline was still too choked up, too overjoyed, too overwhelmed with conflicting feelings to answer. Instead, she leapt into his arms, hugging and kissing him with such ferocity that she nearly knocked him over.

"Hey, hey. I'm glad to see you, too," he laughed.

"I love you, love you, love you!" Caroline exclaimed, half

sobbing, half laughing, burying her face into his shoulder. "I wish I could find the words. I just can't tell you how much."

"No problem. I'll tell you."

James held Caroline at arm's length and gazed into her eyes, drinking in her loveliness, reminding himself that it was all real and that she was his.

"I don't want us to be apart ever again," he said softly, his expression serious, almost solemn. "I'm going to graduate in a couple of weeks, and afterwards, I'll go right up to Maine with Phil. As soon as the countess closes L'Elegance for the summer, you'll fly up and join me. And that'll be the end of that."

Caroline looked alarmed. "The end of what?" she said.

"The end of this separation nonsense," he said in a husky voice, pulling her into his arms and holding her tight. "We won't ever be apart again."

And for the next three days, they weren't. After spending a few minutes chatting with Selma and a few of the other boarders, James told Caroline to grab some clothes and pack an overnight bag. When she returned with her suitcase, he escorted her to the rental car he had picked up at the airport and drove them across the causeway to Palm Beach. To his parents' mansion on North County Road.

"We're going to spend the weekend Chez Goddard," he said.

"You can't mean at your parents'—"

"Shhhh," he soothed. "They're in New York. There's nobody home but the servants. We've got the whole damn place to ourselves!"

Caroline and James spent a magical weekend at the Goddards' estate, a mansion so palatial Caroline couldn't imagine real people living in it. There was a swimming pool and a tennis court and an eight-car garage. There were luxuriant green gardens and a stretch of beach that was manicured each and every morning. There were rooms of every size, all opulently decorated, a kitchen large enough for a hotel and vast bathrooms of marble and mirror.

How funny life was, she thought a bit ruefully, remembering her Sunday pilgrimages to The Breakers and how sad and forlorn and out-of-place she had felt there, how much of an imposter. Now, here she was, eating off heavy monogrammed sterling silver and delicate porcelain, drinking from crystal goblets, being waited on by respectful servants, swimming on a private beachfront or in the olympic-size pool, strolling on private parklands, and sleeping in a silk-swagged bedroom with the man she loved, the man whose family owned the fabulous estate and its surrounding grounds!

The weekend raced by, and when it came time for James to fly back to Philadelphia, he and Caroline consoled themselves with the fact that in only a few weeks, they would be together in Maine.

"Make these few weeks go fast," she said as she clung to him. They were standing at the gate of the Delta Airlines terminal, and the passengers on James's flight had already boarded.

"I'll try," he said. "I love you, Caroline. So much. So very, very much. More than you know. More than you can imagine."

They held each other tightly, hanging on almost for dear life, neither wanting to let the other go.

"Thanks for the wonderful surprise," she whispered, her throat closing as she felt his grip slacken.

"Anytime. Whenever and whatever your heart desires," he said, kissing her one last time and then releasing her, as the flight attendant came on the loudspeaker urging all passengers to board the plane.

"Gotta go," he said quickly.

"Love you," said Caroline. "More than I ever thought possible."

Watching him walk away from her with his graceful athletic stride, passing through the gate and onto the Boeing 727 bound for Philadelphia, was like losing a part of herself. But soon they would be together, she reminded herself as he disappeared from her sight. All summer long. In Maine. Forever and after.

~ 10 ~

Caroline had never been out of Florida, and her first sight of Maine as James drove her from the Portland airport to Camden on that sparkling June afternoon was as exciting to her as someone else's first view of Paris might have been. Florida's landscape was flat, the vegetation subtropical, the flowers lavish and gaudy. Maine's contours were jagged and hilly, ancient geologic formations that stepped down from a center of pine woods to elegant stony beaches. Its flowers were the old-fashioned kind: asters and zinnias in a child's paint box of colors; white and lavender cosmos and demure pastel sweet peas. While Florida's climate was sultry and languorous, Maine's was crisp, often biting, with traces of the briny salt of the sea and of the forests of dark green pine that studded the rocky landscape.

Camden, overlooking the green islands and white sailboats that dotted Penobscot Bay, was a picture postcard of a New England town, ruled by white church steeples and American flags snapping to attention in the brisk sea breezes. As James drove his Healey through its narrow, twisting main street bustling with residents, visitors, and tourists, Caroline noticed a number of small shops selling mass-produced souvenirs as well as a variety of handmade items.

"There's quite a community of craftspeople living and working in the area," James said when she asked about the shops. "In fact, Phil's girlfriend, Jennie, is a quilter—and a Camden native."

Weeks before, James had told Caroline that Phil Bradley, his fraternity brother at Penn, would be spending the summer in Maine, too, as his parents owned a bed-and-breakfast inn in Camden.

"Phil majored in accounting, and unlike yours truly, he actually enjoys working with numbers," James had explained during one of their nightly phone conversations. "He's going to keep the books for the inn and do some accounting for a couple of other local businesses."

Caroline looked forward to meeting Phil and his girlfriend. The idea of having friends her own age, of socializing with them, of being a member of a close-knit group, appealed to her. She had grown up alone, and she had lived alone until James had come into her life. Sharing their love with friends would be a way of amplifying it and enriching it.

"I can't wait to meet them," she told James, putting her hand on his leg as he continued to drive.

At a high point in the road, just as the busy center of Camden began to thin out, James turned into a short driveway. There, set back from the street, screened by huge elm and pine trees, was a large, whitewashed brick house with gleaming black shutters. Giant columns supported an overhang that shaded a wraparound veranda, and dormer windows added grace to the roof line. Nestled just to the side of the house was a small cottage. James stopped the car in front of its entrance and turned to Caroline.

"This is the carriage house I was telling you about." He beamed. "Like it?"

Caroline could barely express her feelings. The cottage was quaint and picture-perfect, an enchanted doll's house. Its clapboard exterior was painted white, the shutters on the windows a dark, glossy green. There was a swing in the yard, a small herb garden, a border of bright yellow marigolds, and on the postage-stamp-size porch, comfortable wicker furniture with blue canvas cushions piped in white. A majestic elm cast shade, and a stone bird bath drew red cardinals and brown sparrows.

"Thank you for finding it," she managed, kissing James on the cheek. "But are you sure we can afford it?" Anxieties about money were never far from her mind.

James nodded.

"I won't be earning very much, but I do have the income

from a small trust fund. It's not all that much, but we'll be able to squeak by," he said.

"I guess this must seem incredibly small to you," said Caroline, looking at the cottage and thinking of the Goddards' oceanfront mansion in Palm Beach.

"It seems like a palace to me," said James, looking at her tenderly. "I'll be sharing it with you."

He always knew what to say and how to make her feel adored, Caroline thought. How lucky she was to have met him, how blessed by fate the day he walked into L'Elegance.

"Who owns the big house?" she asked, turning to him and putting her hand in his.

"Cissy McMillan. She's a New York decorator. Her great-grandfather was a sea captain who built the house in the 1850s. The carriage house was added at the turn of the century."

"Does she live here?" Caroline asked.

"On and off. Her family's been summering Down East for four generations, but Cissy's a very busy lady. When she's not designing interiors for the rich and famous, she comes here to unwind. She's looking forward to meeting you, by the way."

Caroline felt her heart skip a beat as she imagined herself in the company of a woman who decorated the homes of the rich and famous. Yes, she had sold ball gowns and cocktail dresses and lingerie to plenty of wealthy and well-known people at L'Elegance, and yes, she had managed not to embarrass herself or James at Kendall Lawson's birthday party, but she still felt traces of her old insecurities whenever she imagined herself socializing with such people. *Someday I'll feel that I belong,* she told herself as James helped her out of the car. *Someday I'll forget about Patterson Avenue and leave all those bitter memories far behind . . .*

She gazed at him as he took her by the hand and led her up the path to the carriage house. In khaki shorts and a white polo shirt, he looked like something out of a magazine. His broad shoulders tapered to a slim, tight waist, and his long legs were tanned and well proportioned. His golden hair was slightly bleached by the summer sun, and his blue eyes seemed in harmony with the high sky and the hue of the deep water of the bay. Every time Caroline looked at him, she felt a jolt of intermingled pleasure, surprise, and excitement that this staggeringly handsome and relentlessly romantic man had fallen madly in love with her. No dream she had ever imagined came close to this reality, this extraordinary joy. Was it too good to be true? she wondered. Had it all happened too fast? Would it continue? *Could* something so wonderful, so unbelievably blissful last?

"Home sweet home," said James, jollying her out of her dark thoughts. "Don't you want to see the inside?"

"Of course I do! Is it really and truly ours?" she asked, delight sparkling in her eyes as she took in the scene. She had never imagined such a magical little dwelling. The thought that it would be theirs was almost unbearably glorious. For as long as Caroline could remember, Al Shaw had never owned a decent home, and ever since the fire, her home had been the small room at Selma's boardinghouse.

"Ours! For the whole summer," James said. "I've spent the last week getting it ready for you. I've painted, done a little plumbing, and washed the windows."

Caroline picked up his hands and saw the newly formed calluses and the cut across one of his knuckles—tangible evidence of how hard he had worked to welcome her. He was her lover, her protector, her guardian. Her everything. She kissed the cut and the calluses on the back of his hand and then turned it over and kissed its palm.

"No one has ever done anything like this for me," she said, clearly moved by his thoughtfulness, her eyes full and large and shiny with a combination of joy and excitement as she looked at him.

He kissed her cheek lightly, his lips just barely brushing her face in a gossamer butterfly kiss.

"I know it's corny, and I don't care what the neighbors think, but I'm carrying you across the threshold," he said.

He picked her up in his strong arms and maneuvered her through the newly painted white front door with its polished brass knocker and wicker mailbox. As soon as they were inside, he shut the door behind them, set her down, and took her in his arms.

"I've never been so happy," he said, gathering her to him and kissing her again, this time more deeply.

"Neither have I," replied Caroline, praying once again that her newfound happiness would last, that it wouldn't vanish as it sometimes did in her nightmares.

When James finally let her go, he gave her a tour of the house. The front door opened into a small foyer furnished with a hooked rug with a New England schoolhouse woven into the design; a pine desk with a slanted top; and a rustic pine chair. To the left was a small but well-equipped kitchen, and straight ahead was a living room and dining area. The living room had a stone fireplace already laid with kindling and logs in anticipation of the chilly Maine evenings. The furnishings included a small but comfortable sofa and a pair of wing chairs. The windows looked out on the lawns and trees and, beyond, the blue waters of Penobscot Bay. Rag rugs in bright colors decorated the wide-plank floor that smelled of beeswax polish, and the dining table, which James said had come from an authentic old tavern, was a hearty, scarred antique that spoke of good food and good times. On the steamer trunk that served as a coffee table stood a model boat of perfect proportions, finished in a gleaming white paint with a red stripe running smartly along its hull.

"The *Salt Spray,*" said Caroline, reading the name and looking at James. "It's your boat, isn't it?" She and James had spent hours on the *Salt Spray* during his spring break. The 33-foot Herreshoff was his pride and joy.

"It's also the first model I ever made completely on my own," he said with obvious pride. "Even Caleb said it wasn't too bad."

Caroline bent down to examine it more closely, and on the front of the hull were two small entwined hearts. In one were the initials "CS." In the other was "JG."

"A memento of our first days together," he said, explaining the intertwined hearts. "Caleb scoffed—he's a purist, don't forget—but he allowed me this one little indulgence."

"I'll have to remember to thank him." Caroline smiled as James took her hand and led her out of the room.

Up a narrow flight of stairs the entire second floor was

occupied by an airy bedroom with slanted eaves that met the floor in a charmingly crooked line. Its views were entrancing, as white sailboats skittered across the dark blue water and the green islands of Penobscot Bay beckoned. The room itself was a dreamy evocation of times past. Hand-carved beams crossed the whitewashed ceiling, and a hand-made blue quilt with a motif of hearts covered the plump mattress. A blue-and-white spongeware pitcher filled with white daisies stood on a pine dresser, and a blue rag rug covered the floor.

"Jennie made the quilt and gave it to us for a housewarming present," said James. "Cissy gave us the pitcher."

Caroline was touched by the generosity of people she hadn't even met. People so unlike the ones she had grown up with.

"But they don't know me," she said, still unaccustomed to consideration and affection. The ingrained lessons of her childhood, she now understood, were going to be very difficult to leave behind.

"They'll know you soon enough," said James. "Cissy has invited us over tomorrow afternoon, and we're having dinner with Phil and Jennie tomorrow night."

"And tonight?" Caroline said. She grinned and looked up at him mischievously. She hadn't seen James in weeks and was looking forward to spending their first night together alone.

"Tonight we're having room service." He smiled, as if reading her mind. He pointed to the four-poster bed and the tray of sandwiches and bottle of champagne in an ice bucket on the night table, then kissed her.

"Ummm," she said, as he nibbled on her earlobe. "Splendid idea. But how about an appetizer first?"

"An even more splendid idea," he said, and scooped her up in his arms.

Cissy McMillan stood just over six feet and resembled a stork—all legs and elbows. She had wavy, silver-white hair, velvety unlined skin, and clear light blue eyes. She wore a white blouse, a cotton wrap skirt, sturdy walking shoes, and a vivid slash of bright red lipstick. She looked more like a country wife than the head of a sophisticated decorating firm with offices in New York, Boston, and Washington and clients in the Fortune 500. It was said that Cissy McMillan was the woman with the iron fist inside the chintz ruffle. As she came down the path of the big house to greet Caroline and James, she almost tripped over her King Charles spaniel, Erin.

"Would you believe that I sent this beast to obedience school?" she asked no one in particular as the dog raced in circles and tangled the leash around her ankles even more tightly.

Again, Cissy McMillan almost tripped, and James held out a hand to steady her.

"And he graduated! I should ask for my money back!" she exclaimed, laughing and turning to Caroline as the dog ignored her command to "sit" and then to "stay."

"Hello, Ms. McMillan. It's nice to meet you," she said, extending her hand.

"Well, James was right. He said you were beautiful and you are," Cissy replied, taking Caroline's hand in a firm grasp and looking her straight in the eyes. "Welcome to Camden. It's a pleasure to have you here. You've certainly made James the happiest man in the state of Maine! Now, let's go eat our cookies before they get cold."

Cissy McMillan led James and Caroline up to the front porch of the big house. A white wicker table was laid with a freshly laundered blue-and-white-checked dish towel. On the towel was a frosty pitcher of lemonade, three tall glasses, and a white ironstone plate on which were stacked fragrant blueberry bars, still warm from the oven. Simple as the arrangement was, it was almost irresistibly appealing.

"It's almost too beautiful to touch," said Caroline. She was accustomed to the countess, whose aesthetic preferences ran to the extravagant and the elaborate. She had never realized that simple things, arranged with a discerning eye, could have their own kind of elegance.

"Nonsense. It's to enjoy," said Cissy McMillan briskly, reaching for the pitcher and pouring three glasses of the pale yellow lemonade. The drink, filled with chipped ice in which floated the pulp of freshly squeezed lemon, was lightly sugared, refreshingly tart. The blueberry bars, with their golden crust laden with cooked fruit and its oozing dark purple juice, were singularly delicious, and Caroline said so.

"Made from our local wild blueberries," Cissy said. "There's a blueberry patch on the hill right behind the house. I'll show you just where to find them."

The three of them chatted about Maine, about James's boat models, and about Cissy's decorating business, and Caroline found herself relaxing completely, even offering amusing anecdotes about Countess Tamara and the goings-on at L'Elegance.

"This Countess What's-Her-Name sounds like a piece of work," Cissy laughed. "But I'm glad you brought up your job at the shop, Caroline."

"You are? Why?" asked Caroline.

"Because I've gotten myself in a bit of a pickle," said Cissy. "You see, I own a small building on Main Street. For the past six years it's been run as a bookshop, but the lease is up and the couple who've been renting it have informed me that they're planning to move to Oregon." She paused to sip her lemonade. "So now the shop's empty, and I'm trying to decide what to do with it. A number of the local craftspeople have expressed interest in it, but the rent's pretty steep for them. Still, I would like to give them an opportunity to display and sell their wares."

Caroline nodded. She was drawn to this woman who, unlike the countess, was successful *and* reasonable.

"One solution would be to turn the place into a crafts shop and run it myself," Cissy continued. "But I don't have the time—or the expertise."

"The expertise? Come on, Cissy. You could run the White House with one hand and the Pentagon with the other," James teased.

"As a matter of fact, I probably could," she said, only half joking. Then she turned serious again. "But the truth is, I'm really much too busy to dabble in shopkeeping. Overcommitted is my middle name! In the next two weeks alone, I've got to be in six different states."

"Is the traveling fun?" Caroline asked, thinking that her trip to Maine was the first time she'd been on an airplane, the first time she'd been anywhere outside of Florida.

"It depends on the client," Cissy McMillan said. "Some of them become friends. Some of them are a real pain in the ass. But I expect you know that, Caroline, after working in Palm Beach."

"Oh, she's seen everything," James concurred.

Caroline laughed.

"The good, the bad, and the ugly," she admitted.

"Caroline can handle anybody," said James. "Working for the countess has really been an education!"

"James told me you're going to be looking for work while you're here in Camden. That gave me an idea," Cissy said. "What would you think about running a crafts shop for me?"

"You want me to *run* it?" Caroline said, wanting to be sure and glancing at James, who nodded.

"Why not?" said Cissy. "I'm only going to stay open for the summer. You've had some experience, both at L'Elegance and at that gift shop in Lake Worth. I'll pay you on the same terms that the countess did, if that's agreeable to you."

"That would be wonderful!" Caroline said. "It's exactly the kind of job I hoped to find here. But I never imagined it would be so easy." As the word "easy" crossed her lips, she felt that familiar twinge of foreboding, of fear, a profound sense that nothing good came easily. That everything, sooner or later, had a price.

"Good. Then it's settled," Cissy said briskly. "I believe in trusting my instincts when it comes to people. I liked you the minute I saw you, Caroline. You're straightforward. No baloney. You'll fit in just fine with the folks here in Maine."

Phil and Jennie lived in an apartment in an old barn, about a five-minute walk from the carriage house. Phil was taller than James and broader, with lively brown eyes that danced behind wire-rimmed glasses and a bushy ginger beard. He greeted Caroline with a bear hug, while Jennie stood next to him and smiled.

"Ah, so I finally get to put the face with the voice," Phil said, delighted to meet Caroline after talking to her on the phone several times.

"It's great meeting you," she replied.

"And I'm Jennie," said Jennie Armstrong, introducing herself as soon as Phil let Caroline go. She held out a welcoming hand. She was barely five feet two, slightly plump and very pretty. She had cinnamon-colored hair worn in a long braid that fell down her back to her shoulder blades, light green eyes fringed with reddish blond lashes, and a sprinkling of freckles across her cheeks and nose. She wore no makeup and smelled faintly of vanilla. In faded overalls and a plain white T-shirt, she had the fresh, unforced allure of a model in a J. Crew catalog. "We're going to get you acclimated right away with a real Maine dinner—steamed lobsters, baked potatoes, coleslaw, sliced tomatoes, and cold beer," she said, listing the menu and leading the way to a wooden deck built off the side of the barn.

In the yard next to the deck, a bed of coals burned in an open pit, and a battered, galvanized tin washtub held ice, water, and bottles of soda and beer. Potatoes in foil jackets baked on the coals, and a big black-and-white enameled lobster steamer stood ready. James opened the soda and beer and passed them around as Phil poured an inch of water in the lobster steamer and placed it on the hot coals.

"Steaming is best," he told Caroline as they waited for the water to come to a boil. "It concentrates the flavor. Besides, if you just boil them, you end up with a puddle of water on your plate."

"James said that you worked in a really glamorous place in Palm Beach," Jennie said to Caroline when Phil finished his lecture on lobsters.

"Glamorous from the outside. Not so glamorous from the inside," laughed Caroline, glancing at James, who came over and put his arm around her.

"Have you spoken to Cissy yet?" asked Jennie.

Caroline nodded.

"She offered me a job," she said. "I've agreed to run her crafts shop for her. She told me that she was more or less talked into opening a shop."

"I know. I'm one of the culprits," Jennie confessed. "There are a lot of young people around the state who are into crafts and produce really excellent work. We approached Cissy about opening a shop dedicated to nothing but the best—a real showcase for what we do. Cissy is known for her 'America First' style of decorating as well as for her high standards. We thought, if we could get her to sponsor us, it would give us the image we need to get our work shown and sold."

Jennie's enthusiasm was contagious, and as she spoke, ideas began to race around in Caroline's mind, ideas that she would speak to Cissy McMillan about in the morning.

"I don't know anything about crafts, but I do know something about selling," Caroline said.

"Not to worry," said Jennie. "We can teach you all you need to know about crafts. Besides, James told us that you can sell anything. An absolute whiz, he said."

"I don't know about *that,"* said Caroline, blushing and hoping that James hadn't oversold her.

"Well, I do! She's a genius!" said James, squeezing her shoulder and pulling her close to him.

"Lobster's on!" called Phil. He plucked the potatoes from the coals and removed the red crustaceans from the steamer. He placed them on a large wicker tray lined with newspaper and carried the tray, the piping hot potatoes, and the still-steaming lobsters to the deck where a table was already set with plain white dishes and large white napkins. Platters of slaw and tomatoes beckoned. They sat down to eat, and Jennie bowed her head to say grace.

"My father's a minister," she told Caroline when she had finished. "I grew up thanking God before every meal, and I still think it's a wonderful, small ritual. A way to bring family and friends together."

Caroline had a sudden stab of memory: the terrible meals

of her childhood. There were never any friends and barely even a family. She had sat down to the table to endure Al Shaw's drunken shouts and curses, hammering fists and kicking feet. Her stomach had clenched in fear, and very often she had gobbled her food and stuffed herself to quell her anxiety. Jennie's few words of thanks offered a pause, a moment for reflection, and set a mood of relaxation and pleasurable anticipation. At that moment, Caroline decided that even though she had never been particularly religious, she would adopt Jennie Armstrong's "small ritual."

The meal passed with conversation about Phil's summer jobs and his plans to continue his education in accounting in order to become a CPA; about the new quilt designs, some traditional, some quite unconventional, that Jennie was creating; about James's apprenticeship and the intricacies of working with kiln-dried teak and mahogany, the differences between solid hull and plank-on-frame construction, and the patience required to accurately reproduce to scale the complex rigging of three-masted clipper ships. They also spoke about Caleb Jones, an African-American whose family had lived in Maine for generations and whose great-grandfather had been a harpooner on the whaling boats that had plied the Maine coast; and about Caleb's wife, Mildred, also a Maine native and the newly appointed superintendent of schools for the Camden area. After helping Jennie and Phil with the dishes and thanking them for a great dinner, Caroline and James walked home slowly, hand in hand, enjoying the winey crisp Maine night air.

"This is going to be the best summer of my life," she told James when they arrived at their front door.

"The first of many 'best summers,'" he amended. "When we're in our eighties, we can argue about which one was really the best."

Caroline glanced at him. She could see him at eighty, lined but still handsome, bringing her a rosebud and making plans for another wonderful summer, another delightful adventure. And she could see herself, wrinkled but still energetic, holding his hand and smiling up at him.

They lit a fire in the fireplace and made love in front of it, the flames casting an orange glow across their bodies, the heat triggering an intensity of feeling that lingered long after the embers had died out.

Cissy's phrase had stuck in Caroline's mind, and it was her own idea to name the shop "The State of Maine." But it was Jennie's contacts that allowed her to display the work of many of the state's best craftspeople. Everything offered for sale in the shop was made by hand. There was elegant, sturdy glassware from a works in central Maine powered by a waterfall; colorful rag rugs hand-woven in Damariscotta; sweaters knitted from the lanolin-rich wool of locally grazed sheep; pottery, glazed and unglazed, in simple or sophisticated designs; Jennie's delightful quilts in sizes ranging from crib covers to king-size; and a sample of the exquisite model boats handcrafted by Caleb Jones and his apprentice, James Goddard, and available by special order.

Cissy, whose clients often sent their private planes for her, spent as many weekends as she could in Camden and gave Caroline a thousand ideas for creating attractive and appealing window displays. Her decorator's eye was apparent everywhere in the small shop.

"Things need space," Cissy told Caroline, arranging glassware on a simple platter. "They need room to breathe. And don't be afraid to mix," she added, showing colorful pottery dishes with hand-stenciled enamel mugs. Caroline listened and observed and realized that she was learning as much from Cissy as she had learned from the countess. Education, she realized, didn't take place only in classrooms and colleges.

Through Cissy's longtime friendship with the editor of the local newspaper, an article about the shop appeared. It featured photographs of The State of Maine's intriguing window displays, its airy interiors, its high-quality, handmade merchandise, and its beautiful young manager.

"You're getting famous," James teased Caroline when her photograph appeared in the paper. "First the *Shiny Sheet,* now this."

The article caused a surge in sales, and business at The

State of Maine continued to increase as the summer wore on. Caroline soon hired a part-time assistant. Phil taught her how to keep the books, something the countess had always handled herself at L'Elegance, and James gave Caroline the idea of holding an open house every Saturday so that craftspeople from around the state could drop by and meet their customers and show their work in person. By the beginning of August, The State of Maine was no longer something Cissy McMillan had allowed herself to be dragooned into but a profit-making operation, and Caroline was able to give James another check to help settle her debt to him.

"I feel like a creep taking money from you," he said, refusing to take it, the way he always did.

"Well, you shouldn't. That dress from Celeste's was a business deal. A loan. And I want to pay it back," Caroline said.

"But I don't need the money," he said.

"I insist," she said quite seriously.

Unwilling to argue with her further, he took the check and put it into his shirt pocket, and Caroline knew when she got her bank statement that he had deposited it into his own account.

On Sundays, their days off, Caroline and James swam and played tennis, sailed to nearby islands for impromptu picnics, walked down to the wharves to gaze at the magnificent windjammers whose cruises began and ended at Camden, and bought fish and seafood straight from the fishing boats. They picked wild blueberries and made them into pies and bars from Cissy's recipes. They grew tomatoes and corn and planted basil and parsley, petunias and geraniums. In the evenings, they snuggled at home in front of their fireplace or attended performances by the Camden Shakespeare Company and concerts by the Bay Chamber Music Society. They became close to Jennie and Phil and frequently shared dinners, walks, and bicycle tours with them.

It was Tuesdays that were most special, though. Tuesday was the day of the week that James had first walked into

L'Elegance, and ever the romantic, he never let that particular day pass without marking it in some way. One week Caroline awoke to a cascade of rose petals on her pillowcase and a passionate love letter propped against her coffee cup. The next week James arranged a midnight sail complete with champagne and caviar, and the one after that, he took her on a walk to a secluded, secret waterfall that poured fresh, beautiful water into a clear pond. There, in the long, languorous twilight, they made love in the sweet-smelling green glade.

"When will you run out of ideas to celebrate our anniversary?" Caroline asked, lying in his arms.

"Never," he said flatly. He propped himself up on his elbow and looked down at her. She was beautiful. No, she was exquisite from the top of her head to the bottom of her toes. And there was not one mean bone in her body, not one nasty thought in her mind. He could barely believe that he had had the incredibly good fortune to meet someone so perfect inside and out. His expression as he thought over what she meant to him was serious and intense, and there was a profound depth of emotion in his voice that Caroline had never heard before as he spoke. "I want us to have a real anniversary," he said. "I want to marry you, Caroline. Now. Right away."

"Marry me? Right away?" she asked, feeling almost breathless.

"Yes," he said, touching her face with his lips. "Before the summer ends."

"But what about your deal with your father? Won't your parents be upset? I haven't even met them yet . . ." she said. James had told her all about the conversation in the library in Palm Beach and about the deal he had made with his father.

"I'm not worried and you shouldn't be, either," said James. "My parents will be thrilled to have you in the family."

"You're sure?" asked Caroline.

"Of course I'm sure! How could they not adore you?" he assured her. "When they get to know you and find out how wonderful you are and how happy you've made me, they'll fall head over heels in love with you just the way I have!"

Caught up in James's certainty, Caroline began to plan her wedding.

First, there was the business of the guest list. Friends were easy. Families were not. Phil and Jennie would be invited, of course, as would Cissy McMillan and Caleb Jones and his wife, Mildred. Then there were some of the craftspeople with whom Caroline and James had become friendly over the summer and a couple of the men with whom James went sailing occasionally. Caroline also wanted to invite Francesca Palen, with whom she still corresponded and without whom she would never have met James, but she was in California and unable to come, as was the countess, who was summering in Europe.

As for the Goddards, they had registered shock and displeasure when James had telephoned them in Locust Valley to tell them the news. Charles had angrily reminded his son that he had agreed to wait until the summer was over before making any important decisions. Dina simply wept and told James that he was throwing his life away. They both made it clear that they wanted no part of Caroline Shaw, and nothing James said could change their attitude. As a result, Caroline and James were left with a thorny problem: Should his parents be invited? Or not? If they weren't, would they then have even more to hold against Caroline? And if they were, would they show up? And if they did show up, how would they behave? Would they smile and at least pretend to be happy for the newly-weds? Or would they cast a dark cloud of disapproval over the joyous day? Caroline had no idea and even James didn't know. He wondered if he had miscalculated: they were not treating Caroline like one of the family as he'd promised her they would. Just as he was a mystery to them, they were turning out to be quite an enigma to him.

And what about Caroline's own parents? She wanted her mother by her side as she pledged herself to James. Or, at least she realized, thinking it over more carefully, she wanted her fantasy of what her mother could have been. For Mary Shaw had often not been there for Caroline on important occasions. Not the day Caroline became a girl scout. Not the day she graduated from high school. Not the day she landed a job on Worth Avenue. Mary Shaw had been much too preoccupied with her own problems to be able to share her daughter's pleasures and triumphs. What Caroline did know was that Al Shaw would not be welcome at her marriage to James. There was no place for violence and drunkenness and misery at a ceremony celebrating their happiness. But how could she invite her mother without inviting her father? She was in a quandary about both sets of parents and wasn't sure how to handle the situation. James was far more decisive about it.

"I say we invite my parents and sister," he advised. "If they don't want to come, let them stay home. If they show up and they're unpleasant, I'll deal with them. But I really believe they'll come to love you just the way I do."

His words touched Caroline because she knew how much he wanted them to be true.

"You're sure they won't mind the *way* we're getting married?" she asked. "I had the idea that they're the kind of people who'd want a big church wedding and a grand reception for their son."

"I would think they'd be thrilled with a simple affair," he assured her, "especially after Emily's three-ring circus. My mother said she almost had a nervous breakdown planning it."

"You make everything sound so easy," Caroline said, laughing with him, grateful for his confidence, even though she didn't quite share it. "Now that you've solved the problem of your parents, what should we do about *mine?*"

James had a solution for that, too. "Tell your mother you'd really like her to be there, but that you'd prefer it if she came alone. She'll understand, and if she doesn't, well, she doesn't."

Mary Shaw did understand, but when Caroline called back to issue her formal invitation, her mother begged off. She said that she'd broken her arm at work and was in too much pain to travel to Maine.

"Broke your arm at work?" Caroline asked. "Sitting at a desk in an insurance office?"

Not likely, Caroline knew. More likely was that Al Shaw had lashed out at her mother yet again. Why she continued to protect her husband and stay with him was an enigma to Caroline, something she simply could not comprehend.

"Your parents may not be coming but mine are," James had announced after speaking to the Goddards. "So's Emily."

"Are you glad, my love?" Caroline asked James. For all his bravado about not caring whether his family attended the wedding or not, he did care, Caroline knew. He cared very much. For, as independent and nonconforming as he was, James loved his parents and sister and longed to find a way to resolve the differences between them.

"Actually, I'm very glad," he replied.

His positive attitude swept Caroline along in a tide of sweet anticipation and almost giddy delight as she and James planned a wedding just for themselves, just for their own tastes and preferences.

"Nothing fancy," James kept saying. "Everything beautiful. Just like you."

They arranged for Jennie's father, the minister at the Presbyterian church in Camden, to officiate at the noontime ceremony. The reception, which was to be held on Cissy's lawn, was being catered by the owners of the gourmet shop that was housed in the building next door to The State of Maine. Caroline's wedding dress, a classic but summery long-sleeved, princess-style, white linen gown that was overembroidered in tiny seed pearls and featured a small train, was handmade by Susan Lorentz, another local craftswoman and friend. James would wear a white linen blazer, light blue and white pin-striped shirt, navy blue slacks, and navy tie.

"I'll be in charge of the rings," he insisted when the subject came up. "I want them to be a surprise."

The Goddard family arrived the afternoon before the wedding and checked into a nearby inn. James invited them to come to dinner at the carriage house that evening, thinking it would be an ideal way to break the ice.

"That's sweet of you, dear," Dina Goddard told her son when he issued the invitation. "But won't your fiancée have too much to do before the wedding?"

"Her name's Caroline, Mother," James reminded her. "I'm going to marry her tomorrow. Don't you think it's about time you called her by her name?"

Dina sighed. "Really, James," she said. "Your father and sister and I have come all this way. Let's not be cross with each other, hmm?"

"No, let's not," James replied. He did not want to fight with his family on the night before the most important day of his life. He wanted things to go smoothly; he wanted his parents to love Caroline just as much as he did, even though their attitude toward her had, thus far, been disappointing. "Now, you're coming to dinner tonight, right?"

"Of course, we'll come," said Dina. She was furious that James had presented the wedding as a *fait accompli,* but she was more than a little curious about the salesgirl who had maneuvered her son into marriage. By the oldest trick in the world, no doubt.

"Great. Dinner's at eight. This is Camden, so dress casually," said James. "Tell Dad and Emily that Caroline and I are really looking forward to seeing them. You, too, Mother."

From the moment the Goddards crossed the threshold of the carriage house, Caroline felt their frigid antipathy toward her. She also noticed that James seemed oblivious to their disapproval. Either oblivious or unwilling to accept it.

"Everybody, I'd like you to meet Caroline," James said

proudly as he guided Caroline over to meet his family for the first time. Perhaps he truly didn't notice, thought Caroline, acutely aware of the chill in the room. Perhaps he was just accustomed to their superior, snobbish attitudes and that the way they were treating her was the way they treated everyone. Or perhaps he was so convinced that they would love her the way he did that he had blinded himself to reality.

"So this is Caroline," said Dina as she shook Caroline's hand and forced a smile. The girl was beautiful, Dina had to give her that. And she had a sense of style, in her simple blue cotton skirt and matching blouse with navy blue espadrilles that tied at the ankle. Surprisingly, she was as slim as Dina herself was. Was it possible that she wasn't pregnant? Was it possible that James was telling the truth when he said that he was marrying her because he loved her? Even if it was, the match was almost too unthinkable for words, and Dina Goddard inwardly shrank from the mere thought of it because Caroline Shaw represented everything Dina had spent her entire life escaping.

"We appreciate your coming all the way up for the wedding, Mrs. Goddard," Caroline said politely, keenly aware that the woman who was about to become her mother-in-law felt no motherly affection for her whatsoever.

"Nonsense, dear. Maine isn't exactly Mozambique," replied Dina, knowing that she sounded snippy but unable to contain herself. She shuddered at the thought of the mismatch James was walking into with his eyes wide open.

"Still, it was nice of you to come." Caroline smiled, trying to put a good facade on things, hoping that in time James's family would, if not love her, at least come to accept her.

"James *is* our son," said Dina coldly.

"And Caroline is about to be my wife," James said, intervening and drawing Caroline toward his father. "Dad, I want you to meet Caroline."

"Yes, yes. A pleasure, young lady," said Charles, who astonished his wife by planting a kiss on Caroline's cheek. A connoisseur of beautiful women—especially beautiful young women—Charles Goddard couldn't deny that his son had picked a knockout. But what else other than beauty was his son about to drag into the family? Charles wondered. Kyle Pringle had been enough of a blemish on the Goddard name. But a wife who was devoid of social connections, who had no experience with wealth or the responsibilities it brought, who probably had no idea what Goddard-Stevens was or did? How on earth was James ever going to make something of himself? And what would happen to Goddard-Stevens if he saddled himself with such an inappropriate wife? Thoughts of the mess James was about to make of his life and how he might intervene swirled half-formed through Charles's mind. He and James had made a deal—and James had unilaterally broken it.

"Em, I want you to meet Caroline," said James, throwing an arm around his sister.

Emily Pringle appraised Caroline from head to toe, as if she were a rival instead of a soon-to-be sister-in-law. Like her parents, she assumed that her brother was about to embark upon a shotgun marriage.

"We've met before," Emily told James, ignoring Caroline as completely as if she weren't standing right there next to him. The look on James's face held a warning, and she quickly turned and acknowledged Caroline's presence with an artificial smile. "Haven't we, Caroline?"

"Yes, several times," Caroline said, offering Emily her hand, then pulling it back when it was not taken.

"I used to run her ragged at L'Elegance," Emily told James in the same brittle tones her mother employed. "I'd try on everything in the shop, and poor Caroline would run around refolding and rehanging and bringing me fresh glasses of Evian. She was so efficient. I can see why your house is so neat and tidy."

Caroline felt as if she'd been slapped. It wasn't being reminded of her lowly position that so unnerved her. It was the tone. So demeaning, so snide, so vicious and cutting. So unnecessary and gratuitously insulting.

"Actually, *I* do most of the cleaning," James countered

immediately. "Caroline's much too busy. She runs Cissy McMillan's shop for her. It's right here in town. I'm sure you'll want to stop by before you leave town. It's going to be featured in next month's issue of *Beautiful Homes and Gardens,* and one of my boat models has been especially photographed for the article," he said proudly.

Dina and Emily exchanged a disdainful glance that combined a sneer leavened with open disbelief. *Beautiful Homes and Gardens* was *the* elite decorating magazine, its glossy pages and opulent cover prominently displayed on every coffee table from Park Avenue to Worth Avenue.

"I'm afraid we won't be able to, darling. We're leaving right after the wedding tomorrow afternoon," said Dina, not looking the least bit regretful. "Charles is playing golf first thing Sunday morning—some sort of tournament, right, darling?—and I have a breakfast meeting of the historical society. You do understand, don't you?"

"Not really," said James. "Caroline's made a great success of the shop, and you ought to be proud of her. I expect you to treat her just as well as you treated Kyle."

Dina forced a smile.

"Of course we will," she said with a tight smile.

"Beautiful girl! Happy to have her in the family!" boomed Charles.

"We'll have lunch—" offered Emily in a pallid voice.

James smiled, taking their words at face value, and put his arm around Caroline. "Now, what do you say we have a drink before we sample the chicken pot pie Cissy's cook made for us?"

James and Caroline disappeared into the kitchen to make drinks. As soon as they were gone, Emily stole a glance at her mother and whispered, "You'd think she could at least cook."

"What did you expect? Now that she thinks she's about to live high on the hog, she probably won't lift a finger." Dina said.

Minutes later, their hosts reappeared with champagne for everybody.

"I'd like to propose a special toast," James said, lifting his glass and turning to Caroline and embracing her with his eyes. "To Caroline, the woman who has made me the happiest man on earth."

"To Caroline," the Goddards mumbled in unison.

12

When Caroline awoke on her wedding day and looked out the bedroom window, Penobscot Bay had disappeared. All she saw was thick, gray mist. Maine mornings were often shrouded in dense fog, she had come to learn that summer, but she had hoped that this Saturday morning in August, this day on which she was to be married to James Huntington Goddard, would be clear and sparkling. Her disappointment in the weather showed on her face as she turned from the window.

"It'll burn off, you'll see," said James, the eternal optimist, as she climbed back into bed and cuddled next to him. "And if it doesn't? So what? Fog's very romantic. Nothing's going to spoil this day for us. Nothing."

"Not even your parents?" asked Caroline, still upset by their behavior on the previous evening.

"Don't worry about them," said James, getting up and embracing her from behind as they gazed out at the fog together. "I've lived with them my whole life and I know what they're like. They're formal with people they don't know, but they'll come around."

"I hope so," said Caroline, doubting his words, yet wanting to see things from his point of view.

An hour before the ceremony, the fog lifted and a dazzling sun came out. Perhaps, thought Caroline, it was an omen. Perhaps James *was* right about his parents. Perhaps they *would* come around. Still, as she waited in the wings of the church with Jennie, waited for the organ music to signal the start of the ceremony, she observed the Goddards sitting in their seats and chatting conspiratorially among themselves, and shuddered.

"Cold?" Jennie asked, putting a supportive arm around Caroline's shoulders.

Caroline shook her head and shook off the negative feelings the best she could. "Just a little nervous."

"Don't worry. Everything's going to go beautifully," Jennie assured her. "James loves you so much. He won't let anything spoil your day, believe me."

"Not even his family?" Caroline asked.

"Not even them!" Jennie assured her, glancing at the Goddards, so cool, so aloof, so superior, relieved that *she* was not the one who was going to have to deal with them. "How'd it go last night?" she asked. Phil had given his girlfriend a detailed description of the Goddard family, and they had sounded like people to avoid at all costs.

"I passed the first test," Caroline said with a grim smile. "I spent a whole evening with them, and I'm still alive to tell the tale!"

The Reverend Armstrong conducted a moving and inspiring ceremony, speaking of love and God and lifetime commitment. Caroline and James stood side by side, holding hands, united. Jennie and Phil remained nearby, as their maid of honor and best man. When the time came for James to put the ring on Caroline's finger, Phil stepped forward to hand it to his friend.

"With this ring, I thee wed," James repeated after the Reverend Armstrong as he slipped the elegant gold circle on Caroline's graceful finger. He had purchased their unique, handmade eighteen-karat-gold rings from a fabulous private jewelry gallery in Manhattan's Soho. The rings had a matte hammered surface and were shaped in the form of hollow doughnuts. Inside the hollow of each ring was a loose diamond, which, like James and Caroline's love, was a treasure kept secret from the careless, prying eyes of the world. Engraved on the inner surface of the rings were their intertwined initials and the date of the wedding.

"With this ring, I thee wed," Caroline said when it was her turn to put the band on James's finger.

The rest of the ceremony was a blur to Caroline, such was her sheer joy at pledging herself to James, whom she adored with such intensity that she felt overwhelmed, dizzy. It wasn't until the Reverend Armstrong pronounced them husband and wife and invited James to kiss the bride that it finally registered. She had done it! *They* had done it! She was Mrs. James Goddard! Tears of joy ran down her face as she turned to kiss him.

"I love you," James whispered as he was about to embrace her in front of their guests. His eyes, too, were brimming with tears of joy. "I adore you. You and only you. Forever."

"Forever and after," she responded, then melted into his arms and surrendered to her first kiss as Caroline Shaw Goddard.

The sun burned hotter than usual for Maine in August, but there was plenty of chilled champagne and wine and even ice-cold beer, especially for Phil who drank nothing else, and trays of appealingly presented canapés. As the reception got underway on Cissy McMillan's lush, emerald green lawn and people began to circulate, everyone was happy and even ebullient. Except Dina Goddard, who surveyed the guests and scowled.

"Aside from Cissy McMillan, there isn't a single person of consequence at this reception," she whispered to her husband. "What's more, I'm surprised that someone as sophisticated as Cissy would serve beer at a wedding reception. A tad pedestrian, don't you think, Charles?"

Before he could respond, Cissy McMillan responded for him.

"You may call it pedestrian, Mrs. Goddard, but I call it considerate," she said in her no-nonsense, New England tone, having apparently overheard Dina's remark. She had met the Goddards several times during the renovation of Emily and Kyle Pringle's Manhattan apartment and had thought them pretentious and coldly ambitious. "One of my guests is a beer drinker. I like to treat *all* my guests with courtesy."

"Of course. You're perfectly right. I just didn't realize—" said Dina, forcing a smile. Cissy McMillan was just the kind of person she went out of her way to cultivate. "And speaking of guests, Cissy, it was awfully nice of you to give James and his bride their wedding reception."

Cissy arched an eyebrow. "Well, Caroline's parents couldn't. And James's parents wouldn't."

Dina's mouth opened in a silent O. She appeared stunned by Cissy McMillan's directness—momentarily.

"Charles and I weren't consulted," she said, recovering.

"And if you had been?" asked Cissy, who did not wait for a reply but moved away from the Goddards to join the other guests.

The reception lasted for two hours or so, but the real fun didn't begin until everyone but Phil, Jennie, and Cissy had left. Phil took out his guitar and strummed love songs to the newlyweds while Jennie and Cissy sang backup. It was nearly sundown when Cissy finally said, "Enough's enough. Let's leave the lovebirds alone now, shall we?"

Caroline and James thanked their friends, gathered their wedding gifts, and took them back to the carriage house.

"Want to open them now?" James asked as he and Caroline sat on the living room sofa and regarded the brightly wrapped packages stacked on the dining table.

"Why not! We can check out our loot," teased Caroline.

James walked over to the pile, lifted one of the packages, and shook it.

"Weighs a ton," he said. "Crystal, I bet."

"Go ahead and open it," she urged.

He brought the box over to her and planted it in her lap. "No. You."

She sighed and began to tear off the wrapping paper. "Our first fight as a married couple," she laughed.

James had been right. The gift *was* crystal—a large carved bowl from his parents and sister. French crystal from the old firm of Baccarat, James told her, considered the best in the world. A costly and thoroughly impersonal gift, something from one stranger to another. But it wasn't the Goddards' only gift to the newlyweds. There was an envelope resting in the bottom of the bowl.

"You open that one," Caroline said, handing James the envelope. "It might be personal."

The envelope contained a check—for $10,000—and it was made out to James Huntington Goddard. There was no indication at all that he was married, that he had a wife, and that her name was Caroline. The gift was for him and him alone.

"My, that's very generous of your parents!" Caroline gasped, looking over his shoulder.

James looked at her, his expression stony. He was clearly furious, his normally sunny disposition poisoned. The check was a blatant slap in the face to the woman he loved.

"Not to *my* parents! To them, this is peanuts. What my father would call 'chump change,'" said James, thinking of the extravagant gifts with which his parents had welcomed Kyle Pringle into the family. But it wasn't only the amount on the check that disturbed James; it was the insult to Caroline, the fact that her name hadn't even been included on the check. He was enraged by the contrast between the way his parents had treated Kyle and the way they were treating her, crushed by the gulf between his fantasies and this bitter, inescapable reality. Without another word, he proceeded to rip up the check into tiny bits. Then he threw the pieces into the fireplace.

"What on earth are you doing?" Caroline exclaimed as she watched the little pieces of paper char and then burn.

"My father always says 'Money talks.' Well, I'm talking. I'm telling them that I didn't like the way they treated my wife today," he said. "Money is what they understand. They'll get the message when they see that the check hasn't been cashed."

Then the darkness left his face and he took Caroline into his arms. "Look, I didn't intend to upset you. You mean everything to me," he said as he stroked her cheek. "But as long as I'm around, no one—got that? *no one*—will treat you with anything but respect."

She hugged him tightly and thought about their future. Despite James's assurances that she would be welcomed into the Goddard family, it was now clear—at least to her—that that welcome, if it *ever* came, would be a long time in happening. She also wondered uneasily about his gesture. Tearing up the check was grand and melodramatic, to be sure, a rich boy's statement of independence. But Caroline had grown up without money, without waterfront mansions and expensive little sports cars and summers in Maine. To her, $10,000 was a fortune, a cushion to fall back on in times of need, a nest egg that could well be the difference between survival and desperation. There was no telling what the future would bring, no telling when the money the Goddards had given them might be crucial. It seemed to her hasty and reckless for James to have destroyed the check in such a cavalier manner. But, still, how could she fault him? The check had been made out to him. The money was his, and she, more than most people, understood complicated and thorny relationships with difficult parents.

"We don't need their money anyway," James said, instinctively understanding what had been running through her mind. "I've been earning money this summer and I've got my trust fund, too, remember? My grandmother left it to me and my sister. The income's in my name, and I can use the money however I like. Which reminds me."

"Of what?"

"Of our honeymoon. How does Paris grab you?"

"Paris? How do you think it grabs me!" she exclaimed, grateful that their discussion of the Goddards was over—temporarily. She kissed him all over his face—his cheeks, his eyes, his nose, his lips. Then she pulled away. "But how can we go to Paris? I've got the shop and you've got your work with Caleb?"

"We'll go in three weeks, after Cissy closes The State of Maine and my apprenticeship with Caleb is over. The countess isn't reopening L'Elegance until after Labor Day. So that gives us a little window of opportunity. What do you say, wife?"

"I say, 'I love you.' "

"And I say, *'Je t'aime.'* "

"Ummm, you're so continental, Monsieur Goddard."

"Damn right, Madame Goddard."

"Madame Goddard! I still can't believe we're married."

"Believe it. Because I am about to take you to our marriage bed and seal the deal," James said with a twinkle in his blue eyes.

"I wonder if it will feel different now that we're married?" Caroline mused as they walked arm in arm up the narrow staircase.

"Not different. Better," said James. "Much better."

~13~

Marriage inspired James to be even more romantic than before, and Caroline's new life as his wife was a festival of attention, affection, and indulgence. Not a day passed without a declaration of love, a small surprise, an unexpected present, a sentimental token. There were volumes of romantic poetry that he read to her aloud, uniquely configured shells that he had collected from the beach, picnic dinners that he produced seemingly on a moment's notice. And then there were his "anniversary gifts"—celebrations that became a cherished ritual. On the first Saturday after their wedding, he arrived at the carriage house after a day's work at Caleb's studio with a single red rose.

"Happy anniversary, Caroline," he said, handing her the flower. "A red rose to honor the happiest day of my life. Only this time, it's a true anniversary we're commemorating, not some cooked-up occasion."

"You're an incredible romantic, do you know that?" Caroline said, then kissed him.

"Sure," James laughed. "I'm a regular Mr. Romance."

"A regular James Q. Romance," she teased.

"A walking, talking Romance, Inc," James laughed.

"Yes, that's you exactly." She smiled. "Romance, Inc.

The florist's best friend!" Then her expression turned serious, "Have I told you how happy you make me?" she said as she set the rose down on the dining table and cradled James's face in her hands.

"Yes, but I don't mind hearing it again."

"You make me very, very happy, Romance, Inc."

"This is just the beginning," James said tenderly. "You'll see."

On the second Saturday after the wedding, James arrived at the carriage house at the end of the day with two red roses.

"Happy anniversary, Caroline," he said.

"And a happy anniversary to you, Romance, Inc." Caroline smiled, using what had quickly become their private pet name for him and leading him upstairs.

Inspired by her husband's romantic tendencies, Caroline, too, had planned something special for their anniversary. She had rushed home from The State of Maine to arrange a tray of sandwiches and a frosted pitcher of minted iced tea by their bedside. She had also covered Jennie's blue quilt with a bower of daisies.

James looked at her, a glint in his eye.

"A roll in the daisies?" he asked.

"At least one," replied Caroline, winking at him and unfastening the top button of her blouse.

On the third Saturday after the wedding, after a tiring day of helping Cissy close up The State of Maine for the winter and packing for her weeklong honeymoon in Paris, Caroline waited for James to return home from Caleb's studio—with her roses, she guessed. She smiled as she thought of her romantic husband dashing over to the florist before they closed and asking for the most perfect flowers in the shop—three of them this time. Or, knowing James, maybe even three dozen, she thought, recalling the time he had surprised her by coming down from Penn to Lake Worth.

As organized as she normally was, the carriage house was a mess, littered with suitcases and cartons and newspapers. Between getting ready to leave Maine and packing for their trip to Paris and trying to find a place for them to rent back in Palm Beach, there just didn't seem to be enough hours in the day to accomplish all there was left to do.

Frazzled, exhausted, and feeling a bit chilled by the damp Maine air, Caroline still managed to smile, thinking of their third anniversary. She had something to tell James, and she wanted to create a special welcome for him. She lit a fire and put a batch of blueberry bars into the oven, the last batch of the season, she thought wistfully, recalling that she and James had picked the few remaining wild berries just the evening before. Then she made a pitcher of lemonade, just the way Cissy's cook did, and put it into the refrigerator. She hadn't become much of a cook, despite her many attempts to learn over the summer, but she *had* mastered the art of making blueberry bars and iced tea and took pride in her preparations.

She returned to the living room and sat down in front of the fireplace and waited for James to come home. As she stared into the flames, she was transported not to the Shaws' house in Lake Worth, which had been engulfed by fire, not to the misery of her childhood but to the last time she and James had made love in front of the fire. She felt warmed by the memory, safe in it. She reflected, too, on how dramatically her life had changed since James Goddard had walked into L'Elegance that fateful March day. Who had she been back then? she wondered. It was almost impossible to remember, barely possible to compare that girl with this woman. She thought back. She had been frightened. Inexperienced. A girl who had never tasted the love of a man. A girl who had never seen the world. Now she was a woman. A wife. A lover. A businesswoman. A friend. And about to be more, much, much more . . . and all because of James.

The afternoon light faded and Caroline switched on a small lamp. She checked her watch. It was nearly seven o'clock, and James was usually home by six-thirty—even on their weekly anniversaries, when he stopped at the florist first. Where could he be? She wondered what might have detained him. Had he come up with some other delicious surprise for her?

Caroline laughed at herself as she remembered the last

time she'd worried about James. She had nearly driven Selma crazy wondering why he hadn't called from the fraternity house at eight o'clock as he always did during the early days of their courtship. He'd been on a plane to Florida that time. What was it this time? she asked herself. Had her Romance, Inc. gone off on some lovely romantic errand? Would he be knocking on the door any minute, carrying some delightful trinket? Something he had made especially for her? Or perhaps something Parisian as a token of things to come? Or maybe a going-away-from-Maine present? Or perhaps he was bringing Phil and Jennie over for dinner as an anniversary surprise?

Caroline smiled to herself as she let her dreams, still one of the mainstays of her life, unreel. The possibilities were entrancing.

By seven-thirty, she began to worry in earnest. James wasn't home, and he hadn't telephoned. He'd know that she'd be half frantic with concern, and he would never be so inconsiderate of her. She finally called Phil and Jennie, but there was no answer over at the barn. She dialed Cissy's number, too, even though she wasn't sure whether or not their neighbor might still be in New York on business. Then she telephoned Caleb Jones.

"He left here 'bout five-thirty," Caleb said in his distinctive Maine accent. "Should'a been over at your place by now."

"That's what I thought, Caleb," said Caroline, becoming even more alarmed but trying not to worry James's friend and mentor. "Oh, well. I'm sorry I bothered you," she said. "I'm sure he'll be home soon. There isn't much that can happen to a person in Camden, is there?"

"No, there sure isn't," he chuckled.

Caroline hung up and sat back down by the fire. She debated with herself about whether or not to call the police and ultimately decided to wait another half hour before doing so. She glanced at her watch. She was sure she'd hear James's car in the driveway any second.

Eight o'clock came. Then eight-fifteen. And eight-thirty. At 8:40, Caroline walked to the phone and was about to summon the police when she heard a car drive up.

She ran to the front door.

"Happy anniversary to you, too!" she exclaimed as she opened it, throwing her arms open wide and suddenly feeling silly for worrying about her husband. "And where have you been—"

Caroline stopped in midsentence. Her hand flew to her mouth. She was silent for a moment. Then she screamed.

James Huntington Goddard was not standing at the front door with three long-stemmed red roses. He was lying in the county morgue. According to the tall, thin police officer who handled his difficult assignment with as much sensitivity as he could muster, James's Austin Healey had been hit head-on by a drunken driver. Both drivers were killed instantly, said Officer Roiko. James very likely didn't even know what hit him, said Officer Roiko. The car was totaled, but the EMS technicians on the scene were able to retrieve some of Mr. Goddard's personal effects, said Officer Roiko.

Officer Roiko. Officer Roiko. Caroline couldn't focus on any of it except that name. Officer Roiko. For no particular reason that she could think of, it seemed like a funny name. She tried not to laugh.

"About the personal effects," he said again.

"Personal effects?" Caroline parroted, as if in a daze. She didn't hear. Wouldn't hear. Not yet. Maybe not ever.

"Yes," said Officer Roiko. "There was Mr. Goddard's wallet and his checkbook and a sketchbook of drawings of some sort. And there were several roses on the front seat of the vehicle."

"No," Caroline said, shaking her finger at the policeman. "Not *several* roses. Three roses. *Three.*"

She turned away from Officer Roiko, glanced inside the house with its cozy fire and salty charm and beautiful memories. What this man was telling her wasn't possible. It simply was not possible.

She returned her gaze to him but couldn't speak. Instead, she ignored him, walked back inside the house and climbed the stairs to the bedroom, the bedroom she had shared with her beloved for three blissful months, the bedroom in which they had conceived the child he would never know. She had only learned about the pregnancy that morning and had planned to tell James as soon as he got home. He had loved children, she knew, and never tired of saying how eager he was for them to have a family of their own.

Caroline looked around the room, at all the mementos and photographs, at the sheer loveliness of the scene, the loveliness *they* had created. And, inside her, the child they had created. Together.

Nearly trancelike, she turned to face the big picture window that overlooked the lawns and the bay, and walked slowly toward it. Then she stood next to the window, placed her hands over her abdomen, and stared out at the graceful white sailing vessels that dotted the dark, blue water.

"I love you forever," she whispered. "Forever. And after."

And from downstairs came the bitter, acrid smell of burning blueberries.

14

The eulogy was delivered by the Reverend Armstrong in the same church in which Caroline and James had been married. The Goddards flew up to Camden in the Gulfstream jet Charles Goddard used for business trips, and when they arrived at the church, they declined to sit with Caroline, refused to speak to her, did not recognize her presence even with so much as a nod. To them, she had always been a nonentity. Now, with James's death, they had turned her into a nonperson.

Dina and Emily were dressed entirely in black, and Charles wore a dark suit with a somber gray tie. With dry eyes and frozen faces, they filed into the pew next to Caroline's and stared straight ahead at their son's coffin as the Reverend Armstrong conducted the service. When it was over, he announced that there would be no burial ceremony for James but that his ashes would be scattered across Penobscot Bay as per his wife's wishes.

As the mourners filed out of the small Presbysterian church, they extended their condolences to Caroline. Cissy embraced her. Phil hugged her. Jennie wept with her. Caleb and Mildred spoke quietly and comfortingly. Her in-laws waited until she was alone before finally deigning to acknowledge her existence. Charles and Dina faced her while Emily stood behind them, weeping silently and dabbing at her red eyes with a white linen handkerchief.

"Mr. and Mrs. Goddard, I'm so sor—" Caroline began, looking from one to the other.

"Sorry?" Dina interjected, shaking her head in disbelief, as if Caroline had said something entirely inappropriate. She surveyed her daughter-in-law from head to toe and was stunned to see that the girl was as slim as she'd been on her wedding day. Astonishingly, James had been telling the truth: he hadn't married Caroline Shaw because she was pregnant but because he *wanted* to marry her.

"I know how you must feel, Mrs. Goddard, but James and I—" Caroline began, wanting to tell her in-laws about the child she would be bearing that spring.

Once again, Dina did not permit her to finish her thought.

"If James hadn't married you, he would still be alive," she said harshly, her eyes judgmental and her voice chilly with blame.

Caroline was so taken aback that she couldn't respond right away. She just stared at the frigid, perfectly groomed blond woman who had given James birth and marveled at her cruelty.

"If you hadn't trapped my son," Dina continued, "hadn't played off his sympathies, hadn't made him feel that he had to marry you—"

"But I didn't *make* him do anything," Caroline protested, shocked by the sudden, grotesque accusations but eager to defend herself. "And I certainly didn't trap him."

"Why couldn't you have stayed in your place?" Dina went on, as if Caroline hadn't spoken. "Why did you have to push yourself where you weren't wanted? Why did you have to insinuate yourself in my son's life and destroy it?"

Reeling from the onslaught, Caroline somehow managed to gather herself.

"Whatever you may think of me and my motives, Mrs. Goddard, the fact is that your son loved me. Very much," she said firmly. "And I loved him. More than you'll ever know."

With that, her fragile defenses crumbled and she began to cry. Tears streamed down her face and along her throat into the high neckline of her dress. She needed a release from her grief, her accusing mother-in-law and her knowledge that she was carrying James's child—the child he would never see, touch, hold, the Goddards' grandchild. Her emotions overwhelmed her, and her tears turned to sobs. Her shoulders shook helplessly and tears cascaded down her face in a waterfall of grief. Dina Goddard remained motionless where she was standing, making no attempt to comfort her or to console her, making not the slightest effort to reach out to her either physically or emotionally.

"The least you could do is control yourself in public," she said with disgust, turning away from Caroline and leaving the church.

"My wife's very upset," said Charles Goddard. Despite his summer tan, he seemed pale and weary, his physical and psychological power diminished by the sudden, shocking loss of his only son, the heir who would carry on the Goddard name and the Goddard tradition. Now he was alone. When he died, so would the Goddard line. "James would have had a fine future at the firm, once he got that model boat nonsense out of his system," he said, speaking as if in a reverie, as much to himself as he was to Caroline.

"James loved his boats," said Caroline. "But he knew how much Goddard-Stevens meant to you. Despite what you may have thought, he didn't take your feelings lightly. He didn't take *anyone's* feelings lightly."

Charles Goddard's lower lip trembled then and tears flooded his eyes. Visibly moved, he wiped them away with a large white handkerchief, and Caroline realized how much he must have loved his son. How sad, she thought, that Charles had so rarely been able to express his feelings toward James and that James had so rarely been able to warm himself in his father's love and acceptance.

"James cared about Goddard-Stevens," Caroline continued, hoping that she and her father-in-law could at least share a moment of compassion for one another, for the man they had both lost. Perhaps Charles Goddard, in his way, would make up for the pain his wife had deliberately inflicted. "He cared about upholding the tradition of the family, really he did. Just because he loved boats didn't mean he wasn't mindful of his place as a Goddard heir. He was terribly torn about what to do. We spoke about it all the time. He knew his choice would influence the course of the rest of his life. He understood that his inheritance was a valuable one."

At the word "inheritance," Charles Goddard's jaw tightened and his shoulders squared.

"Speaking of inheritances," he said, his expression hardening, "I hope you understand that there will be none for you."

Caroline nodded. "Of course, I understand," she said. The thought that she might inherit money from the Goddards hadn't crossed her mind. The only thing on her mind was her husband's death—and the fact that she was pregnant with the child he would never know.

"The beneficiary of James's trust fund was designated by James's paternal grandmother, and it's Emily," Charles went on, spelling out the terms of the trust in detail, intent on making it clear to Caroline that the Goddard money was carefully tied up, well protected from the grasp of greedy adventuresses.

"I understand perfectly," said Caroline as she dried her tears and attempted to assume the same no-nonsense demeanor that Charles Goddard was displaying. Underneath her surface dignity, she was angry now. Angry that her father-in-law would speak of money at such a difficult time. Angry that he would assume that money was foremost on her mind. Angry that the Goddards had been so quick to judge her—judge her and find her guilty.

"As you well know, Mrs. Goddard and I did not approve

of this marriage, Miss Shaw. Not only will you receive no inheritance from James, there'll be nothing from us. I hope you understand that. I hope you don't plan to come knocking on our door with your hand out," Charles said.

Caroline didn't know which hurt more: Dina Goddard's obscene accusations or Charles Goddard's revolting innuendos about her mercenary motives.

"Miss Shaw?" Caroline repeated with as much venom as she could muster. "Mr. Goddard, however much you may resent me, may I remind you that I was married to your son. My name is Mrs. Goddard. And there's something else you should know. Something I want to tell you—" said Caroline. She wanted him to know that, despite his disdain, she was carrying *his* grandchild, a Goddard grandchild. Wanted him to know that Goddard blood ran in her child's veins and that there would be a new generation of Goddards to ease the burden of James's untimely death. But, just as his wife had, Charles Goddard interrupted her.

"Whatever it is, I don't want to hear it," said Charles furiously. "You have nothing to say that could be of any possible interest to me."

"But, Mr. Goddard, you don't understand," Caroline tried again. "I've been trying to tell you that James and I—"

Charles tightened his jaw and lashed out one final time.

"James is dead. There is no 'you and James' any more. If you intend to play the Goddard widow, carrying on as if you're a part of this family, you will regret it, I promise you. As far as we are concerned, you do not exist, Miss Shaw. Have I made myself clear?"

Without waiting for a reply, Charles Goddard turned and walked out of the church and out of Caroline's life.

As she tried to recover from what had just been said to her, Emily stepped forward and touched her lightly on the arm.

"I know how you must feel," Emily said in a small, choked voice. "I lost my husband, too. And in a terrible accident. Just like James. I'm sorry. So sorry. For both of us."

"Thank you," Caroline managed, still stunned by Charles

and Dina's assault. She stared off into the middle distance, adrift in a world of loss and pain, far removed from the one in which Emily struggled to convey her sympathies.

Standing awkwardly for a moment, not knowing quite what else to say, Emily finally turned away, going off to join her parents.

Caroline watched the three of them cross the church lawn and get into the chauffeured car that would transport them back to the airport, back to the protected cocoon of wealth in which they lived. The isolated cocoon that was defended by high walls and frozen attitudes, by uncrossable moats both physical and psychological, by armies of servants and lawyers all paid vast sums of money to keep out interlopers. They had made it clear that they wanted no part of her. Not then. Not ever. They had never accepted her and now they never would. They had consigned her to a wilderness in which they had no part and no interest. And that, Caroline realized, meant that they wanted no part of her child. James's child. The child and heir who would have meant so much to them.

As Caroline stood alone and bereft in the house of worship where she and James had pledged to love each other forever and after, she turned to face the altar and, sinking to her knees, folded her hands and began to pray.

In the days following the funeral, Caroline packed up James's model boats, donated most of his clothing to the Presbyterian Church drive, and closed up the carriage house. In tears, she wished Caleb and his wife, Cissy and Jenny and Phil good-bye and left for the airport alone. There would be no honeymoon, no trip to Paris, no romantic dinners for two, no moonlit walks along the Seine, no making love under the timbered beams of a charming small hotel. She and James had planned to return to Florida and stay in a modest hotel until they found an apartment in Palm Beach, but now that he was gone, Caroline didn't know where to go or what to do. For a while, Cissy tried to talk her into moving to Manhattan, but she felt too fragile to settle in a new city, especially one as competitive and unforgiving as New York. Phil and Jenny had suggested she stay up in Maine, but she knew there would be few employment opportunities in Camden once the summer season ended and the tourists and summer residents left. Instead, in the end, she decided to go back to Lake Worth.

Florida was where she belonged, she'd decided. The weather was warm and the streets were familiar, and despite her bitter memories, it was the only home she had ever known. She had friends like Francesca and Selma there, and most important of all, she had a job. L'Elegance would reopen the week after Labor Day, and Caroline knew that her job would provide her with money to support herself and the baby. And she was counting on being busy and even on the countess's unpredictability to distract her, to keep her from falling apart with grief.

So back to Florida she would go, but not to her parents, who were still living in Port St. Lucie. Although they had expressed their condolences, Al and Mary Shaw had, characteristically, not been by Caroline's side at James's funeral. Instead, Caroline would go back to the safety of her old room at Selma's, the tiny room that she'd called home before she and James Goddard had met and fallen in love.

On her third day back in Lake Worth, Caroline received an overseas telephone call.

"It's the countess," said Selma, who had answered the phone.

Tamara was winding up her summer in Europe and calling, Caroline assumed, to give her thirty-five errands to do immediately! right now! this instant! before she returned to the States to reopen L'Elegance. Caroline smiled as she took the telephone and looked forward to anything the countess could dish out. Looked forward to being overworked and hassled and badgered. Looked forward to being criticized and corrected and told to "do it over." It would be distraction. It would be therapy and salvation. And, of course, it would mean some desperately needed money. The few hundred dollars in the joint checking account she and James had shared was all that Caroline had in the world, and she often thought of the wedding check that he had torn up. That money, which meant nothing to him, would mean everything in the world to her right now. Ten thousand dollars was a fortune, and it would buy her peace of mind and clothes and food for the baby. If only he hadn't been so impulsive.

Caroline censored her own thoughts. She couldn't allow herself any regrets. Not about any aspect of her marriage to James.

Tamara's voice came through the transatlantic cable, and even before Caroline could quite get out a "hello," she launched forth under full steam.

"Why you little sneak! Getting married in the middle of nowhere without a big splashy party," the countess said. "I've had *The Shiny Sheet* sent to me in London every week, and what do I see? A teensy little column item about your wedding! To James Goddard yet!"

"Countess, there's something I—" Caroline began.

Tamara was having none of it.

"But what on earth are you doing back at that dump in Lake Worth, for God's sake? You're filthy rich now," she continued. "I called the number you gave me in Maine and someone gave me your old number!"

"Countess, there's something I have to tell you," Caroline tried again.

"No, Caroline darling. There's something *I* have to tell *you!* That's why I'm calling! You're not the only blushing bride in this world. I've gotten married, too! To a duke, no less!" She laughed, overjoyed at what she had managed to accomplish. "You may call me Duchess now, Caroline. Isn't that just too much?"

It *was* too much. Caroline knew that the countess was in seven times seventh heaven, but she wasn't up to sharing in anyone else's happiness. Not now. Not yet. She managed an enthusiastic-sounding "congratulations" as Tamara went on and on about the duke's money, the blocks of Mayfair he owned, the antiquity of his title, his lustrous family tree, not to mention his house on Belgrave Square, his villa in the south of France, his island in the Aegean, his country place in Kent—and his aversion to American businesswomen.

The duke, it seemed, was very traditional in his attitudes, and a working wife was not exactly the kind of duchess he had in mind.

"And so, alas, I'm giving up L'Elegance," said Tamara, dropping her bombshell. "Ferdy frowns on such commercial enterprises. He says I won't miss the shop at all, that I'll have lots and lots of charitable activities and a very demanding social life to keep me busy from now on."

Caroline couldn't quite believe what she was hearing, couldn't digest the fact that she had lost her husband and now, suddenly, her job.

"You're not reopening L'Elegance?" she asked numbly, her eyes filling as they so often did since James had been killed. Her voice trembled. "You're actually closing the store?"

"Oh, now don't get all sentimental on me, Caroline." Tamara chuckled. "I know I gave you a rough time now and then, and there were periods when you were dying to find another job. Well, you're free to go now—even to that tart, Celeste—if you want. Wait until she finds out, poor thing. She's a mere countess with a penniless gigolo for a husband, while I'm a duchess with a husband who's positively loaded! So, go ahead and work for her, if you want to. You have my permission and my blessing. See how marriage has mellowed me, darling?"

Caroline's knees went weak and watery and she felt as if she might faint. Her throat was dry and her stomach was queasy with more than just the usual morning sickness. She prayed that she had misheard, had misunderstood.

"What about your lease?" Caroline asked in a voice that didn't sound like her own. "And your clients? And all your merchandise?"

"I made sure to get a sublet clause, so I'll just find another tenant for the space," Tamara replied. "I've already told the realty company to start looking. The clients can shop somewhere else—Celeste's, if they want to look common. As for the inventory, I'll write it off. It'll be a tax deduction. I've got Ferdy now. And *you've* got that adorable James Goddard. God knows, you won't have to work anymore, Caroline. You'll have to get involved socially and do your part for charity, mind you. But good Lord, just think of all that lovely Goddard money!"

The Goddards, Caroline thought ruefully. Their money was hardly lovely. What good was their money when they hadn't shown James the love and support he craved? When they hadn't shown *her* the slightest bit of compassion or sympathy? When they'd made their disgusting accusations, turned their backs on her, and informed her that they never wanted to see or hear from her again? When they hadn't even been willing to listen to what she'd tried to tell them—that she and James were having a baby?

"Countess, I have something to tell you," said Caroline, finally managing to summon up a firm voice. She then went on to tell Tamara about the accident and about the baby.

The countess was stunned by Caroline's news, and as she had many times over the months that Caroline had known her, she revealed a caring and unexpectedly generous side of her personality. Without hesitation, she offered—no, insisted—that Caroline come to London to stay with her and the duke until the baby was born and, perhaps, even after that.

"I can't," said Caroline, after thanking Tamara for her kindness. "I don't have the money for the plane ticket. And even if you sent me one, I couldn't just continue to live off you and Ferdy indefinitely. I have to find a way to support myself and the child. I don't see how I could do that in a foreign country. I think I'd better stay in Florida. My friends are here. The clinic has my medical records for when the baby is born. Besides, it's home."

Home, Caroline thought sadly as soon as she'd spoken the word. Home was wherever James was, and James was no more.

Caroline had lost her husband and her job and even any hope of a civil relationship with James's parents. She was so devastated by the stunning blows fate had dealt her that she took to her bed and stayed there. She couldn't eat and she couldn't sleep, and there were moments when she prayed that God would take her just as He had taken James. She lay awake in her old room at Selma's boardinghouse, overwhelmed by her grief, racked with pain over losing the only person in the world who had ever truly loved her, tormented by the reality that she would never again gaze upon the handsome face of the man she cherished more than her own life. She would never hold him, never kiss him, never make love to him again. She would never feel the texture of his hair, hear the sound of his voice, share his laughter, taste his skin.

Night and day merged into an endless passage of pain. Caroline lay on the bed, wearing one of James's polo shirts and clutching a small, gold-framed photograph of him, taken by Phil on their wedding day. No matter how exhausted she was, no matter how desperate for sleep, her demons would overtake her, forcing her to relive the night James did not return home to the carriage house with her anniversary bouquet; forcing her to agonize over the fact that if he hadn't felt compelled to visit the florist, he would still be alive, just as Dina Goddard had said; forcing her to face the truth—that her beloved was gone, that their marriage was over, that she, riddled with almost bottomless guilt and despair that painfully echoed her unhappy childhood, was alone.

Not quite alone, Caroline would remind herself as she tossed and turned in the squeaky twin bed, whose mattress was so thin she could feel the bedsprings beneath her. No, she had James's child inside her. *Their* child. The child that had been conceived of their passion, a living memorial of their love.

The notion should have comforted her, should have buffeted her from the blow of his death. But it did not. Nothing could. What possible joy could she derive from the baby James would never know, never hold in his arms? Yes, the child would be a part of James. But she didn't want a *part* of her husband. She wanted him! All of him. Alive, and by her side "Forever and after." Wasn't that what they had promised each other? In front of God and the Reverend Armstrong and all their friends?

Why couldn't James have left Caleb's studio ten minutes earlier? she'd torture herself night after night. Or ten minutes later? Why couldn't he have stopped at the drugstore for a bottle of perfume instead of at the florist's? Why hadn't she met him at the studio? They would have stayed to chat with Caleb and then the accident would never have happened. Why did it have to be them? Why did it have to be him? Why? Why? Why?

Sometimes, Caroline wondered if she would go crazy from the pain of second-guessing James's movements that fateful day. Or was it simply from the pain of missing him?

I've got to get out of this bed and find a job, she would admonish herself. *L'Elegance doesn't exist any more. My job doesn't exist any more. I have no money and no way to earn any. I've got to pull myself together and find a way to support myself and the baby.* She lectured herself and tried to pull herself together. *Willpower,* she thought. *All I need is willpower. I have to open a newspaper. Look at the want ads. Bathe and shampoo my hair. Iron a dress and put on some makeup. Schedule appointments and go on interviews. Talk to people and tell them that I need work.*

She had to rejoin the world. Had to stop dwelling on the past. Had to take care of herself and the child that was living inside her.

But it was obvious to Caroline, and to Selma, that she was in no condition to go job-hunting. She had lost her appetite and, despite her pregnancy, she was almost emaciated. Her skin was dull and her hair hung in lusterless strands. She went days without bathing or washing her hair. She lay on her bed in the darkened bedroom, weeping and staring at the ceiling.

Her state of mind became even more bleak when the letter she had written to the Goddards in a desperate attempt to tell them of the child she was expecting came back unopened. Charles Goddard had clearly meant it when he said that the Goddards did not want to see her or hear from her. Ever. To them, people like Caroline Shaw did not count, did not matter. And nothing they could do would ever change that. The realization that James's parents, the child's grandparents, were not even interested enough to open the letter to find out what she wanted to tell them threw Caroline into an even deeper depression.

"You won't eat. You don't sleep. You don't even put on

fresh clothes," Selma told Caroline one afternoon when she came home from the grocery store and found Caroline still in bed, wearing one of James's shirts and weeping over the model boat that rested on the bureau. It was the replica of the *Salt Spray,* the first model James had ever carved, the model of the boat on which they had spent so many blissful moments and the one on which their initials were intertwined.

"I know, I know," Caroline said sadly. "I *have* to get up, *have* to get on with my life, but I miss him so much, Selma. I don't care about anything without him. I just don't care about myself any more."

"It isn't just yourself you've got to think of," Selma said. "There's the baby to think of. The way you've been carrying on, anybody would think you don't care about the child."

Caroline didn't reply. The answer would have been too shameful. Selma was right: she *didn't* care about the baby. Didn't care if it was born or not. Didn't care if it lived or died. She told herself bitterly that she was a victim of fate and genetics and that she was simply carrying on the Shaw tradition of indifference and even hostility toward their own. The Goddards were no better: they didn't care about their grandchild. Caroline told herself bitterly that she didn't want a baby. Not this baby. Not any baby.

She wanted James. And he was never coming back.

Worried about Caroline, Selma Johannas spoke to her other boarders, Helen O'Donnell and Walter Enz. The three agreed: Caroline needed help—and so did the unborn baby. They decided that she also needed her mother, regardless of the Shaws' turbulent family history, and so, Selma Johannas called Mary Shaw and told her what was happening. Caroline's grief was now affecting her physically. She was spotting and having occasional cramps. She refused to go to the clinic, and Selma asked Mary to visit her daughter. Girls need their mother at a time like this, she figured, no matter what's happened between them in the past. What Selma hadn't counted on was that Mary Shaw would show up at the boardinghouse to see Caroline—and that she would bring her husband with her.

"Mom!" Caroline said. She was momentarily jolted out of her depression by the sight of her mother. The two women stood alone in Selma's living room while Al parked the car.

It had been several months since Mary Shaw had last seen her daughter, and she was alarmed by how pale and thin she appeared. Caroline, who had always been plump as a child, now seemed almost skeletal. Her eyes were enormous in her face and circled by dark blue rings. She knew she had to get Caroline to the clinic.

"Caroline, honey, you can't let yourself go like this. You have to take care of your health and your baby's," said Mary, her voice choked with guilt. She was grateful to Selma for calling. She hadn't been much of a mother to Caroline, and she was ashamed that it had taken a phone call from her former landlady to bring the two of them together. She opened her arms, eager to embrace her child, who had suffered a terrible loss, just as Mary herself had years before, when Al Shaw had begun to disappear into black moods and bottles of gin.

Caroline rushed to her mother, all the past hurts momentarily forgotten in the soft security of Mary Shaw's arms.

"I can't live without him, Mom," Caroline sobbed as her mother did her best to soothe her. "I don't know *how* to live without him. He made me feel better than I am, smarter, prettier—"

"Shhh," Mary soothed, stroking her daughter's long, lank hair. "You're smart and pretty all on your own. I've always known that."

Caroline pulled away and looked at her mother. "Then why didn't you ever tell me?" she asked plaintively. "Why didn't you ever make me feel as special as James did?"

Mary shook her head. She had no reason—and every reason. "You know how difficult things have been with your father all these years, honey. Being a wife to him has taken just about everything I had. And then you had to go and call the police that day, and we lost the house and Al went to jail and our lives went straight to hell. I'm so sorry that I couldn't be what you wanted. It's just that Al—"

"What about Al?" came a masculine voice.

It was Caroline's father. He had entered the living room and was standing in the doorway with his hands on his hips. *He looks halfway presentable for a change,* Caroline thought. He was clean shaven and his eyes were clear, and he smelled not of liquor but of some kind of shaving lotion. He was wearing blue slacks and a white shirt instead of his usual jeans and T-shirt. *Has he gotten his act together—finally—or is there some hidden agenda behind the transformation?* Caroline wondered. She couldn't help be suspicious. Almost everything her father had ever said and done had caused her to distrust him.

"Hello, Caroline," he said, politely.

Caroline nodded but made no move toward him.

"Sorry about what happened to your husband," Al said. "I hear you've had a bad time of it."

She eyed her father warily, unsure of his motives.

"What's this?" he said, moving toward James's model of the *Salt Spray,* which Selma had set on the coffee table the day before, hoping to lure Caroline out of her bed and downstairs into the living room.

"Why do you ask?" said Caroline, feeling the need to protect James's work from her father, who was capable of destroying anything near at hand when in one of his rages.

"Just askin'," said Al, sounding defensive and examining the boat closely. "Whoever made this sure knew what he was doin'. This is first-class work."

Caroline felt herself soften toward her father, just for a moment. Al Shaw had once been a skillful woodworker and master cabinetmaker, she knew, and his praise of James's work touched her.

"James made it," she explained. "It's a replica of the sailboat he owns. Owned." The tears began again then, and she made no attempt to wipe them away.

"Your mother says this James Goddard came from a big-shot family over in Palm Beach," Al Shaw went on, uncomfortable as always with emotion, clueless about how to soothe his daughter's pain. "I said to myself, Boy, my kid sure knows how to pick 'em. She goes to work on Worth Avenue and hooks a rich one."

Caroline turned away from her father. He sounded just

like the Goddards. She hadn't "hooked" anyone. She had fallen in love with James, and he had fallen in love with her. But then her father—like the Goddards—would never understand that people could have relationships that didn't involve anger and hostility and resentment and greed.

"Is there a point, Dad?" Caroline asked impatiently. She was too upset to put up with what she knew was coming: Al's rich man/poor man routine. She'd been hearing it all her life, every time he'd launch into a tirade about *them* and *us* and how it wasn't fair and how *we* were entitled to *their* money.

"My point?" said Al. He seized the opening. "All right. I'll get to the point. Mary tells me you're pregnant with this guy's kid."

"That's right," said Caroline, momentarily repulsed by the thought that the child she was carrying—James's child—would have Al Shaw for a grandfather. Al Shaw *and* Charles Goddard. She shuddered.

"Well, I was wonderin'," said Al, his eyes shifty as he lit up a cigarette. "How much are the Goddards givin' you? To support yourself and the kid, I mean? I bet there's enough left over to help out me and your mom."

Caroline's jaw dropped. So her father had come about money, she realized. Not because he particularly cared about her. Because he thought there might be something in it for him.

"The Goddards aren't giving me anything, not that it's any of your business," she said.

"Hey, hey. I'm just askin'," said Al. "I *am* your father, don't forget. I gotta look after my daughter's welfare, don't I?"

"Since when?" Caroline said. "You haven't given a damn about me since the day I was born. You've been too busy drinking and pissing my mother's salary away in bars and beating her up when you had nothing better to do."

"Caroline!" Mary Shaw was shocked at her daughter's outburst. Caroline had never spoken that way to her father's face. But then this was a new Caroline, she saw. Despite the drawn expression and sickly pallor, this was a more mature, self-assured Caroline.

"Look, I was only askin' about the money," Al Shaw protested. "Like I said, a man's gotta look out for his family. You say the Goddards aren't givin' you anything? I say that stinks. I say you should call them. Or get yourself to a lawyer and have him call. They owe you something—"

"Dad! Stop!" said Caroline. She could not bear the thought of facing the Goddards, of getting into what would certainly be a long, ugly, and draining legal battle with them over money. They'd told her to get out of their lives, and she'd realized that she had no real choice except to obey them. She'd rather earn her own living. At least it would be hers.

"Why the hell should I stop?" Al argued. "The Goddards have plenty of cash. I hear they're loaded."

"Where do you hear that?" Caroline asked. Al Shaw hardly ran in the same circles as Dina and Charles Goddard.

"Oh, around," said Al in his crafty, cagey way, his eyes shifting. "You should at least make them give you a regular allowance or something. That way, you'd be set up for life."

Caroline shook her head. "I have no intention of calling the Goddards, and I have no intention of having a lawyer call them," she said.

"What's the matter? You afraid?" Al asked. "You afraid they'll think you're beggin'? Well, you wouldn't be beggin'. You'd be askin' for what's yours. I say get on the phone and call 'em. Tell 'em you're havin' their son's baby and you need money to feed it. Tell 'em you're—"

"Stop! I can't listen to this anymore!" Caroline cried, putting her hands over her ears. "I want you to leave, Dad. Please."

"Oh, yeah? Why's that?" said Al. "You don't want me around now that you married into that fancy family. Is that it? You ashamed of your old dad?"

Caroline looked at her mother imploringly. "Please, take him home," she begged Mary. "I'm not feeling well. I can't deal with him. Not today." She clutched her abdomen and grimaced in pain.

"You were always an uppity kid," Al Shaw went on,

shaking a finger at his daughter. "Always thought you were better than everybody."

"Please, Dad, I just asked you to leave," Caroline said as her face contorted and she winced in pain. The occasional cramps she'd been having for the past few days had become more severe as she argued with her father. She wanted him out of Selma's boardinghouse. She wanted to go back to her room and lie down.

But Al Shaw refused to leave.

"You think I'm a crazy old man, don't you?" he sneered. "Well, I think *you're* crazy for not calling up the Goddards and getting some of their money. It's not right that those people think they can just ignore us—"

"That's enough!" Caroline cried out, finally fed up with her father's speeches about entitlement and "those people." All he cared about was himself, about making others pay for his misfortunes. She had had enough. "I want you out of here!" she tried again. "I've just lost my husband, don't you understand that?"

Suddenly, a bolt of pain seared Caroline's abdomen, and she doubled over and sank to a chair.

"Caroline! What is it?" asked her mother, who kneeled beside her.

Caroline gasped and shook her head. She couldn't speak. Pain was ripping through her.

"It must be the baby!" said Mary Shaw as she helped Caroline up. "Al! Go get the car! We've got to get Caroline to the hospital!"

"You know better than to order me, Mary," he said, not budging. "A second ago, your precious daughter said she wanted me out of here."

"Al, please. Can't you see? She's sick," said Mary in her placating tone.

Al shrugged and went to get the car.

By the time Caroline got to the hospital, the cramps had become even more severe and she had begun staining. After what seemed like an endless wait, during which she thought she couldn't bear the pain or the uncertainty of her condition any longer, she was examined by a doctor in a curtained-off cubicle of the emergency room. She wondered if she would lose the baby, but didn't have the strength or the will to ask. She was in agony and she didn't care if she or the child made it through the ordeal, didn't even care what they did to her. She thought she'd be happy if she died. Then she'd be with James again.

She felt someone giving her a shot, and then another set of hands lifting her onto the gurney and propelling her forward. There were voices and faces and worried expressions, mingled with "You'll be just fine" and "We'll take good care of you." None of it mattered to Caroline as she allowed all of them to do whatever they wanted to her. She felt as if she were sinking one minute, floating the next, her body a sea of contradictions. Eventually, there was weightlessness, a feeling of surrender and peace, and soon, darkness—

Twenty-four hours later, a woman Caroline didn't recall having seen before was standing over her.

"Good morning," she said. She was Asian, petite, and very pretty, wearing a spotless white coat and a slash of vivid, red-orange lipstick. A stethoscope hung from around her neck. Her amazingly black, shiny hair was cut to chin length, and her eyes sparkled behind gold-wired glasses. "Welcome to the land of the living."

Caroline blinked and looked around the room, which, she was surprised to see, she was sharing with three other patients.

"Where am I?" she asked. She was still groggy. She had no idea what day it was or what time. All she knew was that when she moved, her abdomen ached. She winced in pain as she adjusted her position in the bed.

"You're in the hospital, and I'm Dr. Lu," said the woman, who reached out to shake her hand. "I operated on you the day before yesterday. You're going to be a little sore for a couple of days, but nothing like what you experienced when you were admitted."

Suddenly, it all came back to Caroline. The cramps, the argument with her father, the searing pain, the trip to the hospital's emergency room. And suddenly, the question she had been unable and unwilling to ask sprang to her lips.

"The baby? Is the baby okay?"

She looked at Dr. Lu, anxiety clouding her expression. For the first time since James was killed, Caroline realized, she cared deeply what happened to her child. *Their* child. Hers and James's. How could she have been so blind, so unfeeling? This child represented a rebirth, a second chance, a gift of life for the one she had lost. As tears prickled at her eyes, she knew with shimmering clarity that, more than anything in the world, she wanted this baby. James's baby.

"The baby? Is the baby okay?" she asked again, her eyes pleading with the woman who stood before her.

"The baby's fine," said the doctor as she touched Caroline's hand.

The tears came freely then, tears of relief and joy and hope, tears that signalled a commitment to herself and to the child she nearly lost.

"You're very lucky, Mrs. Goddard," said Dr. Lu. "I don't know what you've been doing to yourself, but despite your lack of interest in your diet and overall health, your baby has survived."

"My husband died recently," Caroline said, wanting to explain why she had neglected herself and her child.

"So I understand, but you're still alive and so is your child. This baby must really want to be born."

"I *want* it to be born," said Caroline.

"Then I suggest that you begin to take care of yourself," said Dr. Lu. "You must eat three balanced meals a day, and when you get stronger, you must do some very careful exercise—such as walking. No running, no lifting, no exertion. If you have a job, you're going to have to ask for a medical leave. I don't want you to have the stress and strain of commuting or standing on your feet or having to deal with job-related pressures. Your baby is all right—for now. It's going to be up to you to keep it that way."

Caroline nodded, grateful that her child was safe, willing to do whatever it took to keep it that way.

"Is there anyone to help you over the next several months?" Dr. Lu asked. "A relative? Or a friend?"

Caroline thought for a moment. Her mother had her hands full with her father. Tamara was in Europe. Francesca had her job at The Breakers, where she had recently been promoted to associate director of public relations. There was only Selma, who had been there for her whenever she needed her.

"Yes," Caroline said. "There is someone."

"Good," said Irene Lu. "Have them pick you up tomorrow morning. We'll want to keep an eye on you for one more day."

Caroline nodded once again.

"I want you to come back in two weeks to see me," Dr. Lu added. "And if you begin to experience any problems, any at all, any cramps, any twinges, any spotting, you're to call me right away. Is that clear?"

"Very clear," said Caroline, seriously. Then she managed a smile. "I don't know how to thank you."

"I'll tell you how you can thank me," said the doctor, speaking in a pleasant but firm manner. "You can follow my instructions and start taking care of yourself and your child. I can't guarantee that you'll carry this baby to term, but there's a lot you can do to swing the odds in your favor."

"I'll do whatever it takes," Caroline vowed. "I want this baby, Dr. Lu, much more than I realized."

As Dr. Lu turned to leave the room, she stopped and turned back.

"By the way," she said. "The staff has been wondering, and so have I. Are you one of *the* Goddards?"

Caroline was puzzled by the question and wondered what made Irene Lu ask, but she knew what the only answer could possibly be, and she shook her head.

"It's the same name, but we're not related," she said quietly, feeling sad and ashamed and looking down at the white, hospital sheet that covered her.

Selma arrived at Caroline's hospital room at ten o'clock the next morning. She stood beside Caroline as the nurse helped her into a wheelchair, and she accompanied her as she was wheeled to the hospital's front entrance. While Caroline sat in the chair and waited for Selma to bring the car around, she glanced up at the impressive, obviously new wing of the hospital, the wing in which she had spent an arduous few days. Engraved in the gray granite above the doors was a plaque boasting the name of the donors whose gifts had made the new building possible. It read:

The Dina and Charles Goddard Pavillion

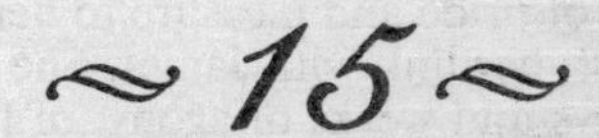

Health and money were the two concerns that now dominated Caroline's life. Following the printed menu suggestions that Irene Lu had given her, she shopped for dairy products, fresh fruits and vegetables, fish and poultry and lean meats. Obediently, the way she had always done everything, she followed Dr. Lu's orders, eating well and regularly and exercising carefully. At first, with Selma's help and on thin, wobbly legs, she walked half a block. Then she increased the distance gradually until she could walk eight blocks all by herself. She spoke to her mother on the telephone but refused to speak to Al, telling Mary that the doctor had ordered her to avoid any kind of stress. She read and watched television and, once a week, spoke to Tamara, who made a point of calling from London. The countess, now the duchess, was filled with concern for Caroline and her baby and bubbled with all kinds of gossip about the fashionable folk with whom she was associating in Europe.

"I don't know what I'd do without you," Caroline told her. "You cheer me up so much. I really don't know how I can thank you enough."

"I do. I want to be the baby's godmother," said the duchess, never at a loss for an idea.

When Caroline had explained that Selma had already claimed the position, Tamara was undaunted. "No problem," she said. "Tell this Selma person that I don't mind sharing the job."

"I'll tell her," Caroline laughed, always surprised by the unpredictable woman whose inability to have children of her own had given her a soft spot for other people's offspring.

Caroline's health gradually improved during the months of her pregnancy. Her thin frame began to fill out. The color and shine returned to her hair, and her complexion was more beautiful than it had ever been. Her swelling belly became a source of pride and pleasure to her, as it was her link with the past, her link with James. She was still often teary, but the days and weeks of agony, of lying in a dark bedroom, were over as she began to deal with the practical problems of being a single parent. Her mother managed to send her a small monthly check, and she depended on that money. Still, she knew she could not count on her mother indefinitely, and she did not want to have to ask friends for help. She had never been a charity case, and she did not intend to become one now.

"I've got to figure out a way to earn some money," she told Selma one November afternoon. "Dr. Lu said I can't go to work, but there must be something I could do at home, some way I could support myself."

Selma nodded. She had fended for herself for years with the modest income from the boardinghouse, but she was at a loss when it came to advising Caroline on business matters.

"What would you think about my selling James's boat models?" Caroline asked. The idea had been floating around in her mind. It was time to put it to the test of reality.

"It sounds like a good idea. If you can find customers," Selma said.

"James was planning to sell them anyway. I know they're worth something because Caleb said so, and I'm pretty sure there are customers out there," said Caroline. "I remember that when *Beautiful Homes and Gardens* ran a photograph of one of the models, several people called The State of Maine, wanting to know where they could buy it. I only have two left, but I thought maybe I'd take a small ad in *The Shiny Sheet* and see what happens."

What happened were three telephone calls and one appointment with a man named Kenneth Draper. On the day before he came, Selma and Caroline carefully dusted off the models that James had carved while he was in Camden and placed them in Selma's living room on the coffee table. Caroline, remembering Tamara Brandt's strategy of pampering her clients, made a pitcher of minted iced tea and bought an assortment of cookies. The boardinghouse was hardly L'Elegance, she knew, and her budget was hardly the countess's, but she would do the best she could. The doorbell rang promptly at three o'clock, and Kenneth Draper stood on Selma's front porch with a woman he introduced as his wife, Linda.

Caroline invited the Drapers inside, and after she offered them refreshments, she learned that Kenneth Draper was a retired plastics manufacturer who had been a lifelong sailor.

"Grew up in northern Michigan and learned to sail on the lake," he said. He went on about his first boat, a Sunfish, and about how, as his business grew, his boats did, too. There had been an Ericson 32, a Valiant 40, and a Hinckley Sou'wester 50. The names were familiar to Caroline—she had heard them all from James—and she felt a wave of warmth as she imagined him describing them to her. Kenneth studied the two models James had made, both of which were replicas of famous racing boats—*Ticonderoga* and *Intrepid.* As he assessed them, Caroline pointed out their finely detailed features and the high-quality workmanship. She conveyed to Kenneth Draper all the things that James had conveyed to her.

But as riveted as Kenneth Draper was by the models, his wife, Caroline couldn't help but notice, was bored and restless. She looked out the window, then around the small room, and constantly glanced at her watch. Caroline was afraid that Linda Draper might get so bored that she would insist her husband leave before he could make up his mind about buying one of the models.

"Would you like to look at a magazine?" Caroline asked Linda Draper.

"Love to," she said, smiling. "You don't know Kenneth, but when he gets involved with his beloved boats, time means nothing. We could be here for hours!"

Caroline nodded.

"I know just what you mean. My husband was the same way."

She gave Linda Draper a copy of *Beautiful Homes and Gardens,* the issue in which The State of Maine had been featured, and continued to answer Kenneth Draper's questions. She realized how much she had learned from James and concealed her excitement when Kenneth Draper finally shook his head and said he would purchase the *Ticonderoga* model for $1,200.

"Now he'll have to build another case!" said Linda Draper, getting up. "I don't know where we're going to find the space for all these boats!" She looked affectionately at her husband.

"We'll find a space," he told his wife with a wink as he wrote out a check.

"I'll pack up the boat for you," Caroline said, feeling extremely pleased with her first sale.

As she said good-bye to the Drapers, Linda Draper asked her about the article on The State of Maine in *Beautiful Homes and Gardens.* "I wish we had that kind of store here in Florida," she said. "There were five or six things I'd adore to own."

"Which ones?" asked Caroline curiously.

"The lace shawl is exquisite and so is the quilt with the hearts," said Linda. "And those handblown glass candleholders and—"

"Hey, hey," Kenneth Draper laughed, interrupting his wife. "It's a good thing Mrs. Goddard didn't have all that stuff on hand today." He turned to Caroline. "Linda's a world-class shopper," he explained. "I'd be out a lot more than $1,200!"

"Oh, now Ken," said Linda, who winked at Caroline. "I

only looked at the magazine because I was bored with all that boat talk. I'm afraid I'm just another wife who yawns while her husband waxes poetic about genoas and spinnakers."

The Drapers left the boardinghouse hand in hand, and as they did, they left behind them an idea. Caroline wondered if, perhaps, she should offer merchandise other than model boats—merchandise that would appeal to women like Linda Draper, boat widows who had plenty of time on their hands to shop while their husbands got lost in the intricacies of ships and ship models.

Caroline took part of the money she'd earned from her first sale and placed a second ad in *The Shiny Sheet.* There were four responses, but only one of the telephone callers was interested enough in the *Intrepid* model to make an appointment to come and see it. And he didn't show up.

"That's retailing," Caroline told Selma with a shrug as the two women drank the lemonade and ate the cookies Caroline had bought in anticipation of the man's visit. "It used to happen all the time at L'Elegance. Women would call to have a dress put on hold, and then they'd never show up to even try it on."

Her third ad, however, resulted in an appointment, and this time the caller did show up.

"The workmanship's great, but I guess I'm not really interested in the *Intrepid,"* said Brian Howards, the owner of an automobile dealership just outside of Palm Beach. He had brought his wife, Janine, to the boardinghouse one evening and stayed for over an hour while he examined the model in detail, asking scores of questions about the workmanship and the material. His wife rolled her eyes and flipped through the copy of *Beautiful Homes and Gardens* that Caroline had left out on the coffee table as her husband talked boats and models.

"This embroidered linen blouse is just gorgeous," said Janine Howards, showing Caroline the photograph in the story on The State of Maine. "I'd sure love to buy one just like it."

"Shush, Janine. I'm here to shop for me," said her

husband. Then he turned to Caroline. "I have a J-44, and what I'd really like is a model of her. Could I commission one? Is the craftsman a local fellow?"

Caroline felt the tears prick behind her eyes, but she swallowed them back and shook her head.

"Unfortunately, he passed away several months ago," she explained. "But I could contact the man he worked with up in Maine. May I call you tomorrow and let you know if he'd be interested in replicating a J-44?"

Brian Howards accepted the suggestion, and as soon as he left, Caroline telephoned Caleb in Maine. She told him what she had begun to do, and she asked him if he could make a J-44, and if so, how much it would cost and how long it would take. She also asked him if he would ship her additional models from his inventory—models she could sell for him out of Selma's living room. He was enthusiastic about the idea, and within weeks, the boardinghouse was filled with Caleb's skillfully crafted models.

"You're quite the businesswoman," said Selma as Caroline used the money she earned from the sale to Brian Howards to place an ad in *Soundings,* the widely read boating newspaper.

"I'd be an even better businesswoman if I offered something for the women, too," mused Caroline.

As boating enthusiasts continued to respond to her ads, Caroline realized that their wives and girlfriends *were* bored by the boat talk. It happened over and over: the men got lost in the world of boats; the women yawned and fidgeted and flipped through magazines. She realized that she was missing an opportunity by not offering merchandise for them. While the men talked specs and fittings and brightwork, the women could shop, too, and Caroline decided to put her idea into action. She would start with some of the best-selling items from The State of Maine, items that she could offer on consignment.

She telephoned Jennie, who was happy to send some of her heart quilts to Florida for the high season. She called Susan Lorentz, who had made her wedding dress. Susan had been working on some hand-embroidered sheer linen blouses, perfect for the warm weather, and had an inventory of a dozen and a half.

"Could you send me six?" asked Caroline. "I'll see if I can sell them here."

Caroline also called some of her other contacts from The State of Maine. There was a vendor in Wiscasset who distributed soaps and bubble baths made with all-natural essences; a woman in Ogunquit whose floral potpourri had been very successful with the summer tourists; and a French lacemaker who had settled in Bangor and made the frilly collars and cuffs that had sold so well. All were happy to find an outlet for their products during the off-season, and Caroline was careful to keep the pricing both reasonable and varied. There were low-priced items and more extravagant choices. That way, a woman could buy a gift for someone else or perhaps treat herself to a small indulgence.

Now, when the men came to look at the boat models, their wives and girlfriends also had something to look at—and to purchase. Selma's boardinghouse wasn't L'Elegance and never would be. And James wasn't alive to make more boat models. But the ones made by his friend and mentor were bringing pleasure to people, just the way James had hoped, and the custom commissions for Caleb came in slowly but steadily. Caroline had found a way to make money, to support herself and her child, to distract herself from her mourning, and to bring happiness to others.

The boat models were sold one by one. The items for the women, Caroline quickly noticed, sold in multiples.

"These are the most beautiful things! So romantic!" the women said of the elegant feminine merchandise. "And original, too! You don't see items like these anywhere else in south Florida!"

As April—Caroline's due date—approached, she was hardly rich, but she was no longer completely penniless. She purchased a modest layette for her baby, as well as a second-hand crib at a yard sale. For the first time since James died, she allowed herself to dream again. Now her dreams centered on the child that was hers and James's. Sometimes the child was a girl, a beautiful baby with James's golden locks and blue eyes. Other times it was a bouncing boy, an energetic child with dimples and a mischievous grin. Always the child radiated health and happiness, just as Caroline herself did these days. At her last check-up, Dr. Lu had complimented her on the way she had followed her instructions.

"I didn't have any choice," Caroline told her. "I wanted my baby to live."

Two weeks before Caroline was to give birth, Selma received an unexpected phone call.

"It was a lawyer," Selma explained breathlessly, putting down the telephone. "He represents a developer from Palm Beach who's going to tear down some of the buildings in the neighborhood."

"And?" Caroline asked. "What did he want?"

"It's what his *client* wants," said Selma. "He wants to buy my property so he can put up one of those high-rise condos! He's offered to pay me a lot of money to move out of here!"

Caroline was stunned by the news. "It sounds like a wonderful opportunity," she said. "But you've lived here for almost thirty years. Won't you mind moving out?"

Selma shook her head vehemently. "Hell, no!" she said. "I'm ready to move. I can't have my godchild seeing me in a place like this!"

The lawyer called again later that day. At Caroline's suggestion, Selma turned down his offer. She held out until the developer raised his offer three more times.

At 8:00 A.M., on April 12, Caroline started to have contractions. The pregnancy that had begun with tragedy and then almost ended in a miscarriage concluded easily, as if to recompense her for what she had been through. She was in the delivery room for three hours, and just before noon, her baby was born. Irene Lu put the child into her arms, and as she held her baby for the first time and saw traces of James in the shape of the eyes and the curve of the mouth, tears came to her eyes. This time, not tears of sorrow. This time, tears of joy.

"A boy," she whispered. "A little boy."

Three weeks later, recalling that Emily had been the only one of the Goddards to extend any kind of condolences, Caroline dialed her Park Avenue number. Even though the Goddards had made it plain that they wanted nothing whatsoever to do with her, she wanted them to know about the baby. They were the child's grandparents after all. A maid answered the telephone and told Caroline that Emily would be in Europe for six months. Caroline left a message, asking Emily to call her.

She never did. And the second letter Caroline wrote to the Goddards telling them about their grandson also came back unopened. She and Jack were on their own, she realized, with clarity and finality. And they would make it—without the Goddards or their money.

Part Two:

Romance, Inc.

Five Years Later

16

"Romancing The Client"

by Roz Garelick

Caroline Goddard's eighteen-month-old boutique, Romance, Inc., located at 218 Okeechobee Boulevard in West Palm Beach, doesn't have customers. It has clients—and more and more of them every day. Ms. Goddard, it seems, has a growing business on her hands. We visited her earlier this week and talked to her about the secrets of her success.

"The client is queen," maintained Romance, Inc.'s twenty-six-year-old proprietor, who opened her shop devoted to items associated with love and romance after three and a half years of selling such merchandise from the living room of her West Palm Beach condominium. The widow of James Huntington Goddard, whose family has maintained homes in Palm Beach since the 1930s, Ms. Goddard had previously worked at L'Elegance on Worth Avenue before pursuing a retailing enterprise of her own. "My husband was the quintessential romantic," she confided. "He took enormous pleasure in creating a romantic environment, in making even the most ordinary circumstances come alive with romance. He had a gift, really, and I wanted to share his gift with others, to allow other women to experience what I had experienced, to spread the spirit of romance."

Ms. Goddard went on to explain that she got the idea for her shop when she was selling her late husband's model boats. She noticed that the wives and girlfriends of her clients were bored while their boat-obsessed mates decided on the details of a purchase.

"I began with a few items—blouses, potpourri, heart-shaped throw pillows—and found that the romantically oriented merchandise sold more quickly than the boats," said Ms. Goddard, a honey-haired beauty, as she showed off a newly arrived line of soaps and bath products in rose, lavender, and lily-of-the-valley scents; a lace coverlet, delicate as cobweb and handmade in Maine; stacks of romance novels, piled invitingly in wicker baskets; and towels and sheets, decorated with hearts and flowers. "With the help of a few friends, I was able to rent space here on Okeechobee Boulevard, and little by little, my business has grown."

Grown indeed. On the day of our visit, the simple but very elegant shop was bursting with activity. Several of the clients remarked that they found the shop's decor unusually appealing. The interior of Romance, Inc. is painted white. A motif of hearts and rosebuds runs along the wainscoting and is also stenciled onto the whitewashed floors. Merchandise is attractively displayed and color themed. At the entrance there is a section of sachets, nightgowns, lingerie, and candles, all in pale violet. Along the left wall are peach-colored lamp shades ("To cast a romantic glow," explained Ms. Goddard), as well as soaps, hand towels, and embroidered linen napkins in a matching hue. The displays change weekly as new shipments arrive, so that there is always fresh merchandise for the shop's regular clients, who receive a ten-dollar gift certificate with every $100 purchased. Ms. Goddard's stylish taste and attention to detail is further revealed by the pink shopping bags with the name of the boutique reproduced in her own handwriting in shiny, red-lacquered letters. Gift wraps are equally seductive: pink tissue is wrapped with red ribbons tied into a bow and always finished off with a fresh rosebud.

Romance, Inc.

"As you can see, the shop is dedicated to romance," said Ms. Goddard, offering a client a cup of jasmine tea and a freshly baked lemon wafer. "I want to make Romance, Inc. a comfortable place for women to shop for men, for men to shop for women, and, perhaps most importantly, for women to indulge themselves."

It looks to us as if Caroline Goddard, who juggles running the shop with raising her handsome and energetic five-year-old son, Jack, has a bright, bright future.

—*The Shiny Sheet*
Palm Beach, Florida

The article appeared just before Valentine's Day and featured a flattering photograph of Caroline, standing in front of Romance, Inc. and holding the chubby little hand of her blond, blue-eyed son.

"Jack looks adorable, doesn't he?" Caroline asked, as she handed Selma *The Shiny Sheet,* folded to the article. It was eight o'clock in the morning, and Selma had arrived at Caroline's apartment to help dress Jack and take him to school. Since she had sold her boardinghouse to the developer for more money than she had earned in all the years she'd been in business and moved with Caroline to West Palm Beach, Selma Johannas had proven to be a godsend once again. From investing three thousand dollars to help Caroline open Romance, Inc. to taking care of Jack while she was at work, Selma had provided Caroline with unconditional, almost maternal, friendship. Caroline, in turn, had taken great pleasure in watching the older woman's transformation since the sale of the boardinghouse. Gone were the ratty slippers and tattered bathrobes! Over the months, Selma had begun to pay more attention to herself, treating herself to well-made clothes, having her hair done professionally, and gradually realizing that, although she had never been married and never expected to be, she might at least find a man to keep her company. Perhaps Romance, Inc. had cast a spell over Selma, too, Caroline thought to herself.

Selma studied the photograph in the newspaper and smiled.

"Yes, Jack does look adorable," she agreed, always proud of her godson. "And you look every bit the successful businesswoman."

Caroline sighed. "I'm a *busy* businesswoman," she said, gulping down the last of her coffee and reaching for her attaché case. "We're having a special Valentine's Day promotion today—discounts on merchandise, plus a drawing for a day at Elizabeth Arden. The winner will get a free facial, herbal wrap, manicure, the works."

Selma shook her head. "You're really something, you know that?" she laughed. "You're going to make that store the talk of Florida."

"If I don't kill myself first," said Caroline, who was bracing herself for a hectic day at the shop. Between the Valentine's Day promotion, *The Shiny Sheet* article and the fact that Marcia Platt, her part-time assistant, was in Toledo tending to her sick mother, she knew she'd have her hands full.

The truth was, Caroline Goddard enjoyed having her hands full—*needed* to have her hands full. Work and motherhood had eased the loneliness she felt since James was killed. They were more than distractions: her child and her shop were her salvation.

She adored Jack with a fierceness of which she hadn't thought herself capable. He was her life force, a living, breathing connection to James, a part of the man she had loved so deeply and so desperately. Sometimes when Jack would smile his dimpled smile or flash his mischievous blue eyes at her, the resemblance to James was so profound it stung, and Caroline would find herself blinking back tears. But mostly Jack brought her joy, and she thought she must have been out of her mind during those weeks of blackness and depression following James's death to have cared so little about him that she almost lost him, too.

They were a little family, Caroline thought, and Jack was as outgoing a child as Caroline had been introverted. He loved playing with his school friends; with Selma, whom he saw every day and adored; with Tamara, his other godmother, who visited him with the duke and fussed over him as if he were Prince Charles; with his mother's clients at the shop, where Selma sometimes brought him after school; even with his mother's parents. When he would ask about his paternal grandparents, about the Goddards, who didn't even know that he existed because they had made it clear they wanted nothing to do with Caroline, his mother would kiss him and say simply, "Your daddy's parents live far away from here, sweetheart. Far away."

"Will they ever come to see us?" he would ask.

"No, darling," Caroline would answer. "I don't believe they will. But we don't need them. We have enough love on our own, don't we?"

"Yes, Mommy. All the love in the world," Jack would say, responding as if Caroline had engaged him in a little game.

"That much?" Caroline would ask feigning surprise.

"More!" he would exclaim, throwing his arms around her. Then he would smile and move on to another subject. He was a happy, well-adjusted child, and Caroline promised herself she would see that he stayed that way.

And work? Work had been more than a tonic for Caroline in her grief. Work had helped her regain her self-confidence—the confidence that James had instilled in her every day of their brief time together. *He* had shown her how to get her job back at L'Elegance. *He* had introduced her to Cissy McMillan and encouraged her to run Cissy's shop. *He* had always been there, cheering her on, exhorting her to be the best she could be, telling her that she had brains and talent as well as beauty and could accomplish whatever she chose—including having a store of her own. Work had given her back herself, Caroline often thought when she reflected on the past several years. They had been difficult years, and a day did not pass that she didn't think about James, miss him, wish he were by her side. But work—first selling out of the boardinghouse, then from her living room, and finally opening Romance, Inc.—was something Caroline could control, something she could make bigger and better, something that wouldn't abandon her. Not as long as she never let up, never let it slip away.

"Mommy!" Jack ran into the kitchen where Caroline and Selma had been chatting. His head was a mass of golden curls, and his blue eyes twinkled. "Can I have lunch at the store today? Selma can bring me there after school. Right, Selma?"

Caroline gazed at her son and felt a wave of love wash over her. Yes, she was anticipating a hectic day at the shop. And, yes, she would be shorthanded. But she could deny her son nothing. Even more she could not deny herself any opportunity to spend time with him.

"Of course, you can," she said, bending down to take him in her arms. "We'll have the ham sandwiches on croissants from Uncle Pierre's. Would you like that, sweetheart? As a special treat?"

Jack nodded enthusiastically. "Can I go to Café Pavillion with you to buy them?" he asked, hoping to ride along on the ten-minute drive between his mother's store and Worth Avenue. Ever since he had been a baby, Caroline had taken Jack to Pierre Fontaine's popular patisserie. He enjoyed being fussed over by Pierre almost as much as he enjoyed sticking his finger into Pierre's cage full of tropical birds!

"We'll see," said Caroline, getting up from the kitchen stool. "Now, I've got to run, you two. I'll see you both at the shop around noon, okay?"

"Sure, Mom. See ya," said Jack as he kissed his mother good-bye.

"Don't run yourself ragged at that store," warned Selma, who relished the chance to visit Romance, Inc., the only business in which she had ever owned even a part. The very idea of proprietorship made her chuckle, as she hardly thought herself as a big-shot investor. "By the way, can I enter your contest?" she asked as Caroline was nearly out the door. "I could use a face-lift, but a free facial at Elizabeth Arden would tide me over until then."

Caroline laughed.

"The drawing is open to *all* the clients of Romance, Inc.," she called out. "Even the clients who double as my son's godmother."

Jack's other godmother also decided to pay Caroline a visit late that morning. Tamara bustled into the shop, trailing the gardenia scent of a powerful French perfume, and carrying her copy of *The Shiny Sheet,* folded to the article about Romance, Inc.

"Did you know about this article?" asked Tamara.

"Roz interviewed me, but I didn't know when the article would appear. Or *if* it would," said Caroline as two clients entered the shop.

"May I help you?" Tamara asked, taking over without even a glance at Caroline.

"Yes. I'm interested in the rose-scented guest soaps," the first woman said, picking up the display bottle. "I want some for myself and some to be shipped to my sister-in-law in Washington."

"Of course," said Tamara, taking down the client's name and address.

The second woman lingered at the display of romance novels. She was looking at the cover of a book by Julie Garwood.

"It's brand-new," said Caroline, who made a point of reading what she sold. "I loved it, and all our clients who have read it have raved about it."

"I've never read a romance," said the woman hesitantly, fingering the book, her eyes riveted by the cover, "even though some of my friends say they're a fabulous escape."

"Nothing wrong with escaping," said Caroline with a smile. "We encourage our clients to indulge themselves, and we reward them when they do. We offer a free sachet with every book."

"Free?" The woman's eyes brightened.

"Absolutely. You have a choice of a mimosa, lavender, or rose scent," said Caroline as the woman reached for her purse.

When the two clients carrying their distinctive Romance Inc. shopping bags left, Tamara turned to Caroline. "Aren't those the same sachets we had at L'Elegance?"

"Yes. Except instead of being covered in ivory silk, I asked the manufacturer to cover them in either red or pink satin," replied Caroline.

"You obviously know a good thing when you see it," admitted the duchess, who now spent the season in Palm Beach with her husband. Waltzing into town every February and shopping Worth Avenue like a lady of leisure afforded her the exquisite delight of one-upping the despised Celeste, who was still a prisoner of her own business, consigned to supporting the elegant but penniless count in his endless rounds of golf and bridge. "Although you also ought to have some covered in prints as well. Florals would be best," said Tamara as she looked around the shop with her eagle eyes and found nothing else to criticize.

Caroline nodded. She loved prints. So did most of the women she knew. It was a good suggestion. Tamara's ideas usually were.

"Won't Ferdy be upset that you're here? *Again?*" asked Caroline, trying to stifle a laugh. "I thought he refused to allow you to work."

"He thinks I'm at the hairdresser," said Tamara, who then drew herself up to her full five feet two inches and added, "Besides, what he doesn't know won't hurt him. You don't think I tell my husband *everything* I do, do you?"

Caroline smiled and watched the duchess take charge of the shop, manipulating and cajoling her way to a sale, just as she used to do at L'Elegance. She may have upgraded her title, but she's still basically the same lovable countess, Caroline thought, as she recalled how annoyed Tamara had been when she'd learned that Caroline had opened Romance, Inc. without her knowledge—or her advice.

"How could you have gone ahead without consulting me?" she had asked, obviously feeling slighted.

"You told me Ferdy was opposed to your having anything to do with business," Caroline had said.

"Ferdy's back in the Middle Ages when it comes to

business," said the duchess. "He thinks that business is for men and that women shouldn't bother their pretty little heads about making a living."

"I would expect that one of these days you plan to drag Ferdy into the twentieth century," said Caroline, hearing the undertone of frustration in the duchess's tone.

"Kicking and screaming, to be sure, nevertheless, just as soon as possible!" said Tamara. She loved her title and all that went with it, but being a duchess, she was learning, was only half a life. "But it's obvious to me that one day you're going to want to expand Romance, Inc. You've got a very good thing here, and you're *almost* as clever a merchant as I was. Mark my words, Caroline. Okeechobee Boulevard isn't big enough for you and Romance, Inc."

Caroline could hear the longing in Tamara's voice: the longing to be involved, the longing to be part of the everyday pleasures, excitement—and frustrations—of running a business. She missed the grit, the thrill of the sell, the spirit of competition—and the sense of possibility. She was clearly thinking big on Caroline's behalf, and although Caroline didn't say so out loud, she herself had just begun thinking of opening a second store. The idea of marketing romance that had started out as a way to make desperately needed money was finding a much more enthusiastic response than Caroline had ever dreamed. Now, with *The Shiny Sheet* article validating her work in print, Caroline felt more than ever that Romance, Inc. had potential that went far beyond one successful, but small, shop.

The idea of expanding excited her—and frightened her. She didn't want to get carried away, didn't want to bite off more than she could chew. Cautious and prudent, the result of a deprived childhood lived in the shadow of relentless financial difficulties, she had decided to move slowly and carefully. She wanted more time to consider the idea, more time to be absolutely certain that she was making the right move. Expansion was a big step, and she didn't want to move ahead without being sure that she'd be able to handle the demands of two shops, the increased financial responsibilities, the added pressure on her already limited time.

* * *

At 12:15, Selma arrived at Romance, Inc. with Jack in tow. The shop was busy with lunchtime shoppers and browsers, and Caroline was grateful for the interruption. She hugged her son as she greeted Selma.

"Can we go to Café Pavillion now, Mom? For the ham sandwiches?" asked Jack. He was perpetually hungry. A walking appetite, Caroline had once affectionately called him.

"You're not going anywhere, young man," the duchess interjected. "Not without a great big kiss for your godmother."

Jack allowed himself to be bear-hugged and kissed by Tamara. He even agreed to mind the store with her while his mother slipped out to buy lunch.

"Don't you want me to get the sandwiches?" asked Selma as Caroline was exiting the shop through the rear door.

"No, thanks," said Caroline. "To tell you the truth, I could use a break and some fresh air. I'll drive over to Pierre's and be back in a jiffy. Tamara will watch the shop while I'm gone—of that I have no doubt!"

Pierre Fontaine's life had changed dramatically since the day Caroline and James had met at L'Elegance and first sipped cappuccino at Café Pavillion. His wife, Chantal, had died after a protracted illness, leaving Pierre to handle the restaurant and patisserie himself. The demands of running it alone were becoming more of a drain as he got older, and as a result, he depended more and more on the advice of his son, Jean-Claude, who had a successful restaurant of his own in New York and who occasionally flew down to Palm Beach on weekends.

Pierre and Caroline had become quite friendly now that she, too, had a business to run. In the quiet moments just before both shops opened, they often shared a cup of coffee and talked over their business and personal dilemmas. Pierre had been very supportive of Caroline in the days and weeks following James's death, but now, five years later, he wondered silently why she was still alone, why she didn't date, why she seemed to avoid even the very notion of becoming involved with a man. Caroline, in turn, had helped Pierre mourn Chantal, and because he had raised a son of his own, she often found herself asking his advice on the subject of bringing up a boy.

"My Jean-Claude was a little hothead as a child. Impulsive, temperamental but very, very innovative," said Pierre, reminiscing fondly. "And the years haven't changed him one bit! The minute he arrives, he lets me know in no uncertain way that he has no patience for Palm Beach or the people in it. *Provincial* is the nicest word he has to say about anyone." Still, Pierre was unable to resist bragging about Jean-Claude's trendy and oh-so-chic Manhattan restaurant, Moustiers, his best-selling cookbook, *Cuisine de L'Amour,* and his celebrity-studded social life. "Despite all of it, Jean-Claude's a good boy and a fine person. Successful as he is, he never hesitates to come and help me. He's a grown man with a busy life in New York, but he hasn't grown too big for his boots. He still cares about his papa."

"And you obviously care very much about him," said Caroline wistfully, thinking of fathers like Al Shaw who didn't care.

Caroline drove east to Palm Beach. She found a spot on Worth Avenue, not far from the storefront that L'Elegance had once occupied, parked the car, and hurried into the café. Pierre seemed especially glad to see her and greeted her with even more exuberance than usual.

"There's someone I've been wanting you to meet," he beamed. As he ushered Caroline back toward Café Pavillion's sleek European-style kitchen, Marcel Chabert, Pierre's longtime executive chef, stormed out of the swinging door. His normally pleasant countenance was flushed, and seeing Pierre, he threw his *toque* to the floor and stamped his foot.

"C'est fini!" he exclaimed. "I am leaving this instant! You will never again see me at Café Pavillion!"

"Marcel, what's wrong?" asked Pierre.

"You know perfectly well what's wrong! It's that son of yours and his crazy ideas! *Quiche* with sun-dried tomatoes! *C'est execrable! C'est un catastrophe! C'est . . ."* Marcel sputtered, throwing his hands into the air. His outrage was so great that words deserted him.

"Calmez-vous, Marcel," Pierre said. "I know that some of Jean-Claude's ways are untraditional, but we've been very successful with the new specials."

"Papa, let him go if that's what he wants," said a tall, breathtakingly handsome young man who followed Marcel out of the kitchen. Caroline recognized him instantly.

"See? He's trying to drive me away!" shouted the plump, mustachioed chef who had worked for Pierre for fifteen years.

"You flatter yourself, Marcel," the young man said testily. "This has nothing to do with you. It has to do with the menu and with giving my father's restaurant a bit of freshening up."

"Freshening up?" Marcel's face reddened even more deeply and he became positively apoplectic. His hands waved in extreme agitation and sweat formed on his brow. "Café Pavillion is French! We serve French food, not *fashion* food. Sun-dried tomatoes! Ha!" he said, spitting out the last words.

Pierre reached out and took his chef by the arm.

"Come, Marcel. Let's go to my office and have an espresso and talk things over," Pierre said diplomatically, leading the chef toward the back of the restaurant.

Jean-Claude Fontaine shook his head and turned away from the two men. Then he noticed the young woman who had obviously heard the entire explosion. She was quite the beauty, he thought, suddenly forgetting about *quiche.* She was slender and hazel-eyed. Her hair was the sumptuous golden-brown color the French call *châtaigne* and she was wearing a casually stylish wheat-colored gabardine suit. She must be Caroline Goddard, he realized, the woman his father spoke of so often. Just that morning Pierre had mentioned that she would probably be coming to the café to pick up lunch.

"You must be Caroline," he said, pronouncing her name with a French accent. "Papa said you were beautiful, but not *this* beautiful." He took a step toward her and bowed slightly. *"Enchanté,"* he murmured. With that, he reached for her hand and, raising it to his lips, kissed it, letting his mouth linger on her skin.

Caroline felt the blood rush to her face and she quickly withdrew her hand. She was thrown by the compliment, completely flustered by the kiss on the hand, caught off balance by the way Jean-Claude Fontaine's very presence made her feel. Now that she was face-to-face with him, she understood why famous women were falling all over him. He was about her age, Caroline guessed, and as handsome as a movie star. He was just over six feet tall. His dark olive shirt, its sleeves rolled up to reveal strong forearms flecked with dark curly hairs, was tucked into cream-colored linen slacks that traced his slim hips and long legs. His dark, wavy hair was tied back in a ponytail, and he had almond-shaped green eyes, a wide sensuous mouth, and a cocky smile.

"And you must be Jean-Claude," she replied, having recognized him from the photograph on the cover of *Cuisine de L'Amour.*

"How did you know?" he asked, his eyes finally pulling themselves away from her body and looking directly into hers.

"Your father described you," she replied dryly, unwilling to let him know that she was aware of how celebrated he was.

He smiled, well able to imagine what his father must have said.

"Demanding, temperamental . . . ?" he suggested.

Caroline nodded.

"Among other things," she laughed.

"I suppose you heard our little squabble?" he said, referring to the *contretemps* with Marcel.

"They could hear *you* in Tampa," Caroline replied. He was flirting with her, she knew, and while part of her enjoyed it, another part wanted to flee. Jean-Claude Fontaine possessed tremendous animal magnetism, and it frightened her even as it thrilled her. Since James's death, she had shut off all thoughts of the opposite sex, all feelings of desire and longing. At first her denial had been a natural extension of her grief. Over time it had become an ingrained response.

"I suppose they could." He grinned ruefully. "What do you think they're saying about me in Tampa?" He tried to mimic her American pronunciation but it came out Tahm-pah. Very French.

"They're saying that you'd like to add a few new specials to your father's menu but that Marcel doesn't share your appreciation of sun-dried tomatoes." She smiled.

He shrugged.

"In Tahm-pah, they probably never tasted a sun-dried tomato," he said disdainfully.

"I've never tasted a sun-dried tomato," she admitted.

He shook his handsome head.

"Nor *escargots* or *foie gras* either, I suppose," he said sadly. "What a terrible pity. I'm going to have to do something about that, something to broaden your horizons beyond pizza and hamburgers, *ma chère . . ."*

Before she could think of something to say to defend herself, Pierre emerged from his office, a more composed Marcel behind him.

"Marcel is willing to try your *quiche,"* Pierre told Jean-Claude. "But he insists that you demonstrate the recipe exactly."

"I absolutely insist on demonstrating it because if he doesn't follow my recipe precisely, the *quiche* will be as uninspired as everyone else's," announced Jean-Claude, almost as imperious as Tamara at her haughtiest. "In addition, I also insist that Marcel actually taste it. So that he will understand the balance I'm looking for in the dish . . ."

Caroline watched Jean-Claude as he discussed the recipe with his father and Marcel. He *was* temperamental, she thought, and it was easy to imagine him strutting around his own restaurant, barking orders. He knew his own mind, and she admired that. But it wasn't his mind that was causing her face to flush and her pulse to race. It was his suave Continental manner, his overt sensuality, his almost arrogant awareness of himself and his appeal. As she watched him speak and gesture and command the absolute attention of the two older men, she had two thoughts simultaneously: that she didn't ever want to be alone with him . . . and that she wanted very much to be alone with him.

She dealt with her emotions the way she often did when

they became too threatening: she turned her thoughts to her business, to Romance, Inc., a realm in which *she* felt complete confidence, a realm in which *she* was in total control. Always creative when it came to her shop, she suddenly had an idea that she knew would bring Romance, Inc. some welcome publicity and, she could almost predict, new clients.

When the three men finished their discussion, Pierre turned to Caroline.

"I see you've met my shy, modest son," he said.

"Yes, and as a matter of fact, I—" She looked at Jean-Claude, hesitated, and then, clearing her throat, forged ahead. "I was wondering, Jean-Claude. Do you intend to be in Palm Beach for very long?"

"Just for the weekend," he replied, caressing her with his eyes, making his appreciation of her obvious. "Why? What do you have in mind, *chérie?*"

He grinned at her, perfectly aware that he made her nervous and enjoying it. He relished the effect he had on women, especially beautiful women.

Caroline cleared her throat again. "I was going to ask you if you could give me an hour or two of your time on Saturday," she said.

Jean-Claude turned to his father and Marcel. "Do you believe that? She's propositioning me!"

The three Frenchmen laughed while Caroline blushed.

"Please," she said, when their laughter—and the color in her cheeks—finally subsided. "What I'm proposing, Jean-Claude, is that you and I become involved in a—"

"Whatever you're proposing, I accept," Jean-Claude interrupted, and the men began to laugh again.

"This is serious!" Caroline chided. "I'm talking about business. I'd like to stage an event in my shop—"

"Ah, yes. Where you sell romance but never indulge yourself," said Jean-Claude, apparently repeating an observation that Pierre must have made.

Caroline straightened her shoulders and made a deliberate decision to ignore the remark. Her personal life was none of his business!

"Since you're the best-selling author of *Cuisine de L'Amour*—a book we've been selling very well, by the way—I thought you might like to make an appearance in my store," she explained. "The clients would be delighted to meet you. All you have to do is stay for an hour or so, talk with them, and sign books. It would be great for business—for both our businesses."

Caroline grew more and more excited as she explained her idea. Her cheeks glowed and her eyes sparkled, and the burst of energy and enthusiasm added a new, vibrant dimension to her All-American beauty.

Jean-Claude looked at his father and shrugged.

"American women are so passionate—about their *work*, aren't they, Papa?" he asked.

Pierre laughed. "And this one is as tenacious as she is lovely. She does not give up, Jean-Claude. So you might as well say yes."

"I have never *not* said yes to a beautiful woman," confessed Jean-Claude. "Although I must admit that I don't much care for Palm Beach women. They're stuffy and set in their ways and they don't like change. Not even a few sun-dried tomatoes here and there." He glanced meaningfully at Marcel, then back at Caroline. "But for you? Anything."

Caroline took a deep breath. He was a snob. A French chauvinist who looked down at Americans, she could see. But she had made an offer and he had accepted. There was no going back now. And, besides, his appearance at Romance, Inc. would certainly attract attention—and business.

"I think we'll be able to sell a lot of books," she said in her most businesslike tone.

"I have no doubt about it," he said with certitude.

After she and Jean-Claude had finished arranging the logistics of his appearance at Romance, Inc., he took her hand and, once again, pressed his lips gently to it, this time holding it far longer than was really necessary. She could smell the scent of his cologne and found the fragrance intoxicating. Or was it Jean-Claude himself? His nearness? His proudly flaunted maleness?

Thoroughly flustered, Caroline withdrew her hand more abruptly than she really meant to, said good-bye to the three men, and hurried out of Café Pavillion.

It wasn't until Caroline was in her car and pulling out of the parking space that she remembered why she had come to the café in the first place.

"Lunch!" she gasped, applying the brakes. She got out of the car and ran back to Café Pavillion where her take-out order was waiting.

"Did you forget the sandwiches? Or was there another reason you came back, *chérie?*" Jean-Claude said flirtatiously as he handed her the elegantly packed picnic.

"I forgot the sandwiches," said Caroline, clutching the shopping bag. "What other reason could there be?"

Jean-Claude shrugged provocatively.

"I can think of one or two . . ." he said, his tone making it quite clear that ham sandwiches weren't what was on his mind.

Caroline turned bright red and looked down at the floor.

"See you Saturday," she mumbled, and almost ran out the narrow flowered passageway to the street. She could feel his green eyes on her, laughing at her, no doubt thinking her completely provincial and . . . so *American.* She felt revealed and exposed and chalked the feeling up to the fact that she had forgotten the lunch. It had nothing at all to do with wanting to see Jean-Claude Fontaine again, she told herself. Nothing at all.

~17~

Like Caroline, Jean-Claude Fontaine had begun working at a young age. He had started out in the kitchen of his family's inn near Moustiers-Sainte-Marie, a tiny village of less than six hundred people located in Haute Provence, a rural paradise of blue skies and crystal-pure air northeast of Marseilles and northwest of Nice. Safely removed from the crowded beaches and traffic-choked streets of the Côte d'Azur, Moustiers is surrounded in spring and summer by fields of fragrant rosemary, wild thyme, lavender, immense sunflowers, almond trees, and hillsides carpeted with blue and pink alpine flowers. The village itself is composed of narrow cobblestoned streets and shuttered, picture-perfect houses featuring traditional terra-cotta–tiled roofs and window boxes spilling bright flowers. The local honeys, olive oils, black truffles, handmade cheeses, and candies are well known and exported throughout the world, but it is the ceramics—the faïence, pottery, and porcelain—that have spread the name of Moustiers throughout the world.

Jean-Claude's family traced its roots in Moustiers to the sixteenth century, and his parents, like their parents before them, owned and ran an inn and adjoining patisserie. He worked summers as a busboy, waiter, and all-around kitchen help. After his high school graduation, he found an apprenticeship in the kitchen of *Les Santons,* the best restaurant in Moustiers, where, under an autocratic chef of the old school, he learned to julienne carrots into perfect slivers and mince onions into tiny, equal-size pieces. He showed a sensitive palate and a definite talent and, despite his occasional run-ins with other staff members, was promoted to assistant to the *saucier,* learning to make the stocks, reductions, and glazes that produced the finely flavored and harmoniously balanced sauces of the *cuisine classique.* When he was offered a job in a two-star restaurant in Aix-en-Provence, the chef at the restaurant where he'd been working encouraged him to take it.

"It's an opportunity you can't pass up," he told Jean-Claude. "Besides, with you gone, there'll be peace in the kitchen."

"And fewer reservations in the books," retorted Jean-Claude.

Jean-Claude, doing his best to keep his menu ideas to himself and not cause the rest of the staff to mutiny, did well in his new position, and his job in Aix led to an offer from a star chef in Lyons. By his early twenties, he was becoming known as a member in good standing of the international band of gypsies, mainly but not always French, who staff the better hotel kitchens and ambitious restaurants throughout the world. He picked up English from two lively Americans who had come to learn traditional French cooking methods in the kitchen in Lyons. He was experimenting with unfamiliar herbs like coriander and spices like turmeric to which he had been introduced by a Vietnamese sous chef. And because he considered America the "big time" when it came to making his reputation, he dreamed of leaving his beloved France, going to the States, and being reunited with his parents.

The year he turned twenty-eight, he moved to New York City where he worked at Tribeca's Montrachet and then, raising the money through investors who knew of his abilities, opened his own restaurant, Moustiers, on Eighteenth Street and Park Avenue South. Located just a block away from Union Square's renowned farmer's market, Moustiers became a mecca for with-it foodies, and Jean-Claude Fontaine, the French chef who experimented with American, Asian, and even African ingredients and seasonings, became a media star in a media-crazed city. Moustiers received four stars from the *New York Times*. Jean-Claude's photograph was on the cover of *New York* magazine accompanied by a rapturously lyrical review. He landed a book contract, and his editor, no more able to resist Jean-Claude's appeal than any other woman, suggested the title: *Cuisine de L'Amour*.

As busy as Jean-Claude was with his professional life, he

did not neglect his personal life. His year-and-a-half live-in romance with the actress Britt Roman began when she was starring on Broadway and had been brought to the restaurant by the show's producer. When Britt left the show and went to Vancouver to shoot a movie, Jean-Claude's on-again, off-again liaison with TV anchor Julie Chang was a gossip column staple. And his dates with supermodel Tysen Taylor gave the paparazzi plenty of photo ops. By the time Caroline met him, he was already a celebrity chef on a par with Wolfgang Puck of Spago's, his name a magic lure to a gourmet-obsessed country, his ego enormous, his personality fiery, his appeal to women notorious.

Jean-Claude's appearance at Romance, Inc. drew local residents as well as women vacationing in the area. They came in groups, they came in pairs, they came alone. The important thing was that they came, and when they came, they bought. After they chatted with Jean-Claude and asked him to sign copies of his cookbook, they stayed and bought more: scented soap, a bottle of toilet water, a tie or a silk scarf for their husband or boyfriend.

Even the duchess, who was madly in love with her beloved Ferdy, wasn't immune to Jean-Claude's appeal. She trilled as he welcomed her in his romantic French accent, gazed deeply into her eyes, and kissed her hand. Selma, who always insisted that she was long past the age for romance, fluttered a bit as he complimented her on her big brown eyes. Cynical, tough-talking Roz Garelick, who'd been divorced three times and announced whenever possible that romance was for the birds, blushed when he asked her if she'd ever eaten *quenelles* by candlelight. Clients who planned to buy one book purchased three—as long as Jean-Claude autographed them. Romance, Inc. was thronged all afternoon with women anxious to get close to the dazzlingly handsome, blazingly sensuous French chef, competing to touch him, to speak to him, to capture, even for a moment, his undivided attention.

"And this one?" said a woman in a red jacket, pushing a third copy of *Cuisine de L'Amour* toward Jean-Claude. "Just write 'For Marilyn, passionately.'"

Jean-Claude smiled and did as she asked, patiently signing books, posing for snapshots, allowing himself to be kissed, hugged, and flirted with, and generally conquering every female heart in Palm Beach. *He may look down at people here,* Caroline thought, *but he certainly doesn't object to the women whose hands he's kissing.* She was also impressed at what a good sport he was being and how he had gone out of his way to help her. He had an international reputation as a chef, and his book was already a top seller. An appearance at Romance, Inc. probably meant little to him and yet, there he was, allowing himself to be lionized and not doing such a bad job of returning the affection. *If he romances the people who eat at his restaurant the way he's romancing my clients,* she thought, *it's no wonder Moustiers is such a smash.*

Initially, he had committed to spending an hour in Caroline's shop; in the end, he stayed for four. Every cookbook in stock had been sold and other items—the fragrances, the lacy boudoir pillows, the padded satin lingerie hangers, the floral printed stationery, the frilly nightgowns, silk slippers, and come-hither bras, panties, and negligees—had flown out of the store. Even before she added up the receipts, Caroline knew that Romance, Inc. had set a sales record that day.

"You really didn't have to stay so long," Caroline told Jean-Claude after the last woman had finally left and she had closed the shop. They were seated in the small stockroom, sharing a cup of tea.

"I know I didn't," he said with his usual self-assurance. "But you wanted me to stay, didn't you?" He looked right at her, directly into her eyes, challenging her to deny his statement.

"Well, of course, I did. That is, I only meant . . ." she stammered, floundering in her own confusion.

"You meant that it was good for business, right?" he supplied, deciding to take mercy and rescue her.

"Yes. That's exactly what I meant," said a relieved Caroline, grateful for the lifeline he had sent out and able, once again, to express herself sensibly. "Your appearance did wonders for sales. I can't thank you enough."

"I enjoyed it. I love women, I love to please them," he said. Then he paused for a moment, holding her eyes with his.

Caroline willed herself not to blush, reminded herself that European men were different from American men—more flirtatious, more open in their feelings about women, more at ease with their own sensuality. She had just seen him operate all afternoon long with Romance, Inc.'s clients, showering them with charm, flattery, and compliments. She told herself that his remark was simply part of the suave Continental way he related to every female that crossed his path. There was nothing personal intended—and nothing personal received. She cleared her throat and got back to business, the subject with which she felt most comfortable.

"I can tell you right now that we've set a sales record today in just the few hours that you were here," she said.

"Then I'd say you owe me a debt of gratitude," said Jean-Claude.

"I certainly do," she agreed.

"*Bon!* Then you'll have dinner with me tonight," he said. He moved closer to her, and she could feel the warmth of his body and smell the tantalizing scent of his cologne.

She shook her head. "Not tonight. I'm—"

"You're what?" he asked, his eyes teasing, seductive. "Not hungry?"

"No," she laughed. "That's not it."

"I wondered. Since your idea of lunch is a ham sandwich," he smirked.

"What's wrong with ham sandwiches?" she asked, annoyed by the put-down. "They came from your father's café."

"True. But Café Pavillion is hardly known for ham sandwiches," he said. "They're only on the menu for—" He stopped himself, not wanting to insult her.

"For provincial Americans?" she filled in.

He pretended to be offended by the words she had put into his mouth.

"Let's just say that I'd like to cook for you and make

something really special," he said. "Are you planning to be in New York any time soon?"

"No," she said. "I'm not."

He looked unhappy. "What about the debt of gratitude? I intend to collect on it."

"I *do* owe you," she conceded.

"Then we have a date. The next time you come to the city," he said firmly, as if the fact that she had no plans to visit Manhattan were a mere trifle that couldn't possibly interfere with his wishes. He drew even closer to her and touched her knee with his. She jumped at the contact. His nearness, his *maleness,* was now almost impossible for her to ignore. It had been so long since she touched a man, been touched by a man, and Jean-Claude Fontaine, she guessed, was well-versed in the art of touching.

"Caroline?" he prompted with a pouty smile, reaching out and putting his finger under her chin and tilting her head so that she had no option but to look into his eyes. "We *do* have a date, don't we?"

"Yes," she said reluctantly, the word barely audible. Then she looked away from him and reminded herself that there was nothing to worry about. She had never been to New York, she wasn't planning to go, not now or ever, and she would never have to pay her "debt." Relieved, she smiled at him. "I'm looking forward to it," she lied.

"You should. I'm a genius in the kitchen," he said. Then he looked directly into her eyes and added, "And in other rooms, as well . . ."

Dina Goddard had been busy all day long. Her flight from New York hadn't arrived in Palm Beach until noon. Then there'd been a meeting with the household staff, a session with her personal trainer, and a long and ultimately unsatisfying consultation with a highly touted new decorator about remodeling the pool house. Before she knew it, it was four-thirty. She was just reminding herself to call Renato's, the trendy Italian restaurant on the Via Mizner, for a reservation that evening, when the telephone rang.

"It's for you, Mrs. Goddard," said the maid. "It's Mrs. Rittenbacher."

Dina took the call in the library, where James had had his talk with his father about his future. How long ago that seemed now, Dina thought, as she walked toward the telephone that rested on a leather-topped antique desk. Charles Goddard had avoided the room since his son's death, but then Charles had withdrawn from so much of life. He had instructed Dina not to entertain unless absolutely necessary. He had shown very little interest in Emily, and most surprising to everyone who knew him, he had even withdrawn from his business, from Goddard-Stevens, the firm that had been his true pride and joy and reason for living.

He had been too depressed to concentrate on work, he confided to Dina, too defeated now that he had no heir to take over the company when he was gone. And so he had escaped from work, spending an inordinate amount of time at his various clubs, playing cards and golf, and, he admitted, doing nothing but wasting time. Cards were a distraction. So were eighteen holes. So was the Scotch—first at five o'clock, lately as early as noon. Dina worried about her husband's drinking, about his state of mind, and kept telling herself that he would emerge from his dark moods and odd behavior. She even wondered from time to time about whether Charles should consider consulting a psychiatrist, although, of course, she had never dared say anything. Then, two years ago, he had astonished her, as well as the executives at Goddard-Stevens, by announcing that he had hired an executive named Clifford Hamlin to take over the day-to-day operations of the firm. Charles explained that he would devote himself to training his new second-in-command the way he had planned to train his son, James. He further said that Hamlin, a managing partner of the respected investment firm of Osborne & Praeger, was the man to whom he would entrust the company's present—and future.

"I hope you know what you're doing, Charles," Dina had told him after she had given a dinner party to formally introduce Clifford to the other Goddard-Stevens partners and to their colleagues and competitors on Wall Street.

"Clifford Hamlin is certainly brilliant and charming, but he's an outsider, after all. Not one of us."

"Us?" Charles said bitterly, pouring himself a post-prandial cognac. "'Us' isn't the same now that James is gone. There's no one in the family to take over at Goddard-Stevens. No one."

No one, Dina Goddard thought to herself as she sat at the desk in the forlorn-feeling library—the very room that had been James's favorite room of the house—and prepared to take the phone call. Poor Charles. He seemed to have reached the end of the line and could see no other way to continue.

"Yes?" she said distractedly as she picked up the receiver.

"Dina, darling. It's Betsy."

Betsy Rittenbacher knew that she was taking her husband's career and her own social future in her hands when she dialed Dina Goddard's number. A longtime friend from Locust Valley and Palm Beach, Betsy and Bennett Rittenbacher had, along with everyone else in their social circle, heeded the Goddards' edict: Never bring up the subject of the woman who had married their son, James. Never! Never even mention the girl! Don't refer to the marriage or even to the fact that it had once existed! The Goddards made it perfectly clear that Caroline Shaw and anything to do with her was a strictly forbidden subject.

Betsy had never even begun to understand what Dina and Charles had against their daughter-in-law. James had obviously fallen madly in love with her, and as far as anyone knew, she had been, for the few brief months of their marriage, an exemplary wife. She wasn't a gold digger, a streetwalker, or an ax murderer, after all, but nevertheless Dina and Charles acted as if she were a threat to their very lives. So what harm could there be in chatting about her now and then? How could it hurt to refer once in a while to James's few months of marriage?

Betsy didn't know and couldn't figure it out. But she was not about to cross her powerful friends; not when her husband worked for Charles Goddard and not when she herself served on two committees that Dina chaired. And especially not when she thought about Vanessa Eliot, Miranda's mother, who had once dared invoke the name of Caroline Shaw in Dina's presence. Vanessa was peremptorily dropped from the Goddards' dinner parties, and her husband, a leading financial analyst who often consulted for Goddard-Stevens, was never called on for his services again. Dina and Charles had simply frozen out the Eliots, acting as if they didn't exist, banishing them from their circle. The rest of Dina and Charles's friends, frightened and appalled, never dared utter Caroline Shaw's name or even refer, however obliquely, to her existence for fear of receiving the same treatment.

It seemed ludicrous, almost demented, really. More than just a little bit over the top. But Betsy, mindful of her social position and her husband's future, had, like everyone else who wanted to remain in the Goddards' orbit for social, personal, or business reasons, obeyed the bizarre edict, and Betsy had never once discussed Caroline with Dina or even, for that matter, referred to James's marriage. Not even after she'd heard through the grapevine that Caroline had opened some sort of store in West Palm Beach. But all of that was before *The Shiny Sheet* article! Before Betsy had seen that photograph and read the caption! Never mind what Dina and Charles Goddard had said. Never mind what Dina and Charles Goddard might *do*. Betsy Rittenbacher *had* to make the telephone call. Simply had to! The whole surreal situation had gone on far too long. It was too outlandish, too strange, too silly.

"Betsy, darling, I was just about to call you," said Dina in the warm, affectionate way she had with people who mattered to her. "Charles and I only just got into town this afternoon, and I've been up to my neck. I've barely even had time to open the mail."

Betsy cleared her throat. "There's one piece of mail you might want to open right away," she said.

"Oh, you mean the letter about the Leukemia Foundation gala?" said Dina, shuffling through the stack of envelopes on the desk.

"No, not the gala," said Betsy. "You and Charles subscribe to *The Shiny Sheet,* don't you?"

"Yes, of course," said Dina, "but I really haven't had a minute to wade through all those back issues that have piled up while we've been away. As a matter of fact, I've already instructed the maid to throw them—"

"Don't!" exclaimed Betsy, interrupting her friend.

"Don't what?" said Dina.

"Don't let the maid throw them out," said Betsy. Then she inhaled deeply and went on. "Actually, Dina, I think you might want to make a point of finding the February ninth issue."

"Why? Is there some truly delicious gossip I've missed? Some fabulous scandal? Did someone run away with her chauffeur? Or end up in bed with a Great Dane and a saxophone?"

Betsy hesitated. There was still time to retreat, still time to pretend that nothing had happened. She wondered if she was about to make a huge mistake, if she was really doing the right thing by telling Dina Goddard what she had learned. Obviously, and as incredible as it might seem, nobody else had.

"Well, what is it?" Dina said eagerly.

Betsy took a deep breath. She could feel her heart hammering in her chest. If she went ahead, there would be no going back, not ever. Her husband's career was in the balance . . . her own social status . . . their financial future and their standing in Palm Beach society. . . . She thought it over for a moment, took a deep breath, then she took the plunge.

"There's a story about a shop on Okeechobee Boulevard," she began. "It's called Romance, Inc."

"In West Palm Beach? What about it?" said Dina, mystified.

"Its owner is James's wife, Caroline."

"Betsy!" Dina snapped icily, the iron gates slamming down. "I thought we made it clear! I thought you knew better than to—"

"Dina, listen to me," Betsy said, her heart beating even

faster as she prepared to deliver the news. "There's more to it than just a newspaper article."

"With that girl there always is," said Dina coldly. "I don't want to hear another word about her. I haven't had to hear her name in years, and I don't intend to start now."

"Yes, you do, Dina," said Betsy. "Because Caroline Shaw is the mother of a little boy." She paused for dramatic effect. "*James's* little boy."

"Ridiculous!" exclaimed Dina.

"No, Dina, it's true," said Betsy. "The child's name is Jack and he's five years old. He looks exactly like James. He's your grandson, Dina. Yours and Charles's."

"It can't be! It's not possible!" said Dina Goddard. "Surely someone would have told us, would have said something."

"You wouldn't let us mention her name. You wouldn't let anyone talk to you about—"

Betsy Rittenbacher heard her friend gasp only distantly as the telephone slipped out of Dina's hand, crashed to the desktop, and then clattered to the floor.

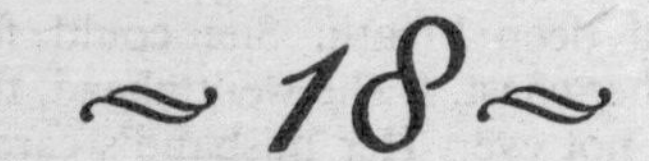

For the first time since James's death, Charles did not drink after dinner, sipping Scotch until he fell into a leaden, almost comalike sleep. Instead, he spent the evening reading and rereading the article by Roz Garelick about a local shop named Romance, Inc. in the February 9th issue of *The Shiny Sheet.* When he wasn't reading the text, he stared at the photograph of the five-year-old child. A child the mother had never bothered to inform him existed. A boy. The five-year-old that Betsy Rittenbacher said was James's son. His and Dina's grandson. His son and the heir to Goddard-Stevens.

Charles studied the child's features, the shape and length

of his limbs, the curl and lustre of his hair, the structure of his face, the set of his features, and the cast of his smile until he knew them by heart. He knew instinctively, deep in his soul, in the very marrow of his bones, that the child carried Goddard blood. His head, however, did not permit him to be entirely convinced. He had suffered too much pain, too much devastating disappointment.

Between Kyle Pringle's dishonesty and James's accident, Charles felt that he had borne far more than any man's fair share of destiny's slings and arrows. For years he had felt suffocated and even on the verge of being destroyed by emotional pain. At times, though he had never said a word to Dina, he had even wondered whether he might be fodder for some head shrinker. Now, of course, because of Betsy Rittenbacher's telephone call, things were suddenly, magically different. Or were they?

That Sunday night, Charles Goddard had gone to bed late, but he had not slept. He had lain awake, tossing and turning, mulling over his options, debating with himself what to do, how to proceed, when to make his move, and exactly what that move should consist of. Yet at the same time he kept cautioning himself, warning himself to hold back, not to get too far ahead of himself. It was essential, he constantly reminded himself, not to get his hopes up before he knew for certain, beyond the shadow of any doubt, whether the boy—Caroline Shaw's five-year-old, the child she had deliberately kept concealed from the Goddards—was really James's child. Was Jack Goddard *really* a Goddard? Did Goddard blood truly flow in his veins? Was the Goddard line still alive? Or was he a sad, beaten old man grasping desperately and pathetically at straws? What he needed was proof—solid, incontrovertible proof.

At five A.M., Charles finally gave up on sleep and left the bed he had not shared with his wife since the birth of their second child. He got dressed and went directly to the glass-enclosed solarium of his Palm Beach estate. As the sun rose over the Atlantic Ocean, casting a dazzling array of colors onto the shimmering water, Charles Goddard sat, sipping coffee, and staring out to sea, thinking back, thinking ahead.

When Dina had told him of Betsy Rittenbacher's phone call the previous evening, he had been stunned at first, disbelieving, thrown completely off balance. When she had shown him *The Shiny Sheet* article and the photograph of the boy, he had experienced an electric jolt of emotions, an intensity of feeling he hadn't experienced since his son's death. Suddenly, the blurry, Scotch-induced fog in which he had been drowning himself, the depression, the listlessness, burned off in a bright, incandescent blaze of possibility. Could it be that James's wife had given birth to a Goddard? To *his* grandson?

The possibility was simply too exquisite to accept on face value and Charles, a hardheaded businessman, did not intend to let himself be suckered in. What if this were a trap? Some kind of a ploy by the girl to get her hands on the Goddard money? What if, after all these years, it was another trick to insert herself into a family that didn't want her? Suppose this was her crackpot idea of some kind of blackmail plot? Charles told himself that he would have to proceed carefully.

First, of course, there would have to be guarantees of the child's bloodlines. Solid, iron-clad, positive, inarguable verification. What did he really know of this Caroline Shaw anyway? he thought, as he gazed out at the ocean, his hopes rising and falling with each wave. James himself had admitted that she was nothing but a shop girl from Lake Worth. A local from the wrong side of the tracks, although a beauty, he had to admit, who had used that beauty to ensnare his son and lead him to his death. She had no background, no pedigree, no social standing, no money. And, no doubt, there had been other men in her life before James had come along and after he had died. Most likely, there had even been other men while James was still alive. You could never tell about people, especially ambitious, young women, Charles mused, as he recalled some of his own more inappropriate liaisons during his wild youth. Perhaps this boy—"Jack," the newspaper said—was the product of an adulterous affair. Or perhaps he was result of some tawdry one-night stand with a waiter or a salesman or a gas station attendant she had picked up in a bar somewhere. Perhaps he was only a foolish old man wanting to believe the unbelievable. Perhaps the child wasn't a Goddard at all.

But what if the boy *is* a Goddard? Charles couldn't help ask himself over and over, coming back to the tantalizing possibility that he was not the last in the line but had an heir. What if he and Dina had a grandson to carry on the family name, a grandson to insure the future of Goddard-Stevens? What then? The answer was obvious: The child would have to be taken in, to be brought up on Goddard standards with Goddard traditions instilled in him from the earliest possible moment. He would have to be trained, educated, and formed in the Goddard mold so that in every way he could project the Goddard vision and the Goddard outlook that Charles and Dina had spent their lives burnishing and perfecting. The child was only five. It certainly wasn't too late, although every moment counted from now on.

The very idea caused Charles Goddard to become agitated, and he found himself getting up from his chair, pacing back and forth, then padding across the room to the wet bar in the library and pouring himself a Chivas Regal. He knew it was hardly cocktail time, but he didn't care. His nerves jangled and his heart raced. He needed to steady himself—or to celebrate. He still didn't know which. As he picked up the heavy crystal glass, he realized that he needed a clear head. The decision he was about to make was the most important of his life, and suddenly the smell of the amber-colored liquor made him feel nauseated, sick at his own weakness, disgusted by the way he had withdrawn from the world after James's death. There might be a Goddard heir. He had to know, had to find out, had to be certain once and for all. He could not live with doubt or suspicion or possibility. There was only one way to find out what he needed to know. One.

He threw the untouched drink down the sink and, squaring his shoulders, made his decision. He walked toward the desk, the desk where Dina had taken Betsy Rittenbacher's call. He sat down, opened his sport jacket, and pulled his wallet from the left-hand pocket. He reached inside the buttery-leather billfold and pulled out a business card. He took a deep breath and dialed a phone number with a Palm Beach County area code.

It was only 7:15 in the morning, but Ted Aronson was available to his clients at all hours of the day and night—even on weekends. Constant availability—along with absolute discretion and confidentiality—were among the "special services" that made Ted so valuable to his employers. A freelance private investigator ("researcher," as he preferred to be termed), Aronson specialized not in sleazy adulteries and second-rate crimes but in the information-gathering needs of corporate and personal clients. Over the years, he had performed several jobs of a delicate nature for the chairman of Goddard-Stevens. They ranged from background checks on prospective employees to top-secret financial profiles of rival companies and deep digging into the personal, sexual, and social lives of would-be business associates. Ted Aronson did not skulk around in alleys or snoop into garbage cans. He was, instead, a master of data, a genius at romancing his computer into finding out whatever his clients told him needed to be found out.

He answered his phone that Sunday morning, exchanged pleasantries with Charles Goddard, and listened carefully while Charles explained what he had in mind. He added that he trusted that Ted would know how to obtain the information—and would be able to get it discreetly. Once Aronson provided the assurances his client desired, Charles Goddard got on with his request.

"I'd like you to check into the birth of a baby," Charles said, speaking slowly and deliberately. "Born five years ago. To a Caroline Shaw Goddard. The child's name is Jack. Jack Goddard," he continued. "I believe that he was born somewhere in or near Palm Beach County. The girl is from Lake Worth, so I would try the hospitals in the area first. I want to know the details of the birth—the date, time, circumstances, everything you can lay your hands on."

"I understand," said Ted, quickly making notes on his password-protected Compaq as his client spoke. "You'll want a birth certificate and the relevant hospital records."

"Exactly. How long do you think it will take?" Charles asked.

Ted Aronson considered the question. His clients were always in a hurry, but they paid him handsomely, so he saw to it that they were never dissatisfied with his work.

"Not very long," he told Charles Goddard. Hospitals were open seven days out of seven and computers knew no time zones, weekends, or holidays. "Twenty-four hours or so."

"Good," said Charles, "I look forward to hearing from you tomorrow at about this time."

"I'll call you then," promised the "researcher."

Step one had been taken, Charles told himself, hanging up the telephone and, for the first time since James's death, feeling in charge of his own destiny and that of his firm. Step two was already taking form in his mind as he picked up the notes he had made for his meeting that morning with Clifford Hamlin, Goddard-Stevens's managing director. Cliff had flown in from New York the night before. He would be spending the weekend with the Goddards at their Palm Beach estate.

Clifford Hamlin was known as the dark prince of Wall Street, a gambler who loved to take risks—and reap the rewards. He was remarkable, as Dina Goddard had once pointed out, for his brilliance and his fearlessness. Men tended to idolize him and did their best to emulate him; women were intrigued by him and did their best to seduce him. He was a thoroughbred in appearance: tall and very lean with a fine-featured face dominated by watchful, slightly wary catlike gray eyes. Wavy auburn hair brushed the collars of his hand-tailored suits, and his voice, soft but assured, carried no discernible regional accent. He was commanding in public appearances, decisive in meetings, delightful at dinner parties, a demanding but fair boss. He dined in the best restaurants, ordered his wardrobe from

Saville Row in London, was a patron of the ballet, and lived in an art-filled penthouse on upper Fifth Avenue overlooking Central Park. Yet underneath the exterior elegance of his life, there was a sad, almost moody side to him, and just below the surface of the polished facade he presented to the world, he radiated the subtle but unmistakable aura of long-ago pain, the result of the single, defining trauma of his early childhood.

Clifford, an only child, grew up not on Manhattan's Park Avenue or in London's Belgravia, but in Blue Ash, Ohio, a bleak midwestern town where the men spent their lives working for one of the area's three employers—the paint factory, the coal mines, or the machine tool plant—and their wives did their best, on limited budgets, to provide decent homes for their husbands and children. Clifford's father, like his father before him, toiled in the paint factory. Every night Frank Hamlin came home coughing blood, sick and half crazed from the toxic fumes he had inhaled all day long. He didn't smoke, had never touched a cigarette or a cigar, and yet, while still only in his thirties, he died of lung cancer.

As a boy of seven, Clifford was left alone with his mother, and it became his responsibility to take care of her. Limited vision, a result of childhood diabetes, caused Virginia Hamlin to depend on her son for everything—shopping for groceries to paying the bills. He virtually became his mother's eyes, and he came to see the world from her point of view. For the rest of his life he would always have a particular sympathy for those who had struggled, and despite the fact that he and his mother scrimped along on welfare and his father's insurance, he did not indulge in self-pity. He sustained himself with the memories of a loving father and his parents' extremely close and unusually affectionate marriage. He looked at their lives and the contrast between what could have been and what was and decided that *his* life would be different because he would *make* it different.

An intellectually gifted child, Clifford could add and subtract at the age of three. He seemed far more mature than other boys his age, and as president of his class throughout elementary school, he quickly showed leadership qualities. While other kids, unwilling or unable to resist the limited opportunities that awaited them, slid indifferently through school, Clifford studied hard. He was a voracious reader whose trips to the library supplied entertainment, education, and diversion as he spent the evenings reading to his mother. The principal of the Blue Ash School was aware of Clifford's gifts, and when Clifford entered high school, he arranged to place him in the area's accelerated program.

"Your son needs to be challenged," he told Clifford's mother. "The program is free. Clifford will be bused to the school every day, but he will be at home every night. The school was established by the state especially for children with Clifford's talents."

The principal also contacted The Beacon, an organization that funded research projects devoted to finding a cure for blindness and provided the blind with volunteers who helped them in their daily lives. Two such volunteers now helped Virginia Hamlin during the hours that her son was away at school, taking her on her errands and to her doctor's appointments.

"You don't have to worry about your mother. You can concentrate on your studies," the principal told Clifford.

Exposed to other children who were equally bright and motivated and taught by the best teachers in the Ohio school system, Clifford took his first step away from the limitations and dismal prospects of Blue Ash. He studied with the same zeal as always, received excellent grades, and at sixteen, when his mother, still only in her forties, died, he distracted himself from the second great loss of his life with the satisfactions of running. At five-thirty every morning, he would run five to six miles around the school track in the gray, murky predawn. Nothing kept him from his routine. Not fatigue, nor the bitter cold temperatures of the Ohio winter, nor the solitariness of the sport. He was driven to excel at running just as he was driven to excel at his studies.

Excellence became his weapon—against vulnerability, against loss, against the two tragic deaths that had shadowed and scarred him.

By the time he received a scholarship to Ohio University, Clifford Hamlin was an outstanding student and a state champion marathoner. At eighteen he had the appearance of a sleek racehorse—long, lean limbs, aquiline Roman nose, pronounced cheekbones, penetrating gray eyes, wavy auburn hair. He had grown into a hauntingly handsome but intense and somewhat enigmatic young man who reminded many girls on campus of a brooding Heathcliff, a tragic romantic hero filled with pent-up passion. He rarely spoke of his background, and the sadness he radiated along with his brilliant class records and his athletic feats caused him to become a heroic, almost mythical figure on campus.

He majored in economics and graduated summa cum laude. Goal-directed as always, he intended to use his mathematical ability to earn enough money to create a life that would contrast with the one he had left behind. The day after his graduation, he passed his stockbroker's exam on the first try. Within the week, he was hired by the Dayton branch of Osborne & Praeger, a medium-size brokerage firm with four other offices in the Midwest. He was the only person he knew from Blue Ash who wore a suit and tie to work.

Clifford Hamlin excelled at Osborne & Praeger just as he had excelled in everything else he had ever done—and he pushed himself just as hard. He was the first to arrive at the office in the morning and the last to leave in the evening. He took graduate courses in accounting and financial analysis and learned the differences between the value-investing and market-timing approaches to investing, the intricacies of the Elliot wave theory, and the significance of Alpha and Beta risk ratings. From them he formulated his own market philosophy, a sophisticated blend of technical analysis and economic fundamentals. He did not neglect the personal basics of business and, alone and unattached, constantly wined and dined his clients, remembered their birthdays and anniversaries, and managed their money as if it were his own, ruthlessly cutting their losses and aggressively leveraging their gains.

When he wasn't working, he was running—five to six miles a day through the woods near his small suburban apartment. And when he wasn't running, he was donating his spare time to The Beacon. Clifford, who had spent the evenings of his childhood reading to his mother, now read to other visually impaired men and women. He also visited the blind in their homes, took them to the bank, the drugstore, the supermarket, doing for others what he had grown up doing for his mother and what, when he had been away at school, volunteers from The Beacon had done for her.

Clifford seemed to spend all his time working for others, and his personal life often took a backseat to his public activities. Men found him impressive but somewhat of a loner. Women were attracted to his good looks and extreme competence, seduced by the notion that they and they alone could tear him away from his relentlessly hectic schedule and bring out his softer side. He was decisive and charismatic, ambitious and aggressive, and over the years, there had been romances, some even fairly serious: a stockbroker from the office, an actress he met while browsing in the biography section of a bookstore, a biologist to whom he'd been introduced by one of the other brokers at Osborne & Praeger. He did his best to respond to them and to open himself to them, but the magic he had seen between his parents never happened for him, and just as he had decided long ago never to settle for whatever life happened to hand him, he would not settle when it came to romance. He was holding out for true love, which he'd know when he saw it because he'd seen it every day of the first seven years of his life.

In his first year at Osborne & Praeger, Clifford earned the distinction of becoming the highest-earning broker in the office, outperforming far more experienced men and women. In his second year he was promoted to office manager, and in his fourth year he was transferred to the company's main office in Chicago. When Osborne & Praeger acquired a firm headquartered in Philadelphia, he was named a vice president and relocated to a four-bedroom brick Georgian on Rittenhouse Square.

Several years later, when Osborne & Praeger had become a prestigious niche player on Wall Street, Clifford was third in influence, with only the firm's two founding partners, Leland Osborne and Bartlett Praeger, standing above him in the company's hierarchy. Both men valued Clifford highly and understood his importance to the company and its future. They paid him extremely well, gave him handsome year-end bonuses, and promised him a place at the very top of the firm when that day came. Therefore, six months after James's death, when Charles Goddard offered Clifford the managing directorship of Goddard-Stevens on the morning of his thirty-sixth birthday, Clifford thanked Charles politely but told him quite frankly that his offer was not nearly attractive enough.

"Leland and Bartlett have both assured me that I am going to be on the executive committee of Osborne and Praeger one day," he told Charles confidently. "In the meantime, I'm a senior partner *and* a profit participant, and I'm very happy where I am."

Charles Goddard was unaccustomed to being denied. Determined to get the man he felt best suited to help him guide Goddard-Stevens into the end of the twentieth century, he approached Clifford Hamlin several more times over the next year and a half. Even though Charles sweetened his original offer considerably, Clifford turned down his second and third attempts in a similar manner. Charles's fourth offer, however, was not to be rejected quite so automatically.

"You've been turning me down for almost two years," Charles reminded Clifford as they lunched together in the private dining room at Goddard-Stevens's New York headquarters. A view of the dramatic canyons of Wall Street and the sparkling waters at the foot of the Statue of Liberty beckoned alluringly from outside the large windows, but neither man even looked up as the older man spoke and the younger one listened. "As you will no doubt recall, I started pursuing you just after James's death, after I realized that I would not be able to hand the day-to-day operations of the company over to my only son. Since then, even though I have twice improved my terms, you've continued to turn me down, been determined to stay at Osborne and Praeger. Why, I can't begin to fathom, considering the exceedingly generous offers I've made to you over the years."

"I've stayed because I'm well treated and well paid and because I have a long, productive past and an excellent future there," said Clifford, repeating once again to Charles Goddard the assertions that had been made to him. "I realize, of course, that Goddard-Stevens is a major firm with a fine reputation, but I've never seen the slightest reason to make any move."

"I think I can give you that reason," said Charles, who had invited Clifford to lunch with a new proposition carefully considered and worked out. "James has been dead for two years now. I have no heir and, given my daughter Emily's inability to find a suitable husband, no reason to hope for one anytime soon. If you agree to become managing director of Goddard-Stevens, I will not only pay you more than you currently earn at Osborne and Praeger, I will offer you something that neither Leland Osborne nor Bartlett Praeger would be willing to match, something that I never had the opportunity to offer my own son—ownership of the firm when I step down or die or should in some way become incapacitated. I never intended to make that offer to anyone outside the family, and I don't intend to make it to you again. You have a choice, Clifford, and I insist you make it right now. You can accept my proposal or you can continue to work at Osborne and Praeger and be an employee for the rest of your life."

Charles Goddard sat back in his chair and held Clifford's eyes with his own. Charles had just played his trump card. He knew that he had made Clifford Hamlin the proverbial offer he could not refuse. There was silence as the two powerful men faced each other.

Although Clifford's expression remained noncommittal, his mind raced. Both Leland Osborne and Bartlett Praeger had children who would one day inherit the firm. No matter how well he did or how much money he earned, Clifford understood, he would always be an employee. If he accepted Charles Goddard's offer, he would be rich, seriously rich—and in complete control of a firm that would be entirely his. Unlike his parents, he would be at the mercy of nothing and no one.

He cleared his throat and, giving no indication of the emotion he felt, quietly accepted Charles Goddard's offer.

Leland Osborne and Bartlett Praeger were shocked and disappointed when Clifford told them he was leaving the company. However, mindful of their own children, they were able to make no counterproposal nearly as compelling as Charles Goddard's offer. They wished Clifford well and, after some hard-nosed negotiation, agreed that his clients, if they so wished, could go along with him to Goddard-Stevens. Every one of them—with a solitary exception—chose to move their accounts. However, Tamara Brandt told Clifford that, although he had tripled her wealth in the years that she had been his client, she would not follow him to his new position at Goddard-Stevens with his other clients.

"It's not personal. You know I adore you," she told him, informing him of her decision.

"Then what is it?" he asked, stung. He felt far more rejected than was completely reasonable. As always, he hated to lose. Even one client. Even one account.

Tamara shoved her chin into the air and firmed her expression.

"I will have nothing to do with that particular firm. Nothing!" she announced, informing him that her account would remain where it was at Osborne & Praeger.

"Nonsense. What's wrong with Goddard-Stevens?" asked Clifford, unable to understand Tamara's violent dislike of the firm he had just joined. Not only had he made a great deal of money for Tamara over the years but she had always sworn that no one else would ever handle her finances.

"Because Charles Goddard is an unmitigated bastard, and I will not allow him to make one penny off me," she said. "And, Cliff, if I were you, I'd be very careful working for that man. *Very* careful. He's dangerous."

"Dangerous?" Clifford knew that Charles Goddard was a tough businessman. Wall Street was filled with tough businessman. Still, Tamara sounded as if there was a personal vendetta involved. He wondered what Charles Goddard had done to her.

"He almost destroyed someone I love," said Tamara, thinking of the cold, rejecting way he had treated Caroline when she'd been pregnant with Jack. "What's more, he refuses to deal with reality. He and his wife insist on seeing the world they want to see. They won't hear anything that conflicts with their own view of things. Nothing. They want to live like ostriches, with their heads buried deep in the sand." She was referring, of course, to the Goddards' rigid exclusion of Caroline—and of Jack—from their lives, and to the way they had cruelly returned Caroline's letters unopened.

"Who did Charles Goddard almost destroy?" Clifford asked.

"I'm not telling tales out of school," said the duchess, suddenly becoming mysterious.

Clifford knew better than to press her further, but he found it hard to imagine that Charles Goddard, a hard-headed, nuts-and-bolts, dollars-and-cents businessman, would refuse to deal with anything, no matter how distasteful or distressing. Nevertheless Tamara was adamant, and despite Clifford's further gentle questions on subsequent occasions, she clammed up and balked at revealing anything more. She saw no reason to violate Caroline's privacy. If the Goddards wanted to live in an ivory tower of unreality—without the adorable grandson who would have meant so much to them—then that was their choice. Their choice and their loss.

Like everyone else who knew Tamara Brandt, Clifford Hamlin was aware of her dramatic, highly exaggerated way of expressing herself and of her vehement likes and dislikes of people. He wondered from time to time who Charles Goddard had almost "destroyed"—and how—but the duchess always refused to say. Was it merely hyperbole? Or did the duchess know something about the Goddards that he didn't? Clifford couldn't quite decide, and he had no way of finding out. Nevertheless, despite her outspoken loathing of Charles Goddard, Tamara's portfolio had grown into a sizable one, and Clifford didn't intend to let it slip out of his hands. Not the dark prince of Wall Street, who never met a client he couldn't land, a portfolio he couldn't increase.

When Charles and Dina invited him to Palm Beach for the weekend, Clifford telephoned the duchess from his New York office. He arranged a face-to-face meeting with her ("for old times' sake") in which he planned to convince her to move her account to Goddard-Stevens. In addition, Clifford, who always thought several steps ahead, had another goal: he planned eventually to acquire the duke's account as well.

Five-year-old Jack Goddard looked forward to Sundays the way other children look forward to Christmas. Sunday was the day of the week when he was spoiled beyond all reason. On Sundays, when Romance, Inc. was closed, his mother brought him over to visit Aunt Tamara at the opulent oceanfront estate where she and Uncle Ferdie spent the winters—the oceanfront estate where he could swim in her pool, make sand castles on her beach, and feel as if there was nothing in the world he couldn't do, nothing he couldn't try. What's more, his godmother always had a little surprise for him—a toy, a video game, a book, an article of clothing, something. Going to see Aunt Tamara on Sunday afternoons really was a little bit like Christmas, Jack thought as he contemplated what kind of surprise she'd have for him *this* Sunday.

"Mom, can we go to Aunt Tamara's *now,*" he asked Caroline with the sort of fidgety impatience only children experience and only they can get away with expressing. He had wandered into his mother's bedroom, where she sat at her desk poring over a set of spreadsheets. She had a meeting with her bank the next day about a loan. She had decided to open a second shop—she would need to borrow the money to rent and decorate it and to fill it with inventory. Jack tapped her on the shoulder, hoping to pull her attention away from her work. "Pul-eeee-ze?" he asked, drawing the word out into three syllables designed to pull at the heartstrings.

She looked at him, then at her watch, and shook her head.

"It's only one o'clock, sweetheart. Your Aunt Tamara usually expects us at two-thirty," said Caroline, who enjoyed her Sunday visits to her former employer almost as much as her son did. While Jack would amuse himself in the pool or on the beach, she and the duchess would chat about Romance, Inc. Or, to be more precise, the duchess would *lecture* Caroline about Romance, Inc., for, despite her elevated title and exalted status, Tamara Brandt desperately missed her days at L'Elegance and longed to be back in the retailing business. More than anything, she loved to sell. She yearned to manipulate, cajole, and flatter clients into buying one more gown, one more handbag, one more pair of gloves.

"Oh, come on, Mom. Please? Can't we go early today?" Jack beseeched his mother, charming her with James's sea-blue eyes. When she didn't say "no" immediately, he continued his plea. "I'll bet you anything that Aunt Tamara wouldn't mind. She loves it when I come over."

Caroline smiled at her son, the love of her life, the one person for whom she would do anything. His absolute certainty that he would be loved and accepted by Tamara Brandt and everyone else he knew struck her as both odd and touching, so different was the level of his self-confidence from hers as a child.

"You know, she *might* be busy," Caroline chided Jack, who, in his exuberance, occasionally forgot to take other people's needs into consideration. "It's possible that she and the duke aren't ready for company until two-thirty."

Jack pondered his mother's remark, turning it over in his mind, then grinned mischievously, just as his father had whenever he was contemplating one of his romantic escapades.

"The duke's probably playing golf, so Aunt Tamara will be all by herself. Let's just *go* there and see what happens!" he said animatedly. "Let's surprise her the way she's always surprising me! Everytime I go there, she gives me a different present!"

Caroline laughed and ruffled her son's blond hair. How could she resist? How could she refuse him?

"All right, but I'm going to call first. To make sure it's okay that we come a little earlier than usual. It's rude just to burst in on people."

"Oh, don't call, Mom. It'll ruin the surprise," said Jack, capturing her heart with his excitement.

He had a point, Caroline knew. Calling ahead *would* ruin the surprise. And the duchess *did* love seeing him—no matter when or where. What was the harm in showing up at her house an hour or so early? If it was inconvenient for Tamara, they could always leave and return later.

"All right," she said, giving in and setting her papers aside. "But if your godmother is busy, we'll have to leave and come back later. It's not polite to interrupt people, do you understand?"

Jack regarded her, then smiled his father's dimpled smile. "Sure, Mom. I understand," he said, then shrugged. "But I don't know what you're so worried about. Aunt Tamara is never too busy for us."

Clifford had known Tamara Brandt since she had been Pearl Branowsky, the foundations buyer at Marshall Field, and he was an ambitious, up-and-coming young stockbroker in the Chicago office of Osborne & Praeger. She had appeared in his office one Friday afternoon with $500 in cash—a "walk-in" who told him that she expected him to invest her money and make her independently wealthy. He managed to keep a straight face, and he considered her a flake—at first. Soon his skepticism turned to admiration as he observed the way she stopped by the office each and every Friday, payday, with more money to add to her tiny account—and the way she shrewdly maneuvered her career, single-mindedly elevating herself from foundations buyer to buyer for better dresses to buyer for the *crème de la crème:* the couture department.

Over the years, she had never stopped improving herself.

She had changed her name to Tamara Brandt ("It's better for business, don't you think?" she had commented at the time), moved east, married the count, and opened and closed her own retail shops with a determination Clifford could only marvel at. As she rose in the world, he had helped her boost the assets in her account from a niggling bookkeeping annoyance to substantial six figures. He had attended her first wedding, attended her housewarming in Palm Beach, consoled her when the count left her for Celeste, encouraged her when she opened L'Elegance, and shared her triumphant satisfaction when she had met and captured the affections of the duke. He enjoyed her tremendously and, therefore, permitted her to tease him, bully him, and generally tell him exactly how to run his life.

As he and the duchess sat together, having lunch in the shaded loggia overlooking her pool and the Atlantic Ocean beyond, Clifford was glad to see that marriage to the duke obviously agreed with Tamara. Decked in daytime diamonds, she laughed and indulged in scurrilous gossip about her neighbors, most especially the loathed Celeste. As a uniformed butler served them the third course of an extravagant luncheon, Tamara abandoned the society chitchat and launched into her standard refrain: that Cliff was too thin; that he wasn't eating enough; and, most of all, that it was time he found a suitable woman to marry.

"Do you realize that I've been married twice since I've known you?" she said, pushing a second portion of the curried chicken salad in his direction. "Aren't you ashamed of yourself? You're nearly forty, and you haven't even taken the plunge once! Not once!"

Clifford cocked an eyebrow. Whenever he got together with Tamara, he braced himself for the When-are-you-going-to-settle-down-with-a-good-woman routine and armed himself with humor.

"How can I find a suitable woman to marry? *You're* already taken," he said with a deadpan expression which passed the duchess by. The subtler emotions, he had noticed, almost always escaped her.

"Oh, don't be ridiculous, Cliff," she snapped, loading his

plate with another helping of wild rice with walnuts and dried cranberries plumped in red wine. "You really should be married. A man in a position like yours needs a wife to help him entertain, to serve on important charities, to provide him with the right image and the right background. Besides, haven't you heard that married men live longer than bachelors?"

Clifford shook his head in amazement. Tamara was indefatigable. *"That's* an argument you've never thrown at me before," he said.

"Well, it's absolutely, positively true, and there are statistics to back me up," said the duchess. "I told Ferdy all about it the night before he proposed, and look what happened. He married me *and* he thinks he's going to live another fifty years!"

Clifford rolled his eyes and permitted himself the hint of a smile. "You're wonderful! Don't ever change!" he told her.

"I have no intention of changing," she replied. "Ferdy insisted I quit smoking and so I have, as you can see. That's all the changing I intend to do. It's *you* who's due for a little changing. You're a gorgeous creature, with those eyes, that wavy hair, that runner's body. You've got the looks of a Byronic poet, the brain of Einstein and the bank account of J. P. Morgan. You're a catch, as if you didn't know. Women must be falling all over you."

"Not the one I want, though," he admitted.

"Which one? Tell. Tell. Who is she?" Tamara asked leaning forward, her eyes widening in surprise, dying to find out. Had Clifford met someone since she'd seen him last?

Clifford shook his head slightly. He was not about to tell her that there was still no one. If he did, he would get Lecture Number 2a: the one about being too picky.

"You have your secrets," he said, referring to her mysterious comments about Charles Goddard. "And I have mine. Besides, I was hoping that we could spend our lunch discussing something more interesting than my love life," he said.

"Like what? My money?" said Tamara, as she served him more of the yogurt-cucumber-mint dressing.

Clifford nodded. "As a matter of fact, yes," he said. "There's something you ought to know. While Osborne and Praeger's performance has been down four percent for the quarter, Goddard-Stevens's accounts increased by fifteen percent."

Tamara eyed him, did a quick mental calculation, thought for a moment, was tempted, very truly tempted, then reluctantly shook her head. She loved money. But not *that* much. Not enough to betray a friend.

"Look, you don't have to pitch me. You know how I feel about you, about how talented I think you are. It's Goddard-Stevens that I object to—" The duchess stopped in midsentence and regarded the butler, who had suddenly reappeared.

"What is it, Soames?" she asked, sounding irritated. "I'm right in the middle of a very important conversation."

"Excuse me, Your Highness," he said, stepping forward and bending down to speak quietly to his employer, who insisted that he use that form of address. Tamara *adored* being bowed to and addressed as Your Highness, even though she half knew that a lot of people snickered at her and her pretensions behind her back. Still, to Pearl Branowsky, such bowing and scraping was irresistible. "Your guests have arrived."

"Guests? Which guests?" Tamara replied, looking at her watch. "I'm not expecting anyone until two-thirty."

The butler smiled.

"It's Miss Caroline, madame," he said. "And Master Jack."

Jack ran across the emerald lawn, launched himself into the air and landed in his godmother's arms.

"We came early!" he exclaimed, barely able to contain his joy. "Are you surprised, Aunt Tamara? Are you?"

"Very," she said, hugging and kissing him, then glancing at Caroline, who had arrived at the pool and was now standing beside them. Aware that she had intruded, she glanced awkwardly between the duchess and her luncheon companion.

"Oh, Tamara. I'm so sorry to interrupt," she said. "I had no idea you had a guest. It was just that Jack wanted to surprise—"

"Clifford Hamlin is not a guest," Tamara interjected. "He's my broker. Or I should say *was* my broker."

Caroline turned to the man who sat across the table from the duchess and smiled. He was lean and wiry and just under six feet tall. His intelligent gray eyes assessed her, his wavy auburn hair curled over the collar of his white linen shirt, the sleeves of which were turned back to show slender, beautifully shaped wrists.

"So *you're* Clifford Hamlin," she said, extending her hand and remembering the name from her days at L'Elegance. "Tamara says you're a financial genius."

Clifford rose from his chair to shake Caroline's hand. His full mouth curved into a smile as his eyes drank her in and his hand touched hers.

"The duchess exaggerates. As usual," he said. "And you're . . . ?"

Caroline opened her mouth to introduce herself when the duchess cut her off.

"This is Caroline. Caroline *Goddard,"* Tamara said.

"Goddard?" he repeated, his eyes still on Caroline. She wore a sunflower yellow bikini over which a sheer white cotton beach wrap half revealed, half concealed a slender, toned body. Her tawny hair glistened in the midday sun, and her warm hazel eyes glinted with life and curiosity.

"Yes, *Goddard,"* the duchess responded before Caroline could. "Caroline is James Goddard's widow. Caroline, Clifford is the managing director of Goddard-Stevens. He works for Charles Goddard now."

Involuntarily, at the very mention of Charles Goddard's name, Caroline took a step backward. She did not want to be near anyone who was close to James's father, the man who had banished her from his world, the man who had hurt her as no one ever had—not even her own father.

"Charles and Dina invited me for the weekend," Clifford explained. He was acutely aware of Caroline's retreat and wondered what there was about him that offended her.

Caroline maintained her distance and struggled to keep a

pleasant expression on her face. Clifford Hamlin was Tamara's guest, after all. Still, he worked for her former father-in-law, ran his company, was staying at the Goddards' Palm Beach estate. He was the enemy, she told herself. A man to be very wary of. As they looked at each other, both of them curious and uneasy, Jack wiggled out of the duchess's lap. His ears had pricked up at the sound of the name "Goddard."

"Mommy, who's Charles Goddard?" he asked.

"He's your daddy's father," Caroline answered quickly, ruffling his golden hair with her hand, hoping the answer would suffice.

Jack looked up at her thoughtfully and considered her reply. He turned the information over in his mind.

"Does that make him my grandfather?" he asked, after a moment. He knew that Caroline's parents, whom he saw every month or so, were his grandparents, that Mary was his grandmother and Al his grandfather.

Caroline paused for a moment.

"Yes, he is," she said reluctantly, cornered into the admission.

"Then why did that man say Charles Goddard invited him to Palm Beach?" Jack persisted, pointing at Clifford. "You told me my Goddard grandparents lived far away. Too far to ever see us."

Caroline swallowed hard. She had known this day would come eventually, known that her son would find out that his grandparents owned a vacation home in Palm Beach, known that Jack would be forced to face the fact that his father's parents didn't know he existed because they hadn't wanted to. She was speechless, flustered, unsure of how to respond to her child, whom she wanted to protect at all costs.

"Well, darling, perhaps Mr. Hamlin meant—" Caroline began.

Clifford glanced at her and saw her evident distress. Aware that he had inadvertently told Caroline Goddard's son something the boy was not supposed to know, he interceded.

"Your mother's right. Your grandfather lives in New

York," he told the boy, the jolting realization flashing through his mind that just as Jack did not know his Goddard grandparents, the Goddards, astonishing as it seemed, did not know about Jack. He wondered how that could be. It seemed so strange, so very, very out of the ordinary. He also noticed the obvious affection between Tamara and Caroline and wondered if the beautiful young woman standing before him could be the "someone I love," the person whom Charles Goddard had, according to the duchess, "almost destroyed."

"But you said he invited you to Palm Beach. I heard you!" Jack protested, looking up at Clifford. "You said that you were here to visit him."

"I'm here to visit Tamara," Clifford said, the dimensions of the bizarre mystery about the unknown grandson—and Goddard heir—still swirling in his mind. "She's one of my favorite people in the world."

"She's one of *my* favorite people," Jack said, distracted from his curiosity and pacified by Clifford's explanation. "And I'm one of her favorite people, right, Aunt Tamara?"

"Of course you are," said the duchess as she gave her godson a hug and a squeeze. "Now, how about a swim? Soames will watch you while you're in the pool."

Jack hugged his godmother, waved good-bye to Caroline and Clifford Hamlin and sped off toward the kitchen to find Soames.

"Soames!" he called out as he went. "We're going to take me swimming!"

Caroline sighed as she watched Jack disappear into the house to search for Soames. She knew Jack, knew that the questions were not over, that one day soon he would bring up the subject of Charles Goddard again. He would remember what Clifford Hamlin had said, would want to know about the grandfather who was in Palm Beach. She wondered what she would say. Wondered what she *could* say. She did not want to lie to Jack—and she did not want to hurt him.

Clifford Hamlin's voice interrupted her thoughts as Jack

and Soames emerged from the house and headed for the pool.

"I'm sorry. I had no idea that Jack didn't know," he said, apologizing. He got up and pulled out a chair for Caroline.

She sat down but did not speak. How could she? Her every word would get back to Charles Goddard, she was sure, and she didn't want that. If only Clifford Hamlin hadn't nearly burst the fragile bubble she had constructed for her son. How she resented him for that—and for his alliance with Charles Goddard, the man who had dismissed her and disdained her and condemned her to a solitary and forlorn pregnancy that had almost ended in the death of her child. His apology had seemed genuine, and his expression seemed to be one of concern. But no matter how caring he appeared to be, she couldn't forget where his allegiance would lie. She knew there was a very good chance that he would go back to Charles and tell him about Jack. She shuddered as she tried to imagine Charles's response to the fact that he had an heir. Would he explode with anger that he hadn't been told about Jack? Or would he shrug off the news with indifference, relegating his grandson to the oblivion to which he had condemned Caroline?

"There's something you should know, Cliff," said the duchess, as Caroline and Clifford continued to eye each other, cautiously sizing each other up. "Charles Goddard has no idea that he has a grandson."

"I realize that he doesn't," he said, aware that Charles had made him managing director of Goddard-Stevens only because there was no Goddard heir to succeed him. "What I don't understand is *why* he doesn't," he said. "It's the most peculiar thing I've ever heard."

Caroline nodded. It *was* peculiar, but as James had said so many times, the Goddards, despite their surface polish, were peculiar people.

"When James died," she said, deciding he should hear her side of the story before he went back to the Goddards and heard theirs, "his parents made it very clear that they didn't want anything to do with me. They informed me in no uncertain terms that didn't want me in their lives. Me—

or anything to do with me. They were afraid I was after their money."

"And were you?" he asked, now able at least to imagine why Charles and Dina might not have wanted to remain in contact with their daughter-in-law. James's marriage had been extremely brief, and Clifford wondered for a moment if Caroline Shaw was some kind of an adventuress, the kind of attractive young woman who would use her beauty to end up in the right bed and, eventually, to parlay her charms into a wedding ring and a share of a rich family's fortune.

Caroline shook her head.

"No, I wasn't," she snapped. "James and I lived modestly. We didn't need or want anybody's money." Her eyes filled with tears as she recalled the nightmarish scene that had taken place at James's funeral in Camden five years ago. The hurt was still there, still alive inside her, no matter how hard she tried to pretend it had faded.

"Then what made the Goddards so sure that your motives were mercenary?" asked Clifford.

"James said that it was due to their suspicion of outsiders and the fact that they themselves tended to see things primarily in financial terms. They made it obvious that they hated me. Dina Goddard accused me of causing James's death. Charles Goddard was convinced I was only interested in money. When I tried to tell him I was pregnant, he refused to let me speak and warned me not to come to him with my hand out. When I wrote them a letter to tell them, it was returned unopened. Then after Jack was born, I called Emily, but she was in Europe. I left a message and she never returned my call. So I wrote the Goddards another letter, this time telling them the details of their grandson's birth. But that letter, too, was returned unopened. The message was crystal clear, and I finally decided that if the Goddards didn't want to have anything to do with me or with Jack, so be it. I vowed never to put myself through that kind of humiliation again and certainly never to expose Jack to their contempt. At this point, I want to keep him as far away from them as possible. Not that that's been difficult considering their complete lack of interest . . ."

Clifford listened attentively to the amazing story, trying to decide if she was lying or, at least, dramatizing. Still, her evident distress spoke to Clifford. And so did the realization that her son Jack was a boy without a father. A boy like he once had been. A memory of his own fatherless childhood pierced the steel shutters he kept drawn over his emotions.

"They won't find out about Jack from me," he said finally, understanding the painful decision she had been forced into.

"Oh, right," she said, highly skeptical of his pronouncement. His loyalty was to Charles, after all, not to a woman he had only just met.

"People who know me know that my word is good," he said, wanting to keep a distance from the complications of the Goddards' family history. In fact, he had always been unwilling to get involved with the Goddards' personal lives. More than once, Charles had implied that Emily would make an ideal wife for him, an oblique suggestion that Clifford had held at bay each time it had been brought up. In addition, from his own selfish point of view, the Goddards' knowledge of the existence of an heir would certainly complicate and perhaps even threaten his own agreement with Charles.

"So you say," she said, seeing Tamara nod energetically, backing up Clifford's words.

"I wish you'd believe me. You see, I think I can understand the difficult predicament you're in," he replied, holding her eyes with his for a moment. Her allure was obvious and so was her determination. She was bringing up her child without the Goddards' help. He admired her independence and self-respect and wanted to know more about her.

"Can you?" Caroline replied in an almost icy tone.

Clifford looked at her and decided against an explanation—at least for the moment.

"Did you grow up in Florida?" he asked suddenly, wanting to change the subject, wanting Caroline to view him in a different light—as a man who had more to him than his association with Charles and Dina Goddard.

"Yes," she said. "But not in Palm Beach."

"Nearby?" he asked.

She nodded.

"On the wrong side of the tracks," she said wryly and proceeded, at Tamara's urging, to tell him about Patterson Avenue, how she met the duchess, and how she became interested in retailing. He listened with intense interest, encouraging her with questions and occasional perceptive comments.

Before either Caroline or Clifford realized how much time had passed, the duchess pushed her chair away from the table.

"That key lime pie did me in," she said, yawning. "Jack's not the only one who needs a nap."

Caroline glanced at her watch. It was almost three-thirty. Jack had gone swimming, eaten lunch, taken a walk on the beach with Soames, then returned to the pool again. By two-thirty, he was so tired that his eyes drooped and he could barely hold his head up. Soames had taken him inside for a nap.

"And it's time I woke Jack and took him home," said Caroline, rising from the table. She had left her work half-finished and wanted to get her figures in order before her Monday meeting with the bank.

"Suppose you let him sleep a little longer. Could you take some time to show me Palm Beach?" Clifford asked unexpectedly.

Caroline hesitated. She had a great deal of work to do, and she wasn't anxious to spend any more time with someone who was so close to the Goddards.

"Just because he works for Charles Goddard doesn't mean you have to hate him," the duchess chimed in, reading Caroline's mind. "And you know I'd love to keep Jack a while longer."

"I would have thought you'd already seen Palm Beach," Caroline said coolly, holding Clifford's gaze. From his clothes and manner and what she had heard about him over the years from Tamara, she imagined him to be well-traveled as well as wealthy.

"Oh, I've seen Palm Beach all right," he said. "If you count the Delta Air Lines terminal, Interstate 95, and the Goddards' estate. Of course, if you don't want to . . ."

She was about to make an excuse when she suddenly remembered the old saying, "Know thine enemy." Impulsively, she decided to take him up on his invitation.

19

Caroline offered to drive Clifford Hamlin in her car.

"We'll use mine," he said, clearly a man who was used to being in charge. He escorted her to the gleaming black Bentley he had hired for the duration of his stay in Palm Beach and introduced her to the driver, a uniformed, gray-haired man named Franklin. "Now, why don't you tell Franklin where he should take us," he said.

"Let's start with Seagull Cottage," she said, unaccustomed to the role of tour guide, but determined as always to do her best. The historic house, she told him as Franklin rolled the car out of the duchess's driveway, was the first Palm Beach home of Henry Morrison Flagler, the founder of The Breakers. "Then we'll go next door to the Flagler Museum and drive south to Mar-A-Lago."

"Donald's place," Clifford said.

Caroline turned to face him.

"You're on a first name basis with Mr. Trump?" she said, not exactly surprised.

"I'm one of his three thousand best friends," Clifford replied in a dry, amused tone.

Caroline smiled, appreciating his humor, but conscious of the necessity of being extremely careful around him. Clifford Hamlin owed his career and his future to Charles Goddard, a man who despised her, and she felt more than a little uncomfortable with him. Just as she was unaccustomed to being a tour guide, she was also unaccustomed to the extreme luxury of a $125,000 automobile and somewhat intimidated by the man sitting beside her, a man from the extremely sophisticated and, to her, rather mysterious world of high finance. Enclosed by the plush, cocooned luxury of gray glove leather and deep pile carpets, the climate automatically controlled, outside noise blocked out, the lush vistas of Palm Beach passing outside the tinted windows, Caroline had to keep reminding herself that Clifford Hamlin was not only someone who unexpectedly had immense power over her and Jack but who was, despite what he had said at lunch, a potential enemy.

"And this is Villa Flora," she said as she continued to point out the sights. "It was built in 1920 for the financier Edward Shearson." She directed his attention out the window as Franklin drove past the Mediterranean-revival-style mansion.

"One of the founders of Shearson, Hammill," commented Clifford, who knew his Wall Street history.

"One of his great-granddaughters was a client at L'Elegance."

"L'Elegance—" Clifford mused as the Bentley moved down South County Road. He had often heard Tamara speak of it—and of the extraordinarily hard-working and talented stock girl she had originally hired more or less as a favor to a friend—in the years she was still his client. "It was on Worth Avenue, wasn't it?"

"Right around the corner, as a matter of fact. Would you like to see it?" Clifford nodded and Caroline told Franklin to make a right turn onto Worth Avenue. When they arrived at the storefront, now a jewelry store, where L'Elegance used to be, Caroline pointed out the window.

"Right there," she said as Clifford Hamlin followed her gaze. "That's where the duchess used to outfit the rich and infamous of Palm Beach." She did not mention that it was also the place where she had met James, where she had discovered that happiness was possible for her after all. Even after all these years, she still felt a catch in her throat when she thought of James, when she spoke his name, when she recalled their all-too-brief time together, whenever a smile or an expression of Jack's came from nowhere to remind her of him. Her words trailed off as she lost herself in memory and emotion. Seeming almost to sense her sudden sadness, Clifford quickly moved to focus her attention on the present, on matters over which she had control. It was a technique that had worked well for him over the years.

"And what's that?" he asked, pointing to a large, beautifully landscaped building as they continued to cruise along the length of Worth Avenue.

"The Everglades Club." Caroline replied. "Very posh. The Goddards are members."

Clifford nodded. "I understand Charles spends a good deal of time there when he's in Palm Beach," he said as he assessed the stately, imposing clubhouse, a Palm Beach institution known for its wealthy members and its exclusionary admission policies.

"The family also belongs to the Palm Beach Polo and Country Club," said Caroline, recalling the things James had told her about his parents.

"The Polo Club? Isn't that where Kyle Pringle died?" asked Clifford.

Caroline nodded.

"James said that it was a freak accident. Something about a problem with the saddle's girth. He said that no one ever really understood it because Kyle was such an accomplished horseman," she replied. Then her tone changed, and she seemed to retreat once again into a private space and speak to herself. "I don't understand why anybody should die young. I'll never understand that."

She was speaking of James Goddard now, Clifford knew.

"I'm sorry about your husband," he said, thinking briefly of his own father who had also died young. "Forgive me for bringing up Kyle's name. It was thoughtless of me."

Caroline turned to him. His auburn hair seemed dark in the shaded interior of the car, and his gray eyes with their long lashes were serious. For an instant, their eyes met and she had an impulse to trust him, to believe that he was genuinely interested in her and her life with James. Instead, aware of the need to be on her guard with the managing director of Goddard-Stevens, she resisted the impulse and summoned a half smile.

"It was a long time ago," she said softly, not wanting Clifford Hamlin to know her deepest thoughts, not about James or anything else.

"You mentioned earlier that Romance, Inc. is in West Palm Beach," Clifford said a few moments later.

"I'm flattered that you remembered the name of my store," she said, surprised that he had paid such careful attention to what she had said.

"I'd like to see it," he replied, not overtly reacting to her comment. His memory—for figures, facts, dates, names—had been one of the reasons for his immense success.

"Why not?" she said. "It's about ten minutes from here." At Caroline's directions, Franklin continued along Worth Avenue, then made his way up Cocoanut Row, onto Royal Palm Way, across Royal Park Bridge, and over to West Palm Beach and Okeechobee Boulevard, a busy, commercial thoroughfare.

"There," she said, pointing as they neared the shop. "It's right across the street." She felt a surge of pride as she looked at the brightly decorated store. *Her* store. The store she had fashioned from her dreams, from hard work and thin air and the help of her friends. The store she had made a reality and was now contemplating expanding. At that thought, she glanced at her watch. The afternoon was fading, and she still had to finish going over her figures for tomorrow morning's meeting with the bank.

"Am I keeping you from something?" he asked. He had noticed her anxious glance at the time. "I really would like to see the store if you can spare a few more minutes." He made it sound as if she would be doing him a tremendous favor.

"Of course," she said, trying not to be taken in by his interest, "but then I really do have to get back. I still have some work to finish."

"We won't stay long," he assured her. "Pull over, Franklin," Clifford commanded the driver. "We'll be getting out for a few moments."

Franklin maneuvered the Bentley in front of Romance, Inc., and held the door for Clifford and Caroline. She unlocked the front door to the shop and invited Clifford inside. It felt strange to be bringing a man into the store on a Sunday. A man she hardly knew. A man who worked for Charles Goddard. In a way she felt not as if she were showing him a store but as if she were showing him her dreams and her innermost secrets.

"Here it is," she said, a little self-consciously, not knowing what a successful financier like Clifford Hamlin would think of her ultra-feminine shop, with its sensuous emphasis on romance.

He walked inside and surveyed the interior of the store, saying nothing at first, simply making note of the design, the layout, the merchandise, and nodding occasionally. His intensity both puzzled and intrigued Caroline, and she was curious to know what he was thinking.

"Obviously, you're very creative," he said finally, speaking to her but not looking at her as he continued to examine the store.

A compliment, Caroline thought with perverse pleasure, somehow certain that Clifford Hamlin was a man of few compliments.

"You have a flair for merchandising *and* marketing," he added, taking in the inviting displays, the brochures that offered clients a ten percent discount for every hundred dollars' worth of purchases, the pasteup of a forthcoming ad on the desk in Caroline's small office behind the selling area. "Not a small thing in business these days. I can see why your clients like it. You've created more than a store here. You've created an environment. An atmosphere. A destination for shoppers. Tamara mentioned that you're thinking of opening a second shop," he said, finally turning toward her.

"Actually, I'm doing a little more than just thinking about it," Caroline said, aware of his gray eyes on her. "I've got a meeting with the bank tomorrow morning. Hopefully, they'll give me a loan to open a second store."

"A smart decision," said Clifford. "You ought to make your move right now, before somebody comes along and steals your idea."

"Steals it?" she asked, a bolt of anxiety shooting through her. She had never considered the possibility of being stolen from. She had never had anything worth stealing. And Romance, Inc. was *hers.* She had created it, planned it, struggled to make it happen, hovered over it day and night. She was consumed with it; the shop represented *her,* her thoughts, her dreams, her ideas, and it was also a memorial to James, her one great love. Nothing in her life, except for Jack, meant nearly as much to her. The thought of someone *stealing* it filled her with terror and with an intense determination to protect her idea. "I hadn't considered that possibility. Perhaps I need to move ahead with my expansion plans even more quickly than I thought."

"You should before someone else does," he replied. "Although, of course, I haven't seen the numbers."

I have the spreadsheets with me, Caroline thought. *Do I dare show them to him? Do I dare trust him with the information?* He could run to Charles with it, she realized. On the other hand, Clifford Hamlin was a gifted, highly regarded financier, capable of overseeing a firm as renowned as Goddard-Stevens. He ought to know more than a little bit about business plans. Why shouldn't I pick his brain? she decided.

"Would I be taking advantage if I asked you to take a look at my spreadsheets?" she asked. "I'd be willing to pay whatever your fee is—"

He didn't let her finish the sentence.

"I'd be happy to take a look at them," he offered without comment. She obviously had no idea that his fee usually ran into seven figures. "And there's no charge."

"Thank you. I'd be very grateful for your advice," said Caroline, relocking the front door of Romance, Inc. Clifford Hamlin had been instrumental in the building of Tamara's fortune. Why not hers?

"Then you shall have it," he said, taking her arm and walking her back to the waiting car, gleaming like a black diamond in the tropical sun.

When they had settled back into the Bentley, Clifford turned to Caroline.

"Why don't we discuss Romance, Inc.'s finances over a drink?" he asked. "Is there somewhere by the water? I don't know about you, but I could do with a view while I work."

Caroline nodded. She knew just the place—it had been one of James's favorites, and she hadn't been there since his death.

"There's the River House," she said. "But it's twenty minutes away in Palm Beach Gardens."

Clifford Hamlin glanced at his watch.

"We have time," he said, giving Franklin the name of the restaurant.

"You don't have to get back to the Goddards'?" Caroline asked, raising an eyebrow. He had said something about a dinner party that evening.

"Yes, but not yet. It's still early," he said.

Franklin pointed the Bentley in the direction of Interstate 95 and made his way north to Palm Beach Gardens.

The River House, a popular restaurant among both locals and tourists, was set along the Intracoastal Waterway. Inside was a bar and a dining room; outside, tables and chairs were set up on a charming flowered deck where patrons could enjoy a drink and an unobstructed view of the water. When Caroline and Clifford were seated, Clifford told the waiter to bring two margaritas, with extra wedges of lime and coarse salt along the rim of each glass.

"This is exactly what I had in mind," he said, leaning back and putting on a pair of dark sunglasses. For a moment he watched in silence the majestic procession of boats that were making their way up and down the Intracoastal. Caroline wondered once again what he was thinking, but his concealed eyes and unrevealing expression gave no clue to his thoughts. He was, she thought, remarkably handsome, resembling the English actor Jeremy Irons, with his fine, sensitive face, clear, pale skin, lustrous auburn hair, and elegantly chiseled bone structure. He was lean and finely honed, a complete thoroughbred. She imagined that he had grown up in a world as exclusive and as refined as James's.

However, unlike James, who hadn't fit into the world in which he had been born, Clifford Hamlin seemed destined to assume his place in the aristocracy. The silence was verging on the awkward when the waiter arrived with their margaritas.

"Shall we drink to something?" said Clifford, turning to her as he raised his glass.

"How about your visit to Florida?" she replied.

Clifford shook his head. "I'd rather toast Tamara," he said with a wry smile.

"The duchess? Why?" asked Caroline.

"Because she introduced us," he said with a brief smile, his eyes obscured behind the dark lenses as he turned toward her. "And because I'm glad she did."

Caroline, astonished by the unexpected words, was at a loss for a response. She lowered her eyes and took her first sip from the frosty, salted glass. She felt the tequila surge through her, and the sensation was warm and exciting. She took another swallow, aware that Clifford Hamlin was looking at her, seeming almost to study her from behind his dark glasses. Was he trying to decide if she was the gold-digging slut the Goddards had undoubtedly described? she wondered. Had he believed her account of her experiences with the Goddards or had he dismissed it? Was he glad to have met her so he could run back to Charles and give James's father a full report on her? Did he view her as a potential client, another notch on his professional belt? Or was something else—something invisible and so far unspoken—happening between them?

It was Clifford who broke the silence.

"Now. About Romance, Inc.," he said, the brief moment approaching something very close to intimacy suddenly gone. "Let's take a look at the numbers."

Suspicion still filling her mind, Caroline nevertheless retrieved the folded spreadsheets from her tote bag and handed them to Clifford. He studied them carefully, and for a long moment he was silent, lost in thought. Caroline, her fantasies running riot, was afraid that he was searching for the words to tell her that her notion of expansion was ridiculous. Feeling anxious and embarrassed at the picayune size of her business and imagining how contemptuous this major deal-maker, this friend of Donald Trump, must be of Romance, Inc., she waited for him to speak.

"How much of a loan are you going to request?" he asked, making no comment whatever about what the figures told him. Or didn't tell him.

"A hundred thousand dollars," she said, doing her best not to sound tentative.

He shook his head.

"Ridiculous," he said, folding up the spreadsheets and handing them back to her.

"You don't think the bank would grant that?" she asked, now feeling small and insignificant and way out of her depth. The insecurities of her childhood had a way of coming back to haunt her at the most unexpected and most inopportune moments.

He shook his head.

"A hundred thousand's not enough," he said. "You should ask for two hundred. Minimum. Your cash flow and projected earnings would permit you to carry that much debt."

"But that sounds like so much money," protested Caroline.

Clifford shook his head.

"It will be a stretch, but you can certainly manage it," he said. "One of the main reasons small businesses fail is undercapitalization."

Caroline had been apprehensive about asking the bank for a hundred thousand dollars. In fact, she had lost sleep over the idea of being responsible for so much money. Now Clifford Hamlin, the man that Tamara called a financial genius, was telling her to double her request. He was, she knew very well, absolutely right about undercapitalization. Romance, Inc. had almost gone out of business in its fifth month. Caroline simply did not have enough money to pay vendors, insurance, sales help, advertising bills, stationery expenses, and taxes. She had had to go to Cissy and Selma for additional money.

"Two hundred thousand dollars is a lot—" she said, weighing his comments. "Although you're perfectly right about undercapitalization."

"If you want to expand, you're going to have to do it right," he said. "Your basic expenses will all double. But that's only the barest minimum you have to plan for. You've said that you want the second store to be in a more upscale location, which means your rent will be higher. You will need to furnish and decorate it, and you will need to hire an architect to guide the plans through the local planning commissions as well as a contractor to actually do the installations. Once the store is ready to open, you'll need a manager you can trust, someone you'll have to pay more than you'd pay an ordinary sales clerk. And you've said that you want to upgrade your merchandise and carry more of it. In addition, there will be advertising costs, legal and accounting expenses, one mailing to your current client list and another to potential clients in your new location, a computer program for inventory control, a more sophisticated telephone system, and, of course, the cost of your own transportation back and forth between the two stores."

Caroline sighed.

"I hadn't taken all of that into consideration. But, of course, you're right," she said, feeling slightly overwhelmed by the complexities Clifford had just laid out. Opening a second store would be a much bigger proposition than she had imagined. She had thought of opening the second store on a shoestring, the way she had done everything in her life. "Maybe I shouldn't be quite so aggressive. I don't want to bite off more than I can chew."

"If you don't expand, someone is going to steal the idea. I can almost guarantee it," he told her. "And if someone does, by the way, you'll need to factor in potential legal expenses."

She rolled her eyes and laughed.

"Are you saying that I have no choice except to expand?" she asked, suddenly realizing that in making Romance, Inc. successful, she had built a kind of trap for herself.

"Look, Caroline, everyone always has choices. But the

reality in this case is that you don't have much of a choice. Not if you want to remain in control," he replied.

Caroline regarded him.

"You like to be in control, don't you?" she asked suddenly, blurting out the question.

He took off his dark glasses and looked at her with his catlike gray eyes for a long moment.

"I insist upon it," he replied, motioning for the check.

Caroline did not reply. She realized that in Clifford Hamlin's world, control was everything.

As they left the River House, he continued giving Caroline a brief lesson in the basics of retail finance. He was so engrossed in their conversation as they stepped into the waiting Bentley that he did not notice Perry Madison, the manager of Goddard-Stevens's Palm Beach office, wave at him as he waited for his own car to be brought around.

By the time they had returned to Tamara's estate, Clifford had convinced Caroline that he was right: if she were going to expand, she would have to do it properly. She would ask the bank for two hundred thousand dollars and explain her ability to repay the loan in exactly the same words that Clifford had, using cash flow estimates, profit margins, and sales projections. Still, even though she felt more or less in command of the new vocabulary she had learned from him that afternoon, her palms were damp and her throat was dry as she imagined sitting down with the loan officer.

"Are you all right?" Clifford asked as the Bentley swung into Tamara's driveway.

"I'm just a little anxious," she admitted. "I don't want to make a fool of myself at the bank."

"It's the bank that will look foolish if they deny you the loan," Clifford told her. "One day you'll look back on this and laugh at yourself. This is small potatoes. You're destined for big things, Caroline. Remember that."

It was the second personal remark Clifford Hamlin had made that afternoon, and Caroline once again had trouble believing he was sincere. What was his real agenda? she wondered, wishing she weren't so suspicious of him, yet unable to help herself. What was behind the kind words and friendly advice?

She shook his hand, said good-bye, and exited the car through the door that Franklin held open for her.

"I want you to tell me what happens at the bank tomorrow," Clifford called out to her.

"You're staying at the Goddards," she reminded him. "I can hardly call you there."

"I'll call you," he said firmly. "You can count on it."

Clifford arrived back at the Goddard estate at seven-thirty. Dina and Charles Goddard, dressed for the dinner, were waiting for him. They knew he had been lunching with a former client and they wanted to know where he'd been since then. He was almost late for the dinner party they were giving in his honor.

"I've been exploring Palm Beach," he explained, going upstairs to the guest suite to change for dinner.

Minutes later, as he stood in front of the bathroom mirror, he realized that he hadn't told his hosts the truth, that what he had been exploring had not been Palm Beach but feelings he had thought closed off to him. He was taken with Caroline Goddard and asked himself why. She was lovely looking, of course, and as bright as any of the women he went out with. But there was more to it than that. Caroline had affected him in a way he found as disquieting as it was thrilling.

When he finally made his way downstairs, the first guests were just arriving. Among them were Perry and Eleanor Madison, and they were standing in the foyer, drinks in their hands, chatting with the Goddards. As Clifford Hamlin entered the area, the conversation abruptly halted and all four people turned toward him.

"You looked as if you were having a good time at the River House," Perry Madison said.

The man's remark took Clifford by surprise, but his face remained expressionless.

"Yes, as a matter of fact, I was," he replied.

20

Charles Goddard listened carefully as Ted Aronson reported the information he had gathered on the birth of Caroline's child. It was just after eight o'clock on Monday morning when Ted's call came; as usual, Aronson had handled his assignment promptly and efficiently. Dina was at the club, playing tennis, and Clifford had left for the airport. Aside from the servants, Charles was alone in the house, and as he sat in the study off his bedroom, he gave Ted Aronson his full and undivided attention.

"The child was born nearly six years ago, on the morning of April twelfth," Ted began. "The precise time of the birth, which took place at Regional Hospital in Lake Worth, was 11:42. The birth weight was eight pounds, twelve ounces."

Regional Hospital, Charles thought with a twinge of irony. The very hospital to which he and Dina had donated millions of dollars for a new, state-of-the-art maternity wing.

"According to the records of the attending physician, an Ob-Gyn named Irene Lu, the pregnancy was a complicated one, but the delivery went smoothly," Ted continued. He was a bit squeamish about discussing such personal, such *feminine* matters, and they certainly were not in his customary line of work, but he pressed on without revealing his discomfort. Charles Goddard was his client, after all. His well-paying and very powerful client. "Mrs. Goddard stayed in the—"

"Mrs. Goddard," Charles muttered, interrupting Aronson's recounting of the specifics of Jack's birth. He still found it difficult—no, nearly impossible—to recognize Caroline Shaw as his late son's wife, as a member of *his* family, a member of the *Goddard* family. He found it even more incredible that she would keep the existence of his grandson a secret from him.

"May I continue, sir?" said Aronson.

"Yes. Sorry. Please go on," Charles urged, wanting to know more. Desperate to know more.

"As I was saying, Mrs. Goddard remained in the hospital for two and a half days after the delivery," Aronson said.

"Were there any visitors?" asked Charles, wondering whether the child's "father" had been to see the boy in the hospital.

"Yes, one," Aronson replied. "A woman named Selma Johannas. It was also Miss Johannas who brought Mrs. Goddard—and her son—home from the hospital."

Charles's heart had leapt in his chest when he'd heard that Caroline's only visitor had been a woman—not some stud from a nearby gas station or pizza place. Was little Jack Goddard James's son after all? *His* grandson? *His* heir? The possibility, once inconceivable, was becoming more and more plausible. Charles paused for a moment, thought about Step two, and then spoke to Aronson in measured tones.

"I want to extend your assignment, Ted," Charles said. "I'd like you to research this matter further. I assume there are some kind of tests to determine paternity?"

The question confirmed what Ted Aronson had suspected since Sunday, since his first words with Charles Goddard twenty-four hours before: that the chairman of Goddard-Stevens wondered if he had a long-lost grandson.

"Yes, there are blood tests," he replied simply. "I'll need a sample of the type you wish to match, though."

"No problem. As you've no doubt guessed, I have reason to think that this child might be my grandson. James's blood type is on file at Lenox Hill Hospital in New York," said Charles. "Am I right in suggesting that if you check the baby's blood type and it matches James's, the child is my grandson?"

"A blood test will show if your son and Jack have the same blood type, not whether or not James was the child's father. Only a DNA test will prove paternity, and we'll need a sample from James to run one. Is there any chance that you have some of your son's hair, for example?" said Aronson in his cool, professional manner, despite the highly charged nature of the assignment.

Charles thought for a moment. "I believe that my wife kept a baby memento book for each of our children," he said. "These books contained locks of the children's hair."

"Good. If you can get me a sample of your son's hair, Mr. Goddard, I'll begin the DNA—"

"You'll have your sample as soon as I can messenger it to you," Charles interrupted. "In the meantime, I'd like you to proceed with the blood test right away so we can at least determine if my son's type matches that of the boy."

"Will do," said Aronson.

"I'd also like you to go and see the boy," Charles went on. "Talk to him. And take a photograph of him."

"Talk to him, sir? About what?" Aronson had no problem operating a camera, but he didn't have an inkling how to talk to a six-year-old child, nor the inclination.

"Yes, talk to him," Charles instructed. "He must be in nursery school or kindergarten or something. Approach him during his playtime or as he's leaving school. Ask him about his friends, something of that nature. I want your impression of him. Does he seem poised? Intelligent? That kind of thing. Then take his picture. I want more than just a newspaper photograph. You understand what I'm saying, don't you, Aronson?"

"Yes, of course I do," Ted replied, knowing only one thing: that Charles Goddard, one of Wall Street's most respected—and feared—investment bankers, was obsessed with a little boy named Jack, a boy who could turn out to be a Goddard.

While Charles Goddard and Ted Aronson were discussing Jack, Caroline was sitting at a conference table in a hushed office across the Causeway. Things were not going well. The two gray-haired, gray-suited, gray-complected bankers refused to see the potential in Romance, Inc.

"It's not that your numbers aren't adequate, Mrs. Goddard," one of them admitted, shaking his head. "It's just that our bank doesn't see much of a future in a retail enterprise that caters to the frivolities of women."

"Frivolities?" Caroline repeated indignantly. She was furious at the chauvinistic way she was being treated, but she did not want to lose her temper. *That* was Tamara's style, not hers. "Believe me, gentlemen. What we sell at Romance, Inc. is hardly frivolous. Unless, of course, you term merchandise that makes women feel good about themselves 'frivolous.'"

"Look, Mrs. Goddard," said the other man, as he tugged on his left earlobe. "As we've said, your figures look fine. But here at United Palm Bank & Trust, we generally approve loans to businesses of a more . . . more conservative nature."

"You mean you're turning down my application for a loan?" Caroline asked, wanting to compel them put their decision into words of one syllable.

The two men nodded in unison.

"I'm sorry," said the first.

"Perhaps on another occasion—" suggested the second, wanting to keep the door open.

Caroline was terribly disappointed, but she kept her feelings in check and the expression on her face businesslike. She gathered her papers, returned them to her attaché case and stood.

"Thank you for your time," she said, shaking the hands of the two men, who then rose from the table, told her they were glad she chose to approach United Palm Bank & Trust, and escorted her out of the bank.

Some financial wizard Clifford Hamlin is, she thought as she stormed down the street to her car, got in, and wondered if he would really call her as he said he would. She doubted it.

But Clifford Hamlin did call—almost as soon as he got back to his office at Goddard-Stevens's New York headquarters at four-thirty on Monday afternoon. His secretary had dozens of messages for him to answer, and his schedule was jam-packed with meetings until seven o'clock that night, but the first moment he was alone in his large, impressively furnished corner office, he dialed Caroline's number at Romance, Inc.

"How did it go with the bank?" he inquired, glad to hear her voice.

"It didn't," she replied curtly.

"They rejected your loan application?"

"That's exactly what they did."

Was it disappointment he heard in her voice or distance? he wondered. Or both?

"What reason did they give you?" he asked.

"Oh, something about the frivolity of my merchandise," she said sarcastically. "They liked the numbers, but not the product."

"Well then, screw them," said Clifford, surprising Caroline with his angry tone. "Banks can be very stupid, trust me. No imagination. I told you they'd like your numbers, though, didn't I?"

"Sure, but what good did it do me? I didn't get the money I need," said Caroline. "What's really frustrating is that the bankers admitted that the numbers were good. 'Impressive' was the word they used."

"You've got to keep plugging," Clifford advised her. "You may have to try several banks before you find one that's sympathetic. One turndown from a bank means nothing."

"I hope you're right," she said, suddenly picturing him sitting at his desk at Goddard-Stevens. She recalled his lean, sinewy body, his wavy auburn hair, his self-assured manner, his absolute confidence in his own abilities. And she remembered how he had expressed confidence in her abilities as they'd sipped margaritas at the River House. "Frankly, I'm surprised that you called," she added.

"I was interested," he said. "I *am* interested." The question was *why,* Caroline thought but did not say. What, exactly, did he have in mind? Was he spying for Charles Goddard? "Have you arranged to meet with more banks?" he asked.

"Yes, I have," she said. "Aside from my son, Romance, Inc. means everything to me. I intend to see that it succeeds."

"I don't doubt that it will," he said. "Now—oh, excuse me a minute. Yes? What is it, Margaret?" Clifford's voice stiffened slightly as his secretary tapped on his office door, then entered carrying a stack of files and pointing to her watch, behaving like the taskmaster he had hired her to be. "Look, Caroline, I'm sorry but I'll have to cut this short," he said, returning his attention to their phone call, albeit briefly.

Before Caroline could tell Clifford that she, too, had a business to attend to and would, therefore, have to get off the phone, she realized that he had already hung up!

"I'm sorry to interrupt, Mr. Hamlin," Margaret Frith said, as she set the files on the corner of Clifford's large mahogany desk. "But you asked me to remind you about the meeting with the Holloway Corporation. They've just arrived and are waiting in the executive conference room."

"Fine, but what are these files, Margaret?" he asked, disappointed that he couldn't have spent more time talking with Caroline, but directing his thoughts back to business.

"The dormant accounts you asked about the other day," she replied. "The accounts department has been going through our computer system and weeding out the files with little or no activity over the past few years. You said you wanted to go through them to decide what to do with them."

Clifford nodded. He had chosen well when he had hired Margaret Frith, a well-groomed but spinsterish woman in her fifties who was as serious about her job at Goddard-Stevens as he was about his.

"Thank you, Margaret. I'll take a look at them just as soon as I have a chance," he said, patting the stack of files, getting up from behind his desk and moving toward the door. "Now then, let's get on with the Holloway group."

Caroline had never been to New York City, and when her Delta Air Lines jumbo jet descended over the East River and then landed at La Guardia Airport that mid-March morning, she felt her pulse race. She had had mixed feelings about the trip; she was enthusiastic about meeting with various vendors to negotiate private label deals for Romance, Inc., but the thought of a week away from Jack was almost more than she could bear. Still, the idea of spending time in Manhattan with Cissy McMillan and of having dinner with Jean-Claude Fontaine had nudged her out of the depression that had plagued her since early March, since the anniversary of the day she had met and fallen in love with James Huntington Goddard.

The memories of their meeting, of their first few dates, of their courtship and subsequent marriage in Maine, had come rushing back to Caroline, as they did each and every March since James died. To compound her doldrums, she had been turned down by each of the three different banks she had approached for a loan.

"We don't think your business is viable in the long run," one banker had told her.

"A chain of stores selling romantic merchandise? Frankly, I don't see it," another had scoffed.

Even more depressing, the naysayers among the bankers hadn't all been men. The female vice president of the West Palm Beach Banking and Loan Company had actually said, "Surely, one store is work enough for a single mother. Why saddle yourself with two?"

Having to pitch her idea to one negative-thinking banker after another had been humiliating and terribly wearing on Caroline, and so when several of her New York-based vendors—a fragrance house, a garment manufacturer, a tableware vendor, an importer of household linens—had agreed to meet with her, she had thought the trip might be good therapy and telephoned Cissy to ask if she might stay with her for the week.

"Of course you can stay with me," Cissy had said, speaking from her East Seventy-seventh Street townhouse. "I've only been inviting you to New York ever since we met, remember?"

Caroline couldn't help but recall Cissy McMillan's kindness when she and James had rented the carriage house in Camden.

"Of course, I remember," she had replied, with a mixture

of sadness and gratitude. "And I'm looking forward to seeing you again. Very much."

The meeting with the garment manufacturer went very well, and Caroline negotiated a contract for them to make blouses, nightgowns, and negligees with a Romance, Inc. logo. Similarly, the tableware company agreed to a deal whereby they would produce a line of Romance, Inc. dishes, flatware, and stemmed glasses. The meeting with the importer of linens ended with an agreement to confer again. There were unresolved issues of deliveries and prices still to be worked out.

Caroline was buoyed by her meetings with the vendors. She handled herself professionally and was able to get almost all of what she wanted in terms, merchandise, and promises to work together on additional projects. The rejections by the banks for a loan to expand her business fell into perspective and temporarily took a backseat to her excitement over her plans for the future.

"I have no doubt that Romance, Inc. will grow," Caroline told Cissy as they dined together in the older woman's beautifully paneled dining room, the table set with traditionally designed tableware, similar to the kind Caroline would soon be offering at Romance, Inc.

"Neither do I. You have the look of a tycoon," Cissy laughed, the lines around her sharp, intelligent eyes crinkling.

"A tired tycoon," Caroline admitted with a laugh.

Cissy nodded. She hadn't said anything, but she was worried about Caroline and could see the sadness beneath the almost frenetic activity. She could sense how much she still missed James, missed his presence in her life. Still, she thought that Caroline was somehow clinging to her loss.

"And a lonely one?" prompted Cissy.

"Sometimes," admitted Caroline.

"You miss James, don't you?"

Caroline nodded.

"All the time," she said.

"I hope you won't think me intrusive, but I'm basically a

blunt New Englander and I don't know how to say what I'm thinking except to just say it," Cissy began. "But I think you're in danger of becoming a professional widow."

"That's not true!" exclaimed Caroline, wounded by the words and appalled by the image they conveyed.

Cissy disagreed.

"I can sense you pining for James. I can almost *feel* it," said Cissy, pressing on. "Every time his name comes up, you get teary. Good heavens, Caroline, he's been dead for over five years. You have to put the past in its place. I don't think James would have wanted you to halt your life in its tracks. You're still a young woman. A young, beautiful woman."

"I haven't halted my life in its tracks. I have Jack. I have Romance, Inc."

"But you have no life of your own. No personal life. James was an extraordinary young man. He was madly in love with you, and you with him. But that was years ago. It's time you came out of the perpetual mourning you seem to determined to wallow in."

Caroline was silent. Cissy's words *were* blunt and, although she didn't mean them to be, hurtful. And Caroline resented them. She loved James, adored him. Of course she missed him. Anyone would.

"You're angry with me, aren't you?" asked Cissy. "You think I'm devaluing your marriage, don't you?"

"No," said Caroline instantly. Then she reconsidered. "Yes," she admitted. "I don't want anyone to devalue James."

"But I haven't devalued James. I was talking about *you,*" Cissy pointed out. "I understand your devotion to Romance, Inc., but it's high time for some man to come along and romance *you.*"

Caroline mustered a smile. Now that her moment of hurt had passed and she had had a moment to think over Cissy's words, she had to acknowledge that Cissy had a point. James had been wonderful and her time with him had been blissful, but she had been very young and so had he.

"I've always thought of James as my only love," she

mused. She had been fat and unpopular, and no boy had ever looked at her. Until James with his blue eyes and golden hair had come along—

"Perhaps it's time to begin to think of him as your *first* love," Cissy said.

"That will be quite an adjustment," said Caroline, sensing very deep down that, despite her initial rejection of Cissy's words, her friend was telling her something important.

"Then there's no time like the present to start making that adjustment. Tell me, when's the dinner with the Frenchman?" Cissy ventured in her direct, no-nonsense tone. Caroline had told her about Jean-Claude, who had been calling her regularly since his appearance at Romance, Inc. She had also told Cissy about the overt and discomfiting way he had flirted with her and about her reluctant promise to have dinner with him if she ever came to New York.

"Tomorrow night," said Caroline with obvious trepidation.

"Where's he taking you?" Cissy asked, her eyes twinkling with mischief. "Somewhere cozy and candlelit, I hope, where he can whisper sweet nothings into your ear."

"Not so fast!" Caroline warned, holding up her hand. "Jean-Claude and I are just friends—two people with a mutual goal of earning a living. His appearance at the store helped *my* sales and the sales of his cookbook."

"Friends? How nice for both of you," Cissy said, skepticism written all over her face. She had read about Jean-Claude Fontaine in the gossip columns, dined at Moustiers, and knew of his flamboyant love life. She found it almost impossible to believe that any woman—even one as determined to avoid romance as Caroline Goddard—could resist such a man. "Where is this dinner going to take place?"

"At Jean-Claude's loft in Soho. I'm going there tomorrow night and he's cooking me dinner."

Cissy rolled her eyes. Dinner alone in a Soho loft with an Adonis who could cook!

"Oh!" Caroline exclaimed suddenly, glancing at her watch. "It's nearly Jack's bedtime, and I haven't called him yet."

As she jumped up from the table to use the phone in the living room, Cissy called after her, "Give him my love. Again."

Caroline missed Jack terribly and spoke to him every morning and every evening. She was enjoying herself in Manhattan with its frantic pace and cosmopolitan aura, but she longed to have her son's arms around her, longed to hear his little voice.

"Hi, sweetheart," she said when she reached him just after eight-thirty. "Is Selma helping you get ready for bed?"

"No, we're reading," he said. "It's a book about Brett Haas."

"Who?" asked Caroline.

"Aw, Mom. Don't you know anything?" Jack sighed, somewhat exasperated by his mother's ignorance. "Brett Haas used to play third base for the Atlanta Braves. Now he's on TV whenever the Braves play. He does the play-by-play. The book we're reading tells all about his life."

"Sounds interesting," Caroline fibbed. Baseball was her least favorite sport and biographies of sports stars at the very bottom of her reading list. Perhaps because Al Shaw had been a baseball fan, or perhaps because she thought the game relentlessly dull and painfully slow-moving.

"We're just at the best part!" Jack went on, excitement causing his voice to rise. "Brett is about to hit a home run to win the final game of the World Series! Right over the left field wall!"

"How do you know he hits a home run?" Caroline asked.

"Because I've read this book sixteen times," Jack said matter-of-factly. "Selma bought it for me last week."

"I bought you something, too, sweetheart," Caroline said, her tenderness toward him nearly overwhelming her.

"For me? You did?" he asked excitedly.

"Yup. At a very famous toy store in New York called FAO Schwarz."

"You bought me a toy?" he asked, his curiosity mounting.

"I'm not telling! You'll just have to wait until I get home," she said. "You always say how much you love surprises. Well, your present from FAO Schwarz is a surprise, okay?"

"Okay," he said with slight disappointment. "When are you coming home?"

"Not for a few days," she replied. "But soon, darling. Soon. I miss you and love you and can't wait to see you."

"Me too, Mom. And when you get home, I'll read you the Brett Haas book. I know practically every word in it. You'll love it!"

Caroline laughed. "If *you* read it to me, I'll love it," she agreed. "Now, let me talk to Selma, would you, Jack dear? I want to say good night to her, too."

Jack handed the phone to his godmother and scurried into the kitchen for a glass of milk and a chocolate chip cookie.

"Everything go okay?" Caroline asked Selma, to whom she spoke every day, checking on Jack.

"Everything's fine," said Selma, who didn't sound fine at all.

"Selma, what is it?" Caroline asked with alarm. "I can sense something in your voice."

Selma Johannas sighed. She didn't want to worry Caroline, not when she was all the way up north in New York, and not when there was probably nothing to worry about.

"Selma? Please tell me," Caroline urged.

"Well, there was this man. He approached Jack as he was leaving school today," Selma said.

"A man? What man? Who?" Caroline asked, her body tensing.

"I don't know. I never saw him before," said Selma. "I was waiting at the curb in the car. I saw him walk over to Jack—not to any of the other kids, just Jack—and begin talking to him. I got out of the car to interrupt their conversation, but Jack was already moving away from him. He said that he told the man that he wasn't allowed to talk to strangers. Your son listens to you, Caroline, which is something a lot of parents *wish* they could say about their kids."

Caroline considered what Selma had just said. Her son

was a special child. She didn't doubt that for a moment. But she did wonder about the stranger—what did he want with Jack? Why did he speak to her son and not to the other children? Who was he? What did he want? Would he be back?

"Keep a close eye on Jack, will you, Selma?" she asked. "He's so precious to me."

"To me, too. I won't let anything happen to him, as God is my witness," said Selma resolutely. "Besides, there's probably nothing to worry about."

"You're right," said Caroline.

She hung up the phone and went into the living room where coffee was set out on a tray.

"Everything all right at home?" Cissy asked.

"I suppose so," Caroline said, and left it at that. There was no need to spoil Cissy's evening by burdening her with needless concerns.

"Good," Cissy said. "Now, let's talk more about that dinner date of yours tomorrow night."

"What about it?" Caroline asked, her mind still on Jack and the stranger who'd spoken to him.

"I was wondering, do you think you'll need a chaperone?" Cissy arched an eyebrow. She was teasing her friend. Or so Caroline thought.

Back in West Palm Beach, Selma wasn't sure if she'd done the right thing or not. She hadn't told Caroline about the photograph she'd seen the man take of Jack before he approached him. She didn't want to upset Caroline while she was away and could do nothing about the situation.

As Caroline lay awake in one of Cissy McMillan's guest rooms, her thoughts fixed on the mysterious man who had spoken to Jack after school, the private line rang in the study of Charles Goddard's Palm Beach estate. The photographs Ted Aronson had taken and messengered to his client confirmed what the newspaper photograph had revealed: that the child had Goddard eyes and a Goddard mouth.

"Yes?" Charles said expectantly. He had been waiting anxiously for Ted Aronson to call, knowing that he would hear from the private investigator the moment the results of the blood test were known.

Ted Aronson uttered three words to his client—words that would change the lives, not only of Charles and Dina Goddard but of Emily Pringle, of Clifford Hamlin, of Caroline Goddard, and, most of all, of little Jack Goddard.

"It's a match," Aronson said, and waited for his next assignment.

~21~

The conjunction of Prince and Mercer is a prime Soho location, equidistant from Dean & DeLuca's gourmet heaven and the glorious and giddily expensive shopping along West Broadway. Art galleries, upscale restaurants, and the downtown branch of the Guggenheim museum all converge at that corner, and it was there, on the top floor of a building that once manufactured sewing machines, that Jean-Claude Fontaine owned a partially renovated loft. Reached by a rickety industrial-size elevator, the hunter green lacquered metal front door was protected by a Manhattan minimum of one Medeco lock, one Fichet lock, and a Fox police lock bolted to the floor. Jean-Claude opened them in sequence, letting Caroline in. She studied him for a moment, trying to square her memories of the charismatic but temperamental Frenchman with the even more seductive reality.

His face, from the high-carved cheekbones to the olive complexion to the deep cleft in his chin, was even more handsome than she remembered. His shiny, almost coal black hair was tied neatly back into its customary ponytail, and he smelled of cologne, the same intoxicating scent she recalled from Palm Beach. She told herself that he was a modern-day Casanova and she was completely indifferent to his allure.

"Chérie," he murmured, looking deeply into her eyes and lifting her hand to his lips. "It's been too long since we were together."

Caroline raised an eyebrow. The come-on was outrageous, even for Jean-Claude.

"It hasn't been *that* long," she reminded him wryly, taking her hand back. She had made up her mind not to become flustered nor to allow Jean-Claude to get to her the way he had at their previous meetings. He was a famous chef and a best-selling author—the kind of man who believed his own press clippings and had a smooth line for every woman he met.

"It's been long enough that I've been looking forward to spending the evening with you," he replied suavely, reaching out for her hand and ushering her into the loft.

"We're not spending the evening together. We're having *dinner* together," she corrected him, taking back her hand yet again. She decided that it was time to change the subject, and she commented on the tantalizing aromas of wine and herbs emanating from the kitchen area of the loft.

"Something smells wonderful!" she said.

"You like my cologne?" he asked, smiling down at her provocatively.

Didn't he ever let up? she asked herself.

"I meant the food," she replied. "It smells delicious."

"Of course it smells delicious. It will *taste* delicious as well," Jean-Claude said with his usual arrogance. "But first the tour then the food."

He took her arm and walked her farther inside the loft and paused for a moment.

"Before," he said, pointing to the shabby, paint-chipped side toward the windows. "And after," he added, indicating the serene, gorgeously carpeted and furnished rear portion of the large, lavishly windowed space.

Caroline couldn't help but laugh. In three words, Jean-Claude had described the loft to a tee. Putting his arm around her shoulders, he showed her around.

"We'll start with the 'after.' Then we'll work our way to the 'before,' " he promised with a smile, guiding her across the floor and opening the door into a large, splendid area.

To Caroline's surprise, it was a bathroom, a masterpiece of design and decor, worthy of inclusion in the glossiest of magazines, sheathed in granite and mirror and flooded with natural illumination from a large skylight. A mini-bamboo forest was the backdrop for a large, dramatically raised square tub on whose wide edges stood an array of bath gels, dusting powders, toilet waters, loofahs, and sponges. A pile of thick white terry towels, fluffy and perfectly folded, awaited the bather. Just outside the bathroom was a king-size bed, low to the floor, covered with a linen spread in a neutral putty color. Cubes filled with books and topped with modern reading lights and small vases of daisies stood on either side, although the impression Caroline received was that very little reading took place here. The arrangement was very sensuous, very sexy—just like the man who stood beside her. She tried to convince herself once again that she didn't really notice the bed or Jean-Claude's virile, masculine body and warm, intimate touch as he showed her around the attractive but unconventional open-plan space.

"And now the 'before,'" he announced when they got to the kitchen at the other end of the loft. It had not yet received the attentions of his architect, and it looked, Caroline commented, as if it hadn't been touched since Herbert Hoover was president.

"A real antique," agreed Jean-Claude, showing Caroline the chipped, old-fashioned sink, the squat refrigerator with a coil on top, and the battered, once-white enamel stove, which had three burners on top and a tiny oven whose handle, long ago broken, had been replaced by a strand of twisted wire.

"I'm surprised that a restaurant owner wouldn't renovate his kitchen first," she said, astonished by Jean-Claude's pathetic excuse for a kitchen.

"The truth is, I'm around kitchens every minute of the day. The last thing I want to do when I'm home is cook." He glanced over at the large, inviting bed and bath, and Caroline understood instantly what Jean-Claude wanted to do when he got home.

"Then why are you cooking for me?" Caroline asked.

"Because you're someone whose idea of lunch is a ham

sandwich." He smirked. "I didn't want to traumatize you with the taro root–mousseline ravioli with wild mushrooms in truffle oil and brown butter that I serve at Moustiers. At home I can make something more—"

"Basic?" she prompted. "For a provincial American?"

Jean-Claude smiled.

"For a very beautiful provincial American," he replied, his eyes appraising her. She was wearing a well-cut suit with a sensuous silk blouse, a provocative combination of businesswoman and woman. She was surprisingly youthful looking, he thought, considering that she had been married and given birth to a child. She was full of contradictions, this Caroline Goddard, a refreshing change from the brittle, sophisticated Manhattan women he had become accustomed to.

Caroline's cheeks flushed under his compliment and his gaze. Despite her resolve to remain cool, and despite her conviction that his words were automatic, the well-practiced flattery of a jaded seducer, his charm, and his magnetism exerted an almost irresistible pull. He was so at ease with his sexuality, so confident of his attractiveness. As she watched him extract the cork from a bottle of white wine, she pushed down her own automatic responses to him and concentrated on the sense of unreality she felt about even being here with him. This was the dinner that she had been sure would never happen. She had never imagined that she'd be in New York when he'd first invited her, when he'd demanded that her debt of gratitude be paid. But now here she was, alone with him in his Soho loft—just the two of them, young and healthy and attractive, male and female, with a distinct, almost palpable, erotic *buzz* crackling in the space between them. Caroline did her best not to notice.

"Will you really be able to cook us dinner in *that?*" she asked, motioning to the decrepit stove as he inserted the corkscrew into the cork.

Jean-Claude nodded. "Believe it or not, I've cooked in spaces smaller and not as well equipped. And *older!*" he said in his French accent, as he handed her a glass of wine, a Sancerre, crisp and pleasantly chilled.

"Really? That seems hard to believe," Caroline said,

accepting the glass. "*I* certainly couldn't do much in this kitchen, but then I'm not much of a cook. Jack and I would starve except for frozen food and the microwave."

Jean-Claude made a face and groaned.

"Microwaves," he sneered. "All I can say is that you're very lucky that I've taken pity on you and invited you for a *real* meal."

"So, tell me, what are you preparing for this poor, badly fed American tonight?"

"*Canard braisé au vin rouge,* madame," he said, bowing as if he were the maître d' in an impossibly luxurious restaurant. "Duck. Braised in a red wine sauce."

Caroline sighed, contemplating the delicious treat awaiting her.

"I think I've just died and gone to heaven," she said, collapsing into one of the canvas director's chairs at the rustic pine table near the kitchen and inhaling the scent of the red wine, thyme, and onions in which the duck was cooking. "This is such a luxury for me," she said and then, not wanting to give him any opening, added, "To be cooked for, I mean."

She leaned back in the chair, sipping her wine as Jean-Claude moved toward the stereo and inserted a CD of some of Mozart's late quartets. When he had issued the invitation, he had made Caroline promise to let him do all the work, and exhausted from her hectic day, she was having little trouble obliging. He had set the table with white pottery dishes and bubbled glasses, handmade, he said, near Moustiers. There were candles and a small flask containing red and purple anemones. Crisp linen napkins were folded at each place. Cissy, thought Caroline, would be impressed.

Jean-Claude stood at the small butcher-block counter, and Caroline watched as he peeled the first fresh asparagus of the season and set them on the stove to steam. He was an extraordinarily handsome man, and Caroline was still finding it hard to believe that she was here with him in his loft. Only that morning at Cissy's she had seen a photograph of him in the *New York Post* attending a movie premiere with film actress Regina Quinn. And the day before, there had been a Liz Smith column item about his dates with glamorous advertising executive Marilee Sterling. She was Caroline Shaw, she reminded herself, someone who'd grown up on the wrong side of the tracks, not someone who ran in the fast lane. So why was she here? What did Jean-Claude Fontaine see in her? Another conquest? Another notch on his belt? Or was he simply being a dutiful son and doing his father's friend a favor?

"So how was your day in New York?" he asked, interrupting her musings. "I can tell you that mine was a nightmare. The pastry chef threatened to quit!"

"Why? Did you insist that he put sun-dried tomatoes into the apple tart?" Caroline teased.

"Not into the apple tart!" he said, feigning horror. "Into the *crème caramel!*"

They laughed together for a moment, sharing the joke.

"My day wasn't a nightmare. But it was long. And tiring," she said, watching him squeeze a lemon and whisk its juice into a deep green olive oil, adding some finely chopped tender shoots of chive and then pouring the lemony emulsion over the asparagus. In his black polo shirt, open at the throat, and the tight-fitting jeans that cupped his butt and outlined his long legs, he was larger than life. No wonder women lined up. No wonder he had caused such a sensation when he had appeared at Romance, Inc. As her contemplation of his sensuality and attractiveness edged into an area that made her uncomfortable, she looked down into her wine and ordered her brain to shift into a more proper, more familiar conversational focus. Instead of allowing herself a fantasy or two about him, she retreated to the safety of her business and told Jean-Claude about her day. "I've been in and out of showrooms looking for special items for my store. It's hard enough to find really beautiful and unusual things without fighting New York traffic—"

"*And* New York manners," he added, finishing her sentence for her. "It sounds to me like you've certainly earned a good dinner." He opened the oven door to check on the braising duck. "Here, taste," he commanded, holding a wooden spoon with some of the fragrant, slightly reduced sauce to her lips. She tasted it carefully but said nothing.

"Well?" he demanded, crossing his arms over his chest and waiting for the compliment he knew was coming.

She rolled the sample of sauce around on her tongue and swallowed thoughtfully as he preened, sure that she was groping for words to describe the wondrous flavors she had just experienced.

"It's sort of tasteless." She finally shrugged.

"Tasteless?! My *canard braisé au vin rouge?!"* Jean-Claude exploded in disbelief. He immediately took the spoon and lifted it to his own lips, carefully analyzing the red wine sauce. *"C'est exquis!"* he exclaimed. "Why would you—" Then he did a double take and realized that he'd been had. "Very funny, Caroline," he chastised. "Very funny."

"I couldn't resist," she admitted, perfectly aware that he wasn't accustomed to having his creations criticized. "Am I forgiven?"

He paused for a moment, needling her as she had needled him.

"Only if you tell me what you *really* think," he bargained, offering her another spoonful.

"Sheer bliss," she replied with a smile, the concentrated, intense flavors of wine and herbs mingled with poultry juices still on her tongue. "No, on second thought, it's better than sheer bliss. It's sublime."

"Su-bleem," he corrected, instructing her in his language and giving the word its French pronunciation. He bent over again to reclose the twisted wire that held the oven door shut. The duck, he judged, needed to cook for just a few more moments. He placed the platter with the asparagus on the small table along with a basket containing a slim, crusty, golden-brown *baguette* wrapped in a linen napkin, and indicated to Caroline that it was time for them to have their first course. As she sat down, he lit the tapered ivory candles, poured them each another glass of wine, and, taking the chair opposite hers, opened his napkin.

"To our first evening together," said Jean-Claude, raising his wineglass in a toast.

"Our first?" she asked, raising an eyebrow.

"One of many, I hope," he replied, touching his glass to

hers and letting his fingers graze hers for just a moment longer than necessary.

He was really too much, she thought. An outrageous flatterer with one phony line after another.

They sipped the wine, and then Jean-Claude served the first course, placing some of the asparagus on Caroline's plate, an equal amount on his own. "Beautiful food for a beautiful woman," he said.

Caroline smiled. She couldn't help but be pleased by the compliment, even though she didn't delude herself that she was the only one to whom Jean-Claude had said those words.

"Thank you," she said, taking a bite of her asparagus, savoring the fresh lemony taste of the tangy sauce against the grassy flavor of the vegetable. "This is delicious. *Sublеem.*"

He nodded, silently accepting the compliment. For an instant, their eyes met and held. His emerald and rimmed with long, dark lashes; hers hazel, an intriguing mélange of green and brown, the lashes the color of rich tawny sable.

"Perhaps you'll show me how to make it," she said.

"Ah, *chérie,*" he murmured in his sexy accent. "There's a lot I'd like to show you, but how to prepare asparagus isn't exactly the kind of instruction I had in mind."

Caroline smiled.

"You really are outrageous, Jean-Claude, do you know that?" she said.

"Outrageous?" He managed to look offended. "When all I do is speak the truth?"

The man was incorrigible! At a loss for words, Caroline simply shook her head, amazed by his willingness to say everything and anything that might win her over. For the first time since the evening had begun, she couldn't think of a swift comeback. Perhaps, she thought, the wine was beginning to relax her. Besides, it wasn't so bad to be cooked for, not so terrible to hear lavish compliments, not so dreadful to indulge in a bit of teasing badinage. Perhaps it was time to allow herself to enjoy the evening—and the handsome, charming Frenchman sitting across the table from her.

"Everywhere I go in New York people are talking about Moustiers," she said. "Tell me what you do to make it so successful. I know about retailing but almost nothing about restaurants."

"It's not nearly as glamorous as it looks," he said. "In fact, it's very hard work and long hours. I took tonight off to cook for you, *chérie,* but normally, weeknights are all work and no play."

"*No* play?" she scoffed. "What about Regina and Merilee?"

"All right. A *little* play," he admitted, pleased that she had read about him. "But the truth is, I'm often up at five to oversee the fish and meat deliveries, to check that the laundry is delivered, to assure that the flowers have arrived, and that the vegetables are of the very best quality. I have to make sure that my cooks are following my recipes exactly as I created them, to see to it that my clients are given the reservations they desire, to prepare special items for my regulars, to choose the appropriate wines and liqueurs to accompany the food. And then there are consultations with my editor, who is urging me to write another cookbook. And phone calls with the accountant, the agent, my purveyors and suppliers. . . . Well, I think you 'get the picture,' as you Americans say."

"I never realized that you worked so hard," said Caroline, impressed by the myriad of details a restaurateur like Jean-Claude had to attend to—details not unlike those she had to resolve at Romance, Inc. It occurred to her for the first time that she and Jean-Claude Fontaine might have more in common than she wanted to imagine.

"Of course you didn't. You have made up your mind that all I do is escort famous women to movie premieres."

She laughed. "You do find time for that, don't you?"

"There's always time for love," he said. "We French aren't ashamed of our desires, *chérie.*"

She realized he thought her a prude—uptight and strait-laced, someone who would rather die that admit her desires. She tried not to be insulted, but deep down, she had to wonder if, perhaps, she was a bit of a puritan.

"I envy your attitude. Every time I try to imagine myself

falling in love again, I—Well, I just don't want to take another chance," she said. "I know this may sound ridiculous, but sometimes I wonder if I might be bad luck for any man foolish enough to get involved with me."

"Bad luck? Why would you think that?" asked Jean-Claude, looking amazed. The notion seemed preposterous.

"Because James fell in love with me, and within a year he was dead," she said, her eyes filling the way they still did whenever James's name came up.

"Your husband died in an accident," said Jean-Claude, who had heard the tragic story from his father. "You didn't cause it. It just happened. Life is full of surprises. Some are welcome, others aren't." He paused. "This, for example. This is definitely welcome."

"This?" Caroline asked.

"You. Us. Our dinner. It's very welcome," he said, spelling out his thought. "I'm enjoying every moment."

Caroline met Jean-Claude's eyes. She realized that she was enjoying herself, too, something she hadn't done in a long, long time. She had devoted her life to Jack and Romance, Inc.. There had been no time, no energy left over for pleasure. But now, she felt wonderful—feminine and lighthearted and desirable—being in the company of a man again, a young, handsome, charismatic man who was attracted to her or was very, very good at making her think he was.

"So am I," she replied, almost shyly, feeling a sudden heat surge to her cheeks.

"I'm glad. Very glad," he said, and then, eager to dazzle her with his culinary expertise, he pushed his chair away from the table, carried the empty dishes to the sink, and returned a few minutes later with a blue-and-white platter on which he had arranged the duck in the red wine sauce and added some pitted black olives. Small roasted potatoes sprinkled with finely minced parsley surrounded the platter. A cool, lightly dressed salad of crisp, pale green and white frisée arrived next, a perfect, slightly bitter accompaniment. As he served each dish and opened a bottle of Crozes-Hermitages, a deeply flavored yet slightly flinty red from the Côtes du Rhône that he had especially chosen to go with the main course, Caroline could not help but notice the grace with which he moved, the confidence he radiated, the sensuality he exuded with every smile, every gesture. Wanting suddenly to know more about him, to know what he was like *inside,* she asked him if he ever missed living in France.

"Of course," he said. "My roots are there. And to be honest, New York is so superficial."

Caroline laughed. "Palm Beach is provincial and New York is superficial. Is there a place you *like?"*

He laughed, too.

"I don't mean I don't like New York," he explained. "It's just that the people in New York can be very shallow."

"Why do you say that?" she asked, thinking that the few New Yorkers she'd met hadn't seemed shallow at all.

"I often feel I'm being used. It's not a nice feeling, and it doesn't have anything to do with the man I really am," he replied, as she tasted the succulent dark flesh of the duck and the rich sauce in which it had braised.

"And what kind of man is that?"

"A man with strong feelings and traditional values," he said.

Caroline eyed him. "So you're a terrific cook, a notorious womanizer—and a traditional man?" she asked laughing, amazed at the miraculous food that had emerged from the bare-bones kitchen and surprised that such a Continental, sophisticated man would proclaim such down-to-earth values.

"A terrific cook, *bien sûr,* I admit. But a few affairs don't add up to a 'notorious womanizer,'" he corrected her. "And yes, in some ways, the ways that I think really matter, I *am* a traditional man. I want to have roots. I want to belong to someone. I want someone to belong to me. It's the way I grew up. And, in that way, I haven't changed."

"Which means that you're like your father?" asked Caroline, sipping the red wine. A thought of Pierre and Chantal, who had spent a long, happy lifetime together, flashed through her mind. Was that the kind of relationship Jean-Claude had in mind? The one he had seen as he was growing up?

"Very much," replied Jean-Claude.

She smiled at him over her wineglass.

"I apologize if I've misjudged you," she said, still unsure whether she had.

"I accept your apology," he said. "The more time you spend with me, the more you'll see that I'm not the big bad wolf."

"Well, maybe just a wolf."

"Look, Caroline, what if I said that for as long as Papa has been telling me about you, I've wondered about you, wondered about the beautiful young widow who bears the weight of the world on her shoulders. Papa said you never go out, never see men since your husband died. The idea saddened me, *chérie.* Really. So when we finally did meet, I thought, maybe I can bring her back to life. Maybe I can bring her some pleasure." He lingered on the word.

Caroline felt her inhibitions melting under the influence of the wine and the man who sat across from her.

"You see, I want more from you than just a mere flirtation," he said simply. "But then, you feel the same, don't you, Caroline? Haven't you been just as eager to be alone with me as I have been with you?"

She stared into his green eyes and nearly let herself be seduced by them, by the meal and the Mozart and the man himself. He was such a flatterer, such a charmer, that she had no idea of whether or not he was being serious or simply handing her just another line. Still, something in his tone caused her to take him at face value.

"I don't know," she said hesitantly, unwilling to talk to him about her feelings. "But, even if I have, what's the point? You live in New York. I live in Palm Beach. You have a demanding business and a very active social life. I have my own business to run and a child on whom I think the sun rises and sets. I don't see how we could even think of a 'flirtation,' much less anything more—"

"So you admit you have thought about me, too? About us being together?"

"Of course, I have. You're a very attractive man," Caroline admitted, finally meeting his gaze.

They sat silently, their words hanging in the air, which was now filled with tension—emotional and sexual. When the music on the CD ended, Jean-Claude removed their dishes and brought out a bowl of ethereally light passion fruit mousse with thin, crisp lemon cookies and tiny, handmade chocolate truffles that had been rolled in powdered cocoa, along with tiny cups of dark and rich espresso.

They ate and drank silently, each too distracted by their mutual desire to focus on the meal any longer. Jean-Claude wanted Caroline, there wasn't a doubt in his mind or his body, but he understood that Caroline was conflicted over the possibility of their deepening relationship—and even over the fact that she was as drawn to him as he was to her.

Finally, her conflict overwhelmed her.

"It's late and I really should go," she said, pushing her chair away from the table.

"Please, don't. Not yet," he implored, glancing across the loft at the sumptuous bed in plain view from the dining table.

Caroline was acutely aware of the bed, so near and so beckoning; of the magnetic, sensual man gazing at her with longing; of the desire that burned in his eyes; of the fact that it had been nearly six years since she had felt a man beside her. Inside her.

"No, I should go. It would be better for both of us," she said.

"Not for me. It wouldn't be better for me," he reiterated.

He reached out and touched her face. As his fingertips made contact with her cheek, she felt an almost electric charge course through her flesh—an electric charge she had forgotten she was capable of feeling, one that she had imagined she could never and would never experience again. Helpless to stop herself, she reached up and gently took his hand from her face and entwined her fingers through his.

"I don't know how I feel about this," she admitted, as their fingers continued to weave in and out of each other's grasp. "For so long I've told myself that my life will consist of Jack and Romance, Inc. Nothing and no one else."

"Then listen to me," he said. "I *need* to see you again, Caroline. To *be* with you."

She watched their hands, making magic of their own with their continuous touching, and reluctantly slipped hers out of his.

"I'm not ready," she whispered in a suddenly choked voice.

As she backed away, Jean-Claude stepped toward her and reached out once again to touch her face. Then he stroked her hair and moved his hand down her back. She turned her head involuntarily, exposing the nakedness of her neck, anticipated that he would bend to caress it, and allowed him to.

"Jean-Claude," she murmured.

"Très, très belle," he said, his voice husky with desire, holding aside her silky chestnut hair with his hand and kissing the delicate skin on the nape of her neck.

"We shouldn't—" She could feel his masculinity against her, hard and insistent.

"You're so beautiful," he went on, ignoring her mild protests, luxuriating in the feel of his lips on her skin.

Caroline *felt* beautiful, for the first time in a long time. But she feared venturing into a situation she could not handle. Jean-Claude Fontaine was difficult to resist, but he lived and worked miles away from Palm Beach. What's more, he was already a star and, she just knew, poised for further celebrity. Besides, he had a well-documented reputation of going through women as if they were selections on a menu. First the Broadway actress, then the advertising superstar, and on and on the list continued. Would she be just another notch on his belt? Did he really care for her? Could she get involved with him now? Could she? It would be complicated. It would force her to confront her feelings, to deal with a part of herself she had shut away for so long. She was acutely aware of how vulnerable she was and of how agonizing any disappointment would be.

No, she realized with a jolt. No! Now wasn't the time. She had told him the truth: she wasn't ready. She wanted to stay in the cocoon she had constructed for herself. She wanted to be safe, not to reveal herself, not to open herself to a potential letdown. Despite what Cissy had said, James was still the only man in the world for her, the only man she would make love to, the only man she could ever love.

She pulled away from Jean-Claude and announced once again that she was leaving. And this time, he made no move to stop her.

He helped her on with her coat and escorted her out of the building and down to the street, where he flagged a passing taxi. He took Caroline's hand in both of his and, raising it to his lips, kissed it gently.

"One day," he said simply, holding her eyes with his, the meaning of his words clear to both of them.

Then he opened the door of the taxi, helped Caroline inside, and watched as she drove away into the night.

~22~

The evening with Jean-Claude continued to bring back memories of Caroline's early days with James, and she spent most of the night tossing and turning and trying to make sense of her emotions. Cissy's comments, at first hurtful, began to make more and more sense as Caroline had time to contemplate them. Cissy was right: Six years was a long time to mourn. Too long? She was still in her twenties, by any standards, still a young woman. Had she tied herself to a past and created fantasies that reality could not hope to match? Had she constructed an image of James and the bliss they had shared that was so unrealistic that no mortal man could begin to compete with it? Had she built their love into something too idealized, too perfect? After all, what did she really know about men, about relationships with them? She had been isolated and unpopular as a teenager. She had never been invited to parties; never attended a prom; never been kissed in the backseat of a car.

In fact, she had never gone out on a single date in high school. James Goddard was the first and only man who had ever even looked at her. She had, she realized, no other experience against which to compare her brief marriage to an extremely romantic man.

On top of that, her feelings about the Frenchman were utterly conflicted and she felt tied in emotional knots. She was unsure of herself and the way she had behaved. She realized that she had no idea of how a grown woman should act with a man—particularly a man she was attracted to. Had she done the right thing by allowing Jean-Claude to caress her? Or had she unfairly led him on? Had she exercised good judgment by leaving the loft over his protestations? Or should she have stayed? Was she better off keeping her distance? Or was it time she got involved with a man? They were obviously very drawn to each other. But was she ready for a relationship? With him? With a man who lived in another city. A man with a jet-set lifestyle and an overflowing little black book.

The questions gnawed at her, and it wasn't until three o'clock in the morning that she finally fell into a fitful sleep. She would have slept until noon if Cissy's maid hadn't awakened her with a knock on the door.

"There's a phone call for you, Mrs. Goddard," said Colleen O'Malley, Cissy's longtime housekeeper, after tapping lightly on the door of the guest room and opening it just a crack.

"For me?" Caroline asked groggily. This was her last day in Manhattan, and even though there was a lot she wanted to accomplish, she had hoped to luxuriate in bed for a bit longer.

"Yes, a gentleman," said Mrs. O'Malley.

A gentleman, Caroline thought, assuming it was Jean-Claude and that he wanted to talk to her and discuss what had happened between them.

"Would you tell him I'm not available right now?" Caroline asked, wanting to avoid or at least postpone having to confront her feelings. She would need time to sort out how she felt about Jean-Claude and how she wanted their relationship to proceed.

Mrs. O'Malley opened the door wider. "He sounded as if he was in a big hurry," she said in her thick Irish brogue. "He didn't so much *ask* to speak to you as *demand* it."

"Did he have a French accent?" Caroline asked.

"No, ma'am," said Mrs. O'Malley, shaking her head.

Caroline raised an eyebrow and pulled herself out of bed, then draped a robe around her and padded into Cissy's living room, where a phone rested on a coffee table.

"Hello?" she asked tentatively.

"It's Clifford."

"Clifford," she said. He had called her several times since they'd first met in Palm Beach, and when she'd told him about her planned trip to New York, he'd suggested they meet for a drink while she was in town. But each time she'd agreed to a time and place, she'd been so plagued with suspicion toward him that she'd called his secretary and canceled their dates. But now here he was on the phone on her last morning in the city.

"I'd like to see you later. Say around six o'clock," he said, his tone determined, as always. Clifford Hamlin, Caroline knew, rarely—if ever—took "no" for an answer. At least, not for long. What she also knew was that his powerful, take-charge manner impressed and excited her, even as it intimidated her.

"I'm afraid it's my last day in New York, and I've got a killer schedule," she said, conflicted about seeing him again.

"I understand killer schedules," he said with a hint of irony as he scanned his crammed appointment book. "As a matter of fact, I've got a dinner meeting at seven. But you could meet me at my apartment at six—obviously, it would be awkward for you to come to the office. Something's come up that we need to discuss."

"Something you can't tell me now?" Caroline asked warily.

"Something I want to discuss with you in person," he said. "What I have to tell you is very important to your future—and Jack's. As well as that of Romance, Inc."

Caroline had to admit that a part of her wanted to see

him again. He was intense, driven, and so brilliant—attractive in a completely different way than Jean-Claude. Clifford challenged her, intrigued her, even as she wondered about his motives. And now, he said he had something to tell her, something important to her future and that of her business, something that might impact on her ability to support herself and her son.

She glanced at the clock in Cissy's living room and calculated how to fit everything into her last day in New York. Later that morning she had a meeting with the fragrance people and, before that, a conference with a manufacturer of imported silk flowers. In addition, she wanted to visit the Fifty-seventh Street branch of Victoria's Secret, as well as a few other boutiques, to look for ideas for Romance, Inc. Then there was the cocktail party Cissy had mentioned.

"Where is your apartment?" she said finally.

"I'm at 1040 Fifth Avenue," said Clifford, brightening at the thought of seeing her again, pleased that he had *convinced* her to see him again. "It's across the street from the Metropolitan Museum."

"Fine. See you at six," she said, and hung up the phone.

She yawned and stretched as Mrs. O'Malley entered the room and offered her some breakfast.

"Just some coffee, please," she told Cissy's housekeeper, already swinging into the rushed Manhattan rhythm as she headed toward the shower. "I've got a busy day ahead of me, and it just got busier."

The meeting over a wholesale florist's showroom on Sixth Avenue and Twenty-sixth Street resulted in an agreement for Romance, Inc. to carry silk flowers themed to seasonal color schemes. It had been conducted at a Formica table over coffee and bagels and was strictly business, dollars and cents, delivery dates and dye lots. The encounter at the West Fifty-seventh Street fragrance house, on the other hand, was more like fun than business. Caroline met with the company's executives and sniffed and smelled her way through dozens of delightful scents, all with the intention of selecting a Romance, Inc. toilet water—a signature fragrance that would embody the shop's philosophy of romance, sensuality, and adventure.

"They're delightful, but I'm so confused!" Caroline exclaimed after sniffing eight different fragrances, looking at over a dozen sizes and shapes of bottles and flacons and examining what seemed like hundreds of varied label designs. "I simply can't choose. They're all beginning to smell the same."

"People can only really appreciate three scents at a time," said Patricia Kent, the company's vice president of marketing. "After that, our sense of smell goes on overload. I'll tell you what—I'll have samples of your favorites prepared for you. Then you'll take them back to Palm Beach and live with them for a while. Think about them, try them out on your clients and your friends. See how they react. Take your time. It's an important decision." Before the meeting ended, Patricia filled Caroline's canvas tote bag with scores of glass vials filled with toilet water samples. Lavender and lily of the valley, jasmine and carnation, rose and violet. Caroline couldn't wait to try them all.

At precisely six o'clock, Caroline entered Clifford Hamlin's opulent, old-world Fifth Avenue building. The marble floor of the lobby was covered with rich Oriental rugs, and antique chairs upholstered with needlepoint tapestry were arranged invitingly. The space was softly illuminated by heavy crystal chandeliers and gleaming polished sconces. Uniformed attendants guarded their preserve, attentive, protective, intimidating. Caroline surveyed her surroundings, and for a moment, she felt as if she were a fifteen-year-old girl again, tiptoeing around The Breakers, hoping she wouldn't be grabbed by the arm and hauled away as an intruder. She quickly admonished herself and remembered that she was no longer fifteen, no longer young and inexperienced, no longer afraid of the wealthy and privileged. Still, as a concierge in a tailcoat strode up to her and asked her whom she had come to see, she felt twinges of her old insecurities and found her palms becoming just a bit clammy.

"Caroline Goddard," she told him. "I have an appointment with Mr. Hamlin. He's expecting me."

The man picked up a telephone and spoke into it briefly. Then he nodded at Caroline.

"Mr. Hamlin is waiting for you, Mrs. Goddard," he said respectfully, leading Caroline along the wide, hushed passage to the paneled and chandeliered elevator. The uniformed elevator man then took her up to the penthouse floor.

"Mr. Hamlin's apartment is to your left," he said when they'd arrived at the top floor of the luxurious building that was home to business tycoons, media moguls, and international royalty.

Caroline nodded her thanks to the elevator operator, who needn't have bothered to provide her with directions: Clifford's apartment was the only one on the entire floor!

Caroline was about to ring the bell next to the gold-lettered #14A, when an Oriental houseman opened the door, nodded, showed her inside, and motioned for her to remain in the formally decorated foyer. It was a large skylit rectangle on whose walls hung a large abstract painting. A long, Japanese-looking polished wood credenza held a massive porcelain vase filled with branches of pink quince.

"Mr. Hamlin will be with you shortly," he said, his speech clipped, the accent British, his stare impassive and impenetrable.

She checked her watch—it was 6:05. Just then Clifford appeared. He was dressed in a dark, perfectly cut suit and wore a discreetly figured silk tie, fastidiously knotted.

"Caroline, so glad you could come," he said warmly, moving toward her and shaking her hand. She was even lovelier than he had remembered—an appealing combination of smartly dressed businesswoman and fresh, All-American beauty. Was he more than simply attracted to her? he wondered. Was the fact that he thought about her, tried to imagine her life with James Goddard, pictured her by his side, fantasized about her in bed, an indication that he was falling in love with her? A woman he'd met only once?

"You said you had something important to discuss with

me," she said. "Something that had to be discussed in person."

"Yes," he said, and motioned for her to follow him down a hallway to his ultramodern yet surprisingly comfortable office. She sat in a leather chair and waited for Clifford to speak.

"Something to drink?" he offered as he took his place behind his desk. A tray of tea and coffee rested on the low table next to her chair.

Caroline shook her head. "No, thanks. I'm fine. You have a spectacular apartment," she said as she surveyed the paintings on his wall. They were abstract, quirky, yet full of wit.

"If you're talking about the paintings, they're by Paul Klee, a Swiss painter of the early twentieth century," he told her, seeing the curiosity in her eyes and responding to it.

"They're intriguing. So is the rest of your office. Did you decorate it yourself?" she asked, admiring the rich leather chairs, the rosewood desk, the floor-to-ceiling bookcases, and the glimpse of the beautifully landscaped terrace just outside. The loft where Jean-Claude had entertained her was homey and casual, filled with the sound of music and the smell of cooking; Clifford Hamlin's residence was spare, immaculate, luxurious, tranquil.

"Yes and no," he said. "I used a decorator and then vetoed everything he wanted to buy for the apartment. I guess you could say I was a hands-on client."

Caroline had no doubt of it. She guessed that Clifford Hamlin was on top and in control of everything he touched.

Such a puzzling man, she thought as she regarded him. He was dashing, smooth, sophisticated in a hand-tailored Saville Row suit, so rangy and taut and full of pent-up energy. He seemed in charge of every moment, so cool, so determined. He intrigued her and he intimidated her—and, despite her continued wariness of him, he excited her.

He began their meeting by asking her about her latest attempts to secure a loan for Romance, Inc.

"Still no takers," she said and was about to be more specific when the black, four-line phone on his desk rang.

"Excuse me a minute," Clifford said and took the call.

Caroline watched him as he talked to someone named Peter about the risks and rewards of commodities trading, then hung up and returned his attention to her. "You were saying?"

"I was about to say that the banks haven't been at all receptive to the idea of a second store," she replied, taking up her thought again. "As a matter of fact, I—"

She was interrupted once more by the ringing of the phone.

"Excuse me. I'll just be a minute," said Clifford, picking up the receiver, then conversing with someone who was either an accountant or a lawyer about a client's tax problem. "Sorry," he said after ending the call. "You were saying that the banks haven't been much help."

"Yes, they act as if Romance, Inc. is some sort of a hobby for me, instead of a bona fide—"

She was interrupted again by the ringing of the phone.

"I'll just take this and be right back to you," Clifford said, picking up the receiver. The conversation had to do with the merger of two frozen food companies. "I apologize. Again," he said with a smile as he hung up the phone. "You were telling me about—"

This time it was Caroline who interrupted Clifford. "Look," she said, speaking politely but firmly, "I realize that you're very busy and that you're squeezing me in between your other appointments. But it was *you* who invited *me* here—to discuss something important, something that affected Romance, Inc. You also said you only had an hour." She paused and glanced at her watch. "It's now 6:25. That leaves us just thirty-five minutes."

Clifford Hamlin laughed, and the act warmed his stark, almost birdlike features. The lines crinkled around his observant gray eyes, and his lips parted to reveal extremely white, even teeth. He really is quite attractive, Caroline thought as she assessed him, then reminded herself that he was managing director of Goddard-Stevens. A man who owed his livelihood to Charles Goddard, her sworn enemy. A man she wasn't sure she could trust.

"Tell you what," he said, moving toward his answering machine and flipping it to the On position. "I'm going to let the next thirty-five minutes' worth of callers fend for themselves."

"I'm flattered," Caroline said wryly, returning his smile. "*Now,* would you like to hear about my adventures with the banks?"

"Very much," he replied, his expression reflecting the pleasure her presence was bringing him.

Caroline gave Clifford a full report of the banks she'd consulted and the responses they'd given her. She also confided that, despite her positive meetings in New York regarding private-label merchandise, she was beginning to lose hope of ever expanding her business beyond the one store.

"Nonsense," Clifford scoffed. "As we discussed down in Florida, you've got to expand before someone steals your idea."

"That's just it—someone already has," Caroline said. "A local reporter friend of mine named Roz Garelick told me there's a woman in Coral Gables who's talking about opening a store very similar to Romance, Inc."

"All the more reason to move ahead with your expansion plans," said Clifford. "It sounds to me as if it's time for you to consult an attorney to trademark your retailing concept."

"Trademark?" Caroline asked.

"Either trademark or register, your lawyer will know which," he said. "Furthermore, it's clear that those spreadsheets of yours, while impressive, just aren't enough. You need a long-range business plan that will offer financial projections as well as your objectives and goals. The problem, as I see it, is that you can't open one more store and leave it at that. You've either got to stick with the one you've already got and hope that the competition isn't very effective, or else open *several* more Romance, Inc. stores. It's one or the other—stay small or expand."

Several more? A *chain* of Romance, Inc. stores across the country? Of course, she'd thought of it. Dreamed of it. Fantasized about it. But first things first; so far, she hadn't even been able to convince a bank to finance a second store.

"Frankly, I'm confused about how to proceed," she

admitted as she sat back in her chair and sighed. Clifford obviously knew what he was talking about, and she'd be a fool not to take advantage of his experience and expertise. "I don't know the first thing about creating a business plan. And I don't know any lawyers who handle trademarks."

"If you like, I'll recommend a lawyer and I'll also volunteer to do your business plan," said Clifford as matter-of-factly as if he'd just volunteered to fetch Caroline a glass of water.

"Why would you do that?" she asked, once again wary of his offer to help her. Was she an assignment that Charles Goddard had given his managing director? Was Clifford Hamlin a friend? Or a spy? Was she putting herself—and Jack—in danger by even being in his presence? He was an incredibly busy man, she knew. The phone had rung several more times since he'd decided to let his answering machine screen his calls, one of which had been from Hong Kong. He was an international financier with multimillion-dollar portfolios to manage. Why the interest in Romance, Inc.? In her?

"Because I want you to succeed," he replied, then went on as if she hadn't asked the question. "How many stores do you envision ultimately? Six? Eight? A dozen?"

Caroline's jaw dropped. He was going too fast for her. "Shouldn't we concentrate on getting the financing for a second store? Isn't that my first priority?"

"The second store shouldn't be much of a problem any longer," he said, a bit mysteriously.

"No? And why is that?" she asked, realizing that he was probably referring to the "something important."

Wordlessly, he reached into his attaché case that rested next to his chair and handed Caroline a manila envelope that bore the name and address of Goddard-Stevens in the top left-hand corner. Her own name was handprinted on the front. She looked at him, unsure of what he wanted her to do.

"Go on, open it," he urged.

Mystified, Caroline examined the envelope again, then opened it slowly. It contained several sheets of paper stapled together. On the paper were columns of numbers. When she read them and the heading on top, their significance nearly sent her into shock.

"Mine?" she asked, slightly incoherent, still holding the papers.

"That's right, yours. It's an investment account that's been set up in your name," said Clifford, studying the bewildered expression on her lovely features. "I discovered the account's existence just this morning. It's one of the reasons I insisted we meet." The other reason, Clifford Hamlin neglected to add, was that he didn't relish the thought that Caroline Goddard would be leaving Manhattan and he wouldn't have seen her again.

Caroline continued to stare at the contents of the envelope, to try to fathom what it signified, how it would impact on her life, hers and Jack's. "It's a list of stocks and bonds totaling two hundred thousand dollars," she managed finally. "In the name of Caroline Shaw. Where on earth did it come from?"

Her first thought seemed unreal, totally impossible. Had the Goddards somehow had a change of heart over the years and decided to give her money? After the way they had treated her? After the way they had ignored her attempts to inform them of Jack's birth? It simply did not seem credible. But who else did she know who had that kind of money?

"It came from your husband," Clifford began, not wanting to prolong Caroline's confusion any longer. "He set up an account for you at the firm before you were married and continued to make deposits after your marriage. He put in some money of his own and added to it checks you had given him to repay a loan of some sort."

Caroline's hand flew to her mouth as she realized the significance of what Clifford was telling her.

"My commission checks!" she exclaimed, suddenly remembering that she had given James whatever money she had made, first from L'Elegance, then from The State of Maine. He had always protested when she'd insisted on repaying him for the dress he'd bought her at Celeste's, the dress that had provoked Tamara Brandt into rehiring her.

But now Clifford Hamlin was saying that James had put the money—her money—into an investment account. At Goddard-Stevens. In her name!

"Your husband specified that the money be invested aggressively," Clifford said. "As a result, thanks to several high-performance stocks, you've done very nicely indeed."

"But he never told me! He never said a word!" said Caroline. "And the Goddards certainly never said anything."

"Your husband probably wanted to surprise you with it. And I would imagine that Charles Goddard didn't even know the account existed," said Clifford.

"Small potatoes, I guess," she said.

He smiled.

"But how did you find out about it?" she asked, still feeling a bit overwhelmed.

"Sheer coincidence. A month ago I asked the records department to give me a list of dormant accounts. Yours was one that landed on my desk. I remembered your maiden name from Tamara's tales of L'Elegance. So, if you want money to open a second store, there it is," he said, gesturing to the papers in her hands. "All you have to do is tell me, and I'll have a check cut for the full amount."

"I don't know. I'm not sure," said Caroline, still trying to process the information she had just been given. James had set up an account for her. The $200,000 she was holding in her hand was yet another gift from him. Tears welled up in her eyes as she imagined him depositing her commission checks into an account at Goddard-Stevens, wanting to care for her, wanting to provide for her, wanting her to have some money of her very own.

Clifford reached into the jacket of his suit, removed a perfectly folded white linen handkerchief, and handed it to Caroline.

"Would you like anything? Tea? Water? Something stronger?" he asked, looking at her tenderly. He hadn't intended to make her cry, after all. But he understood that the moment was an emotional one for her, and he wanted to reach out to her.

Caroline shook her head. "I'm fine," she said, dabbing at

her eyes with his handkerchief. "It's just that I wasn't expecting—"

"I know you weren't," he said.

"I wasn't expecting *any* of this," she went on. "Nor do I know what to believe when it comes to Charles Goddard and his company."

"What do you mean?" he asked.

She looked intently at Clifford. She could accept the part about his learning of her $200,000 by sheer coincidence. But why hadn't he told Charles about the money? she asked herself. Could she really believe him? Charles was the person to whom he had an allegiance, not her.

"You could have gone straight to Charles when you found out that his son had set up an account for me," she said. "And then the two of you could have figured out a way to bury the account, take the money, whatever. And I would never have been the wiser."

Suddenly, Clifford's expression darkened and his gray eyes blazed. "Is that what you think of me?" he exploded, angry at her for doubting his integrity. "That I would conspire with Charles Goddard to steal money from you? Money that your husband invested on your behalf? Is your hatred of Charles so deep, so old, that you can't see it when someone is trying to help you? Do you honestly think I'm so hungry for approval, so desperate for a pat on the back from my boss, that I would risk my reputation? Is *that* what you think of me?"

"I don't know what to think of you," she said softly, her voice trembling.

She let his words sink in, weighed everything he'd just said. She realized that she might be wrong about Clifford Hamlin. He could have gone to Charles and told him about the money, but he said he didn't. The $200,000 was hers—James's legacy to her. What's more, she had no right to hold Clifford responsible for the cruelty that Charles had inflicted on her, did she?

"I'm sorry," she said finally. "This has all come as quite a shock to me."

"I'm sure it has," he said, softening toward her. "Now, let's talk about how your two hundred thousand dollars will affect your plans for Romance, Inc. Where do you envision the second Romance, Inc. will be located?"

Caroline considered the question, then answered as the decision came instantly to mind. She spoke firmly and deliberately.

"I'm *not* putting the money into a second store. I want this money put aside for Jack. For his future. For college. I don't want him to have the kind of pinchpenny childhood I had. If he wants to go to Harvard or Yale, that's where he'll go. If he wants to be a doctor or a lawyer, then that's what he'll be. And this money will help him do it."

"I understand," Clifford said, seeing for the first time that, given a choice between her son and her business, Caroline Goddard was a mother first, a businesswoman second. And given his own deprived background, he admired her tremendously at that very moment.

"Do you understand?" she said, still tearful. She imagined that Clifford Hamlin, like James, had grown up with a silver spoon and all the things that went with it.

"More than you might imagine," he said, offering her a tantalizing glimpse into a part of him he rarely revealed. "But that still leaves us with the matter of your empire," he said as his phone rang yet again. He met her eyes and made a point of ignoring the telephone, letting his machine take the call instead. "As I said, I'm willing to help you, but I should also point out to you that banks aren't the only route to take. You can also approach private investors. I've been thinking about it, and I have a couple of candidates in mind," he said.

"Really? Who?" said Caroline, her eyes wide with anticipation.

"Well, there's a client of mine named Drew Darlington. He's a—"

"I know exactly who he is," Caroline said excitedly. She had read about Drew Darlington in a recent issue of *Fortune* magazine. The billionaire Englishman was said to be as flamboyant as he was successful. His holdings included a chain of video stores in the United States and Britain, as well as a number of publishing companies.

"As I was saying, Drew's a client of mine—a very smart

guy, by the way. He's got a real entrepreneurial spirit, and he's always looking for interesting and innovative ways to invest his money. I've mentioned Romance, Inc. to him, and he was quite enthusiastic. He said he'd love to meet you."

"You're kidding."

"Not in the slightest."

"Well, *I'd* love to meet him," Caroline said, her excitement building. "Who's the other potential investor? You mentioned that you had a couple of people in mind."

"I do. The other candidate is your old friend Tamara. Or, more accurately, her husband."

"Ferdy? He doesn't even like Tamara to *talk* about retailing, let alone go back to it," Caroline pointed out. "What makes you think he'd invest in Romance, Inc.?"

"First of all, we both know that Tamara is itching to get back in the business. I'm betting that if she told him she really wanted to become a partner in Romance, Inc., he'd have to at least *think* about it."

Caroline shook her head. "She says he's living in the Middle Ages."

"Then it's time we helped her drag him into the twentieth century. The duke has more money than he knows what to do with. Perhaps if we approached him together, we could get him to change his mind about women and business."

"He and Tamara are going back to London in a couple of weeks. April first, I think she said. How are we going to—"

"I say we pay them a visit in London, the duke's home turf," Clifford suggested. "I'm planning a trip to Brussels on the eleventh. Why don't you and I fly to London on the ninth and see if we can't scare up some investors for Romance, Inc.? After we meet with Tamara and Ferdy, I'll take you to meet Drew Darlington. And, come to think of it, you should also meet Felicity Kramer, another London client of mine."

"Felicity Kramer?" said Caroline, her thoughts whirring.

"Felicity is a major success story in her own right. Fifteen years ago she published a gift catalog. Now she owns one of the biggest mail order businesses in Europe. You're starting a private label line of merchandise for Romance, Inc. Why not try and interest Felicity in introducing Romance, Inc. products to customers on the other side of the Atlantic?"

"Yes, but London? Next month? What about Jack? And the store. I can't leave Romance, Inc.—" Caroline said, her thoughts blurring together. Between the surprise of the investment account and the sudden suggestion of the trip abroad, she hadn't quite absorbed all that was happening to her.

"Why not? You're a businesswoman who's trying to expand her business. If it's your son you're worried about, it sounds to me as if your neighbor takes good care of him. And, as for running of your shop, you told me you recently promoted your assistant manager. Isn't she capable of covering for you while you're away?"

"I suppose," said Caroline, whose mind raced with possibilities. She had always yearned to travel to Europe, first with James, of course, on their honeymoon to Paris, then after his death, as an independent woman on a journey to the world's glittering capitals. Could she fly to London and meet with Clifford's important clients? Could she ask Tamara and Ferdy to invest in Romance, Inc.? Would the duke be more receptive to the idea once he was away from the distractions of Palm Beach and back in his own country? Tamara had been annoyed when Caroline hadn't asked her to invest in the first Romance, Inc. shop. And she would certainly welcome the opportunity to get involved with retailing again. Perhaps if the idea were strategically presented—with someone like Clifford Hamlin doing the presenting—the duke might actually go for it, too, Caroline thought. And then a doubt clouded her expression.

"The duke and duchess aren't even clients of yours," she reminded Clifford. "Tamara invests her money with your old company, Osborne and Praeger. Ferdy probably has a European firm to manage his investments. What would you get out of the deal?"

"Normally, I'd get a fee for bringing the parties together, but in this case, I'll waive it," he said. "What I'll really get is satisfaction. Seeing you get a brilliant idea off the ground and making it fly." *And making you happy,* he thought but kept to himself.

"That's extremely generous of you, but you have something else in mind, don't you?" She smiled, knowing that Clifford Hamlin didn't get where he was by flying around the world in search of satisfaction. "You intend to persuade Tamara to move her account to Goddard-Stevens and to reel in the duke along with her."

Clifford Hamlin returned her smile.

"I'd better be careful around you. You can read my mind," he said. "The truth is, I *do* want to help you realize your dreams. I also want Tamara's account—and her husband's. I'm not used to losing, Caroline, and I don't intend to start now."

She regarded the man in front of her once again. As driven as he was, as obsessed with success, he also seemed genuinely eager to help her. Was he on the level? Could he be trusted not to steal her Romance, Inc. concept himself? She wasn't even sure if he had kept his word about Jack. How did she know he hadn't told Charles Goddard about his grandson? She barely knew Clifford Hamlin, and yet he had made time for her, turned over money she hadn't even known was hers, said he would help her with a business proposal, said he would help her find the financing for expansion.

"What do you think?" he prodded. "Does a trip to London sound like a good idea to you?"

"It sounds like a wonderful idea, but—" A thousand worries skittered through Caroline's mind. Anxieties about Jack, about the store, about money. . . .

"No 'buts,'" he silenced her. "I'll have my secretary arrange everything." He checked his watch and stood quickly. Caroline's audience with him had come to a close. "Now, don't bring up the subject with the duke and duchess when you see them in Palm Beach," he advised. "I think it's better if we confront them together in London."

Caroline nodded in agreement.

"My job will be to put together your business plan, based on figures you'll provide me with over the next week or so," he continued as he opened his attaché case and took out some papers for his seven o'clock dinner. He scanned them quickly, then looked up at her. "Your job will be to think about where you'd like your second store to be located."

She stood and faced him. "I already know where I want it to be located, because I've been dreaming about it for years," she said resolutely. "The second store will be in Palm Beach. On Worth Avenue."

To celebrate Caroline's last night in New York, Cissy made a reservation at the Four Seasons. As they dined at a poolside table, hovered over by attentive waiters, Cissy told Caroline about the cocktail party she had missed, and Caroline recounted her meeting with Clifford.

"He sounds like someone *I'd* run off to London with," Cissy said dryly, sipping a gin and tonic. "Handsome, sophisticated *and* the bearer of a two-hundred-thousand-dollar surprise."

"Oh, stop," Caroline scolded her friend. "He's just my— Well, I guess I'd call him my financial advisor."

"The same way you'd call the Frenchman your platonic pal?" Cissy teased. "Ridiculous. Both men sound divine."

"You're incorrigible," Caroline laughed.

"No, just realistic," said Cissy.

While Caroline was in a cab en route to La Guardia Airport at seven o'clock the next morning, Charles Goddard was in the dining room of his Manhattan apartment, talking on the phone with Ronald Switzer, his personal attorney. Dina Goddard sipped coffee and listened to Charles's end of the conversation.

"There's absolutely no question about it. We want the boy," Charles was telling Switzer, an experienced trial lawyer whose courtroom triumphs ran the gamut from criminal defenses of celebrities to high-profile custody cases. "He's a Goddard. Our grandson. It's only fitting that we raise him in the Goddard mold."

"Tell me about the mother," said Switzer. "Where does she live? What does she do? That kind of thing. . . ."

"She's an absolute nobody, Ronald," Charles said. "Her father's a drunk who's in and out of unemployment offices.

Her mother's a bookkeeper. They rarely see the boy, I'm told. As for the girl herself, she runs a small store in West Palm Beach. The boy is usually left in the care of some woman they knew from Lake Worth named Selma Johannas. As a matter of fact, at this very moment, this woman is babysitting my grandson while his mother is here in New York, cavorting with God knows who."

"All right. So we can claim she's neglectful of the child," Switzer mused, thinking out loud. "And what about her personal life? Are there men in the house on a regular basis?"

Charles shrugged. "I don't know but I would assume so. She's not exactly unattractive."

Assumptions were not enough. Not in court.

"I suggest you contact your PI and tell him to initiate surveillance of the mother and the boy," Switzer said. "Tell him to provide daily reports—whether she's out of town, how often she leaves the boy alone, and, of course, if there's a man on the scene."

"Will do," Charles said, making a note to call Ted Aronson and give him further instructions. Step three was underway: the makings of a custody suit. Charles Goddard intended for the case to go smoothly and, most of all, quickly. He wanted his grandson. And he wanted his grandson now.

The air was balmy for New York in March, which was why Caroline went without a coat and wore only her navy blue gabardine suit as she hurried onto Delta flight 603 bound for Palm Beach. She had stopped at a pay phone near the gate to call Jack before he left for school and was a little late boarding the plane. Consequently, some of the passengers were already in their seats as she stepped onto the Boeing 727 jetliner, glanced into the cockpit to her left, and then walked toward the back of the aircraft. She had nearly made her way through the first-class cabin when, at the very moment the line came to a standstill, a stocky, broad-shouldered man suddenly got up from his plush, leather seat and snapped his fingers at her.

"Hey, sweetheart," he said in a thick southern drawl.

"How about y'all giving this thirsty boy another Bloody Mary, huh?"

Caroline looked around, assuming one of the flight attendants was standing directly behind her and that the man sitting in first class must have been talking to her. But there was no flight attendant standing behind her. Drunk, she thought. At eight A.M.! She averted her eyes and looked straight ahead.

"Hey, what's the matter, sweetie? You're ignoring me. You girls never ignored me before," said the man, staring right at Caroline and shaking his glass, which still had plenty of Bloody Mary in it.

Good God, she thought suddenly, glancing down at her navy blue outfit, so similar to those worn by the Delta flight crew. *He's talking to me! He thinks I'm a stewardess!*

Caroline pitied the poor flight attendants who had to deal with and behave politely to boorish passengers who snapped their fingers at them and called them girls.

"Hey, babe!" the man called out again. Louder this time and clearly indicating Caroline. "I said, how about—"

Caroline cut him off before he went any further. "Look here, I'm a passenger, just like you are. Not a flight attendant," she said curtly, wishing the line of passengers in front of her would move faster so she could escape the first class cabin and take refuge in her lowly coach seat.

"Well, excuuuuse me," he said, grinning rakishly at her and mocking her rather prim scolding of him. "But you looked like a stewardess to me, with those great legs of yours. Great legs, don't you think?" he asked expansively, addressing the other passengers.

Caroline turned scarlet as the people in front and back of her looked on with amusement, some of them even smiling at the man and acting as if they not only approved of his obnoxiousness but thought it funny.

She averted her eyes again and waited for the line to move. But it didn't. Apparently, one of the passengers toward the rear of the plane was complaining that someone was occupying his seat. Consequently, the rest of them couldn't occupy theirs.

"So if you're not a stewardess," said the man, louder than

before, "how about sitting down next to me and having a Bloody Mary with me? What do you say, huh, sweetheart?"

Caroline turned to face the man. He was thirtysomething, she guessed. *Late* thirtysomething. He had sandy hair—dirty blond, she used to call the color as a kid—and a hard, muscular build. His features could best be described as rough around the edges—the nose had been broken more than once, she surmised; the blue eyes had lines etched around them; the skin bore the stubble of a late night and serious partying; and the clothes. God, the clothes! Nothing matched—the red golf slacks clashed with the orange polo shirt, and the socks were another story altogether: olive green! The guy was obviously color blind.

"No, thank you very much," she told him sarcastically, annoyed at the way he kept calling her "sweetheart." Some men really were chauvinist pigs, she thought.

"Aw, come on," he urged, patting the empty seat next to him. "Nobody's sitting here. I bought 'em both so I could stretch out—or invite a foxy-looking chick like you to stretch out with me. Whichever came first."

Caroline was about to tell him to take a long walk off a short pier when he moved toward her, got his foot caught on the strap of his carry-on bag, and lurched, dumping the contents of his glass all over her skirt—the Bloody Mary, the wedge of lime, even the ice cubes!

"Oh, look what you've done!" she snapped, glaring at him. She opened her bag and searched frantically for a tissue to wipe away the mess he had made.

"Jesus, I'm sorry," he said, offering his already soiled cocktail napkin and attempting to clean her skirt with it.

"Stay away from me!" she shouted, backing as far away from him as she could in the crowded cabin, grateful as the line of passengers in front of her finally began to move.

Before the idiot could do or say anything else, she was out of the first-class cabin and on her way back to her seat. Safe at last!

Once the 727 had reached its cruising altitude and the captain had turned off the seat belt sign, Caroline went to the restroom and cleaned up her skirt as best she could.

Then she returned to her seat. When she got there, guess who was sitting there?

"What'd you do, go looking for a Laundromat?" said the walking color wheel. She was surprised he wasn't wearing a purple jacket to round out his ensemble.

"I went to the lavatory to clean up the mess you made," she said. "And I'd appreciate it if you got out of my seat."

He looked up at her and smiled in a way that *he* obviously thought was winning.

"I came back to apologize," he said, not budging.

"I accept," said Caroline, as she stood in the aisle. "Now, why don't you go back to your two nice big comfortable first-class seats?"

"I was kidding about the Laundromat. I wanted to do more than just apologize. I wanted to tell you I'll pay for the skirt to be dry-cleaned," he said, still planted.

"That won't be necessary," Caroline said, looking around for the flight attendant but seeing none.

"Give me your phone number, and I'll—" he said.

Caroline reached over right in front of him and pushed the Call button. Let the stewardess tell this jerk to get out of her seat.

Just then the captain's voice came over the speakers, advising that there was turbulence ahead and asking passengers to return to their seats and fasten their seat belts.

"I'll catch you later, sweetheart," he said, finally relinquishing her seat and then winking at her. When she didn't respond, he took a long look at her legs, put his fingers in his mouth, and wolf whistled. Every single person in the cabin turned to look.

Caroline was so embarrassed she wanted to open the exit door of the plane and jump out. Instead, she sank down into her seat and reached into her canvas tote in which, along with some reading material, she had placed the sample vials of toilet water she'd been given by Patricia Kent at the fragrance house. Then she pulled out a magazine and buried her face in it for the remainder of the nearly three-hour flight.

When the 727 landed in Palm Beach just before noon, she gathered her belongings and deplaned. She breathed a huge sigh of relief as she passed through the first-class cabin and saw that Mr. Obnoxious had already left.

"Good-bye," she said, nodding to the flight crew as they stood near the exit ramp, sending the passengers on their way.

"Good-bye, and thanks for flying Delta," said the captain. "Hope you enjoyed the flight."

Oh, the flight was fine, she thought to herself. *It was the company that was a little bumpy.*

As she walked down the ramp, she noticed that a horde of women were standing near the gate in the terminal. There was a brunette, a couple of redheads, and several platinum blonds, she noticed, and all of them were wearing . . . well, very little. Had they come to ogle some celebrity? Some rock star? Or maybe one of the movie actors who occasionally flew to Palm Beach for a little sun and fun?

Then she saw that it was her "friend," the Bloody Mary Madman, around whom they were gathered, flirting and giggling and acting as if he were God's gift to women! She couldn't imagine why they would be throwing themselves at a man as revolting as he was!

She had to pass the group in order to get out of the airport, and naturally, he *had* to notice her.

"Hey, you!" he said, suave as ever.

Caroline walked faster but he detached himself from the knot of women and attempted to follow her. She ignored him and walked even faster.

"You with the dynamite legs!" he called.

Caroline tried to move farther away from him, but he lunged toward her. As he did, he knocked her canvas tote bag out of her hand, sending it sprawling to the floor. The vials of toilet water smashed into pieces, spraying fragrance all over the cuffs of his pants—and his size 12 Nikes!

Caroline couldn't help herself. In spite of the fact that she would now have to call Patricia Kent and ask her to send more samples, she threw her head back and began to laugh out loud! The sight—and smell—of this macho jerk, whose sneakers were now reeking of jasmine, rose, and lily of the valley, was too much.

"I guess the score's tied, honey," he said as several of the women who had surrounded him ran over to offer him tissues and handkerchiefs. "In my business we'd be going into extra innings."

"Your business?" Caroline managed, nearly choking with laughter. "And what business is that?" She couldn't imagine this person having any job of consequence, much less a business, despite his two first-class seats. He was probably the idiot cousin of someone who worked for the airline.

"Baseball, the national pastime," he said with a swagger that made the women who had clung to him swoon. "Brett Haas, nice to meet you, sweetheart."

Brett Haas! Good lord, Caroline thought. So *this* was the famous baseball player Jack idolized! This was the Hall of Fame shoo-in, the World Series hero whose bat had made him millions and who was now a television broadcaster for Jack's beloved Atlanta Braves.

He must be down in Palm Beach for the spring training games at Municipal Stadium, Caroline realized. She knew Jack would be delirious if he found out that *she* had met his Number One hero, the legendary Brett Haas. Never mind that the legendary Brett Haas was a crude, womanizing, Bloody Mary–guzzling creep!

"We'll have dinner while I'm here in town," he *told* Caroline, ignoring the other women. "All I need is your name and phone number."

Caroline was at a loss. If she declined his invitation and kept walking, she'd never have to see the jerk again. But if she did *that,* she'd break Jack's heart. And, since he came first in her life—always—she turned to face Brett Haas.

"Caroline Goddard," she said, wincing, as if she were being forced to swallow some foul-tasting medicine. "You can call me at my store in West Palm Beach. Look in the phone book under Romance, Inc."

"Romance, Inc.? What are you, honey, a hooker or something?" He smirked.

Caroline couldn't bear another minute in his presence. She gave him the dirtiest look she could muster and stalked out of the airport.

23

When Brett Haas was Jack Goddard's age, his father, Bill "Hands" Haas, was playing third base in the minor leagues—the *very* minor leagues. Although Bill could field grounders as well as the next guy, he couldn't hit a curve ball to save his life, and his batting average never rose above the Mendoza line. As a result, he bounced from minor league team to minor league team, dragging his pride and his family around the country with him.

"Someday you'll outdo your pop and become a major leaguer," Bill would tell his son, in whose hands he had placed a bat before the boy was old enough to walk.

When Brett was nine, his father gave up on his dream of playing in the big leagues and became a coach with the Mets AAA farm team in Norfolk, Virginia—a job that lasted ten years and provided his wife and son with the stability they craved. It also gave young Brett an opportunity to be around ballplayers, live and breathe the game, familiarize himself with the atmosphere that surrounded baseball—the locker room pranks, the chewing tobacco, the groupies, all of it.

Bigger and stronger than his father and possessing the hand-eye coordination his father lacked, the teenaged Brett Haas could not only hit a curve ball but hit it a mile. A home run–belting third baseman at Randolph High School in Norfolk, he was constantly being scouted by representatives from the major league teams, relentlessly being touted as the next baseball phenom, forever being told he was the hottest, the best, the star.

Such praise tends to swell people's heads, and by the time Brett Haas graduated from high school, a major league contract in hand and the first installment of the money in the bank, his head was the size of Virginia. He had been drafted by the mighty Atlanta Braves, who saw in him what the Royals had seen in George Brett, what the Yankees had seen in Gregg Nettles, what the Phillies had seen in Mike Schmidt: a big, strong third baseman who could not only field his position flawlessly but hit for power, drive in runs, and intimidate the hell out of the opposition.

Once in the big leagues, Brett Haas did not disappoint. His heroics on the field earned him two World Series rings and a sure place in the Hall of Fame. His antics off the field earned him a reputation as a good old boy, who told filthy jokes, partied until dawn, and pursued the ladies almost as doggedly as they pursued him.

One of those "ladies," a nurse named Mary Lou Wheatley, had camped out at his hotel while the Braves were down in Houston for a series against the Astros. Never one to pass up a beautiful woman, particularly one so aggressively willing, Brett, cockier than ever at twenty-seven, spent a torrid four days with Mary Lou, and by the time the team had moved on to Los Angeles for three games against the Dodgers, he had taken up with a stewardess who flew for TWA and forgotten that Mary Lou Wheatley even existed.

And then she reminded him.

Three months later she wrote him a letter telling him she was pregnant.

"What the hell am I going to do?" Brett asked his father, with whom he was very close and shared everything, including his fervent desire never to surrender his bachelorhood.

"You're going to marry the girl, son," Bill Haas replied without a moment's hesitation. "Same as I married your mama."

"You mean my mother was pregnant with me before y'all got married?" asked Brett, who had assumed that his mother, unlike every other woman he knew, was a chaste soul who would never have slept with a man out of wedlock.

"You got that right," said Bill. "And we've been together thirty years."

Brett pondered his father's words and tried to imagine himself married to Mary Lou Wheatley or any other woman for thirty years. He shuddered.

"You've got to do the right thing by the girl," his father advised. "Ain't no doubt about it. You're a big league ballplayer, son. And that's an honorable thing to be. It wouldn't be honorable *not* to marry her, you know what I'm saying?"

Brett did know, and before the day was out, he telephoned Mary Lou and made arrangements for them to be married. He bought them a house in a middle-class suburb of Atlanta and told her he would make the best of the marriage.

"That means no other women!" Mary Lou said determinedly. "If I catch you running around behind my back, I'll get my daddy's shotgun and shoot you!"

Brett had laughed at the time, thinking Mary Lou was just a bit high-strung. He assumed all pregnant women were, seeing as their hormones were out of whack—or so he'd been told by his teammates who'd been through the pregnant wife routine. Then the baby was born—a beautiful, rosy-cheeked, dimpled little girl whom Mary Lou insisted on naming Patsy, after her grandmother back in Abilene.

"Isn't she something?" Brett would ask his buddies on the team as he'd whip out a photograph of his daughter every chance he got.

He wasn't just proud of the little girl who'd been conceived one steamy summer night. He was positively besotted with her. It was Mary Lou he couldn't stand, a fact that became painfully clear to him as the days and weeks following Patsy's birth wore on. Mary Lou, who had been the essence of compliance when they'd first met, had metamorphosed into the shrew of the Western world! She was always barking orders at him—threats, really—and he didn't take kindly to them or to her.

"If I hear that you even looked at another woman while you were on the road, I'll set fire to all your clothes!" she'd warn as he'd leave the house for road trips, which gradually became his escape from the hell at home.

She was forever trying to domesticate Brett, to tie him to her and their child. But she was never loving, never welcoming him home from a trip, never trying to involve herself in baseball, which truly *was* the love of his life, no matter how she ranted and raved about his obsession with the game.

When they had been married only three years, Mary Lou decided that marriage to a superstar ballplayer was no marriage at all. She took Patsy, went back to Texas, and filed for divorce, citing both irreconcilable differences *and* mental cruelty, and demanding—and eventually getting—full custody of her daughter.

Brett was deliriously happy at the prospect of life without Mary Lou, but the thought of seeing Patsy only occasionally devastated him.

"She's going to grow up without me," he complained to his father.

"Not unless you let her," Bill Haas replied. "The law gives you visitation rights. All you've got to do is use 'em."

And Brett did—whenever his playing schedule permitted. Seeing his daughter became easier, though, after he turned thirty-seven, went through yet another operation to repair his torn-up knees, and decided to retire from the Braves and become a play-by-play announcer on the television broadcasts of their games. In fact, when his two-week stint in Palm Beach was over, he intended to spend a full ten days in Abilene with Patsy, who was now an adorable and very precocious ten-year-old. In the meantime, he planned on doing his job behind the microphone and, in his spare time, checking out the chick he'd met on the plane. She was more standoffish than he was used to, but she was beautiful—classy-looking, he thought and wondered how long it would take to work the old Brett Haas charm on her and loosen her up a little.

"Romance, Inc. Good afternoon."

It was close to three o'clock on Saturday afternoon when Caroline answered the phone in her small office at the shop.

"Hey, good lookin'. What's cookin'? Besides those sexy wheels of yours, I mean."

Caroline felt the bile rise in her throat. So Mr. Baseball had called her, after all. God, now what would she do?

"It must be Mr. Haas," she said, her voice dripping with sarcasm. "I'd know those dulcet tones anywhere."

"Well, now, isn't that flattering," he laughed. "I'm downright surprised you remember me, what with the way you took off at the airport."

Caroline rolled her eyes. "Oh, I remember you," she said, wondering how she could forget such a person. "What can I do for you, Mr. Haas?"

"I told you. We're going to have dinner. Tonight."

"Tonight? I couldn't possibly—" she began. Then she stopped herself. There was Jack to think of. When she'd told him she had met Brett Haas on the plane home from New York, he had literally jumped out of his chair and begged her to tell him every detail of their conversation. He would be crushed if he had the chance to meet his sports idol and Caroline didn't give it to him. And *she* would be crushed for him—and guilty to boot! "Well, you could stop by for a drink," she said cautiously.

"So you can get rid of me fast, is that it?" he said.

"No, of course not," she said.

They both knew she was lying through her teeth.

"You think I'm a lush, don't you?" he said.

"No, I only suggested a drink so that we could—"

"Come on, you're thinking about those Bloody Marys I threw back on the plane," he interrupted, then laughed. "I hate to fly, never could deal with it, so I tank up before I get onboard, no matter what time of day it is."

It was Caroline's turn to laugh. This macho jerk with the muscles and the swagger had a fear of flying? The image amused her.

"Thanks for clearing that up," she said, glad he couldn't see the smirk on her face. "How's six-thirty?"

"Sure, sure. Then we'll head out for dinner."

"No, then you'll leave, and I'll spend some time with my son, who I haven't seen in over a week."

"You've got a kid?"

Oh, look, Caroline thought to herself. He's disappointed that we won't be alone. Now he knows he can't maul me the minute he walks in the door.

"Yes, a six-year-old boy," Caroline said. "He's quite a fan of yours."

"Yeah? That's nice," said Brett, feeling a profound yearning for Patsy, who, despite the daily dose of Your-father's-a-no-good-son-of-a-bitch she got from her mother, was a fan of his, too.

"So we'll see you at six-thirty?" Caroline asked, hoping he'd change his mind and say no.

"Yeah, sure. Why not?" he said. "An hour in my company and you'll be begging for more."

"Oh, spare me," Caroline muttered under her breath. The man was so full of himself.

"What's that?" he asked, not hearing her.

"Nothing," said Caroline, who took a deep breath and gave Brett Haas her address.

She hadn't remembered that, with his cropped, dirty blond hair, dark tan, gleaming white teeth, bright blue eyes, and strong, wide shoulders, he was handsome. Or even that he possessed a certain boyishness that wasn't altogether unappealing. And so when he walked in the door of her condo, she was momentarily taken aback by his rugged attractiveness. Then she focused on his fire-engine red blazer and electric blue trousers and, after he opened his mouth, her disdain toward him returned.

"Sweetheart," he greeted her, then patted her on the backside.

She batted his hand away, stepped back, and gave him the nastiest look she could muster. She would have let him have a piece of her mind too if Jack hadn't come running into the foyer, flushed and breathless with excitement.

"Are you really Brett Haas?" he asked, knowing the answer but too awed to believe it.

Brett ruffled Jack's golden hair and grinned at him. "I'm really Brett Haas," he replied, barging into the living room without an invitation and surveying the room. "And are you really Jack Goddard?"

"Yeah, but how'd you know my name?" asked Jack, who, eyes shining, tagged along behind his hero.

"Your mom told me." Brett eyed the sofa and made himself comfortable. He stretched out across it and threw his feet, Nikes and all, across the chrome and glass coffee table.

Caroline couldn't control her anger at his boorishness. "Would you mind taking your feet off my—"

"How about a soda, huh, Caroline?" Brett asked, either oblivious to or unaffected by Caroline's displeasure with him. He turned to her son, while she went to the kitchen to fetch him a Coke. "So tell me, Jack, how do you think the Braves are gonna do this season?"

Jack hopped onto the sofa next to Brett and proceeded to make every moment with his famous guest count. He told Brett what he thought of the players, the manager, the coaches, even the trainer! Then he jumped up and ran out of the room.

"Where do you think you're going?" Caroline asked, not wanting to be left alone with Brett, even for a second.

"To get something, Mom. I'll be right back," said Jack, who scurried into his bedroom.

"Hey, babe. Come sit." Brett patted the sofa cushion next to him. "I want to get reacquainted."

Caroline stiffened. "I think I'll sit over here, thanks," she said, settling onto the chair on the opposite side of the room.

Brett made a face. "What's the matter, sweetness? You afraid of me? Or is it that you're just a little shy around celebrities?"

Caroline scoffed. "Has it occurred to you, Mr. Haas, that not every woman on the planet has a desire to throw herself at you?"

Brett thought for a moment, then said, "No, now that you mention it, it hasn't occurred to me. I haven't had a woman turn me down since I was fourteen—and she was my English teacher."

Caroline couldn't help but laugh. "You're too much," she said, shaking her head and wondering where Brett Haas got his extraordinary self-confidence. James had money and charm, Jean-Claude was born with a flair for cooking and a talent for seduction, and Clifford possessed a brilliant mind and a thirst for success. They were all self-confident. But this man—this hick whose only gift was his ability to hit a baseball—was positively in love with himself!

"I'm back," said Jack as he practically leapt onto the sofa

next to Brett. "I didn't want to forget to ask you—will you autograph this book for me?"

It was the Brett Haas biography that Selma had bought Jack and read and reread to him so many times that he knew most of the words by heart.

Brett took the book from the boy, reached inside his blinding red blazer, and pulled out a pen.

"Sure, I'll sign it," he said, then wrote on the inside front cover: "To Jack. Keep rooting for the Braves. And for me. We need fans like you on our side." He signed his name and handed the book back to Jack.

"Oh, man!" said Jack, his eyes growing wider as he tried to read the inscription for himself. "Thanks a million, Mr. Haas."

"What's with the 'Mr. Haas' stuff? Call me Brett. We're buddies now, right, Jack?"

"Right, Brett."

Caroline couldn't remember ever seeing her son look so happy—or so grown-up. His chest swelled with pride as he sat next to Brett, elbow to elbow, man to man. If only his father could see him, she thought with a catch in her throat. If only . . .

"Now, Jack, my pal. How about leaving your mother and me alone for a minute or two, huh?" said Brett, who then winked at the six-year-old.

Jack winked back, clutched his newly autographed book to him and strutted proudly to his room.

"He's a great kid," Brett said, giving Caroline his full attention, eyeing her in her tight-fitting jeans and white linen blouse. *Great bod,* he told himself. *Too bad she's so uptight.*

"Thanks. I think so, too," she said.

"His father in the picture?"

"No. His father died before he was born."

"Sorry. I figured it was a divorce. Take me, for instance. My old lady booted me out three years into the marriage. Not that I wasn't glad to be rid of her. It was not seeing my kid that nearly drove me up a wall."

"Your kid?"

"Yeah, Patsy. She's ten. Lives with her mother in Texas. I'm going there when I finish doing the games here. I try to get down to Abilene whenever I can."

Caroline regarded the man sitting across from her. He was crude and coarse and rough around the edges. But he obviously cared for his daughter, which showed he had a soft side to his personality. And he had made Jack's eyes light up, which revealed that he understood a boy's hero worship and didn't disdain it. Still, he was a womanizer and a jerk, and she wondered how a man like that behaved around a ten-year-old girl.

"Let me ask you something, Mr. Haas," she began. "Would you want men grabbing your daughter's behind and calling her 'sweetheart'?"

He laughed. "You haven't met my daughter," he said. "She's not what you'd call shy. Takes after her dad, I guess. When she grows up, *she's* the one who's going to be grabbing asses."

Good Lord, so the man was raising his daughter in his image, poor girl. Caroline glanced at her watch. He had been there for just over an hour, and she was eager to be rid of him so she could spend time with Jack. Just the two of them.

She rose from her chair. "I'm afraid I've run out of time," she told Brett as diplomatically as she could. "I promised Jack I'd watch a movie with him tonight, and if I don't get started, it'll be his bedtime before he knows it."

"It's Saturday night," said Brett, who did not budge. "What's a foxy chick like you doing watching a movie with her kid on a Saturday night? No boyfriends?"

"None of your business," Caroline snapped.

"It is now," he said, looking her up and down and back again—and making no secret of the fact that he liked what he saw. "You might as well save yourself the trouble of playing so hard to get."

"Oh? And why is that?" She smirked.

"Because you're gonna fall for me, sweetheart," he said as he stood up and walked toward Caroline's front door. "Whether you like it or not."

* * *

Caroline was reading the Sunday morning paper when the phone rang. She answered it and braced herself for a lecture from Tamara, who, she knew, would be dying to hear all about her trip to New York and would be upset that Caroline hadn't called her the instant she'd gotten home.

"Sweetness, how're we doing this beautiful Sunday?"

It was Brett Haas. At eight o'clock on a Sunday morning. Didn't the man ever sleep?

"Fine, thank you, Mr. Haas," she said patiently. "What is it this time?"

"You can lose that tough broad act, for one thing," he said.

"Lose the what?" Caroline said, her voice rising. Brett Haas had a knack for infuriating her. Everything he did and said made her crazy!

"You heard me," he said. "I'm coming over around noon. Tell Jack, okay?"

"Look, Mr. Haas."

"Brett."

"Brett. You were very nice to my son last night. I can't thank you enough for signing his book and making him feel as if you were his friend. But we have plans this afternoon. We always go to his godmother's house on Sunday."

"Not *this* Sunday you don't," he said casually. "Tell Jack I'll be by around noon. Okay, sweet cakes?"

Caroline was about to explain that she did not appreciate his terms of endearment nor his insinuating himself into her weekend time with Jack. She had no intention of spending the afternoon with him. None whatsoever! She had done her part for Jack by introducing him to the legendary Brett Haas. But enough was enough!

"I don't mean to be rude," she said, "but I don't care for the way you speak to me, on top of which we really are busy this afternoon."

There was no response, which surprised Caroline until she realized that Brett Haas had already hung up.

He arrived at 12:15, dressed—for him—almost conservatively. He wore a dark blue suit with a pale blue shirt and a lively red-and-blue patterned tie, and he looked, Caroline had to admit, quite handsome in a weathered, beat-up sort of way. For the first time, she could see why a woman might be attracted to him. A certain kind of woman, anyway.

"My television attire," he explained. "When I'm in the broadcast booth, the network boys like me to look presentable."

"The network boys have a point," replied Caroline. "But you really could have saved yourself a trip over here. I did tell you we were busy this afternoon." The man was persistent, she had to give him that. He obviously wanted to go out with her—badly—and he wasn't taking no for an answer. "As I explained on the phone, Jack and I go to visit his—"

"What's this 'Jack and I' stuff?" he asked as he pushed his way past her and walked into her living room. "I'm not asking *you* to go anywhere. It's Jack I came to pick up. You can do whatever you want."

"Jack?"

"Yeah, you remember him. He's your son. The kid who loves the Braves. I thought he'd get a kick out of going to the game today. The Yankees are coming up from Fort Lauderdale. He can watch the action from the booth with me. What do you say?"

Caroline was stunned. So he hadn't come to see her after all. He had come to see Jack. To take Jack to a baseball game. He hadn't even suggested that she come along, never mind behave as though he wanted her company. So much for his stud act and her supposedly irresistible legs!

Just then Jack bounded in.

"Mom, I thought I heard—"

"Jack, old buddy. We were just talking about you," Brett said, turning to him. "You up for the Braves-Yankees this afternoon?"

Jack beamed and high-fived his famous new friend. Then he looked at Caroline. "Can I, Mom? Can I go with Brett?"

"What about our Sunday visits to Tamara's?" she asked, feeling slightly left out, in spite of herself.

"You can go by yourself," Jack suggested, his eyes sparkling. "When you tell the duchess where I am, she'll be real excited."

Yeah, real excited, Caroline thought as she tried to picture Tamara Brandt's reaction to Brett Haas, a man whose clothes alone would mortally offend her.

"Okay, let's go, buddy," said Brett as he took Jack's hand. "Don't want to be late, right?"

"Just a minute," Caroline intervened. "I haven't given my permission."

"Aw, Mom. Please don't say no," Jack said, his eyes begging her to let him go to the game.

Caroline looked at him and felt a stab of conflict. She knew how thrilling it would be for Jack if she let Brett take him to the game. But what did she really know about this man? That he was an ex-baseball star; that he covered the games on television; that he was a ladies' man, a man who treated women like pieces of meat. How did she know he'd take good care of Jack? Act responsibly with him?

Caroline suddenly thought of the man whom Selma had seen speaking to Jack after school. He hadn't appeared again, but Caroline had vowed that now that she was back from New York, she would keep an extra close eye on her son, make sure nothing happened to him. Jack was the most precious thing in her life. He meant everything to her. How could she possibly let him run off with this . . . this macho idiot?

"Sorry, Jack, but I don't think so," she said, shaking her head.

Brett held onto Jack's hand and wouldn't let go. "I'll take good care of him if that's what's bothering you," he said. "I've got a kid of my own, remember?"

Caroline remembered all right. He had a kid who was going to grab men's asses when she grew up.

"Please, Mom," Jack said insistently. "I promise I'll clean my room and wake up in the morning when you tell me to. I'll do anything you say, only please let me go with Brett?"

He was breaking her heart. Of course, she had to let him go. And then it dawned on her—the real reason Brett Haas wanted to take Jack to the game . . . so he could score points with her! It made perfect sense. She'd been giving him the cold shoulder, so he did the next best thing: he ingratiated himself with Jack.

"I suppose it's all right," she said, reassuring herself that if Brett wanted *her,* he'd never do anything to hurt her son.

"Oh, thanks!" Jack cried, tugging on Brett's hand, so eager was he to get to the ballpark.

"What time will you be bringing him home?" Caroline asked Brett as the three of them walked out her front door.

"When the game's over, sweetheart," he said.

"But he hasn't had his lunch," Caroline said.

"Relax, babe. The hot dogs at Municipal Stadium are out of this world," said Brett. "Jack'll love 'em."

"'Bye, Mom," Jack waved as he walked with Brett to the elevator. "I'll try to catch a ball for you!"

She waved back and blew him a kiss. I'd love to bottle his happiness, she thought to herself. I'd love to freeze the expression on his face and savor it forever.

Caroline spent a few hours at Tamara's. Over iced tea, she explained that Jack was at a baseball game, then told her former employer every detail of her business meetings in New York—and of her social evenings there, including her get-togethers with Jean-Claude Fontaine and Clifford Hamlin. She did not, however, broach the subject of the duke and duchess becoming investors in Romance, Inc. She and Clifford had agreed to wait until they were in London and could present a united front.

"It sounds as if the trip was a smashing success—businesswise and manwise. It's about time you started having a social life of your own," Tamara said.

"You sound just like Cissy," replied Caroline.

"And why not? It's high time you shelved the nun routine," said Tamara, noticing as Caroline glanced at her watch for the twentieth time since she'd arrived. "If you're so concerned about Jack, go back to your condo and wait for him," she advised.

"Would you mind terribly?" Caroline asked. "I'm sure everything's fine. It's just that I can't help worrying about Jack. He's all I have in the world."

"Then it's time he had company. You need another man in your life."

Caroline smiled at the duchess. "I'm working on it, as I told you. But for now, I'd like to go home and wait for Jack."

"Give him a kiss for me," said Tamara. "Tell him I missed him today."

"So did I," said Caroline. "So did I."

Caroline didn't begin to worry in earnest until five-thirty. The game had long since been over, and neither Jack nor Brett had called to say they'd be late. And so she paced, back and forth, back and forth, listening by her front door, watching out the window, hoping her son would be home safe and sound, wondering how long to wait before calling the police.

At 6:25, the doorbell rang. Caroline ran to answer it and saw Jack—wearing an Atlanta Braves uniform—standing with Brett and five other very large men.

"Mom! Look at me!" he exclaimed, rushing to hug her. "Brett bought me the uniform and took me to the locker room and introduced me to some of the guys on the team!"

"The guys on the team?" Caroline asked.

"Sweet cakes, meet Ray Dinkins, Tim Delahanty, Reggie Ballard, Dick Henderson, and Arnie Lister," said Brett as he motioned for his friends to enter the condo. *Caroline's* condo! The man acted as if he owned the place! As if he owned her son!

"I told them you'd cook everybody dinner," Jack said, looking at his mother with pleading, beseeching eyes.

She shrugged. She was powerless when he looked at her that way. Besides, what could she do? Throw them all out when they'd been so nice to Jack?

"Did you also tell them I don't know how to cook?" She smiled as she bent down to kiss Jack.

He shook his head. "Just *pretend* you know how," he whispered. "Do your best, okay, Mom?"

"Okay," Caroline said, and then invited all seven men—including her ecstatic son—to make themselves comfortable while she got to work in the kitchen. Jean-Claude may look down his nose at microwave ovens, but they sure come in handy, she thought as she reached into the freezer for her entire inventory of frozen pizza.

At eight o'clock that evening, Charles and Dina Goddard were just about to sit down to dinner in their Manhattan apartment when the maid advised Mr. Goddard that there was a telephone call.

"It's Mr. Aronson, sir," she said. "You asked me to tell you as soon as he called."

"Yes, quite right," said Charles, excusing himself from the table and taking the call in the library.

"Aronson. What's up?" Charles asked. The private investigator had been calling his client every day with a surveillance report.

"You'll be pleased with today's report, sir," said Aronson. "Not only did Brett Haas, the ex-ballplayer, come by the condo again this afternoon, he took Jack with him when he left and kept him out the entire day."

"So she lets the boy go off with anyone and everyone," Charles mused. First, there was the woman from Lake Worth, Selma Johannas. Now there's Brett Haas, whose hell-raising reputation was well known to anyone who had ever read a newspaper.

"Exactly, sir," Aronson agreed. "But that's not all. When Haas returned with the boy a few hours ago, there were five other men with them. Five members of the Atlanta Braves. The boy's mother is entertaining all of them."

Charles nodded. It was exactly what he expected of Caroline Shaw. *Trash is as trash does,* he thought.

"That's precisely the kind of thing Switzer told us to be on the lookout for," he said. "Men around the house. On a regular basis. For wild parties and such." He allowed himself a smile. "Five men at one time. Things are going far better than I expected, Aronson."

Six hours later, the phone rang in the Virginia ranch-style home of Bill Haas and his wife, Claire.

"Pop?" said the voice at the other end of the receiver.

"Brett? Is that you?" Bill Haas asked after flipping on the

light and glancing at the clock on his night table. It was nearly two o'clock in the morning, and he and Claire had been asleep since midnight. "Anything wrong, son?"

"Yeah, Pop. Plenty."

"What is it, boy? Is Patsy sick or something?" Bill knew how his son adored the little girl, how devastated he'd been if she were ill or hurt. The public thought Brett Haas was a tough guy—a hard-as-nails jock who didn't give a damn about anything but baseball and partying. But Bill knew different. Bill knew that Brett loved his daughter with a fierceness that far surpassed his love for the National Pastime.

"No, no. It's not Patsy. It's me. I'm the one who's sick," said Brett.

"Is it your knees again, boy?" asked Bill, hoping his son didn't need yet another operation on his battered legs.

"No, Pop. It's my heart," Brett said and sighed.

Bill Haas tightened his grip on the phone. The sixty-year-old minor league coach had had triple bypass surgery the year before. Now he feared that his son had inherited his predisposition to heart disease. "Are you calling from the hospital, son?" he asked.

"Naw, I'm calling from my hotel room in West Palm Beach. I just got home from a date."

"A date?"

"Yeah. That's why I'm calling you, Pop. You've always given me good advice when it comes to women."

"Oh, women," Bill said with relief. He smiled at his wife who lay in bed next to him.

"I think I'm in love," Brett announced.

Bill chuckled. "Nothin' wrong with that, son. Who is she?"

"A girl I met on the plane," Brett replied. "It's the damnedest thing. She treats me like shit, but I can't get her off my mind."

"Probably because she treats you like shit," Bill laughed. "You're not used to that kind of treatment from women. Right, son?"

"Damn right."

"Well, maybe that's why you think you're in love with her. Because she treats you bad. You always did like a challenge, boy."

"True, but it's more than that," Brett explained. "She's different from the broads I usually hang out with. She's got class. A real lady, not to mention a knockout. Nothing like Mary Lou, who had stars—and dollar signs—in her eyes. This girl doesn't give a damn if I'm a celebrity. She'd never camp out at a hotel and try to screw her way into marriage to a ballplayer, like my nightmare of an ex-wife did. I'm telling you, Pop, this one knows I'm headed for the Hall of Fame and treats me like shit anyway."

Bill laughed again. "Sounds like you've got it bad, son."

"Yeah, and there's more. She's got a kid. A terrific little boy whose hero is you-know-who."

"Have you told her how you feel, son?"

"Are you kidding? I just met the woman. And, like I said, she hates me. If I start sweet-talking her, she'll kick dirt in my face."

"Since when did you start backing down from a contest?" said Bill, who had always been proud of his son's never-say-die attitude. "I never saw you do that on the ballfield."

Brett was silent for a second or two. Then he asked, "Okay, how should I handle her, Pop? Tell me what to do."

"Keep on seeing her," Bill replied. "Wear her down, just like you used to wear down the best pitchers in the National League. Get in the batter's box and stay there. One strike. Two strikes. Don't bail out. Hang in there. Before you know it, you'll be rounding home plate."

Brett considered the analogy, then thanked his father and said good night.

"Good night, son," said Bill. "Oh, and your mother and I want to meet this young lady."

"That'll have to wait awhile," said Brett. "I've gotta convince her to go out with me first. We haven't even been alone together yet."

"Remember what I said," Bill reminded his son. "Get yourself back into the batter's box and take your cuts. You can't hit a homer unless you step up to the plate."

After Bill hung up the phone, Claire Haas smiled at her husband. "It's possible that this girl really doesn't *like* Brett," she said. "I may be his mother, but I'm not unaware of his faults, one of which is that he doesn't know how to express his feelings."

Bill Haas smiled back at the woman he found as lovely and desirable as the day they were married. "Good thing I know how to express mine," he whispered, then turned off the light, reached for his wife, and expressed his feelings the best way he knew how.

Like Caroline, Francesca Palen had come a long way since the day they'd met in the lobby of The Breakers. Back then, she had been a neophyte, a lowly assistant in the hotel's public relations department, and Caroline had been a shy and unhappy fifteen-year-old.

Francesca had done well at her job, impressing her superiors with her flair for creativity as well as with her organizational skills. Currently the hotel's associate director of public relations, she was next in line to take over the director's job when her immediate boss, Karen Haswell, who was six months pregnant, left to have a baby. But there was always the chance that upper management would hire someone from a competing hotel to run the PR department—and that Francesca would be left out in the cold.

"The president of the hotel has invited me to lunch several times," she told Caroline when the two of them spoke on the phone. "I've heard that he's thinking of promoting me when Karen leaves, but I've also heard that he's not sure I can handle being the head of the department."

"Would you take the job if he offered it to you?" Caroline asked, knowing that Francesca loved her work but found it extremely demanding.

"Would I? In a heartbeat! It's the job I've always wanted."

"Then he *has* to give it to you. That's all there is to it!"

"Well, he might—if I can prove to him that I can pull off this party next Tuesday night."

"What kind of party?"

"A big 'do' for the executives from one of the television networks. Karen will be out of town for a couple of weeks, so she's put me in charge. If I show everybody that I can handle the whole thing, I'm pretty sure I'll get the job."

"Francesca! That's fabulous!" Caroline exclaimed, delighted for her friend. It was gratifying to hear that a woman could work hard at her job and be rewarded. After Caroline's negative experiences with the banks regarding Romance, Inc., she was beginning to wonder.

"And speaking of the party," Francesca went on, "I wouldn't mind having a friendly face there. Want to come?"

"Me? I don't know any television executives," Caroline said.

"Maybe not, but you know *me,"* Francesca pointed out. "I really could use some moral support, Caroline. I'll be running around, making sure Mr. So-and-So has his favorite brand of Scotch, and when I'm not doing *that,* I'll be praying the band I hired doesn't play the theme song of our guests' rival network!"

"Sounds nerve-racking," Caroline commiserated.

"It's all part of the job," Francesca sighed. "But I really would love it if you'd come. Who knows? Maybe there'll be a couple of eligible bachelors for us there."

A couple of eligible bachelors, Caroline thought, rolling her eyes. Two nights before, she had entertained six "eligible bachelors" at her condo, the most ardent of whom had been Brett Haas, who let her know once again in no uncertain terms that he was in great demand among the ladies. God, he'd been insufferable. He had gone out of his way to be nice to Jack, which she appreciated, but did he have to go out of his way to annoy her? He had the subtlety of a Mack truck!

"What do you say, Caroline?" Francesca prompted. "Will you come? It's cocktails and a buffet dinner. Dressy but not formal. You can help me make sure everyone's having a good time."

"Of course, I'll come," said Caroline. She looked forward to doing whatever she could to help Francesca, who'd been one of the first people to help her. Besides, she couldn't remember the last time she'd been to a party. And a dressy one at that.

The following day Caroline was helping a client at Romance, Inc. when her assistant told her she had a phone call. A man. She wondered if it were Jean-Claude. He had been telephoning her nearly every day since she'd returned to Palm Beach. The more they had spoken, the more she found herself thinking about him and the more she found her inhibitions dissolving. She was looking forward to seeing him again the next time he came to Florida.

"Hello?" Caroline answered the phone as her assistant attended to the client who'd been trying on lace blouses.

"Hey, sweet cakes. It's guess who."

Caroline didn't have to guess. After spending an entire evening with Brett Haas, she would have recognized that self-satisfied southern drawl anywhere.

"Hi," she said, trying to muster some enthusiasm. "Don't tell me you want to take Jack to another baseball game."

"No, I want to take *you."*

"I don't care for baseball."

"I didn't mean baseball."

"You just said you wanted to take me somewhere."

"I do. To a party, not a ballgame." He sighed. "Hey, are you always such a pain in the ass?"

Caroline laughed. "Not at all. I just don't respond to your 'charms' the way other women seem to."

"Yeah, and I don't get it. But I'm gonna change it. One more night with me and you'll be throwing yourself at me."

"Sure. Now if you'll excuse me, I've got to get back to my clients."

"Not until you say you'll go to the party with me."

"What party?"

"The shindig I've been invited to. Personally, I'd rather watch grass grow, but a job's a job."

"So this is a business function you're inviting me to?"

"You got it."

"Well, as I've told you, I don't care for baseball."

"Look, it's not a baseball thing. For the third time, it's a party. A fancy party with champagne and caviar and all the trimmings."

"Thanks for thinking of me, but I'm afraid I'm busy that night."

"Bullshit! You don't even know what night it is."

"Oh. Sorry. What night is it?"

"Tuesday. Seven o'clock."

Caroline breathed a sigh of relief when she realized she had a legitimate excuse. "Actually, I really *am* busy that night," she said. "A friend has invited me to a party she's giving."

Brett Haas was silent for a moment. A rarity, Caroline thought.

"Are you there?" she asked, feeling a bit guilty for the way she was treating him. Perhaps she *was* being a pain in the ass. He was attentive. He made her laugh. He was great with Jack. It was just that he was so . . . so . . . arrogant, so full of himself, so—

"Yeah, I'm here," he replied. "I admit it. I'm disappointed. I thought for sure you'd go with me." Hadn't his father advised him to be persistent? To hang in at the plate, take his cuts, and wait for just the right pitch? *His* pitch?

"Then you were mistaken," she said. "Maybe you shouldn't assume things where women are concerned."

"Oh, give me a break with this 'women' stuff," he said, exasperated. "I just thought you might like to hang out at The Breakers. It's a la-dee-da hotel, and all the network boys will be there and—"

"That's the party?" Caroline asked. "The buffet dinner at The Breakers next Tuesday night?" Just her luck. Brett Haas was going to the same party Francesca had invited her to.

"Sure. I'm one of the guests of honor," he said, resuming his relentlessly cocky tone. "I do cover the Braves' games for the network, remember?"

She couldn't possibly forget, as Jack never ceased to remind her since the moment he'd found out she knew Brett.

"That's the same party that I was invited to," she said, resignation in her voice.

"Beautiful. We'll go together," Brett said.

Now it was Caroline's turn to be silent. She didn't know how to get out of this one.

"I'll pick you up at six," he went on, as if she didn't have a thing to say about it.

"Six? The party doesn't start until seven," said Caroline as she tried to imagine herself being escorted to Francesca's important function—a function that could make or break her friend's career—by a loose cannon like Brett Haas.

"Yeah, but I gotta make a stop on the way. We're gonna give Reggie Ballard a ride to the party. He's staying at his mother's while the team's down here for spring training, and according to him, she lives in the boonies somewhere."

"Fine, fine. Whatever," said Caroline, eager to get off the phone and back to her client. She was trying to play down her feelings about going to the party—going anywhere, for that matter—with Brett Haas. If it weren't for Francesca, she'd probably pretend she had the flu. She consoled herself with the thought that he would only be in Palm Beach temporarily, and that as soon as spring training was over, he'd be going back to Atlanta or Abilene or whatever planet he came from.

Brett showed up at the condo at five minutes after six. Jack, freshly bathed and sporting the Braves T-shirt he never took off, answered the door and greeted his idol with several energetic high fives. Brett picked him up and tossed him into the air just as Caroline came in from the bedroom. She was wearing a grass green silk dress with a sweetheart neckline, a tiny waist, and an elegant bell skirt—the dress that she and Tamara had seen in a window at Saks at the start of the season and decided was too delicious for Caroline to pass up.

At the sight of her, Brett placed Jack gently back down on

the ground and looked at his date as if he were X-raying her. And then he gazed longingly at her legs and whistled.

"Ooh, baby. You look good enough to—"

Caroline cut him off quickly—before he said something she'd have to explain to Jack, who was hardly old enough to understand.

"Jack, invite Mr. Haas inside," she said, as she found herself staring at Brett. He was wearing a dark suit, white shirt, and sober tie, and was newly shaved and smelling of a crisp, citrusy cologne. For the second time since they'd met, Caroline could see why *some* women found him appealing in a diamond-in-the-rough sort of way.

"Brett! Brett!" Jack said eagerly, jumping up and down. "Throw me up in the air again! Just the way you did before!"

Brett looked over at Caroline, who nodded her approval.

"One last time," she said, thinking how much and in how many ways Jack missed having a father. To roughhouse with. To talk to. To look up to.

Brett repeated the performance, and when a giggling Jack was safely back on terra firma, he ruffled the boy's hair and patted his backside.

"Okay, kid. Go watch television or something. Your mother and I have a heavy date," he said, then winked at Jack and handed him a thick envelope. "And here are the cards and the highlights video, just like I promised."

Jack whooped with joy as he opened the envelope to find baseball cards autographed by some of his favorite players, as well as a videotape chronicling triumphant moments in the illustrious career of All-Star third baseman Brett Haas. Brett kissed the crown of the six-year-old's blond hair and gently pushed him toward Selma, who had emerged from inside the condominium.

"We won't be home late," Caroline told Selma after introducing her to Brett, who gave Jack's godmother and babysitter the thrill of her life by whistling at *her* legs, too!

Brett pulled the rented Lincoln Town Car away from the condominium complex where Caroline, Jack, and Selma lived, and instead of heading east, in the direction of Palm Beach and The Breakers, he drove west.

"Where are you going?" Caroline asked as she pointed out the car window. "You're driving in the wrong direction."

"We're picking up Reggie. At his mother's, remember?"

Caroline nodded. "Where does his mother live?"

"In Hobe Sound."

"Hobe Sound? That's about an hour from here."

"So? The party doesn't start until seven. We'll be there by eight. We'll make a big entrance. Parties don't start until I get there anyway."

Caroline shook her head. "How on earth did you get so full of yourself?" she asked, wondering how she had allowed herself to go off with this madman. She hoped they wouldn't be too late for the party, as Francesca was counting on her being there.

"Full of myself? Darlin', you ain't see nothin' yet," said Brett as he turned on the car radio and proceeded to sing along—totally off key—with the golden oldies the station was playing.

They were driving for what seemed like an eternity when Caroline finally asked Brett if he knew where he was going.

"Hell, yes," he said, continuing to sing, then reached into his jacket pocket, retrieved a rumpled scrap of paper, and handed it to her.

"What's this?" she asked, doing her best to smooth it out.

"Directions to Reggie's mother's house," he said.

"Now you're showing it to me?" she remarked, and tried to read the words on the piece of paper. They were scribbled in penmanship that made doctors' prescriptions seem legible. Caroline made out an *s, vns,* and *st.*

"You're sure that's an *s?"* he asked when she read him the letters.

"No, I'm not sure at all," she said, realizing that Brett, a resident of Georgia not Florida, didn't have a clue where they were.

"Maybe it's an *e,"* he said. "I sort of remember Reggie saying something about turning east."

"Why don't we stop at a gas station and ask someone?" Caroline suggested, exasperated by his stubbornness.

Brett looked at her as if she'd just suggested he bunt with the bases loaded.

"Brett, we're lost. Admit it," said Caroline, who had lived her whole life in Florida but didn't recognize any of the streets they passed.

"Keep your panties on, sweetheart." He smiled. "Reggie's mother's house is bound to be around here somewhere."

"But why not stop and ask somebody?" Caroline persisted, too concerned about their predicament to scold him about his relentlessly boorish way of speaking to her. "Or are you too macho to ask for help?"

Brett opened his window, stuck his head out, and yelled at the top of his lungs, "Help! I've got a woman in the car who won't lighten up!"

Caroline had to laugh. He was crazy, absolutely crazy. He had no inhibitions whatsoever and did and said whatever he felt like. No thought went unexpressed, no feeling was ever suppressed. In a way, she envied him and suspected that he was a lot more at peace with himself than she was.

Another ten minutes of wrong turns and dead ends passed. Brett swore he knew where he was going, and Caroline swore they'd never get to Francesca's party, and each of them swore at the other. And then they found themselves on a dark and uninhabited road whose only building was a deserted farm stand and whose only light emanated from the brilliant starlit sky.

Brett pulled the car off to the side of the road, slammed on the brakes, and brought the Lincoln to a stop, pitching Caroline abruptly forward in her seat. Then he turned off the ignition.

"What on earth are you doing now?" she asked, certain that they would never reach Reggie Ballard's mother's house—or The Breakers.

"I'm stopping the car, obviously. We're lost." Brett shrugged.

"So you admit it!" Caroline said.

"I admit it," Brett said, then grinned his puckish, mischievous grin. He's like a child, Caroline thought. A big, unmanageable, adorable—

Adorable? She stopped herself. Brett Haas? He certainly

wasn't dull. She had to give him that. And he didn't give a damn what anybody thought about him, which was admirable in a way. But adorable?

"Caroline, baby, what do you say we make our own party?" he said, leaning back against his seat and gazing out his window at the stars in the night sky.

"I say we should go to the party we were invited to," she said. "We're both expected there."

"And do you always do what's expected of you?" He turned to look at her and noticed that the moonlight made her profile seem etched in ivory.

"I suppose so, yes," she confessed.

"Well, I don't," he said, sitting up and reaching to turn the radio back on. "Great station, huh? I love oldies."

He began to sing along with the Isley Brothers' rendition of "Twist and Shout" as Caroline watched in amazement. This overgrown kid didn't seem to care that dozens of network executives—his bosses—were awaiting his arrival at an important business function. Was he irresponsible or just spontaneous? Full of rebellion or full of fun? She didn't know. She knew only that they were as different as two people could be.

"Oh, listen! They're doing a whole 'twist' number," he said excitedly as he began to hum the melody to "The Peppermint Twist" by Joey Dee and the Starlighters, which was then followed by Chubby Checker's "Let's Twist Again."

"Brett," Caroline tried to get his attention as he wiggled and snapped his fingers to the beat of the music. "Shouldn't we try to get back? We're all dressed for the party and people are—"

"People are meant to enjoy themselves," he interrupted her. "You know, sweet cakes, if you'd loosen up a little, you'd have a lot more fun out of life."

Caroline sank back in her seat and sighed. What else could she do? She was at his mercy. It was either beat him or join him in his lunacy. And since she was a virtual prisoner in the darkness of the deserted street, she began to snap *her* fingers to the beat and sing the words to the song along with Chubby Checker. As a teenager, she'd never allowed herself to sing along with rock 'n' roll songs—at least not so anyone could hear her. No, while her classmates were going to dances, she was home trying to keep the peace between her parents. Maybe it was time for her to let her hair down, to be the youthful, devil-may-care kid she'd never let herself be. Maybe it was time for her to have silly, mindless fun!

"Hey, that's more like it," said Brett when he saw the way she moved to the music. "Now, how about really showing me your stuff?"

"My stuff?"

"What's the matter? You don't know how to do the twist?"

He got out of the car, walked around to her side, and opened her door.

"Come on. Out. Let's go. I wanna see those legs twistin' the night away."

He held his hand out for her and she took it. Before she knew it, she was gyrating to the sound of "The Twist," breathless and laughing and twisting her heart out, right there in the road in the middle of nowhere. And when the twist songs were over, the dance tunes continued: "The Locomotion" . . . "Mashed Potatoes" . . . "The Swim." . . . On and on it went until the station finally broke for commercials.

"Thank goodness!" Caroline sighed, then collapsed against the side of the car. "I haven't laughed so hard in—"

She stopped herself and looked at Brett, who wiped the sweat from his brow and moved closer to her.

"You're pretty damn gorgeous when you laugh," he said, his voice serious suddenly. "But then you've probably been told that by millions of guys."

Caroline shook her head. "Not millions," she said, her eyes locked on his, though she was thinking of James. "Just one."

"He made you laugh like this?" Brett asked, his competitive juices flowing.

"Yes," she said softly. "Just like this."

He was about to lean toward her, to kiss her beautiful mouth, when the radio commercials ended and Dirk, the deejay, announced that he was changing the mood from dance music to romantic ballads.

"Here's an oldie for all you lovers out there," Dirk intoned. "Lenny Welch's 'Since I Fell for You.'"

As the first notes of the song emanated from the car radio, Brett took Caroline's hand in his and pulled her gently toward him.

"I've always had a thing for this song," he said as he wrapped his arm around her waist and began to guide her slowly, sensuously to the music. "But I never figured I'd be dancing to it with someone like you." As it had many times since he'd met Caroline, the realization of how different she was from the other women he had known washed over Brett. She *was* different, so classy, so independent, so self-reliant. The women he usually danced with were groupies he'd pick up outside the ballpark, hangers-on who had nothing better to do than throw themselves at athletes, movie stars, TV celebrities, anyone with a famous name and a fat bank account. He'd never pictured himself with a woman like Caroline; a woman who had scruples; a woman who dressed in a refined, dignified style; a woman who had an educated way of speaking and interests that went beyond shopping and partying; a woman with a career and a son and a devotion to both; a woman who was not impressed by celebrity, certainly not his. No, Caroline Goddard was special, he thought as he held her, oh so carefully, as if she were precious cargo.

Caroline let Brett's remark go unanswered as she placed her arm around him and allowed herself to melt into the song. Into him.

They danced wordlessly, her head against his broad shoulder, her body moving in sync with his. There were no thoughts of his arrogance, her aloofness. Only the music and the stars and the warm night air.

Then, as if on cue, just as the song ended, a cloud passed over them and, as often happens in south Florida, it suddenly began to rain—a brief but torrential rain that soaked their hair, their clothes, and their shoes and sent them scurrying for the shelter of the car. They rushed inside, closed the doors and windows, and watched as the rain continued to pour down, creating little pools of water in the road.

"My hair," Caroline moaned as she tried to squeeze some of the moisture out of its ends. She had spent an hour washing and blow-drying her hair for the party. It was now practically glued to her neck and forehead. "And my mascara must be running down my face!"

"Yup," said Brett, looking at her and laughing.

"And my clothes," she said. The expensive dress she'd bought at Saks clung to her body like wallpaper, and her delicate gold metallic sandals were waterlogged.

"Seems like I got you soaked again," he said.

"Again?" she asked, not understanding.

"The Bloody Mary? On the plane?"

She nodded. That incident seems like ages ago, she realized with a jolt. It was the present she was focused on, the nearness of him, the wetness of them both, the laughter that still echoed through the deserted street.

"Are you pissed off?" he asked, reaching over to cup her chin in his fingers and turn her face toward him.

"My friend Francesca is the one who'll be angry," Caroline said. "She specifically wanted me at the party, and I let her down, Brett."

"We'll make it up to her," he said.

"*We* will?"

"Yup."

"What about your bosses at the network? Won't they be furious that you didn't show up?"

"Probably, but they'll get over it. Most of the time I give them exactly what they want, which is ratings. The rest is bullshit."

He drew her face toward him. She could feel his hot breath on her skin, and she made no move to pull away.

"You're not only gorgeous when you laugh, you're gorgeous when you're wet," he murmured as he stroked her damp hair and then traced her lips with his surprisingly graceful fingers.

She was silent, spellbound by the situation—and by the man whose sheer physical presence she felt helpless to resist. She closed her eyes and waited for him to kiss her. To hell with his boorish manners and offensive language. She had had fun with him—more fun than she'd had in years—and now she wanted him to make the moves he'd been boasting he would make since they'd first met.

But instead of embracing her, he pulled away. It was *he* who decided not to take advantage of the moment.

"I don't think so, baby," he said, removing his hands from her face and placing them on the steering wheel. "I've got a headache." She wasn't going to kick dirt in his face, the hell with his father's advice. No woman was worth being humiliated. Not even Caroline Goddard. He started the car.

"A headache?" Caroline's face turned scarlet and her nostrils flared. "You're the one who's . . . You're telling me you . . . After the way *you* chased *me,* bragging how you were going to get me to fall all over you—"

"I *am* going to get you to fall all over me," he cut her off as he resumed his macho tone, turned on the windshield wipers, steered the car back onto the road and headed—he hoped—in the direction of Caroline's condo. "What I told you right from the beginning was that you were going to beg me."

"Over my dead body," she sniffed.

"Such a gorgeous body," he mused.

"You'll never get close enough to enjoy it," she retorted.

"Don't bet on it, sweet cakes. Everything is going right on schedule. The next time I'm about to kiss you, you'll be begging me not to stop."

"Oh, give me a break," Caroline said. "You're really out of touch."

"See? You've got 'touch' on the brain, honey," he smirked. "Oh, and by the way, I had a great time tonight," he added. "I just wanted you to know."

Caroline answered by turning her back to him and remaining in the position for the entire ride home.

At nine-thirty the next morning, Caroline telephoned Francesca to apologize for not coming to the party and to find out how everything went. But before she could get a word out, Francesca bubbled with questions.

"How on earth did you meet Brett Haas, and where did you two buy such an exquisite—and extravagant—arrangement of flowers?" she asked. "My office looks like a greenhouse! And which of you wrote that adorable note?"

So Brett had meant it when he'd said, *"We'll* make it up to Francesca." If he was sincere about that, was he sincere about making Caroline care for him? she wondered.

"I met him on the plane coming back from—"

"Oh, never mind that," Francesca interjected when Caroline was about to answer her friend's first question. "I've got to tell you that the party was a roaring success but that the network people were terribly disappointed that Brett didn't show up. They seem to think he hung the moon."

"They do?" Caroline asked, amazed.

"Definitely. They think he has a great future as a broadcaster. He's apparently very well respected and extremely well liked not only by viewers but by the television executives who do business with him. They say he's colorful and full of personality and so much fun to be around."

"Colorful? He's nothing short of blinding," said Caroline. "You ought to see him in his red blazer and his orange golf slacks. He's enough to give anyone a headache."

Francesca said she'd take that kind of headache any day.

"What *I* want to know is, does he have a brother at home?" she asked. "A brother who's single and looks like him?"

Caroline laughed. She kept forgetting how famous Brett Haas was and that Francesca, who read all the magazines, including *Sports Illustrated,* knew exactly who he was and what he looked like. "The truth is, I know very little about Brett except that he dances as well as I'm told he used to play baseball."

"Dances, huh? It sounds as if the two of you have gotten pretty cozy," said Francesca. "What's he like?"

Caroline paused for a moment, then told Francesca exactly what she thought, "Macho. Insensitive. Loud. No taste. No manners. Totally in love with himself."

Francesca laughed. "In other words, you're crazy about him."

~25~

Francesca's wrong, Caroline thought as she hung up the phone. *As wrong as a person could be.*

There was no way she could be crazy about Brett Haas. Crude, crass, color-blind Brett Haas? Haa! Francesca might as well tell her that she was crazy about the man on the moon. Sure, she'd enjoyed herself with Brett, letting some of his I-don't-care-what-anybody-thinks-of-me attitude rub off on her, and dancing the twist in the middle of the road in the middle of the night in the middle of God knows where. And sure, she hadn't laughed so hard in years. But it had been late, she'd been tired, and she'd decided she might as well humor him. Besides, Brett *was* macho and insensitive and totally in love with himself, just as she'd told Francesca. He was wonderful with Jack, she had to admit, a father figure the boy so clearly longed for. But a love object? Hardly.

It was Jean-Claude with whom she was preoccupied. He had telephoned from New York the night before and left a message with Selma: he was arriving in Palm Beach the next morning. He would be staying at his father's apartment above Café Pavillion, and if he didn't hear from Caroline to the contrary, he would meet her at Romance, Inc. at six o'clock that evening. Before saying good-bye, he had added, "And please tell Caroline that I would like very much to spend some time alone with her. To pick up where we left off in New York."

To pick up where we left off in New York, Caroline sighed as she recalled the sumptuous meal Jean-Claude had prepared for her at his Soho loft . . . the candlelight and wine and Mozart . . . the low whispers of his desire . . . the feel of his lips against her skin . . . the sensation of his arms around her . . . the almost unbearable excitement of his need for her. She sighed once again as she replayed the scene in her mind, including the moment when, although so tempted to surrender to his embrace, she had pulled away and insisted on going home. To the safety—and emptiness—of Cissy McMillan's guest room and the chaste life she'd carved out for herself.

What will happen when we're together this time? she wondered, as jittery as a schoolgirl before a first date. Had that evening in his loft been a chimera, the vain and foolish fantasy of a lonely woman? Or had it been something more than mere illusion? Had something real, something substantial, taken place between them? Will I feel just as attracted to him? she asked herself. Just as drawn to his dazzling good looks and vibrant sexuality? And what will I do about it? Will I give in to my feelings? Or will I continue to resist, to avoid the pleasure of his touch, his words of affection, his caress?

Caroline didn't have time to sort through the conflicts that pulled her in opposing directions and answer the questions she posed to herself. She had a nine o'clock meeting at the First Ocean Bank of the Palm Beaches in yet another attempt to convince someone somewhere that she and Romance, Inc. were deserving of a loan—a loan that, on Clifford Hamlin's advice, she had upped to $200,000. Thoughts of where the future might lead her and Jean-Claude would just have to wait. Business before pleasure, she thought to herself as she gathered up her attaché case and hurried out the shop's rear entrance.

"Yes," said Richard Clendenon, taking Caroline completely off guard.

He was a chubby, middle-aged man with a ruddy complexion and a red handlebar mustache, sitting in a corner office telling her that the First Ocean Bank had decided to grant the $200,000 loan she was seeking. She was ecstatic—and so lost for words—that she almost threw her arms around him. Instead, she merely pumped his hand in a very grateful and enthusiastic handshake and grinned so hard she thought her face would break. After a moment of speechless surprise, the words returned.

"I can't tell you how happy I am that I brought my business to First Ocean," she told Mr. Clendenon. "The other banks I dealt with weren't nearly as open-minded."

"Their loss," he replied. "The loan committee and I think you've got a good idea here." He paused and cleared his throat, then continued. "I've also discussed the concept of your store with someone whose opinion I often solicit when I'm considering lending money to a retailer."

"Would that be Mr. Owens?" asked Caroline. Reginald Owens was the president of the bank.

"No, Mrs. Goddard. That would be my wife," said Richard Clendenon, the twinkle in his eyes at odds with his serious, bankerly expression. "No one knows more about shopping than she does. She's a world-class expert."

Caroline laughed. "I hope you'll tell her that she's welcome in my shop anytime," she said.

"She's already been there," he said. "Several times. Our house is filled with your merchandise. So's her closet."

Caroline laughed again. "That's wonderful." She beamed. "But wait until she sees the things we're going to stock in the new store."

"Ah, yes. The Worth Avenue branch of Romance, Inc.," he said.

Caroline smiled. "The Worth Avenue branch of Romance, Inc. Gosh, that has a nice ring to it."

"Have you chosen an actual site yet?" he asked.

"No, I haven't. I wanted to wait for the loan to come through before I plunged ahead and spoke to realtors. But now that you've given me a verbal green light, Mr. Clendenon, I might just head over to Worth Avenue right now."

Richard Clendenon nodded, then rolled his eyes. "Worth Avenue," he muttered. "Estelle spends so much time there, she should declare the street her legal residence on her tax return."

Caroline laughed, then gathered her purse and attaché case and stood up.

"Thank you," she said to the banker, shaking his hand one final time. "You've made my day. No, make that my *year!*"

Caroline raced back to the store to spread the good news. She felt elated, and she wanted to share her positive feelings with the people who had been there for her in the days when she'd been so depressed she could barely function. Her friends Selma, Cissy, and Francesca were at the top of her list; then came Jenny and Phil up in Maine. She considered calling her mother, too, then rejected the idea. Mary Shaw hadn't shown much interest in Caroline's business, even though she had a sharp eye for figures and, if she had not been bogged down with an abusive, alcoholic husband and had taken the time to pursue a career, would have made a fine accountant. Caroline considered calling Jean-Claude at the Café Pavillion, but after checking her watch, she realized that his plane would not have arrived yet from New York. She wanted very much to call the duchess, who was returning to Europe in a couple of days, but Clifford had advised her not to discuss the financial side of Romance, Inc. with Tamara until they met with her and the duke in London.

Clifford, Caroline thought. She should tell *him* that her loan had finally been approved. It was he who had suggested she ask for $200,000 instead of $100,000; he who had encouraged her to persist until she found a bank that would be receptive; he who had told her not to give up, not to be thrown by rejection. Of course, she should share her good news with him.

But she had never called him, not at Goddard-Stevens or anywhere else; *he* had always been the one to call *her*. It had been an unspoken agreement between them. Neither of them wanted Charles Goddard to find out about their "friendship," if it could be termed that. Or perhaps, it suddenly occurred to her, it was because Clifford liked to be the one in control, the one who decided if and when he would call. Still, why shouldn't she try to reach him at his office? He was her financial advisor, after all. They were planning a business trip to London together to find investors for her company. What she and Clifford Hamlin did was none of Charles Goddard's business.

Caroline was about to pick up the phone to ask Manhattan information for the number of Goddard-Stevens when it rang.

"Romance, Inc. Good morning," she said into the receiver.

"Hello, Caroline. It's Clifford."

Caroline was taken aback by the coincidence momentarily. She wanted to tell him that she was just about to call him, but she didn't. He still intimidated her slightly, and she was suddenly relieved that she hadn't made the call after all.

"Caroline? Is everything all right?" he asked when she hadn't responded.

"Yes, more than all right, actually. I have wonderful news."

"Your loan has been approved," he said as if reading her mind.

"How did you know?" She was astonished.

"Because a couple of 'no's' mean nothing when you're trying to build a business. All it takes is one 'yes.'"

"Well, I got my 'yes' from Mr. Clendenon at the First Ocean Bank of the Palm Beaches."

"That *is* wonderful news. Now, when we meet with Drew Darlington and the duke and duchess, you'll be coming in with more of your own money."

"You really think they'll go for it?" Caroline asked, her old insecurities surfacing.

"Drew loves a good idea, as I told you. Tamara will be salivating. Ferdy, on the other hand, will take more convincing. Which is why I called you this morning. Have you got those figures we discussed? For the long-range business plan I said I'd draw up for you?"

"Yes. I finished them late yesterday afternoon. Should I overnight them to you?"

"Please. Now about the arrangements for the trip. My secretary, Ms. Frith, has booked us on the Concorde for April ninth. We'll be staying at the—"

"The Concorde?" Caroline gasped. A ticket cost thousands. She had been planning to buy an economy fare. "I can't afford—"

Clifford interrupted. "You're not paying. Goddard-Stevens is picking up your expenses for the trip."

"Oh, right. Charles Goddard will love that," Caroline said sarcastically.

"Charles Goddard has nothing to do with this," Clifford said, eager to reassure Caroline that he was his own man, free to handle his clients—and potential clients—as he wished. "I do what I think is best for Goddard-Stevens. And bringing you to London is best for Goddard-Stevens. As you so astutely pointed out some time ago, I'm engineering this trip, not only to help you expand your business but to service my existing clients and to convince Tamara—and, more importantly, the duke—to let Goddard-Stevens handle their American assets. If I land their accounts, the trip will more than pay for itself."

Caroline couldn't argue with Clifford's logic. Besides, Charles Goddard owed her more than a trip to London. He owed her the dignity he had once tried to strip away from her and the respect he had never once shown her. How ironic it would be, she realized, if Charles Goddard's money helped her turn Romance, Inc.—the business James had inspired—into a successful retailing empire.

"Now, is April ninth convenient for you?" Clifford asked.

Caroline thought for a moment. April 9th was only ten days away. There was so much to do, so many details to take care of. "I've got to check with my assistant here in the shop," she replied. "We have a 'Spring into Romance' promotion scheduled for the tenth, which will involve special discounts on select merchandise. I have to make sure she can handle things alone. And, of course, I've got to discuss the trip with my son and with Selma, the woman who takes care of him when I can't."

"Fine. When you've cleared the date, give my secretary a call and she'll make all the arrangements. You'll fly to New York, and we'll leave from Kennedy together. As for the hotel—" He paused. Caroline could hear a woman's voice in the background. "Yes, Margaret?" he said, speaking to his secretary. "Tell Mr. Goddard I'll be with him as soon as

I finish this call." He paused again and then returned his attention to Caroline. "Sorry. Why don't I have Ms. Frith call you with the details? And congratulations on the loan. It's only the beginning."

Only the beginning, she mused with a sudden sense of pride and accomplishment. Romance, Inc., the *chain* of stores, was becoming more and more a reality. Step by step. Little by little. Just as Clifford had predicted. Just as she had dreamed.

Charles Goddard's office at Goddard-Stevens was at the opposite end of the plushly carpeted executive wing from Clifford's. Nevertheless, even as Clifford was engaged in conversation with Caroline, Charles learned precisely what was being said—thanks to Ted Aronson and the marvels of modern electronic eavesdropping. The private investigator had been providing him with daily reports of Caroline's comings and goings—and those of her male friends. At Charles's instructions, Aronson had spun an intricate web of surveillance around her—from paying her neighbors to spy on her to bugging her phones at home and at work. Unbeknownst to her, her life was no longer her own, her privacy a thing of the past. Aronson knew instantly that Clifford Hamlin's call to Caroline would be explosive information to his client. He called Charles even before the conversation was over.

"It seems that there's yet another man in Mrs. Goddard's life," Aronson told Charles. "Two more, in fact."

"Good Lord," said Charles, thinking of the promiscuity to which his grandson was being subjected.

"It's true, sir," Aronson continued. "Right now, as we speak, Mrs. Goddard is conversing with Goddard-Stevens's managing director."

"With Goddard-Stevens's *what?*"

"Your managing director, sir. Clifford Hamlin."

Charles Goddard was silent for a moment as the information sank in. And when he finally spoke, his voice, calm and controlled, did not betray the shock and rage he felt.

"That's not possible," he told the private investigator. How would they even know each other? Where would they have met? "Not possible at all," he reiterated. Even as he spoke, though, he realized that it *was* indeed possible. After all, what did he really know about Clifford Hamlin's private life? What did he know about what Clifford did and who he saw in his off-hours?

"I have their conversation on tape, sir," affirmed Aronson. "It seems as if Mr. Hamlin and Mrs. Goddard have been in contact with each other for some time."

"Clifford Hamlin? You're absolutely sure?"

"Yes, sir. Very sure. He and Mrs. Goddard are planning a trip together, sir. To London early next month."

Seldom was Charles Goddard speechless, but for the second time in less than five minutes, he could barely utter a word. What would possess Clifford Hamlin, the man to whom he had entrusted the future of Goddard-Stevens, to betray him this way? To take up with the very woman who had destroyed his son. The very woman he planned to sue for custody of his grandson. Clifford was a bachelor, Charles knew. An eligible and, no doubt, very sought-after bachelor. But he hadn't been the slightest bit interested when Charles and Dina had tried to pair him with Emily—and now Charles understood why: Clifford obviously liked to bottom fish. From a poor family of no social status himself, Clifford obviously felt more comfortable with those from a similar background. It was a fact, Charles suddenly realized, that he hadn't taken into consideration when he had made Clifford his offer.

"Mr. Goddard? Are you there?" asked Ted Aronson after several seconds of silence.

"Yes, Aronson," said Charles, regaining his composure. "Now then, you mentioned that there were *two* more men in the woman's life?"

"Yes, sir. The other is a Frenchman whose father owns a business in Palm Beach called Café Pavillion."

"Yes, yes. On Worth Avenue. I know the place," said Charles. "The son owns a restaurant of his own in New York. He's quite a ladies' man, I hear."

"That's right. He's been seeing Mrs. Goddard in New York and in Palm Beach. They're planning a little reunion tonight at her store. At six o'clock."

So Dina was right, Charles thought. The woman their son had married really *was* trash. Attempting to worm her way back into the Goddards' life—and, no doubt, their fortune—via Clifford Hamlin. Openly running around with a French loverboy. Flitting from one lover to another, self-indulgently preoccupied with her own pleasure. Neglecting her son. James's child. *Their* grandson. Charles wondered if Caroline had ever cared for James at all, or if he had merely been her stud du jour, her meal ticket.

"I hope you're pleased with the information, sir," Aronson said, wanting to guarantee that his powerful client would continue to pay the hourly fees he was billing Charles. "Exposing your former daughter-in-law's irresponsility will certainly help with your custody suit."

"That it will," agreed Charles. But pleased with the information? Charles supposed he was. He was certainly pleased with the fact that, thanks to Aronson's surveillance of Caroline's tawdry private life, he was piling up incontrovertible evidence that she was a neglectful, unfit mother, and that custody of Jack should be granted to him and Dina. Judges did not approve of absentee mothers. They did not allow children to stay with mothers who put their careers before their children. And they certainly did not approve of mothers with wild, promiscuous lifestyles.

But pleased about Caroline and Clifford? As Charles hung up with Aronson, he pondered *that* piece of information. His first impulse was to storm into his managing director's office and fire him on the spot. But then he considered the consequences of dismissing Clifford. First, there was the employment contract. The firm would have to pay Clifford millions in severance if he were let go. Second, there was Clifford's ability. He was a brilliant financier who would be extremely difficult—if not almost impossible—to replace. He had increased profits, cut costs, and raised Goddard-Stevens's profile both with the press and within the financial community. Third, Charles had intended Clifford's arrival at the company to send a message to Wall Street that Goddard-Stevens was a vibrant, ever-growing organization that kept pace with the times even as it remained a rock-solid enterprise. Firing Clifford would send the opposite message: that the firm was unstable, its management in disarray, and that Charles Goddard, who had wooed Clifford aggressively and finally won him, had misjudged and made a poor choice.

Well, I'm supposed to have a meeting with Clifford anyway, Charles reminded himself, glancing at his watch. *Perhaps I'll have a little chat with him first, before we discuss Goddard-Stevens business.* He moved toward the phone and buzzed his secretary.

"Yes, Mr. Goddard?" replied Lydia Albright, who had worked for Charles Goddard for over twenty years and had adored and feared him for just as long.

"Please call down to Mr. Hamlin's office again and tell him that I want to see him," said Charles. "Right away."

"I've called several times, sir," Lydia said. "Mr. Hamlin's secretary said he was still tied up on a long-distance call."

Charles scowled. "Then tell her to untie him," he barked.

"Yes, Mr. Goddard."

He hung up the phone and reached for a cigar. Lifting one out of the box, he struck a match and lit the tip of the Cuban cigar, ordered from Montreal and sent by pouch to Manhattan. He smiled as he thought of how Clifford Hamlin, who ran marathons and watched his cholesterol, detested cigar smoke. He leaned back in his chair, drew on the cigar, and exhaled the smoke in a long, gray stream. Then, just as Clifford entered, he inhaled once more and released another stream of smoke into the room.

"Ah, Clifford," Charles said with a killer grin. "So you were able to extricate yourself after all."

Caroline spent the rest of the day planning her London trip. After consulting with her assistant and with Selma, she contacted Jack's school to make sure the trip didn't conflict with any student activities or parent-teacher events. Then she put the figures Clifford had asked her for in the overnight mail drop before getting in touch with two realtors who specialized in commercial real estate on Worth Avenue. Each had locations they were eager to show her.

"A prime corner!" the first one told her, describing the location he had in mind.

"Right next to Chanel!" said the other, indicating a large space adjacent to the famed designer's branch store.

Worth Avenue! she kept shaking her head in disbelief. Having a store there would be the culmination of all her dreams, all her years of hard work. And soon it would be a reality!

She made appointments to look at store space the following day and then waited on clients, closed the shop, and freshened up for Jean-Claude's visit at six o'clock.

At five minutes before six, he arrived. He was dressed in tight-fitting jeans, leather moccasins and a white polo shirt that showed off his strong, muscular body. He wore his coal black hair, not in his customary ponytail but loose and free. As his green eyes swept over her, seeming to caress her, his sensuality almost overwhelmed her.

"Hello, *chérie,*" he said as he stood at the door, a wicker basket in his hand. "Since you can't come to Moustiers tonight, I thought I would bring Moustiers to you."

"Jean-Claude . . ."

Across the street, sitting in a gray Honda, Ted Aronson made a note of the time and snapped a photograph as the son of the owner of Café Pavillion, Jean-Claude Fontaine put down the basket he was holding and took Caroline into his arms.

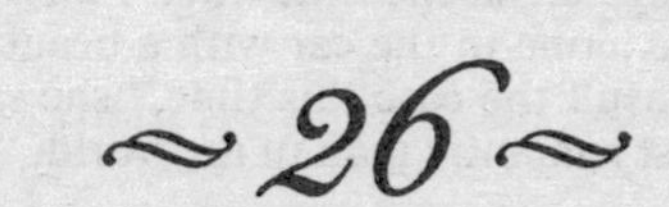

Caroline put her hands against Jean-Claude's chest and took a step backward, away from him. And then she exhaled deeply.

"Come now, *chérie.* Don't tell me you didn't enjoy that kiss," he said. Judging by the way she had yielded to his caress, allowed her mouth to linger on his, she had been just as eager to see him again as he had been to see her.

"I didn't say I didn't enjoy it," Caroline smiled wryly. "I just needed to take a breath."

Jean-Claude laughed. "I did tell your baby-sitter when I called last night that I wanted to pick up where you and I left off in New York," he said. "And we did leave off with a kiss, did we not? With several kisses, in fact?"

Caroline nodded. The memory of their dinner at his loft had remained with her for weeks, and she kept replaying the scene in her mind. She was tremendously attracted to him, there was no doubt about that. And she hadn't been with a man since James died, something Tamara and Cissy never ceased to remind her. It was time to open herself up to life, to other men, she knew. She did have needs, both emotional and physical. But was Jean-Claude the right man? At the right time? For her? He was certainly more appealing than Brett Haas, wasn't he? Wasn't he?

"Yes," she admitted. "And I was very happy when I got home last night and found your message."

"That's nice to hear," he said. "I had hoped to speak to *you,* though, not to your baby-sitter."

"I had an appointment," she said evasively, avoiding his eyes.

"Yes, a party, I understand," Jean-Claude said.

"Actually, I never made it to the party," Caroline said. "My escort got us lost."

Jean-Claude raised an eyebrow.

"Lost!?" Jean-Claude chortled. "That's the oldest trick in the book. We played it all the time when I was a boy—when we wanted to be alone in the car with a beautiful girl."

"Well, that wasn't the case this time," she said, thinking of Brett, the least romantic man in the world. "Not the case at all."

"Chérie. Tu es très naïve," he said, shaking his head. "The guy probably wanted to—"

"Jean-Claude Fontaine," she cut him off. "Is it possible that you're jealous?"

He smiled but didn't answer. Instead, he reached down and picked up the elegant Hermès wicker picnic basket he'd brought with him.

"What about having our *hors d'oeuvres* on the beach?" he

suggested. "We can sip champagne while the sun goes down."

"Sounds wonderful," said Caroline, whose last picnic on the beach had been with James. More than five years ago. Much too long ago. "I'll just have to change my shoes." She looked down at her ivory pumps.

"Leave the shoes in the car and go barefoot," he said. "The sand will feel delicious between your toes."

She nodded, reminded yet once again of Jean-Claude's extremely sensual nature and envying it. Enjoying it.

The two of them walked out of the shop, arm in arm, looking very much to all the world like lovers.

Still in his gray Honda, Ted Aronson glanced at his watch, made a note of the time, and snapped a second photograph. Then he started the engine and followed as Caroline and Jean-Claude got into her car and drove away.

They headed east to Palm Beach, parked on South Ocean Boulevard and took a leisurely walk down to the sea. A light breeze blew off the water, but the early evening air was unseasonably balmy, the sky just beginning its nightly show of blues and reds and yellows.

"The colors are intensely beautiful in Florida, I must admit," said Jean-Claude as he took in their surroundings.

Caroline nudged him gently in the ribs. "Was that really you? Paying provincial Palm Beach a compliment?"

He smiled. "I've always said that the place is exquisite. It's the people I'm not so sure about."

"I see," she said skeptically.

"Although there is *one* Palm Beach person I'm growing very fond of," he added, tightening his grip around her waist.

She could feel his body against hers and became acutely aware of the sexual spell he seemed to cast over her. She found herself longing for more physical contact between them, even as the very idea threw her in conflict.

They found a stretch of beach that was nearly deserted and selected it as their picnic spot. Jean-Claude opened the leather fastenings of the picnic basket, pulled out a vividly colored kilim and spread it across the sand.

"The tables at Moustiers are a bit more comfortable, but the view can't compare to this one," he said, helping her down onto the rug.

"This is perfect, Jean-Claude," she said, smiling up at him as he stood before her, a dark and dashing figure silhouetted against the brilliantly hued sea and sky. "I can't think of a nicer way to end the day. You've obviously gone to a lot of trouble."

"Bien sûr, but it was worth it," he said, reaching into the basket and carefully lifting out a half-dozen small white cardboard boxes, a bottle of champagne, and two glasses carefully wrapped in large, crisply starched linen napkins. "I intend to dazzle you with my culinary artistry—and to prove to you once and for all that there's more to life than ham sandwiches."

"I'm beginning to see that," Caroline replied. "But how on earth did you find the time to—"

"I arrived at Café Pavillion at eleven o'clock this morning, informed Marcel that I would be taking over his kitchen, and proceeded to replicate several of the appetizers I serve at Moustiers," he interrupted.

"Marcel must have had a fit." Caroline winced.

"Let's just say he wasn't amused," said Jean-Claude without guilt. "But then Marcel doesn't have one of the world's great senses of humor, *n'est-ce pas?"*

Caroline smiled. Jean-Claude Fontaine was really something, she thought, knowing she had never met anyone like him. He was a handful, but a witty and charming one, and if he were ever to settle down with one woman— She stopped herself. Would Jean-Claude settle down with one woman? Could he? Would he be able to give up the nightlife and the adoration and the affection of all those beautiful, sophisticated women? He had told her that he aspired to the kind of quiet married life his parents had enjoyed. But did he really? And what about her? Did she want him to?

"Champagne, *chérie?"* Jean-Claude filled the glasses and handed one to Caroline, then joined her on the blanket, sitting very close to her. She could smell his cologne, his skin, him. She did not make the slightest effort to move away.

"To romance," he said as he toasted.

"There you go again," she said. "The Frenchman is relentless in his quest for *l'amour.*"

"That's true, but I was also speaking of your store," he maintained. "Isn't that what you sell there? Romance?"

"Absolutely," she said, and sipped her champagne. It was crisp and dry and bubbly, and she let it linger on her lips, on her tongue.

After Jean-Claude took a sip from his glass, he began to open the boxes of *hors d'oeuvres.* Caroline shook her head in amazement as she surveyed the sumptuous array he had prepared for them. For her.

"Pour madame, I have made an after-work *repas.* Light but provocative, something to tease the appetites," he said with a suggestive smile, displaying the elegantly presented and colorful tidbits. "The selections are: vodka-cured salmon with sour cream and salmon roe on buckwheat blinis; curried chicken mini brochettes; *gougères* flavored with *gruyère* and cayenne. Oh, and one last item: tomato, basil, and red pepper tarts with thyme. *Fresh* tomatoes, you'll be relieved to know."

They laughed together for a moment. It was nice to know that, despite his ego, Jean-Claude also had a sense of humor about himself.

"I can't get over this," she marveled, shaking her head. "I don't know what to eat first."

"Then let me choose for you."

Jean-Claude reached for one of the salmon blinis and brought it to Caroline's mouth.

"Taste," he commanded softly, his voice low and husky, as if it weren't food he was offering but a prelude to a different kind of pleasure, a more intimate sort of indulgence.

Caroline parted her lips and let him feed her the cool, smooth salmon. She closed her eyes as she felt it slide down her throat, as sensual a sensation as she could ever remember. His fingertips lingered on her lips and, without her consciously willing it, she kissed them.

"Ummm," he murmured, moving his hand to cup her cheek and caress her skin.

"Ummmm," she agreed, leaning into him. "Su-bleem."

Caroline meant it. Never had she realized how seductive food could be, and so when he brought, not more *hors d'oeuvres* but his own moist, warm lips to hers, she yielded to him. At first, his kiss was gentle, with the tenderness of a butterfly's wing. Then, with increasing heat and hunger, he opened his mouth wider and explored her lips with the tip of his tongue, tasting her and engraving the shape of her mouth in his memory. In response, her mouth opened and his tongue entered the warm wetness of its interior. She began to lose herself in a world of food and wine, of touch and sensation, a world she hadn't known existed, a world in which men and women, love and desire, meet and merge and finally flame. . . .

Ted Aronson, walking along the shore with a camera dangling from his neck like a thousand other visitors to south Florida, paused on his stroll, pointed the camera at his prey, focused it and snapped a picture of Caroline and Jean-Claude, who were locked in a passionate—and very incriminating—embrace.

They never saw, never noticed, as their kiss spun on and on, drawing them deeper and deeper into utter oblivion.

But then suddenly, a sound intruded on the very fringes of Caroline's consciousness. And another sound. A blaring, incredibly annoying sound. Reluctantly, she and Jean-Claude pulled apart to see what the commotion was all about.

"Was there an accident?" asked Caroline, wresting herself from the spell she'd been under, aware of her pounding heart and flushed face.

Jean-Claude shook his head.

"Some idiot over there is sitting on his horn," he remarked, his tone revealing his annoyance. He and Caroline had been enjoying a beautiful moment in a beautiful setting and some *mauvais type* had to come along and spoil it.

"Who? Where?" asked Caroline, turning around.

"Over there. In the convertible," Jean-Claude said, pointing. Caroline craned her neck to get a better view. Then she saw what Jean-Claude was pointing at: a fire-engine red convertible with several very scantily clad females sitting next to and behind the driver.

"Probably some tourist making a nuisance of himself," she said.

Suddenly, the driver of the convertible caught Caroline's eye and began to wave—and honk his horn at the same time!

"Hey, sweet cakes. It's me!" he yelled.

"Oh, my God," Caroline groaned. It was Brett Haas! What on earth was *he* doing there?

"How about a little decorum out in public, huh, Caroline honey?" Brett shouted over the din of his horn. "Y'all are smooching in full view. Suppose the cops come along? Tell the stud with the ponytail to cool his jets. Palm Beach isn't Coney Island, ya know?"

"Do you *know* that person?" Jean-Claude asked Caroline, appalled. Everything about the clod in the convertible offended the sophisticated Frenchman: the less-than-classy females draped around him, his neon green shirt, his loud horn, and his loud mouth.

She nodded. "Unfortunately. But maybe if we ignore him, he'll go away. Like a bee."

Brett didn't go away. Once he realized it was Caroline whom he'd spotted kissing a man on the beach, he buzzed and buzzed and circled the block over and over, honking and yelling at her each time.

"I can't take this anymore," she said finally, getting up off the blanket. "Let's find a place where we can eat in peace."

Jean-Claude agreed, and as they walked back down the beach, Brett saluted them with a final blast of his horn, accelerated, and sped off in the opposite direction.

"A friend of yours?" Jean-Claude asked with a raised eyebrow.

Caroline shook her head vehemently. "Absolutely not! A friend of my son's."

* * *

The spell having been broken, they decided to finish their picnic within the relatively safer and quieter confines of Café Pavillion at one of the tables by the window. They watched the passersby on Worth Avenue and devoured the rest of the *hors d'oeuvres* and champagne and chatted with Pierre, who sat with them for several minutes.

"He looks tired," Caroline commented when Pierre left them to attend to his dinner customers.

Jean-Claude nodded. "The café is really too much for him to run on his own now. He's too proud to admit it—we Frenchmen are famous for being a bit stubborn—but the time has come for him to either sell Café Pavillion or let me run it."

"Let you run it? You have a very popular restaurant in New York that takes almost all your attention as it is," Caroline pointed out. "I know you find the time to come down here on weekends occasionally, but how on earth would you run restaurants in Palm Beach and Manhattan simultaneously?"

"Oh, it can be done," he said. "It would mean hiring very competent managers in both places. And, of course, it would mean spending much more time in Palm Beach."

"But you hate Palm Beach," said Caroline.

"I'm hating it less and less," Jean-Claude said with a grin that spoke volumes. He took her hand across the table and looked into her eyes. He lowered his voice and spoke to her in an intimate tone: "How would you feel if I spent more time here, *chérie?*"

The question surprised her. She hadn't expected him to be considering a more permanent arrangement in Florida. The very idea of him living nearby, of seeing him more often, of getting to know him better, filled her with excitement and confusion. What *did* she feel about Jean-Claude Fontaine? Was it merely a sexual attraction? Or was there more to it? Time would tell, she knew. Time would tell.

It was nearly ten o'clock by the time she got home, and when Selma opened the door for her, Jack, in his Braves uniform and bare feet, bounded across the living room to greet her.

"Shhh!" he said, holding his finger to his mouth and pointing to the supine figure on the sofa. "Brett's asleep!"

"Brett? What's *he* doing here?" she asked, following Jack's gaze, stunned to see the *mauvais type* stretched out on her couch and snoring loud enough to drown out the baseball game that was blaring away on the television set. She was furious at this latest intrusion into her life.

"It's my fault," said Selma, upset that Caroline was so angry. "He said that you and he had a date. And, of course, Jack was overjoyed to see him. So I let him in."

As Selma went back to her own apartment, Caroline turned off the television set, picked Jack up in her arms, and over his protests, carried him off to his bedroom. She stood over him as he washed his face and brushed his teeth. Then she watched as he changed into his pajamas. When he was snug and safe under the covers, she combed back his golden hair with her fingers and kissed his forehead.

"You're up much too late!" she scolded him.

"But Brett came over. He brought popcorn and soda. We watched an American League game even though I *hate* the American League," he said, his eyes wide, glowing from the attention of a father figure who was also one of his idols.

Caroline sighed.

"What am I going to do about you? And about your friend?" she whispered.

"He's not so bad, Mom. Honest," said Jack, looking at her with wide, adoring eyes. "You really should give him a chance."

"A chance for what?" she said, more to herself than to her son.

"Just promise you won't be so mean to him," Jack pleaded.

"I'm not mean to him," Caroline protested.

"Mom?" He eyed her. "You taught me never to tell a lie."

"I'm not mean to him," she maintained. "I'm just not as fond of him as you are, darling."

"Come on, Mom. He's a neat guy when you get to know him," said Jack, gazing up at her with his big, blue eyes. "Will you get to know him? Please?"

Caroline didn't answer.

"Please?" he said again, this time even more beseechingly.

What could she say? She was putty in his hands.

"All right," she said reluctantly.

"Promise?"

"Promise," she said with a smile.

"Cross your heart?"

"Cross my heart," she laughed, crossing it and then kissing him good night one last time.

Caroline walked back out to the living room, stood over Brett with her hands on her hips, and despite the promise she had just made, glowered at him. How dare he just barge into her apartment and plant himself on her sofa, making himself at home? His hair was tousled, and his chest rose and fell with the calm breaths of deep sleep. He looked like a big, overgrown kid. A big, overgrown, color-blind kid. He was wearing a shiny purple jogging outfit—sweatpants with sweatshirt and jacket to match. It was quite an ensemble.

She leaned over, grabbed ahold of his purple jacket, and shook him. Hard.

"You look like an eggplant!" she snapped.

"Hey, what the— Where am I?" he said, coming to.

He opened his eyes and saw her standing over him. He blinked. And then he grinned.

"Well, well. Look who's finally home," he said, rubbing the sleep from his eyes and then assessing her in her linen suit with its slim lines and short skirt. "Best legs south of the Mason-Dixon line. You're a knockout, you know it, sweetheart?"

"What are you doing here, Brett?" Caroline asked wearily, ignoring his compliment.

"Sleeping, obviously."

"I never invited you," she told him.

"Jack did." He smirked.

"All right. Then try *this* question. Why were you spying on me at the beach this afternoon?"

"Hey, chill out, sweet cakes. All I was doing was driving around with my friends. Then I saw you making a public spectacle of yourself necking on the beach with some Casanova."

"Me making a public spectacle of myself? You were the one who was honking his horn, causing a commotion—"

"Who was that guy, anyway?" he cut her off.

"Who were *your* 'friends'?" she countered. "They weren't wearing much."

"Listen, sweet cakes. Your pretty boy's clothes were so tight they looked like they were glued on."

"Jean-Claude is French," said Caroline defensively. "Frenchmen dress in a very sophisticated, European style. But you wouldn't know anything about *that."*

"No, I sure wouldn't," he said. "What is the guy, a model for perfume ads or something?"

Caroline ignored his sarcasm. "It just so happens that Jean-Claude Fontaine is the most influential chef in New York. He's also a best-selling cookbook author."

"Yeah, and I've invented a cure for hiccups."

"Oh, please," Caroline sighed. "Let's get back to your little friends in the convertible. What, may I ask, do *they* do for a living?"

"I have no idea," said Brett after making no attempt to stifle a yawn. "We didn't have time to talk business, if you catch my drift. We were having fun. F-U-N. Ever hear of it?"

"Now don't you start *that* again," Caroline said. "It's late. I'd really like you to leave. I understand you and Jack had a grand old time and for that I'm very grateful. But the party's over."

Brett rose from the sofa but made no move toward the door. Instead, he grabbed Caroline around the waist and pulled her to him.

"What do you think you're doing now?" she asked, her face smack up against his.

"Whetting your appetite," he said, his arms locked around her.

"For what?" she said.

"For the day you beg me to kiss you. From what I saw on the beach today, you need someone to show you how it *should* be done."

"Oh, really?" she said, deciding to take the bait. "And how should it be done?"

She looked up, closed her eyes and waited . . .

. . . but nothing happened.

Instead, he disengaged his arms and stepped away.

"Nope. That's not a 'beg.' That's an 'ask.' I don't deliver until you *beg,* and your time is running out, honey."

"Oh? And why is that?" she asked, humiliated and frustrated by his Now-I'm-going-to-kiss-you/Now-I'm-not routine.

"Because I'm only going to be in Florida for another week or so. Then it's on to Abeline to see my Patsy."

"Only another week?" Caroline blurted out as Brett turned and headed for the door. She had gotten used to having him around, she had to admit. And ever since she'd met him on that plane, he'd been around—all the time. First, there was the highlights videotape that Jack watched over and over; whenever Caroline walked by the television set, there was Brett, hitting, fielding, mugging for the cameras! Then, there were the impromptu visits to the condo, the sparring, the crude jokes, the laughter—yes, the laughter. Brett had turned her life upside down, and now he was leaving!

"That's right, only one more week. Better grab me while you have the chance, honey," he said, patting her on the fanny. "I may not be as pretty as your beach boy, but I'm sure a lot more fun." He was about to open her front door when she called out to him.

"Brett?"

"Yeah?" He turned to look at her.

"I just . . . Well, what I mean is . . . I don't think I've thanked you properly for the kindness you've shown Jack. He kisses the ground you walk on."

"How about that," said Brett, arching an eyebrow and walking back into the living room. "And you?"

"What about me?"

"Do *you* kiss the ground I walk on, Caroline Goddard?"

"Don't be ridiculous," said Caroline as Brett moved closer to her. She felt her pulse quicken and her face flush. It wasn't as if she were making some kind of admission of her feelings for him, she told herself. It was Jack who adored Brett, Jack of whom she'd been speaking. How could he even think that she—

"Well, I kiss the ground *you* walk on," Brett confessed. "What do you say to that, huh?"

"I say you're playing with me, as usual," she said. "As far as I can tell, *you're* the only one you truly care about."

"You're way off base, sweet cakes, and I'm gonna prove it to you."

"Really? How?"

Brett got down on his hands and knees and began to kiss the white, wall-to-wall carpeting beneath Caroline's feet! She threw her head back and laughed.

"You're impossible!" she said, pulling him up on his feet. When he was standing, he inched closer to her and put his arms around her waist.

"I'm not impossible, and neither is this," he said determinedly, remembering his father's words of encouragement. There would be no backing out now. It was a full count with bases loaded and two outs. He needed a hit and he needed it now.

"Oh? And what's 'this'?" she replied, feeling the hardness of his athletic body against hers and sensing that something was about to happen between them, something that went beyond teasing and taunting and one-upping each other.

"Us," he said, bowing his head slightly, shyly. It was the first time he had allowed himself to be honest with her, to let her know that his attraction to her was more than just physical. "I don't think we're impossible together. I think we're pretty good for each other."

Caroline cocked her head and stared at him. Good together? She and Brett Haas? "Look, Brett . . . as I said, you're terrific with Jack, and I'm sure you have many wonderful qualities, but—"

"But nothing," he said, as he lifted his hand to brush an errant lock of hair off her cheek. His gentleness surprised her, and her expression showed it. "You're special, Caroline. I'd be a fool not to see that."

"Are you being serious for a change?" she asked, not wanting to be played for a fool herself. The truth was, she didn't know how to react to his sudden words of tenderness and affection.

"Very serious," he said. "Let me show you, huh?"

He leaned closer to her, and as he did, Caroline braced herself for one of his patented pullbacks, one of his I-want-you-to-beg speeches. But none came. He cupped her chin in his callused hand and tilted her face up to the light so he could see her better, see her fresh and vibrant beauty. "The face of a princess," he murmured.

In that instant Caroline let her resistance to him go, allowed herself to give in to his attention, to his apparent willingness to admit his real feelings toward her. She closed her eyes and felt his lips brush hers, and the sensation nearly made her knees buckle. He tightened his grip around her waist and pulled her even closer to him. "Caroline," he whispered. "Caroline."

He had just moved to kiss her again, intending the kiss to be the dawning of a new phase of their relationship, when a voice startled them both.

"Mom!" said Jack.

Caroline turned around. Jack was frowning and rubbing his eyes.

"What's the matter, darling?" she asked.

"Mom, there's this monster," he said, looking frightened.

Caroline pulled away from Brett and threw her arms open for her son. As she cradled him and rubbed his back and told him that it was only a bad dream, Brett knelt down to talk to the boy.

"You've got great timing, you know it, kid?" He smiled, ruffling Jack's hair.

"Sorry, Brett, but I was really scared," said Jack, still clinging to his mother. "There was this monster outside in a palm tree and it ate children and grown-ups and—"

"Sounds like a nightmare, all right," said Brett. "I bet I can get you to stop thinking about it though."

"Yeah? How?" asked Jack, his eyes still fearful.

"Come sit on the couch with me," he said as he took Jack's hand and led him over to the sofa. He motioned for the boy to put his head on his shoulder and began to tell him a story.

"Once upon a time, there was a boy who could hit a baseball a country mile," he said, and proceeded to tell Jack Goddard the story of his own life. Within minutes, Jack, who already knew Brett's story by heart, was fast asleep.

"I'd better put him back in bed," Caroline whispered to Brett as she stood over her son, who slept so peacefully. "Thanks for— Well, thanks for stopping over."

Brett rose from the sofa, touched her arm, and walked toward the front door.

"Caroline?"

"Yes?"

"I meant what I said tonight."

"Which was?"

"You heard me the first time."

"I know, but I forgot. Tell me again," she said, fishing.

He looked at her and laughed. "You're never going to give me a break, are you?" he said, his eyes teasing her, flirting with her. "But that's okay. I love a challenge. I didn't win two batting titles by wimping out."

"Now you're equating me with a batting title?" she asked, trying unsuccessfully not to smirk.

He shook his head as he opened her front door. "Compared to you, sweet cakes, those batting titles were a day at the beach." He was about to leave the condo, then stuck his head back inside and added, "Oh, and call your swell babysitter—Selma, isn't that her name?—and tell her you'll need her to stay with Jack tomorrow night."

"Why? What's happening tomorrow night?"

"I'm taking you out on the town. Just the two of us."

"If I say yes, will you promise you won't get us lost on some deserted street in the middle of nowhere?"

"Not unless you want me to, babe. Now, is that a yes?"

"Yes."

The swiftness with which she answered startled her, and as she watched Brett leave the condo, she shook her head in total confusion.

"What just happened here?" she whispered to a sleeping Jack. "I came home on a cloud after spending the evening with Jean-Claude, and then Brett tells me he's leaving town in a week, and I'm so sorry to see him go that I actually agree to go out with him! Maybe Francesca was *half*-right. I'm not crazy about Brett Haas. I'm just crazy!"

Sighing, she shut the door behind Brett and double-locked it.

After he left her apartment, Brett stopped for a moment, trying to remember where he had parked his car. As he paused, Ted Aronson snapped a photograph of him framed in the entranceway of Caroline's building. The ex-ballplayer's clothes were rumpled, his hair disheveled, and his expression satisfied, sleepy, and very happy. It was perfectly clear to the private investigator exactly what he and Caroline Goddard had been up to.

27

Patsy Haas's appendicitis wasn't serious, just sudden—sudden enough to force Brett to telephone Caroline at seven o'clock the following morning to cancel their date.

"I'm outta here on the next plane," he told her from a courtesy phone in the Delta Air Lines Crown Room. "I wanted to take you out tonight in the worst way, sweet cakes, but Patsy's my kid, ya know?"

Caroline did know, of course. If Jack had been rushed to the hospital with appendicitis, she would have done anything to be with him. She not only understood Brett's decision, she identified with it—and admired it.

"I hope Patsy will be all right," she told him.

"Oh, she'll be fine," he said. "Once she sees my face, she'll be all smiles."

Caroline sighed. "You really do think a lot of yourself, don't you?" She laughed.

"You're the one I think about, babe. Twenty-four hours a

day. Which reminds me—can I get a rain check on this dinner we were supposed to have tonight? I'm gonna stay down in Abilene until Patsy's out of the hospital, then I've gotta fly out to San Diego, where the Braves are playing an exhibition game against the Padres. After that, there's a break in the action before the regular season starts. I could swing a quick trip to Florida around the ninth of April, and we could have dinner then. What do you say?"

"I say I'm not going to be here on the ninth," said Caroline.

"Aw, you're not gonna start that hard-to-get bullshit again, are you? I thought we made some headway last night."

"It's true, Brett," she said, disappointment creeping into her voice. "I really am going to be out of town that day. I'm flying to London on business."

Brett was silent for a moment. Then he spoke, his tone gentler, more earnest. "I've gotta see you again, Caroline Goddard. And I want to see that baseball-crazed son of yours, too."

She felt her heart melt as she remembered the touch of Brett's lips and the excitement of his strong arms around her. He was the last man she'd call her "type," the last man she'd expect to have romantic feelings for. But he made her laugh and feel young again, even as his oversized ego and boorish manners infuriated her. And he was certainly the best thing that had happened to Jack, an adult male he could look up to, to turn to when monsters and bogeymen haunted his dreams. He had been so instinctive with the boy, so natural with him. Obviously, he was more than the womanizing jock she'd first thought him. He was intuitive when it came to children, a born leader and motivator, she guessed. Had she really been too stiff with him? Had he been right when he'd told her to loosen up? Liven up? Her friends had all encouraged her to stop mourning James and enjoy herself. With a man. With *men.* Did they see in her the same reluctance to let go, to live for the moment, that Brett did?

"You there, sweet cakes?" Brett asked.

"I'm here," she said with a catch in her throat, not wanting to hang up, not wanting to sever the fragile truce they'd established.

"Good. I'll call you the minute I can get back down there. But in the meantime, I don't want you running around on the beach with Mr. Hairy Chest, huh?"

Caroline laughed. "He's leaving today, too," she said of Jean-Claude, who was flying back to New York around noon.

"Beautiful. I like competition, but not where my woman is concerned."

"Your woman?" She smirked. "What are you, a caveman or something?"

"You heard me. I care about you, sweet cakes. I don't want to lose you to some walking French fry."

She laughed again. "I'll miss you, Brett," she said, shaking her head at his "quaint" way of putting things. "I really will."

"Sounds to me like you're getting closer and closer to that 'beg' I talked to you about," he said, then paused. "Caroline?"

"Yes?"

"Take care of yourself, huh?"

"I will. You, too, Brett. *Sweet cakes."*

He laughed and hung up.

As Caroline rested the phone back on the hook, she heard Jack's voice calling her.

He'll be so disappointed that Brett had to leave, she thought, but she also had to admit that Jack wasn't the only one who felt let down. *She* didn't want Brett Haas to leave either. Nor did she want Jean-Claude to go back to New York.

There couldn't be more difference between the two men, she knew. On one hand there was Brett, a diamond in the rough in every way. And then there was Jean-Claude, so suave, so continental, so charming. Unlike Brett, Jean-Claude was comfortable expressing his feelings, and there was no doubt she would continue to see him and that their relationship had potential. But what kind of potential? she asked herself. They lived in different cities, were from different countries. She had a son, he had a bachelor's free and unencumbered lifestyle. It would be very easy—too easy—to fall in love with him, but shouldn't she guard her feelings until she got to know him better? Until she could sort out her feelings for Brett?

As her departure for London neared, Caroline grew more and more determined to put thoughts of her increasingly complicated love life in the back of her mind. What mattered now, as she prepared to leave for her trip, was Romance, Inc.: making a success of her business, her labor of love, her means of support for herself and her child. Clifford had expressed such confidence in their ability to attract European investors.

"You came up with a brilliant concept when you conceived Romance, Inc.," he'd said. "Why not convince some Brits with deep pockets just *how* brilliant?"

Why not, Caroline thought. *Why not indeed?*

London was horizontal where New York was vertical. It seemed to Caroline to be a series of villages that had haphazardly grown into one another over the centuries to form a complex, modern city. The buildings were lower than those in New York, the streets cleaner, and the grounds much greener. In fact, everywhere Caroline looked there were spacious and inviting parks, as well as a profusion of colorful flowers—on stoops, in window boxes, even in planters that surrounded the lampposts. Piccadilly was as dizzying as a neon sign—electric, roaring with traffic, chockablock with shops; Mayfair was discreet, hushed, refined, with expensive-looking townhouses lining its centuries-old streets; Bond Street was Worth Avenue's haute couture sister, boasting the London branches of Cartier, Armani, and Chanel; Sloane Square was filled with trendy boutiques, much like New York's Madison Avenue; and Fulham Road featured avant-garde designers, similar in atmosphere to Manhattan's Soho.

Clifford Hamlin told Caroline that he had traveled to London so often over the past several years that the city was practically a second home to him. He had friends and clients and business associates there, knew its shops and restaurants, and could even—he laughed—speak the language. When they arrived at Heathrow Airport after their flight aboard the slim, sleek British Airways Concorde—a trip, Caroline was amazed to learn, that took only three and a half hours!—he arranged for his regular chauffeur, a silver-haired man named Raymond, to be at their disposal for the duration of their stay.

"What happened to Franklin?" Caroline teased as Raymond took their luggage and helped them into the gleaming black Bentley.

"Franklin only works one side of the Atlantic." He smiled and squeezed her arm.

As it was nearly midnight by the time they left the airport, it was too late for any sight-seeing, and they headed straight for their hotel, the small, elite Stafford's, whose history could be traced back to the eighteenth century and whose clientele read like a Who's Who of international business and society. Booked into adjacent suites, the size and opulence, Caroline guessed, of a similar accommodation in Buckingham Palace, she and Clifford stood in the elegant but somehow cozy corridor between their rooms and said good night.

"Jet-lagged?" he asked, standing close to her.

"A little," she replied.

"Sleep will fix that," he said. "And one of the hotel's incredible chocolate mints."

"Mints?"

"Look on your pillow. In the little box."

"I will," promised Caroline, eager for the treat and looking forward to luxuriating in her suite.

"Remember, our first meeting is at ten o'clock tomorrow morning," he said.

His words brought her back to earth and Caroline gulped, her nerves—and the realization of what she was in London to accomplish—catching up with her. "Who are we seeing first?" she asked.

"Tamara and Ferdy," he said. "I thought it might be a

good idea to try out our dog and pony show on a familiar and, hopefully, friendly audience."

"An excellent idea," she said, relieved.

"I suggest we meet for breakfast in the lobby at seven," he said.

"Seven?"

"Too early for you?"

"No, it's not that. I was planning to get up early anyway. It's just that you said our first meeting wasn't until ten."

"It isn't, but I thought you might like to see a bit of the city before we get down to business."

With Raymond at the steering wheel, it was Clifford's turn to show Caroline the sights—and he did. They only had a couple of hours before their meeting with the duke and duchess, but Clifford made the most of it, whisking an excited Caroline past the Tower of London, where Anne Boleyn and Lady Jane Grey had been beheaded; past the Houses of Parliament, Westminster Abbey, the Victoria and Albert Museum, Madame Tussaud's, Harrods department store, and the Portobello market.

"It's almost too much to take in!" said Caroline turning to him and glowing with the pleasures of seeing a new place for the first time.

"And you haven't seen the palace yet!" said Clifford, putting his hand over hers for a moment and enjoying her delight. She was animated and enthusiastic, and he had to force himself not to take her into his arms right then and there, in broad daylight.

At Buckingham Palace he asked Raymond to stop the car for a moment.

"So that Mrs. Goddard can take a photograph," he explained.

"Jack will be so excited when I show him the pictures and tell him about all this!" she exclaimed, adding that her son, like his father, had a keen interest in faraway places and people.

"He'll be even more excited when you come home with a present for him from Hamleys," said Clifford.

"Hamleys?" Caroline had never heard of it.

"It's the largest toy store in the world," Clifford explained, watching her eyes widen, reveling in the fact that she seemed finally to have warmed to him, to have been willing to let down her guard with him, at least for the moment. "Wait until you see their vintage vehicles."

"Is the store open now?" she asked.

He glanced at his thin gold watch.

"Not yet. It's still early, but we'll make time to go there later. Between meetings, all right?"

She nodded and smiled, aware of all the things he was doing to please her. He was considerate, charming, knowledgeable. I could learn to like this man, she thought suddenly. I could learn to like him a lot. Glancing at him sitting next to her in the spacious backseat of the Bentley, she noticed that he seemed less formal, somehow less intimidating. Even his face seemed relaxed, his expression open and accessible. Perhaps it was being away from the office, she thought, perhaps it was being back in London, a city that he said felt like home. Still, when he took a phone call in the limousine a few moments later—a call from Charles Goddard—the warning flags went up again, and she found herself shrinking away from him. He was too close to Charles, too tied to the Goddards' money and power, too dependent on their largesse to be trusted completely, she thought as she listened to him discuss the international bond market with the man she feared most in the world.

She was surprised when Clifford noticed her discomfiture.

"You've moved away. What is it?" Clifford asked her as Raymond steered the Bentley toward the section of London where Tamara and her husband resided. "Is it the phone call? From Charles?"

"Of course, it is," she said, meeting his gaze.

"But why? When we were having such a good time together? When we were getting along so well?"

Caroline did not answer. She couldn't entirely explain her reaction. It was visceral, irrational, something she couldn't control. Her whole body tensed at the sound of Charles's name, and her suspicion and distrust of Clifford immediately returned at the realization of the close bond between them.

"Caroline?" he said, prompting her for a response.

"I'm sorry," she said. "It's just that—"

"That I took a phone call from Charles," Clifford cut her off. "I run the man's company, Caroline. Why should that spoil our trip?"

"Because it's thanks to Charles Goddard that we're here," she said.

"It's *not* 'thanks to Charles Goddard.' He has nothing to do with the trip."

"He has everything to do with it. The Bentley, the chauffeur, the Concorde, all of it," she said. "They're all bought and paid for by him."

The expression on Clifford's face turned dark, and he pulled back almost as if he'd been slapped. For an instant, he seemed almost to glare at Caroline. Then, without a word, he leaned forward in his seat and lowered the glass partition that separated them from their driver.

"Stop the car, Raymond," he said curtly. "Mrs. Goddard and I are going to have a little chat."

Raymond pulled the Bentley over to the side of the road and raised the partition again so that Clifford and Caroline could speak privately.

"Now you're going to sit here and listen to me," Clifford told Caroline, not making any attempt to stifle his anger. "You've been suspicious of me since the moment we met, always alluding to my allegiance to Charles, always making the assumption that I owe my wealth and success to your former father-in-law." He paused and took a deep breath. "Has it ever occurred to you that I *earned* the Concorde and the Bentley and Raymond? That's it's Charles Goddard who owes me?"

She was so accustomed to thinking of Charles Goddard as all-powerful that the thought had never even dawned on her. Stunned by the notion, Caroline remained silent.

"No, I didn't think so," Clifford went on. "Well, it's true. After James died, Charles's interest in Goddard-Stevens waned, so much so that the company lost much of its luster, not to mention many of its top people. The financial community wrote the place off, pegged it as a ship without a captain, said openly the only way Goddard-Stevens would survive was if Charles installed someone else at the helm."

"And that's exactly what he did," Caroline said thoughtfully, looking at him. "You."

"Damn right. I didn't want the job at first. I turned the man down over and over. But when he essentially offered to hand me the company when he retired or died, I could hardly say no."

"Why not? My husband did."

Once again, Clifford Hamlin looked stung. But he recovered quickly. "Your husband was born into a family with more money than most people dream about."

"And what about *you?* I imagine that you grew up with *two* silver spoons in your mouth."

"Then you imagine wrong. I grew up in a place called Blue Ash, Ohio. My father worked in a paint factory until the fumes killed him before he was forty. After that, it was up to me to support my mother. And I did. We never had new clothes, the house was never painted, and we couldn't afford a car, but we never went hungry and we always had a roof over our heads. Now, every time I get into a chauffeur-driven Bentley, every time I dine in a fine restaurant, I think about those times. And the sense of accomplishment never fades. I *made* myself a success, Caroline. From nothing. And I never cheated anybody to get there."

Once again Caroline was speechless. All her presumptions had suddenly been turned upside down. She had always assumed that Clifford Hamlin had derived his unflagging air of self-confidence from his pedigree, from family money, from an inheritance, financial and psychological, much like James's. Now he was telling her that he was the product of a childhood very much like hers—deprived, lacking, lonely.

Wanting to apologize with more than just words, she reached out to take his hand. "I'm sorry," she said, her fingers grazing his. "But you see I—"

"Yes, I see," he interrupted, seeming not to notice her hand on his. "I see that your husband's family hurt you terribly and that you still bear the scars. But I don't understand what that has to do with me. I took a big risk coming to London with you. Charles threatened that if I went ahead with the trip, he would—"

"He knows we're here together?" Caroline blurted out. She wondered suddenly if Charles also knew about Jack, that he was James's son. Her heart raced as she tried not to imagine the consequences.

"Yes. He knows," said Clifford. "He threatened to break my contract with Goddard-Stevens if I came here with you."

"And yet you *did* come with me," she said slowly. "You came to help me get financing for Romance, Inc., regardless of what Charles said. At risk to yourself and your job—"

"That's exactly right." Clifford let a half smile escape from his lips. "Nobody tells me what to do or how to do it. Especially not when it comes to making money. And Charles Goddard knows it."

Caroline nodded, her eyes filled with a new respect and admiration. Clifford Hamlin had defied Charles, just as James had. He had come to London with her in spite of the potential consequences. And he had fought his way out of a poor, unpromising childhood to make something of himself. He was an inspiration to her and she told him so.

"Then we're clear on all this?" he asked, reaching over to touch her cheek.

She did not back away.

"Perfectly clear," she said.

"Good." He lowered the glass partition and told Raymond to start the car. "Belgrave Square," he instructed the driver. "Mrs. Goddard and I have a business meeting to get to."

Like many men of his generation, Charles Goddard had defended his country in war. But the war he was about to wage against his former daughter-in-law wasn't about politics or property; it was about the future of a little boy named Jack Goddard, a boy he'd never even met.

Ronald Switzer, Charles's lawyer, was hardheadedly realistic about their chances of winning the custody case.

"We have an excellent case, but I wouldn't be doing my

job if I didn't tell you that in lawsuits there are no guarantees," Switzer told his client after Charles had ended his transatlantic conversation with Clifford. "Your investigator did an excellent job of gathering evidence against Mrs. Goddard. The photographs are proof of her promiscuous lifestyle, and those daily time sheets showing how seldom she's home with the boy demonstrate neglect. Look where she is now—in London."

"Any judge is going to have to agree that she's a neglectful mother living an immoral lifestyle. He'll have to see the trips and the men and the running around as proof positive that the woman is an unfit mother, won't he?" Charles wanted to make very sure that Jack would be his, his and Dina's.

"Look, Charles, most likely everything will be just fine," said Switzer.

"I hope so," said Charles, looking worried. There could be no failures, no slipups, no chance that the judge would rule in Caroline's favor. The child was a Goddard. He belonged with the Goddards.

"By the way, did you find out what's going on between your former daughter-in-law and your managing director?" asked the lawyer. "The more evidence we pile up, the better our chances of winning."

"They're in London together. What else do I need to know?" Charles snapped. He had been incensed when he'd learned that Clifford was going abroad with the Shaw woman. He had told Clifford that if he went ahead with the trip, he would be risking his career at Goddard-Stevens and, ultimately, his reputation on Wall Street. His contract, Charles had reminded him, had a "best interests of the firm" clause. "If you choose to spend the firm's time and money on Caroline Shaw," Charles had told Clifford, "I'll have little choice but to invoke that clause and terminate your employment." Charles had neglected to add that once Clifford was fired, he would then take back the reins of Goddard-Stevens himself until his grandson was old enough to assume his rightful place at the helm of the firm.

"As I said, Charles," Switzer continued, "the case looks

very solid. Nowadays, the mother doesn't automatically get custody. More and more often, it's the father who wins."

"Or the grandparents," Charles added.

"Or the grandparents," Switzer agreed. "And in this case, where the grandparents are able to offer the child so much more in the way of care, attention, education, and opportunity, the judge will probably have little reluctance about turning young Jack over to you and Dina."

"Probably?" asked Charles.

"I told you, Charles, lawsuits don't come with guarantees. Nevertheless, you can call off Ted Aronson. His work is over now. The time has come to serve the mother."

"All right, then draw up the custody papers," Charles instructed the attorney. "How soon can they be served on her?"

"As soon as Mrs. Goddard steps back on U.S. soil," Switzer replied.

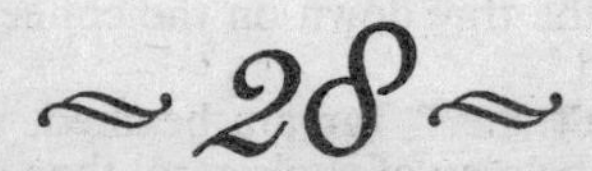

Tamara Brandt had always dreamed of owning a castle in England, but the Georgian mansion in which she and the duke now resided was close enough. A perfectly symmetrical structure with immense windows that flooded the interior with light, the architecturally significant house was entered through a heavy door leading to an imposing center hall. To the right was a spacious kitchen; to the left a large but cozy library. Straight ahead and running across the entire breadth of the house was a living room with four sets of windows overlooking a lush, meticulously maintained garden. The estate was in the heart of London's elegant Belgravia, but it had the feel of a house in the country . . . a very *grand* house in the country.

"Caroline, Clifford, darlings," Tamara cooed as her guests crossed the threshold. She double-kissed Caroline in the Continental manner and then, thrusting out her left cheek, permitted Clifford to kiss her.

"Jolly good to see you both again," Ferdy welcomed them with hearty handshakes. "Even though you've obviously come to get money out of me."

"Now, Ferdy, don't be difficult," cautioned Tamara.

"Learned it from you, my dear. Speak my mind, you're always telling me." Ferdinand Bates, the duke of Karlsborough, was a tall, portly man with pink weathered skin and bright blue eyes. He had the appearance of someone who liked to eat and drink with abandon and who never, under any circumstances, apologized for it. Tamara, in her daytime diamonds, fluttered around him like a lovestruck schoolgirl.

As they made themselves comfortable in the living room, a maid in a starched dove gray uniform and white apron appeared, nearly staggering under the weight of an immense silver tray. It was loaded down with tea, coffee, toast, butter, jams and jellies, slices of lemon cake studded with candied fruits, and a silver bowl containing thick, clotted Devon cream. She set the tray down on the coffee table, curtsied, and disappeared.

"Efficient, isn't she?" Tamara beamed, as Ferdy served himself a larger helping of cholesterol than Clifford allowed himself in a year.

"Well, now," the duke mumbled, his mouth full, crumbs on his waistcoat. "You're here to gang up on me. Isn't that how you Americans would put it?"

"Not quite," Clifford replied. "We Americans would say, 'We're here to make you an offer you can't refuse.'"

Ferdy chuckled. "That sounds interesting."

"It *is* interesting," Clifford said, turning serious. "Caroline and I have come to London to speak to you about her business. About Romance, Inc."

"And I thought you came to London to convince me to move my account to Goddard-Stevens," Tamara said, looking slightly miffed.

"That, too, Duchess. That, toc," Clifford smiled affectionately. "But the truth is, Romance, Inc. is poised for expansion right now. Caroline has done a wonderful job with the shop, but it's time to branch out, to open additional stores."

"Additional stores? Tamara spends entirely too much time in the one store that already exists," Ferdy exclaimed. "She just can't stay away from that sort of thing, even though she knows I don't approve of women operating a business."

"Why is that?" asked Caroline, speaking up for the first time. "Why don't you approve?"

"Because it's not the done thing, my dear," said the duke. "Makes it look as if a man can't support his wife properly."

"That's why? You're worried about appearances?" Tamara asked her husband. "I thought you were above such pettiness."

"I am," he said, blithely defying anyone to disagree with him. "But there's another reason I object to your getting back into business. I want you all to myself. At my age I don't feel like sharing my wife."

Tamara leaned over and planted a kiss on his forehead.

"What if you were involved in a business, too?" Clifford asked Ferdy. "Then you and your wife would have something else to share."

"Me? Involved in a business?" The duke looked positively astounded by the notion. "I've never worked a day in my life. Wasn't brought up to it. I'm a gentleman, you see. One of a dying breed."

"Nonsense," Tamara scoffed. "You run the estates, oversee the managers, superintend the plantings, watch the budgets. You'd lose your mind if you were idle all day long."

"I'd lose my mind if I had a business that sold romantic geegaws," he said.

"'Romantic geegaws,' as you call my merchandise, are incredibly popular in the States," Caroline said. "You might actually enjoy having a hand in a successful business venture, you know."

The duke looked at Caroline as if she had committed a heresy. But then, she was American and he had learned from his wife that Americans often had peculiar opinions. Believed in politicians, gurus, and psychologists, all sorts of dicey charlatans.

"I'm quite content looking after my estates," he said. "Can't just let the inheritance go to pot."

"No, you can't. And that's why we're here," said Clifford, cutting in gracefully. "I understand from Tamara that your investments are all in the U.K."

"Why wouldn't they be?" said Ferdy. "I'm English."

"Because it's usually prudent to diversify," said Clifford. "Leave some of your assets here, move some to America."

"Put some of them in Romance, Inc., you mean," Tamara said, arching an eyebrow.

"As a matter of fact, yes," Caroline answered, then turned to face the duke. "As Tamara may have told you, I started Romance, Inc. almost six years ago, selling out of my living room. The response was so positive that I decided to open a retail store in West Palm Beach. I'm pleased to say that after a few false starts, we've done very well. We have developed a solid base of regular clients, and we regularly draw a heavy volume of business from visitors to the area. At least once a day a tourist tells me she wishes there were a Romance, Inc. store where she lived."

"Poppycock," the duke said as he helped himself to another slice of lemon cake. "Your customers are all women. Can't support a business on just half the population, my dear."

"What about your countryman, Vidal Sassoon?" Clifford interjected. "He did all right for himself."

"Quite right! Brilliant chap," said Ferdy. "Started out as a crimper, I believe. Hadn't thought of that."

"But the fact is that Romance, Inc.'s business doesn't depend solely on women," Caroline pointed out. "Men shop there, too, for birthday and anniversary gifts as well as little indulgences for the women in their lives. You may be interested to know that almost one-third of the names on our mailing list are male. We have a registration program for men to sign up and receive automatic reminders of birthdays and anniversaries. We also alert them to special gift possibilities in the price range they've selected. And, of course, we wrap the gift and either mail it or hand deliver it. Men say that having the legwork done for them makes their lives much easier, and they've come to count on us."

"You don't say," the duke remarked. He glanced at Tamara, who was nodding vigorously.

"It may also interest you to know that Caroline's business is not only booming but on very solid financial ground," Clifford took over. "Gross sales have grown by an average of nearly eighteen percent every year since Romance, Inc. was opened. Which means that even in the recession, business has increased. Profit margins have remained steady and, because Caroline is a hands-on manager and does much of the selling herself, the overhead has stayed low while volume continues to expand."

"Sounds a bit like your experience with L'Elegance, eh, Tamara?" commented the duke, looking over at his wife.

"Exactly," said the duchess.

"Actually, I modeled Romance, Inc. on many of the sales strategies I learned while working at L'Elegance," said Caroline, telling the truth but also shamelessly flattering Tamara.

The duke gazed lovingly at his wife. Her American savvy had been one of the qualities that he had most admired in her. She had seemed such a breath of fresh air, compared to the dotty old bats he knew. Still, he had doubts about Romance, Inc.

"If everything's going so jolly well for your business, Caroline, why on earth are you here?"

"As Clifford said a few minutes ago, Romance, Inc. is poised for expansion," she replied. "It's grown as much as it can in its present location. To put it in the American vernacular, we've 'maxed out.' We can't service more clients unless we open more stores. We can't offer a larger and more varied selection of merchandise unless we have more capital and additional space."

"What Caroline foresees is a chain of shops based on the Romance, Inc. concept," Clifford explained.

"A chain? Good God!" exclaimed the duke. "You'll need plenty of money for that."

"I already have quite a bit of money," Caroline said firmly, thinking of the $200,000 loan she'd just secured. "I need more."

"Then why don't you go to a bank?" asked Ferdy.

"I have," said Caroline. "They've given me a substantial loan, but I need additional financing to accomplish my goals."

"So you've come to me for your 'additional financing,'" said the duke.

"Yes," said Caroline. "And because I would welcome your wife's experience and advice."

Tamara glowed at the compliment and nudged her husband in his amply cushioned ribs. "You see, darling, I'm good at more than being your duchess." She winked at him.

"Quite right," he conceded and squeezed her hand. Then he turned to Caroline. "What's in it for me?" he asked. *"If* I should decide to invest, of course."

"A chance to be involved in a growing, trend-setting business," she replied, going on to mention the private label merchandise she planned to offer her clients, the exclusive items she'd bought at gift fairs, and the promotions and in-store events she would be offering all year long—events that brought in clients and sales and introduced the Romance, Inc. concept to new and different groups of clients. As she spoke, she became more and more energized, more and more enthusiastic. Her eyes sparkled and her cheeks began to glow as she lost herself in her plans for the future. Clifford watched with admiration, marveling at her creativity, at her passion for her business, at her belief in the concept she had built from nothing. The duke, too, was clearly impressed by Caroline's dynamic presentation, but it was Clifford he turned to for an answer to his question, "What's in it for me?"

"I'll tell you what's in it for you," Clifford began. "Not only will you have an opportunity to get in on the ground floor of a unique retailing operation, but you'll be able to put a portion of your assets in U.S. dollars. Having an American investment will protect you against fluctuations in the pound, and we calculate that you will receive at least a ten-percent yield on your investment."

"Ten percent?" the duke repeated. The best quality investment grade bonds were yielding about seven percent.

"Ten percent—not including potential capital gains," said Clifford, going in for the kill.

"Just exactly how much of an investment are you talking about?" Ferdy asked, as the knots in Caroline's stomach tightened. She could sense that the duke was weakening, that he was moving closer to saying "yes" to their proposal, that her dreams of a chain of Romance, Inc. stores might finally be on their way to coming true.

"A million two," she said firmly. Having rehearsed saying the number out loud as she dressed for her day of meetings, she sounded—and felt—confident. "I'm planning to open the first new store on Worth Avenue. There's space next to Chanel—"

"Chanel!" Tamara interrupted, raising her eyes to the heavens and clutching her hands to her bosom. "How utterly glorious! Wait until Celeste finds out!"

"Next to Chanel?" the duke repeated, ignoring his wife's outburst. "Sounds like you have something very substantial in mind."

"I do," said Caroline. "First, with the Worth Avenue store. Later, with other stores. I'm determined to give every woman in America—and perhaps, one day, Europe—a chance to indulge herself at whatever price her budget allows."

"Very ambitious, but a million two is a lot of money," said the duke. "I'd have to have a careful look at your figures."

"That goes without saying," Caroline commented. "Clifford and I have prepared detailed financial statements for you to review before making your decision."

Ferdy reached for his coffee and took several sips. Caroline waited on the edge of her seat for him to say something. Anything!

"Tell you what," he said finally, after clearing his throat. "Clifford and I will adjourn to the library to review the numbers. You two ladies can stay here and gossip."

Caroline was about to protest that she should be present when Ferdy looked over her company's financial statements, but Clifford gave her a glance—a glance that said, "You've done your part beautifully. Now let me do mine." She nodded and watched the two men disappear into the cavernous hallway.

"Bravo," said Tamara, who sidled up to Caroline and threw her arms around her. "You and Clifford were brilliant together. Brilliant."

"Were we really?" Caroline said, remembering the duchess's penchant for hyperbole.

"Absolutely. You two make a formidable combination. I have a feeling Ferdy's going to do it."

"How do you know?" Caroline asked.

Tamara rolled her eyes. "Because I know that man as well as I know myself. He barks sometimes, but deep down he's a pussycat. A very shrewd pussycat. He understands a lot more about the business world than he likes to let on. Anyway, we'll find out in a few minutes whether we're all going to be partners."

But it wasn't a few minutes. Caroline tried not to keep glancing at the grandfather clock in the corner of the room, tried to keep her mind focused on what Tamara was saying, but it was difficult. She was *dying* to know what was going on in the library!

"And by the way, Caroline," Tamara was saying, "whatever happened between you and that football player?"

Caroline smiled. She knew that, sooner or later, the duchess would get around to her favorite subject after Jack: Caroline's love life.

"Baseball player," she corrected Tamara.

"Football, baseball, whatever. The last time we talked, you were fighting the man off."

"I stopped fighting," Caroline admitted.

"Do tell!" said the duchess excitedly.

"What I mean is, I discovered that there's more to Brett than his macho facade. He's terrific with Jack, he's totally unpredictable, and he makes me feel like a teenager."

"A teenager!" Tamara trilled. "How wonderful."

"But then there's Jean-Claude," Caroline mused.

"The Frenchman?"

Caroline nodded. "You remember him from that day he signed books at Romance, Inc.?"

"Remember him?" the duchess snorted. "How could I forget him? Those eyes . . . that face . . . that body . . ."

"Down, girl," Caroline laughed.

"So there's something going on between you?"

Caroline nodded. "We've been seeing more of each other. He's quite . . . intriguing."

Tamara arched her heavily penciled eyebrows. "I'll bet," she smiled lasciviously. "But haven't you left someone out in the boyfriend department?"

"I don't understand."

"Clifford, darling. What about Clifford?"

Caroline stared at the duchess. "What about him?" she said.

"He's obviously mad about you. Anyone can see that."

"Don't be silly. Clifford and I are here on business together. When we finish our meeting with you and Ferdy, we're going on to see some of his clients about—"

"*You* may be here on business, but Clifford has more on his mind," the duchess said. "I've known Cliff a *very* long time, Caroline. I've never seen him look at a woman the way he looks at you."

Caroline felt herself flush at her friend's words. Had she sensed that Clifford was interested in her romantically? And was that the real reason she had kept her emotional distance from him? To avoid an involvement with Charles Goddard's managing director? To fend off a man who was what James might have been? To eliminate the possibility that she would find herself falling in love with the man who had taken James's place at Goddard-Stevens?

"You and Clifford make an awfully good team, you know," Tamara went on blithely. "Once you two started hammering home your points, Ferdy didn't stand a chance."

Caroline smiled. "Clifford is very bright, isn't he?" she mused.

"And eligible," said the duchess.

"And attractive," said Caroline.

"*And* loaded," said the duchess.

Caroline couldn't help but laugh.

"But there's a problem—he works for Charles Goddard," Caroline pointed out.

"Nobody's perfect," said the duchess airily, waving away Caroline's objection.

"Oh, you!" Caroline laughed again. "This is all so crazy. Only a few months ago, I was trying to bury my feelings toward men. Now, I'm trying to sort out my feelings for two very different men!"

"Two? *Three!* Don't forget Clifford," insisted Tamara. "Besides, there's nothing crazy about it. You're long overdue where men are concerned. I'm not a young woman. I've learned that time passes too quickly not to seize the opportunities that life presents."

"Maybe, but juggling several different men is a little much," said Caroline. "I have friends who can't even find one man they really like."

"Look, Caroline. Don't start feeling guilty because you have several suitors," the duchess warned. "When a woman is in bloom the way you are, men sense it—and they're drawn to the scent like bees to honey."

"You *do* have a way of putting things," Caroline observed fondly, not for the first time. She was about to glance at the clock yet again, when she saw Clifford and Ferdy emerge from the library. Finally! After an hour and a half! She tried to read their expressions as they walked toward her, but they were impassive, impenetrable.

"Well?" the duchess asked expectantly.

"Ladies," Ferdy began, "You're looking at the new investor in Romance, Inc."

Simultaneously and without missing a beat, Caroline and Tamara jumped up from their chairs and rushed toward the duke, nearly knocking him over.

"How exciting!" Tamara exclaimed, standing on tiptoe and kissing her husband's rosy cheeks.

"You won't be sorry!" Caroline promised, pumping the duke's hand.

"No, I don't suppose I will be," said Ferdy. "From the looks of those financial statements, Caroline, your business is a bloody gold mine."

Caroline turned to face Clifford, who had been responsible for putting together the financial statements—and for arranging the trip that was already a big, big success.

"Thank you," she whispered to him, knowing that it was

he who had finally erased the duke's lingering doubts and closed the deal.

He nodded and felt his heart turn over at the way she was looking at him. Was it gratitude in her eyes? he wondered. Or something more?

"I hate to spoil the party, but Caroline and I have two more meetings to get to," he said after checking his watch.

"Oh, drat. I was thinking we'd all celebrate with some champagne," said the duke.

"Clifford said they have to leave, Ferdy dear," Tamara reminded her husband.

"Yes, but there's so much to celebrate," said Ferdy, pouting like a child. "There's my investment in Caroline's business *and* my decision to let Goddard-Stevens—*Clifford,* that is—handle a good deal of my investments from now on."

Caroline glanced at Clifford and smiled. So he had done it. He had talked Ferdy into letting him manage his money! Surely, Tamara's portfolio was next.

"We'll celebrate the next time we're in town," Clifford promised his new client as Clifford escorted Caroline out the door toward the waiting Bentley and their next appointment.

The next two meetings were equally successful. Drew Darlington, who served them lunch in his private corporate dining room, was as flamboyant as the magazines portrayed him. Sporting a headful of carrot orange hair and outfitted in a black-and-white striped suit with wide lapels that reminded Caroline of a gangster's wardrobe, Drew was an animated young man always in motion who, after pacing back and forth restlessly while she and Clifford made their pitch, promised that he would consider the possibility of investing in Romance, Inc.

"This trip is turning out to be a great success," she told Clifford as the Bentley took them toward Felicity Kramer's Chelsea mews house.

"It's a success you've *earned,"* said Clifford, happily but practically. His words reminded Caroline of what she'd become over the years: a successful owner of a business with almost unlimited potential. She looked at him, silently grateful for his help—and for his perspective. Once again, his sensible words and his encouraging manner seemed so reminiscent of James and of what he'd meant to her as a very young, very wounded woman. She was older now and more experienced, but she still flowered under the approving words of a man she respected.

Sitting on garden chairs in a sunny conservatory, Caroline and Felicity Kramer, the mail order queen, negotiated an agreement under the terms of which Romance, Inc.'s private label merchandise would be featured in each of Felicity's gift catalogs. Through them, the Romance, Inc. concept would reach a worldwide consumer base of over ten million people.

"Tamara was right." Caroline sighed as she and Clifford relaxed in the backseat of the Bentley after leaving Felicity's office.

"Right about what?" asked Clifford.

"We *are* a good team," she replied, turning toward him.

"The best," he said, then briefly put his hand over hers. "I had a hunch we would be."

"Sort of the way you have hunches about the stock market?" she asked, her tone teasing, lighthearted, intended to dissipate the heat she felt at his touch.

"Sort of." He smiled. "Now tell me, how do you feel after taking London by storm?"

"I'm so excited that I don't know what to do with myself!" Caroline admitted. Her mind was whirling, filled with ideas and plans for Romance, Inc.

"I'll tell you what I usually do when I land a new client or cement an important deal," he said.

"Tell me."

"I spend a lot of money. Nothing like it when you've earned a pat on the back."

"You *are* a genius. That's a brilliant idea! But exactly where should we spend all this money?"

"How about Hamleys?" said Clifford. "This morning you said you wanted to go back to the store and buy your son a present."

"That's right, I did," said Caroline, who realized once

again how thoughtful Clifford Hamlin was. The question came back to her yet again: Why on earth would such a decent human being work for Charles Goddard?

Hamleys was five floors of what seemed to be every toy on earth. There were scores and scores of dolls, including the Catherine Nesbitt replicas of all the royal personnages in British history up to the Princess of Wales, as well as the carefully detailed British Regiment Guards. There were games and sporting goods; traditional wooden toys and state-of-the-art electronic wizardry; a wide selection of teddy bears, among them, the classic Hamleys bear with its bright red waistcoat. But it was the famous Hamleys Vintage Vehicles that captured Caroline's fancy, just as Clifford predicted they would. She knew she *had* to buy one for Jack, but she couldn't decide between a red double-decker bus or a black London taxi.

"Why don't *you* buy him the bus and *I'll* buy him the taxi?" Clifford suggested.

Caroline looked at him. "That's very generous of you, Clifford, but I can't—"

"But nothing. I'm a very generous man," he said.

"No, really. You hardly know Jack," she pointed out.

"True," he acknowledged. "But I know you. Not as well as I'd like to, I admit."

She smiled at him. *Perhaps Tamara was right,* she thought. Perhaps Clifford Hamlin did respond to her. He was bright and sophisticated and so handsome in his smartly tailored suit. She was growing more and more fond of him as the trip wore on, and she continued to see him in different situations and varying moods. Would it really be so unthinkable if they were to become more than business associates? Wasn't it perhaps time that she relied on her feelings toward him rather than on suspicions carried over from a bitter past?

"What do you say we have a celebratory dinner tonight?" he said suddenly as they waited for Jack's gifts to be wrapped.

"I'd love to," said Caroline. "Where? In the hotel?"

"No, actually there's another favorite haunt of mine," he

said. "A restaurant called Wendy Winston's, named for its American owner. It's a little late in the day to get a reservation there, but Wendy's an old friend."

Caroline felt an irrational twinge of jealousy. *What sort of old friend?* she wondered, then laughed at her foolishness. Clifford Hamlin was an extremely eligible bachelor who undoubtedly had lots of "old friends."

"Is it terribly elegant?" she asked, not knowing how dressed up London women got.

"It's casually elegant. You'll probably want to change into something a bit dressier," he replied.

Dressier? Caroline wondered what she was going to do. She hadn't anticipated a dinner date, hadn't packed anything at all dressy. She had only brought two business suits with her.

When the Bentley pulled up to Stafford's, Clifford exited the car and waited for Caroline to do the same. "Coming?" he asked when she didn't move. He didn't want to leave her, but he had to go up to his suite and prepare for his round of meetings in Brussels the following day.

"You go on ahead," she told him. "I just remembered an errand I have to run."

He gave her a surprised look and said he would pick her up at her suite at seven-thirty.

"No," she said firmly. "I'll meet you at the restaurant."

She waved good-bye to him, and when, with a puzzled expression, he disappeared inside the hotel lobby, she leaned forward and asked Raymond to take her to Harrods.

She glows, Clifford thought, as he watched her walk toward their table at Wendy Winston's, the fashionable eatery on Kensington Church Street where he often dined while in London. She was not overly tall but very slim and extremely feminine. Her chestnut brown hair glimmered gold in the flattering chandeliered lighting, her hazel eyes sparkled, and she moved with the grace of a dancer or an athlete. Clifford was aware that he wasn't the only one who noticed her; several other men turned to look at her, their eyes lingering, approving. She had changed from the beige business suit she had worn earlier in the day into a high-necked, long-sleeved, superbly flattering, very dark navy dress of silk jersey that clung sinuously to her tiny waist and swirled around her legs as she walked.

"You look wonderful," Clifford told her as she sat down, his eyes still on the dress that revealed—but did not vulgarly flaunt—her lovely body.

"Thank you," she said simply, knowing that he was right and that she had never looked better. She had bought the dress at Harrods after she'd left Clifford. It was a Jean Muir, and except for the gown James had bought her at Celeste's, it was the most expensive dress she had ever owned. She had seen it from across the floor, had known the moment she touched the heavy, sensuous fabric and noticed the sophisticated cut and seaming that it was going to be perfect. A magical garment making her look taller and slimmer, giving her an air of worldliness that seemed genuine, not borrowed. It made her feel the way the Vionnet-inspired gown from Celeste's had once made her feel so many years ago, and from the instant she slipped it over her head, she knew that she must have it, despite its fierce price.

Over dinner she and Clifford talked and talked, two people eager to know more about each other. Clifford mentioned the enthusiastic way Caroline had spoken of Romance, Inc. at Ferdy and Tamara's earlier that day, her impressive presentation to Drew Darlington, and her meeting with Felicity Kramer. They spoke about Jack and the toys they had bought him, about Clifford's fascination with business and his dedication to the charity work he was involved in. They also spoke about happy marriages.

"It was a long time ago," said Caroline wistfully, thinking about James and her younger self. "Sometimes it almost seems a dream."

Clifford spoke about his parents and their relationship.

"Their marriage wasn't just a marriage. It was a love story," he said. "They truly adored each other, and I felt that affection between them until my father died. It was more than just sexual passion, although, of course, there was clearly that. But they respected each other and honored each other. They showed me what it was like to be happy, to find the one person that could make life complete."

"But Tamara tells me you've never been married," said Caroline.

"That's because I haven't found that one person," he said, looking directly at her.

"I hope you haven't given up," replied Caroline.

He shook his head.

"Not at all," he replied, touching her hand. Then his lips curved in a slight, secret smile. "In fact, I think I'm finally making progress."

Caroline returned to her suite feeling exhausted but exhilarated. She had so much to look forward to, so much to be thankful for. It was hard to imagine that a few short years ago she had been penniless, numb with grief, so desperately unhappy that she had nearly thrown her life away—and that of her beloved son. Now there was Romance, Inc., which seemed as if it might exceed her wildest dreams. There was Jack, whom she adored with a fierceness that continued to surprise and delight her. And there were men—enough of them to arouse her—and to confuse her. Clifford had promised to call her as soon as he was back in the States, and she was eager to speak to him again, to see him again, more than she knew how to tell him—more than she even knew how to tell herself.

What *were* her feelings for him? He was attractive, sophisticated, cultured, eligible, and so very successful. As polished as Brett was crude, as businesslike as Jean-Claude was sensual, Clifford exuded power in a way that both excited and fascinated Caroline. Was he, perhaps, what James might have become if he had lived? There was no way to know, but the possibility was tantalizing and not entirely out of the question. If it weren't for Clifford's association with the Goddards, he would be the catch of the century, she mused, then stopped herself short, wondering how in the world she had suddenly allowed herself to harbor romantic thoughts for, not one, but *three* men!

She thought about their dinner together as she carefully slipped out of her precious new dress. She admired it for a moment before hanging it in the closet, wondering where and with whom she would wear it next. James had been right: expensive clothes were often more than just an indulgence. They could be an investment. An investment in getting a job back . . . an investment in self-esteem. And Clifford had been right, too. There were times when one had *earned* a pat on the back.

She stepped into the fluffy white terry cloth bathrobe the hotel provided for its guests. Too keyed up to sleep, she reached into her attaché case for the gift catalogs that Felicity Kramer had given her, and brought them over to the bed. The covers had been turned down, and there was a small box resting on the pillows. Another of Clifford's favorite chocolate mints, she thought, deciding that she would save this one for Jack. She picked up the box, intending to place it in her suitcase, glanced at it, and suddenly realized that it didn't contain a mint at all.

Cartier didn't sell candy.

Her fingers trembling, she opened the envelope propped next to the box and removed the card inside.

"To commemorate this day," the card read on its top side.

Nestled in the velvet box were a pair of domed gold and diamond pavé earrings with large, lustrous pearl drops. Caroline removed the earrings from the box and fastened them to her lobes, immediately aware of their pleasing weight and superb balance. They fit the shape of her earlobes and the curve of her cheeks as if they had been custom made for her.

"They're exquisite," she marveled as she gazed at her reflection in the mirror.

She picked up the card and looked at it again.

It was signed by Clifford.

Shaking with excitement, Caroline moved toward the phone by the bed and asked the hotel operator to ring Clifford's suite. Her heart raced as she waited for him to answer.

"Yes?" he said.

"They're gorgeous. I mean, they're magnificent!" said Caroline, trying not to babble. "I don't know how to thank you."

"In person would be a good idea."

"Now?" It was past midnight.

"I'll be gone in the morning," he reminded her.

"But I'm in my robe—"

"So am I. Stafford's has the most comfortable robes, don't they?"

Caroline paused, knowing he was teasing her.

"Besides, I'm just next door," he pointed out.

"Yes, but what if someone sees me in the hall?"

"What if they do? They'll probably just nod and wish you a good night."

Caroline thought for a moment, then asked herself why she was being so standoffish, so reserved. Was she really the kind of stiff, uptight woman Brett Haas had accused her of being? *Clifford has just given you an unbelievably extravagant gift,* she told herself. *Now stop being such a wimp and get over there and thank him!*

"I'll be there in a minute," she said. "In person!" she added with a giggle and hung up.

She glanced at herself in the mirror, fluffed her hair, powdered her nose, and pulled the robe tightly around her. Then she tiptoed out the door of her suite, looked left and right, saw that she was completely alone, and went next door, her earlobes sparkling with the valuable jewels she had just been given.

"It's open," said Clifford after she had knocked.

Taking a deep breath, she pushed open the door to his suite. He was standing across the room, his hands in the pockets of his robe, and he looked, Caroline thought, extremely sexy. His wavy auburn hair curled against the back of the robe's collar, his gray eyes were heavy, seductive, and his mouth formed a teasing half smile beckoning her inside, closer.

"I wanted to . . . to thank you," she said, stammering suddenly as she stood by the closed door, her hand still resting on the doorknob, conscious of the lateness of the hour, of being alone with him in a foreign, romantic city far away from home. The atmosphere in the room was almost palpably intense, charged, electric.

"Then thank me," he said, his voice low and commanding, his eyes smoldering.

He willed her across the room and she walked toward him slowly, slowly, as he began toward her. She didn't blink, barely even breathed as they drew closer to each other. When they were only inches apart, they stopped as if by mutual unspoken agreement. For a moment, they studied each other's face.

"Lovely," he murmured, tracing the curve of the precious earrings along her cheek.

Then, with the shadow of a smile on his lips, he bent down and took her face in his hands. He held her eyes with his, and without a word, he leaned closer and kissed her on the mouth, first gently and then with increasing passion, just as she knew he would, just as, she suddenly realized, she had hoped he would. Acknowledging her own longing, she abandoned herself to his touch and his taste and lost herself in emotion and sensation. After a long moment, she remembered the earrings, the glitter of gold, the dazzle of diamonds, the sheen of pearls.

"No one's ever given me anything like them," she murmured, lost deep in his kiss.

"No one?" he asked, sounding slightly surprised.

She nodded. "No one. You're the first."

And at that moment, she truly felt as if he were the first—and she experienced a sense of being fresh, untouched, filled with new and unfamiliar emotions.

Their lips met again and the kiss deepened, whirling her into a vortex of heat and desire. He was lean and wiry, yet so strong, a man of many contradictions, she thought, feeling the exquisitely soft texture of his lips and allowing herself to lean into him, to let her body melt into his. With a hungry sound coming from somewhere deep within his throat, he lowered his hands and unfastened the belt of her robe, letting it fall open.

"I've wanted this from the moment I saw you," he said so softly it was almost a hum.

"I didn't know—" she managed.

"You must have," he said. "You had to—"

Caroline felt her body go limp with surrender. She was dizzy with his touch, reeling from his scent, the sound of his voice.

She heard herself moan as he reached inside her robe to stroke her breasts, to caress the curves of her body.

"You're beautiful," he whispered over and over as his hands moved against her skin.

She opened her mouth to him and luxuriated in the feel of him. She wanted the moment to go on forever, wanted the feeling to go on into eternity.

"Come," he said softly, holding out a hand and turning toward the bedroom.

At his command, she opened her eyes and suddenly saw their reflection in the mirror over the mantle. She was flushed and disheveled, yearning for more, longing to give herself to him, hungering to be part of him. And yet, even as she began to move toward the bedroom, a thought intruded into her consciousness. Clifford Hamlin, the man who was now intimately involved in her business, the man who was now intimately caressing her, was also the man who worked for Charles Goddard. What if their feelings ripened and went even deeper? What if their relationship became even more involved? What if Clifford had to choose between her and Charles Goddard? What would he do? Would he give up millions of dollars and a position of immense power to be with her? If it came down to a choice between her and Charles Goddard, where would Clifford Hamlin's allegiance really lie? She couldn't be sure, didn't want to risk finding out, didn't want to suffer another unbearable loss at the hands of the man who had been her enemy for years.

She straightened up suddenly, took her hand out of his, and closed the robe tightly. She stopped where she stood in the living room of the suite.

"What's the matter? Have I done something? Something you didn't like? Moved too fast?" Clifford asked, looking startled, stricken.

She shook her head and smoothed her hair back into place. "It's not you," she said, her breath coming in deep gasps and her heart pounding. "It's this."

"This?"

"The situation."

"The situation is that I've fallen in love with you, Caroline," he said, taking her into his arms.

"That can't be!" she exclaimed, backing away from his embrace even as she knew that what he said was true. Tamara had known it, seen it, predicted it. And Caroline, despite herself, had responded to it, to him. And she wished she hadn't. The barriers between them were too high, too difficult to vault. How would they deal with their feelings, sort out the complexities of their loyalties? No matter how they felt, no matter the power of the attraction between them, the fact remained that Clifford worked for Charles Goddard. Any personal relationship between them would inevitably be too complicated, too burdened by a bitter history, too fraught with problems. Too dangerous, she warned herself. No, a love affair with Clifford Hamlin would never work out, was out of the question.

"I *said* I've fallen in love with you," Clifford repeated, reaching out to touch her shoulder.

"I know, I know, but, Clifford, what about Charles? How can we possibly be together when he's threatened to fire you because of me? When he despises me so? He's a powerful man, a man who abuses his power. I saw it in the way he treated James. And I saw it in the way he treated me. In the way he doesn't even care that he has a grandson."

"Caroline. Listen to me. Look at me. I'm not afraid of Charles Goddard. Do you hear me?" he said, a hurt urgency in his eyes.

He reached out for her again, but Caroline pulled away from him, took off the earrings and handed them to him, then she walked toward the door.

"But *I* am afraid of him, Clifford. *I* am."

She closed the door firmly behind her as he stood there holding the gift, a devastated expression on his handsome face, a terrible hurt in the depths of his heart.

Caroline slept during most of the flight home. She didn't want to think about Clifford, didn't want to recall the anger and the disappointment in his eyes, didn't want to face the conflicts that raged within her. She wanted her life to be simple again, wanted to get back to Jack and to her everyday life. There was Brett and there was Jean-Claude—she already had enough romantic conflict in her life. There was also Romance, Inc. to think about, the plans to be executed, the decisions, *important* decisions concerning its future, to be made. Above all, there was her beloved son, Jack. He deserved her time and her attention—he deserved all of her and she wanted to give herself to him, to his interests, to his well-being. She already had enough: enough love, enough complications, enough demands.

As the miles separated her farther and farther from London, she told herself that nothing that had happened there counted. It was a phantasm, a *folie a deux*. They had experienced a time out of time, and she and Clifford had simply been carried away by the distance and the excitement of being far away from home and collaborating in a project that had been more successful than either of them had imagined. By the time her plane landed in New York, she told herself that what she and Clifford had thought was love was nothing more than a chimera of their imaginations. When she saw him again, everything would be back to the way it had always been, and business, not romance, would be the tie that bound them.

The second leg of her flight arrived in Palm Beach International Airport at close to four o'clock in the afternoon. She gathered up her purse and her attaché case and hurried down the ramp toward the airport gate and the baggage carousel, hoping there wouldn't be much traffic when she finally got into her car and drove to her condo. She was eager to get home, eager to see Jack, the one constant in her life, eager to hold him and kiss him and hear what he had done during their days apart, eager to show him the photographs she had taken and the surprises she and Clifford had bought him at Hamleys.

Once inside the airport, she was standing by the baggage claim area when a heavy-set man in a nondescript suit stopped her.

"Mrs. Goddard?" the stranger asked. "Mrs. Caroline Shaw Goddard?"

"Yes," she said, startled, wondering how he knew her name.

"I have something for you," he said. He thrust an official-looking document into her hands and disappeared into the crowd.

"Mrs. Goddard?" the stranger asked. "Mrs. Caroline Mae Goddard?"

"Yes," she said, startled, wondering how he knew her name.

"I have something for you," he said. He thrust an official-looking document into her hands and disappeared into the crowd.

Part Three

~

Threshold

Seven Months Later

~29~

"Mommy, what's 'cus-tiddy?' "

Caroline gasped and felt as if she'd been kicked in the stomach. Jack had finally asked her the question she'd been dreading. In the months since she had been served with the papers declaring that Charles and Dina Goddard were suing her for custody of her son, she had walked an emotional tightrope, struggling to protect him from the cruel realities of the situation, yet at the same time fighting to keep him with her, fighting to win a battle her own lawyer warned her would be more than uphill. Every time she looked at Jack, held him in her arms, watched him sleep, heard him whoop and holler and cheer at his beloved baseball games, she died little deaths at the gruesome but very real possibility that she would lose him forever—to people he had never even met.

"Why do you ask, darling?" she said, ruffling his hair and trying not to fall apart in front of him. They were sitting at the kitchen table, eating dinner together. Or, at least, Jack was eating. Over the past few months, Caroline had been too anxious to eat, too distraught over the monstrous action her former in-laws had taken, too consumed with the realization that, despite his promises, Clifford had obviously betrayed her and told Charles about Jack. She had lost weight—and sleep—and her friends were worried about her.

"One of the kids in school said that my grandparents were trying to get 'cus-tiddy' of me," he replied. "He said he heard about it from his parents."

Caroline forced a casual smile as her heart broke into a hundred tiny pieces. " 'Custody' means the right to take care of somebody," she responded, as if merely teaching

Jack the definition of a new word, wanting desperately to avoid further explanation.

Jack nodded thoughtfully, then asked, "But why did he say the part about my grandparents?" He looked up at Caroline, his expression so innocent, so trusting, so loving. "Grandma Mary and Grandpa Al don't take care of me. You do."

Caroline took a deep breath. It was time to tell Jack, she realized, time to stop shielding him from the truth about his other grandparents. He would find out sooner or later, she knew. From a classmate at school, from a client in the store, or from some inquiring newspaper reporter. No, it was time he heard what was going on. From her. In a way that he would understand. In a way that wouldn't traumatize him.

She inhaled once again and began. "Remember I told you about your daddy's parents?" she said. "The ones who lived so far away that they couldn't ever come and see you?"

Jack thought for a moment, then nodded. "My Goddard grandparents," he said.

"That's right, sweetheart. Well, they're older now, and they've realized how much they missed by not having such a wonderful boy in their lives," she continued, determined to present James's parents in a positive light to her son, conscious of not wanting to poison him against them in case they were to win custody. . . . She stopped herself whenever the thought clouded her mind. They wouldn't take Jack away from her. No one would. Not ever.

"You mean they're coming to visit me?" Jack asked, seeming confused—and slightly apprehensive.

"It's possible," she said. "It's also possible that they might want you to visit them. And stay for a while." Her throat tightened and tears pricked at her eyes. No, she couldn't say anymore. There was no reason to. She wasn't going to let the Goddards come near Jack, let alone win custody of him. "But it's nothing for you to bother about," she added quickly. "In the meantime, we have lots of exciting things to look forward to. Aunt Tamara and Uncle Ferdy are coming back from Europe next week, which will mean we can start visiting them on Sundays again. And Mommy's new store on Worth Avenue will be open the week after that, just in time for Thanksgiving."

What Caroline didn't mention was that the custody hearing was scheduled for the Monday after Thanksgiving. After months of postponements, bureaucratic snafus, and legal maneuvering, the judge had finally set a court date, and while Caroline was hardly looking forward to going up against Charles and Dina Goddard and their formidable phalanxes of lawyers, she also knew that if the outcome went against her, if the judge ruled in the Goddards' favor, she would not accept the judgment passively. She would do something—anything—to keep her son with her. Appeal the decision . . . Take Jack away somewhere . . . Change their identities . . . Whatever it took to keep her child with her, she was more than willing to do. Even if it meant giving up Romance, Inc. Even if it meant abandoning her friends, the three men who seemed eager to court her, and the way of life she had painfully constructed for herself day by day, month by month, in the years since James had been taken from her.

"And Aunt Tamara is planning a delicious Thanksgiving dinner for us," she went on cheerfully, wanting to end the conversation on an upbeat note. "She's going to have turkey and stuffing and we'll have so much fun—"

But Jack seemed preoccupied, lost in his own thoughts.

"Mommy?" he interrupted, tugging on the sleeve of her blouse. "What if I don't like my Goddard grandparents? What if I don't want to visit them, even for a few days? What if I just want to stay with you instead?"

Caroline stared at her son, nearly overwhelmed by the love she felt for him, by the sheer terror at the thought of losing him, and by her inability to convince him that he was safe and promise that his stable and love-filled life wouldn't change. She couldn't reply to his questions. She didn't have the answers. Not yet.

Her throat closed once again, and words eluded her. What could she say to him? she wondered. How could she tell him that his father's parents were cold and unfeeling and capable of a kind of cruelty she could never have imagined? How could she reassure a six-year-old boy that his future would be secure, that she would always be able to protect him from people like Charles and Dina Goddard?

She couldn't, and in the end, the only words that came to her were the ones she knew to be true, beyond a shadow of a doubt, beyond any decision a judge might make, beyond any despicable action the Goddards might take against her.

"I love you, my darling," she said by way of an answer to his questions. "And I always will."

Despite the success she had made of Romance, Inc., Caroline rarely thought of herself as a person with a great deal of courage. Yes, she had built her business from nothing, and, yes, she was raising Jack by herself. And, yes, she had even reinvented herself, metamorphosing from the shy, insecure ugly duckling of her youth into a vibrant, creative, beautiful woman who not only drew the friendship and loyalty of other women to her but attracted members of the opposite sex as well. Still, it wasn't until the Goddards threatened to take Jack away from her that she realized just how much courage she did have, how much fight she was able to muster, how much inner strength she truly possessed.

It would have been easy to wilt into defeat and surrender, to fade into despair and self-pity, to shrink from the daunting task of taking on the powerful, rich, politically connected Goddards. But she didn't. She had too much at stake to retreat into a cocoon of fear and depression. She didn't care what the battle cost, whether she had to ask for money, what indignities or humiliations she had to suffer, she would keep her son—or die trying.

And so on the day after her return from London, she had arrived at her shop on Okeechobee Boulevard at seven A.M., sat at her desk, and pored over her client list, searching for names—important names, prominent names, influential names, names of people who could help her in her fight to keep her son. With none of the hesitance or tentativeness that had crippled her in the past when approaching people she thought above her socially, she picked up the telephone and called, determined not to suffer in silence. She was facing the struggle of her life, and she was not going to give up or to give in.

First, and most important of all, there was Gwen Harding, whose husband, Douglas, was a well-known Palm Beach attorney. She insisted on arranging an appointment with him that same afternoon, and then, a battle strategy already forming in her mind, she called several other clients and acquaintances: Leslie Oberman, a social worker; Robin Valk, a corporate vice president; and Suzanne Gunther, community relations director of the public library—women whose testimony on her behalf would surely impress the judge. And then there was Myrna Lydig, Jack's pediatrician, and Kathy Nester and Jill Moss, his teachers at school, whom she asked to write letters pointing out what an involved parent she was and how destructive it would be to Jack if he were removed from the parent and the lifestyle that had been his since birth. In addition, there were her closest friends: Selma, Francesca, Cissy, Tamara, Jenny, Phil . . . all of whom promised to help her in any way they could. She called Jenny's father, the Reverend Armstrong, who had presided over her wedding ceremony. She and the minister spoke every other week, and Caroline found his words a great comfort, as she did her nightly prayers, in which she begged God not to take her child, pleaded with Him not to punish her for the time six years earlier, when, devastated by James's death, she had neglected herself and nearly lost Jack before he came into the world.

Caroline also called her mother, who rose to the occasion and offered her daughter comfort and moral support. Despite their complicated relationship, Mary Shaw loved Caroline and Jack and found it impossible to imagine why on earth the Goddards would try to come between them. Even Al Shaw made an effort to be there for Caroline, although his attempts at comforting her usually involved his characteristic bitter litanies about the tyranny of the rich and the victimization of the poor.

"I told you those Goddards would try to shit all over you," he'd rail.

Douglas Harding proved to be an honest and decent man, an attorney with a heart and a conscience and a habit of taking his client's causes as his own. He was a dignified, gray-haired man, pleasant and approachable, who had a no-nonsense way of telling Caroline the score, even when it was painful. He wanted her to understand just exactly what she would be up against.

"The truth is, everyone agrees that you're a wonderful mother to Jack. In addition, your financial position is inarguably more than adequate for Jack's every need. There's absolutely no doubt you're fully capable—both financially and emotionally—of raising him," he said to her just after taking the case and looking at the letters of support she had gathered. "But there's another truth, as well—that Charles Goddard is a very formidable opponent. We know that those photographs of his lie and that his private investigator undoubtedly embellished the time sheets, but he's got money and power and, most crucial of all, desire. He wants Jack, Caroline, and he wants him badly. He's letting us know that he'll do anything and everything to get what he wants."

"So will I," Caroline said resolutely. "So will I."

"Good. You're going to need that kind of strength and determination. We'll fight just as hard as we can," said Douglas Harding. "But before we really roll up our sleeves, I have to tell you that I can't make you any promises. The judge *should* decide in your favor, but life is often unfair. Judges are often unfair, even irrational. I want you to understand that you might lose."

Caroline nodded soberly. She had never thought of the Goddard custody motion as a trifling nuisance suit she would easily win.

Douglas Hardling cleared his throat and continued.

"I also want you to understand that the Goddards' case against you is based in part on their contention that you lead a promiscuous lifestyle, that there are several men in the picture."

Caroline took a sharp intake of breath as she thought of Jean-Claude and Clifford and Brett. She had taken her friends' advice and allowed herself to stop mourning James, to begin to see other men, even let herself love them. Was she going to have to pay for having a life of her own by losing Jack?

"Are you saying that I have to live the rest of my life alone in order to keep my child?" she asked. The thought seemed grotesque.

Douglas Harding shook his head.

"What I'm saying is that until this custody case is resolved, you will not spend time with any of these men," he warned. "You will behave like a nun, purer than pure. If you want to speak to your male friends, speak to them over the phone. But no in-person contact, nothing written, no secret rendezvous. I don't want to provide Charles Goddard or his investigators with one more bit of ammunition. Is that clear?"

"Perfectly clear," Caroline said. She would miss Jean-Claude and Brett, miss them terribly, but ever since she had realized that Clifford had betrayed her, she had refused his telephone calls. She looked her attorney straight in the eye. "Now then, you mentioned something about a fight. Where do we begin?"

Harding smiled. He admired his new client and genuinely hoped he could win the case for her.

"Right here," he said. He patted the stack of magazines on his desk. There were back issues of *Life, Look, Time, Newsweek, Fortune, Business Week,* and more. "Have you ever heard the old saying, 'Behind every great fortune lurks a crime?' " he asked.

Caroline nodded. Her father quoted it often, and for the first time since she'd been served with the custody papers, she felt a glimmer of hope, a hint of possibility.

"I've hired someone to look into the all-mighty Goddard family," Harding explained. "I don't know what we'll find, but I'm willing to bet that somewhere in Charles's past is something he'd rather not have people know about. Maybe there's even more than one something. And maybe whatever it is didn't happen all that long ago."

During the months preceding the court date, Charles Goddard felt like a caged lion. He was tense, edgy, restless.

He didn't like the postponements and continuances and roadblocks that were standing in the way of his getting what he thought he truly deserved: custody of his grandson. He didn't like them at all, and as the months passed without resolution, he became more and more insecure and apprehensive about the outcome of the suit. Every time he spoke with Ronald Switzer, he felt even more anxious, even more unsure of the final result of the hearing. Switzer had a winning record in custody cases, Charles knew, but the lawyer had also made it clear that he couldn't guarantee a victory, that no one could, and that he wouldn't put himself in the position of making any promises. Switzer's inability to make an absolute guarantee of victory unnerved Charles, made him impatient and fearful, made him eager to take matters into his own hands.

One of the matters that especially gnawed at him was Clifford Hamlin's trip with Caroline Shaw to London in April. He had confronted Clifford about the reason behind the visit, of course, but his managing director had remained infuriatingly closemouthed on the subject, saying that their meetings in London involved confidential business matters. As if his loyalty were to that woman, for God's sake, instead of to Charles, to the firm. And so when Clifford was in San Francisco meeting with several of Goddard-Stevens's important West Coast clients, Charles had ordered Clifford's office searched—thoroughly. What the search unearthed were the financial statements Clifford had drawn up for Romance, Inc. in preparation for the London trip, as well as letters of commitment from the duke regarding his investment in Caroline's company and from Drew Darlington, who had, in the months since Caroline and Clifford had made their presentation, decided to proceed with a substantial investment in Romance, Inc.

Charles was stunned when he analyzed the financial data Clifford and Caroline had presented to prospective investors. Romance, Inc. was not only a bona fide success, it was nothing less than a gold mine! His former daughter-in-law wasn't the poor, struggling, single mother he had supposed. She was the founder of a retail business with an almost limitless horizon. According to the file in Clifford's office, she was currently planning to let her lease on the West Palm Beach store lapse and open a much larger, more ambitious shop on Worth Avenue, right next door to Chanel! What's more, she and Clifford were already exploring the possibility of opening branch stores in Miami, Atlanta, and Dallas.

Charles sat at his desk and read and reread the contents of the file. He couldn't get over it. Caroline was well able to provide for her son, that much was clear. His own case, largely—but not entirely—based on the superior financial assets the Goddards could offer Jack, might not be as foolproof as he had imagined. The crucial question was, how would a judge evaluate the importance of her business success? Would the fact that Caroline Shaw was impressively self-supporting make a judge less likely to award custody of Jack to Charles and Dina?

Charles mulled over the information for the next several days. It wasn't like him to act impulsively. He preferred to weigh his options, calculate his risks. If the judge wasn't impressed by Charles's argument about the Goddards' superior financial wherewithal, he would still have to take serious note of the mother's neglect of the boy, the proof of her promiscuous lifestyle, and the fact she kept Jack's very existence a secret from his grandparents for nearly six years. Perhaps those issues would be enough to tilt the decision toward the Goddards. Perhaps he had nothing to worry about. Perhaps he was being too pessimistic and anxious. Perhaps . . .

On the other hand, if he took action . . . if he somehow arranged for a business problem to arise . . . a mishap or some kind of financial reversal . . . if he saw to it that Romance, Inc.'s owner was actually in financial difficulty and unable to provide for her son . . . his victory would be assured.

The thoughts came quickly, and Charles felt his excitement build. Why rely on lawyers? he realized. All they knew was talk, talk, talk, but no ironclad guarantees. When he needed something important taken care of, he had other resources, didn't he?

* * *

It was the nights that were the most painful for Caroline as she awaited the custody hearing. The days were hectic with work—running her shop on Okeechobee Boulevard, preparing for the opening of the Worth Avenue store, meeting with the architect, decorator, and contractors, making sure that the construction progressed on schedule, attending to the thousand and one details that arose with building, furnishing, and stocking a new store. But at night, after Jack had gone to bed and she was alone, she feared she would drown in her anguish, in her loneliness.

She missed Brett and Jean-Claude. They had given her pleasure, made her feel cared for, represented a new beginning, and in a sense, had brought her back to life. After six years of mourning James, she had finally let herself explore the possibility of new love—and now she couldn't see them—either of them—until Jack was truly hers. When she had told them of the custody suit, each had immediately offered to drop everything and come to Florida and help. Then, when she had explained that her lawyer had forbidden her to see them, she had felt their longing for her as keenly as she had felt hers for them.

Jean-Claude called to console her, saying how much he missed her, how much he wanted to see her again. Brett bombarded her with phone calls and sent Jack souvenirs from every ballpark he broadcast from during the long and grueling baseball season.

"Soon," she told Brett, just as she'd told Jean-Claude. "Soon we'll be able to see each other and decide exactly what there is between us. But right now there's only Jack."

As for Clifford Hamlin, he telephoned her, too, but each time he did, she refused to speak to him. He had betrayed her trust by telling Charles Goddard about Jack—and the betrayal was too raw, too painful to even think of letting him try to explain his motives or defend himself. She missed him though, missed the person she'd *thought* he was. But whenever he called the shop, she avoided him.

"Tell him I'm busy," she instructed her assistant.

And when he called her at home, she was brief.

"I'm sorry, but I'm late for an appointment . . ."
Eventually, Clifford stopped calling.

As elegant as the first Romance, Inc. shop was, the Worth Avenue branch, which was to become the company's flagship store when the lease in West Palm Beach was up, was absolutely spectacular. Caroline retained the red-and-white scheme of the original store, but with the help of her interior decorator and a theatrical lighting designer, she had taken what was simple and elegant and transformed it into something romantic and seductive with an originality that made it unlike any shop anywhere. Her idea was not to provide merely a selling space but a theatrical experience. A customer entering the shop would be transported out of everyday concerns and feel as if she were the sole star of a sumptuous fantasy come magically to life.

The red hearts and flowers motif was continued, but gauzelike scrims now concealed the walls, their sheer fabric stirred into constant, subtle motion as a result of concealed air ducts. An elaborate, computer-controlled lighting system similar to those used in Broadway shows allowed the white scrim to appear pink, peach, shell, ivory, aqua, violet, pale yellow, or bud green, depending on the current season and display theme. Large green plants in immense terracotta pots and curved French chairs upholstered in white velvet formed the only "decoration." Displays were subtly spotlit, and dressing rooms were flatteringly lit and equipped with specially ground mirrors so that every woman automatically looked her very best. So original was the conception and so superb the execution that several magazines were already vying for the first publication rights. Even before the store opened, the architect's sketches for the design of the Worth Avenue shop had been featured in a trade magazine and was the talk of retailers around the country.

Construction was nearly completed on the afternoon that Caroline met Francesca Palen there after work. Francesca, who had been promoted to director of public relations at The Breakers, was eager to see the new Romance, Inc., and when she stepped inside, she shook her head and whistled.

"Do you realize that this store is going to be Worth Avenue's crown jewel?" she asked, almost bowled over by what she saw. "It's an absolute showplace!"

"I'm glad you like it," Caroline said, sounding pleased but subdued. She was more than just happy with the way the store was turning out, but there would be no real pleasure or excitement until Jack was truly hers.

"So, what are you going to do to show it off?" Francesca asked.

"Show it off?" asked Caroline somewhat numbly. She was preoccupied with judges, courts, and lawyers.

"You've got to throw a party," said Francesca. "Invite all the movers and shakers in town and get the media to cover it. A terrific party is free advertising. *Particularly* when you have a one in a million venue like this that people are dying to see."

"I suppose you're right," said Caroline.

"I *am* right," Francesca said firmly. "You know, old friend, when you were fifteen years old and had stars in your eyes, I told you that you were a VIP-in-training. Well, the training's over. You've worked hard for years, and you just can't walk away from your accomplishments now that it looks like Romance, Inc. is really taking off. This snazzy store of yours puts you in the big leagues, as your pal Brett Haas would say. I know you've got other things on your mind these days, but you need to pay attention to Romance, Inc., too. Making this store the talk of the town is a good way to start."

Francesca was right, Caroline knew, and, although planning a party was the last thing on her mind, she set a date for the last Tuesday in November, arranged for a caterer and a florist and a string quartet, made up a guest list, and contacted television producers and newspaper and magazine editors. Her business was the one bright spot in her life. With Francesca's advice, she decided that she would make the party the most glittering, talked-about event of the new, young season.

It didn't take much to track Ray Lyons down. The bandy-legged groom with a gambling problem and a penchant for cheap whiskey was living in Port St. Lucie, Charles knew. The last time Ray had tried to blackmail Charles, he had had the nerve to telephone the chairman of Goddard-Stevens at the office, and Charles had traced the call.

"I need money," Ray had told Charles.

"I gave you money," Charles had barked. "And then I told you to stay the hell away from me."

"You didn't give me enough," Ray protested. "Killing someone is expensive, but keeping quiet about it is going to cost you even more."

"You've been paid," Charles snapped. "In full. Now crawl back under your rock and leave me alone."

And Ray Lyons had left Charles alone. But as the custody hearing loomed, and Charles's anxiety over whether he would actually win the case grew, it was he who sought Ray out.

"You want more money from me?" Charles said when he reached the stableman.

"That's what I told you," said Ray sourly, not the least bit surprised that Mr. Big Shot had come to his senses.

"Good. I've got another job for you, and it must be completed right away," said Charles. "I'll pay you half of the money up front and the other half after you do the work."

Ray was about to demand that he be paid the rest of what he thought he was owed on the last job when Charles named his figure.

Ray was dumbstruck. It was more dough than he'd ever had in his life. *With money like that I could pay off all my debts and then some,* he thought greedily.

"What do I have to do this time? Kill somebody else?" he asked, instantly leaping for the bait.

"No," Charles said brusquely. He did not want Ray to talk to *anyone* about what he'd done—not even to him. "There's a store in Palm Beach. On Worth Avenue. It's called Romance, Inc., next to Chanel."

Boy, this Charles Goddard gets me to all the right places, Ray Lyons snickered to himself. First, the Palm Beach Polo and Country Club. Now, some swanky store on Worth Avenue.

"What do you want me to do when I find this Romance, Inc.?" he asked Charles.

Charles allowed himself a small smile.

"Light a match," he said.

~30~

The ringing of the telephone on Caroline's night table jolted her awake at quarter to two on the morning of Tuesday, November 22. By two-thirty, she had frantically dressed, called Selma to come and stay with Jack, and driven to Worth Avenue just in time to watch three truckloads of firefighters turning hoses on what was going to have been her triumph: Romance, Inc.'s flagship store. Instead, what she witnessed was the destruction of a lifelong dream.

Flames licked high into the night sky, making a dancing, taunting mockery of her aspirations. The wall of heat radiating from the red-hot center of the blaze assaulted her, stinging her eyes, and the acrid scent of smoke filled Caroline's nostrils with the smell of despair. All she had worked for, all she had struggled toward, the one and only bright spot in the recent months of hell, was gone, reduced to smoldering rubble. Destroyed in ash and flame, incinerated in a fiery maelstrom of nothingness. Memories of another fire, a fire that had burned down the house she'd grown up in, rose up with a ferocity only a bitter and traumatic past could produce. She recalled the ugly fight on Patterson Avenue, her mother's screams, her terrified call to the police, her father's threats, his curses, his fist as it came toward her face.

"We're not sure what started it, Mrs. Goddard. We're going to have to conduct an investigation," said the fire chief, his voice finally impinging on Caroline's consciousness.

"Investigate?" she said, still lost in the brutal images

from the past, dazed by the enormity of what was happening to her in the present.

"We don't know what caused the fire. I understand that the store was undergoing construction. Is that correct?"

"The construction was finished. *Just* finished—except for the painter's final touch-ups. I'm giving—well, I was *planning* to give—the opening night party for the store next week," Caroline said, thinking suddenly that she would have to notify the 250 guests she had invited that there would be no party, no store, no Romance, Inc.. She stared blankly at the charred space that was once her dream, dimly aware of the dimensions of her loss—financial, personal, psychological. She wasn't crying, she wasn't hurt, she wasn't even afraid. She was numb. In shock. Overwhelmed.

"Maybe oily rags were left around," the fire chief surmised. "Maybe there was a short in the electrical system. It could be just about anything when you're talking about a building that's under construction."

Caroline thought of the expensive, innovative lighting system she had had custom designed for the shop; of the high-tech, state-of-the-art computer system that would track sales and inventory; of all the wires and cables, switches and fuse boxes the electrician had so painstakingly installed. She wondered if her father had been right all those years ago when he'd called her uppity and told her she was reaching past herself. Did she really think she was too good to be Al Shaw's daughter? *Was* she snooty and uppity? And was she now, as her father had always predicted, paying the price for her aspirations, her unfulfillable expectations?

"There's also the possibility of arson," Caroline heard the chief say. "Do you know of anyone who thinks he's got a score to settle with you?"

Caroline felt her throat go dry and her stomach churn. How could she tell a perfect stranger about her father? About his curses and his threats? About his sneers and accusations? About the violence he had always resorted to when he couldn't deal with his frustrations and disappointments? Besides, Al Shaw couldn't have done it, could he? He was living in Port St. Lucie. In recent years he seemed to have changed. He visited Caroline more often and acted as if he were genuinely fond of Jack. He had managed to control his drinking reasonably well, and he had been able to hold a steady job. He might not be the best husband in the world, but he was an improved one, according to Mary Shaw.

"Do you know someone who might want to hurt you?" the fire chief asked again, waiting for her answer.

"No," she said in a voice that didn't sound like her own as she wondered about her father, wondered how deep the changes really went. "I can't think of anyone."

Charles Goddard paid Ray Lyons the way he always did. On time and in cash. Untraceable cash.

"Now get lost," said Charles, handing the groom the thick envelope as the first fingers of dawn lighted the sky. He loathed the little man, despised his weakness for gambling and horses, but found him necessary on occasion. And, Charles knew that despite Ray's many faults, he was discreet. Over the years Ray Lyons had proved that he knew how to keep his mouth shut.

Ray had no more respect for Charles than Charles had for him. *All front and bluster,* he thought, *and inside, rotten to the core.* He looked at the powerful financier as they stood in the dark on the grounds of the Goddards' Palm Beach estate and sneered.

"Until next time, right?" he said.

He put the envelope into the pocket of his jeans and, on the way back to Port St. Lucie, decided that he deserved a night out on the town. He had money in his pocket, and he was in the mood to spend it. He knew just where he'd go, too. The Horse Shoe wasn't one of those high-class yuppie bars with fancy mixed drinks, cable television, and Michael Bolton on the jukebox. It was a workingman's bar with beer on tap, a pool table, dim lighting, a friendly group of regulars, and a bartender who poured with a heavy hand.

The Horse Shoe was the kind of place where Ray Lyons felt comfortable. The kind of place where he would be sure to run into people he knew. The bar would be closed for Thanksgiving in a couple of days, but tonight it would be hopping. And the same went for the weekend, when all the regulars would be there . . .

At nine o'clock on Wednesday morning, the day before Thanksgiving, less than a week before the custody hearing, Caroline sat in Douglas Harding's office. Although she had been home to see Jack, to shower and change clothes, she had been up for two straight nights and looked it. There were deep circles under her eyes and hollows beneath her cheeks. The smell of smoke was still in her hair, and an unmistakable air of despair hovered over her as she briefly told her lawyer everything she knew about the fire that had destroyed her store.

"Burned to the ground," she said in an empty, uninflected tone of voice. "Everything's gone. *Everything.*"

"I'm so sorry," he said sympathetically. He paused for a moment, trying to compose words that he hoped would not sound too harsh. He had bad news for Caroline, and the timing of it could not be more inappropriate. He looked into her sad, bereft eyes and couldn't proceed, couldn't speak.

"You have something to tell me? About the report your investigator was putting together on the Goddards?" she asked. Even in her own pain, he noticed, she was aware of his discomfort and tried to help him out.

He nodded.

"There are rumors and innuendos about how the Goddard family made its money and how they found their way to Wall Street. There are also all sorts of whispers about how Charles Goddard became sole proprietor of the firm and the circumstances under which his partner left," he said.

"Are these rumors and innuendos evidence we can take to court on Monday?" Caroline asked.

Doug Harding sighed.

"I wish they were," he said. "People are willing to talk about Charles Goddard behind his back, but no one will *swear* to anything. Not in front of a judge."

"People are afraid of him," said Caroline, remembering that even James, his own son, feared him.

"He's a very powerful man," confirmed the lawyer. "As for his wife, the investigator found out that Dina Goddard was not exactly a Park Avenue debutante when she met Charles. She came from a lower middle class family somewhere in New Jersey."

"Being from a lower middle class family isn't illegal," said Caroline, finishing the sentence. "And it certainly wouldn't disqualify her as a potential caretaker for Jack."

"Nor would lying about her background in the society pages," concluded Doug Harding. "I'm sorry, Caroline, but we seem to have come to a dead end. The letters of endorsement you've gotten are going to help, as is the testimony from Jack's teachers."

"But that's not enough?" asked Caroline with a sinking feeling.

"I wouldn't say that. You never know how a judge is going to rule. It's impossible to predict which evidence he'll respond to. That's why we've left no stone unturned in presenting your side of the case," the attorney said.

"But our position is weak, isn't it?" she asked.

Doug Harding was silent for a moment.

"There's your business travel and the men you've been seeing," he said, referring to the Goddards' allegations. "And, of course, the fact that you never told the Goddards about Jack."

Never told them! The words outraged Caroline.

"I *tried* to tell them!" she exclaimed. "I wrote to them twice. Both times they returned my letters unopened. And I called Emily. She never returned my call."

The lawyer looked surprised.

"They contend that they had to find out via their friend Mrs. Rittenbacher, who claims she found out about Jack from an article in *The Shiny Sheet.*"

"Via Mrs. Rittenbacher and *The Shiny Sheet?*" asked Caroline, stunned. "It was Clifford Hamlin, Goddard-Stevens's managing director, who told Charles."

Doug Harding shook his head.

"Clifford Hamlin had nothing to do with it, according to the court papers and to Mr. Hamlin himself. In fact, he's written to me several times. He's offered to be a character witness on your behalf."

Caroline felt the breath go out of her. How could she have misjudged Clifford? Assumed he was guilty without even listening to his side of the story? She had treated him terribly—cast him out of her life after he had done so much for her. She would have to make it up to him, tell him how sorry she was as soon as possible, and hope that he would forgive her.

"About those letters you say you wrote to the Goddards," said Doug Harding. "Did you keep them?"

Caroline smiled bitterly.

"Yes, I did," she nodded. "I kept them in a locked drawer in my desk, which had just been moved over to the new store." She paused and took a deep breath. "They were burned in the fire. Destroyed along with everything else."

The lawyer was quiet. The letters would have been an important piece of evidence. Without them, Caroline had no tangible proof of her efforts to inform the Goddards of the existence of their grandson.

"It doesn't look good, does it?" asked Caroline, understanding that the fire had cost her not only her store but crucial evidence that might have helped balance the scales in her fight against the Goddards.

"It's not as bad—" the attorney began, reacting to Caroline's distraught expression. Then he stopped himself in midsentence and shook his head slowly. There was no point in lying to her. "You're very astute and very brave, and I don't want to insult you by being less than completely honest," he said. "No, Caroline. I'm afraid it doesn't look good."

That evening, Caroline telephoned Clifford.

"I don't know how to begin to apologize," she told him, relieved that he was at home and grateful that he didn't hang up on her the moment he heard her voice. "My lawyer and I had a meeting today. He happened to mention that it was someone else who informed the Goddards about Jack. Someone named Betsy Rittenbacher."

"I tried to tell you," said Clifford, his voice racked with emotion. "But you wouldn't listen, wouldn't even take my calls. You just made up your mind that I had betrayed you and shut me out of your life without giving me a chance to explain."

"I know and I'm ashamed of myself, ashamed of the way I behaved. The truth is, I did to you exactly what the Goddards did to me when I tried to tell them I was pregnant with Jack and they refused to listen to me, to even acknowledge me. I, of all people, should have been sensitive to your feelings, and I still can't believe that I was that cruel. The only excuse I can offer is that I've been out of my mind with worry. Losing Jack will kill me, Clifford."

"I know," he said softly. "That's why I contacted your attorney about being a witness on your behalf."

"Yes, I heard, and I thank you, Clifford. From the bottom of my heart—for that and for being on my side. Through everything," she said, thinking that beneath Clifford Hamlin's cool, slightly aloof exterior, his character was pure platinum.

"I *am* on your side," he confirmed. "And I always will be. I hope you know that now."

"I do. Really. But I wish there were something I could say to express my apology, some way I could make it up to you," she said.

"There is," he replied, his tone brightening. "When this case is over, I'd like to see you. Here in New York. Or, if you'd prefer, in Palm Beach."

"I'd like that, Clifford. I really would," she said.

Thanksgiving was the worst holiday of Caroline's life. There wasn't much to be thankful for, after all. She had lost her glittering new store, was about to lose her son, and whatever happened after that didn't matter to her. She and Jack spent the day at Tamara and Ferdy's beautiful estate, but despite her forced smile and determination not to impose her desolate mood on anyone, Caroline could not think of anything except Jack and the coming trial. The turkey tasted like sawdust, the cranberry sauce like cotton, the vintage wine like vinegar. She could not keep her eyes off Jack as he took three helpings of everything, played with the new video game Tamara had given him, bounded into and out of the pool half a dozen times, and even managed to inveigle Ferdy into a spirited round of hide-and-seek.

The *last,* she kept telling herself. The word haunted her thoughts, punctuating every sentence like a death knell. The *last*— The last holiday she would spend with her adored child. The last visit with him to Tamara and Ferdy's. The last time she would watch him swim in their pool. The last night she would give him his bath, read to him, tuck him into bed, and kiss him good night. The time wasn't measured in months anymore, nor in weeks, but in hours. The trial was scheduled for Monday, and on Monday, she feared that the judge would find her wanting, find her inadequate, find her an unfit mother, and take her child away from her—forever and after.

Behind her sunglasses her eyes brimmed with tears, and her heart felt like a stone in her chest. She sat alone, off to one side on the terrace, watching the festivities go on around her, watching Jack charming everyone in sight. Her boy . . . her precious darling . . . her reason for living . . .

"Are you all right?" Tamara asked, knowing the answer. She had been devastated when she'd learned of the Goddards' custody suit against Caroline and even more devastated when she'd returned to Palm Beach from London and seen her friend so tortured, so broken by the tragedies she was being forced to face.

Caroline looked at the countess and knew she no longer had the strength to pretend, to go through the motions, to make the effort.

"No," she said. "I'm not all right."

"Maybe not, but you shouldn't give up," said her old friend.

"I know. That's what Mr. Harding said," replied Caroline. "But in the end, even he admitted that it doesn't look good for me."

"What do you expect? He's a lawyer!" Tamara scoffed. "Lawyers are paid to be negative. If they didn't tell you all the things that could go wrong, they wouldn't be doing their job."

Caroline managed a wisp of a smile.

"Then I guess I've got a good lawyer," she said. "I just wish I had something to fight back with. Some ammunition besides letters from people telling the judge what a wonderful mother I am. They seem so pathetic against the evidence the Goddards have against me—not to mention their money and power."

"If only you could dig up some dirt on Charles Goddard," Tamara said. "Something that would destroy the bastard once and for all."

"I know," said Caroline, sounding desolate. "But what? Mr. Harding tried that. There were hints of possible wrongdoings but nothing concrete. Nothing we could use in court."

For one of the very few times in her life, Tamara had no answer, no advice, and there was a long moment of silence as neither woman had the words to express her feelings.

"I wish I knew what to do," Tamara said finally. "I feel so helpless."

"I don't think anyone can help me now," said Caroline, her eyes filling, her heart breaking. "I really don't."

Tamara reached out and took Caroline into her arms.

"I'm sorry," she said, rocking her. "So sorry."

In the safety of Tamara's arms, the tears that Caroline had only barely managed to keep in check all afternoon poured out, and the duchess led her, sobbing and finally out of control, into the house, away from prying eyes.

"Why were you crying?" Jack asked that night as Caroline was tucking him into bed.

"I wasn't crying," she said quickly, trying to avoid his gaze.

"Mom? You always tell *me* not to lie. I saw Aunt Tamara hug you and then I saw your shoulders shaking," said Jack, his big blue eyes, so much like James's, unwavering. "Is it cus-tiddy?"

He had trouble with the word and stumbled over it.

"Yes, darling. It's cus-tiddy," Caroline admitted. The hearing was only four days away. There was no point in playing games with Jack now.

"Don't worry, Mommy. Everything's going to be all right," he said, sounding amazingly like his father. "Just you take my word for it."

With that, Caroline scooped him up in her arms and felt the velvety skin of his plump cheek against her mouth.

The *last?* she wondered. Was this the last time he would make her laugh and cry at the same time? The last time she would kiss him? The last time she would feel his skin against hers? The thoughts were too unbearable to hold for more than a moment. She felt pierced through to her heart, sick to her soul, and held him close to her.

"Mommy! You're squeezing me too hard!" he said.

"I'm sorry, darling," she said, loosening her grip. "So sorry."

"Sorry for what?" he asked seriously.

"Sorry for everything," she said, feeling overwhelmed by guilt and shame and dread.

Not knowing what to say or what to do anymore, she finally let him go and put him back into bed. As she kissed him good night one final time, she noticed that the collar of his pajamas was damp.

From her tears. Tears she would continue to shed for as long as she was forced to live without him.

On Saturday night, after a full day at the racetrack, Ray Lyons bellied up to the bar at the Horse Shoe. Limpy, the bartender, was there and so were all the regulars, guys who worked with their hands, guys who lived on social security, guys like Ray who did a little of this, a little of that, hustling to make a living. Feeling sour, Ray didn't go in for his usual glad-handing. Instead, he plunked himself down next to Al Shaw, who was nursing a cup of coffee at the end of the bar.

"Still off the booze?" asked Ray.

"Doin' my best," said Al.

"I'd offer to buy you a drink. Hell, I was going to buy the whole joint a round," said the groom.

"You came into some dough?" asked Al. The subject of money always caused his ears to perk up.

"Some. Not as much as I thought, though. I just did a job for someone. A big-time job for a big-time guy. I figured I deserved a tip. A pat on the back, so to speak. Instead, I got stiffed," said Ray.

"You mean you didn't get paid for this job?" asked Al, invariably responsive to an injustice.

"Nah. I got paid. But I got *exactly* what we agreed on. You know what I mean? *Exactly.* The way I look at it, this was a dangerous job. The least I deserved was a 'thank you.' You know, a few extra bucks, what with the holiday coming up," said Ray, picking up the shot the bartender had put in front of him and downing the whisky in one swallow. He wiped his mouth with his sleeve and signaled for a beer chaser. "But, shit, you know rich guys. Bunch of cheap pricks always out to screw the workingman."

"Yeah," said Al sympathetically. "They think we're nothing but dirt. Who's the rich guy you did the job for?"

"A Palm Beach swell. You probably never heard of him," said Ray, picking up the beer and draining off half. "Lives in a big, fancy place right on the ocean. Name's Charles Goddard."

"Charles Goddard?" asked Al, astounded to hear that name in the Horse Shoe.

Ray nodded, then finished the beer and motioned for a second shot, this one a double.

"Big shot Wall Street guy," Ray said. "Why? You heard of him?"

Al could be cagey and knew that this was one of the times to keep his temper cool, his mouth shut. He picked up his coffee and took a leisurely sip. He didn't want to seem nosy. Or anxious.

"Practically everybody around here has heard of him. Whadya do for him anyway?" he asked, trying to sound casual.

"Torched a store," said the groom, draining the second shot. "A fancy joint. On Worth Avenue, no less."

"Worth Avenue? In Palm Beach? No shit?" Al said, eager to keep Ray talking.

"Yeah. Very high class," said Ray, wanting to make sure his friend understood that he moved in the big leagues every now and then.

"You know the name of it?"

"Nah. Some kind of ritzy operation is all I know. Just built, too. I could smell the fresh paint. Probably even helped it go up faster," he said, proud of his handiwork.

Al's heart thumped in his chest. He knew his daughter's store had burned down just the other day. Mary had told him. He also knew that Charles Goddard was trying to take Jack away from Caroline. From the *Shaws.* Al's anger began to boil as Ray went on.

"Did anyone see you torch this store?" asked Al.

Ray shook his head.

"No way. I worked in the dark. Got in and out of there in less than ten minutes. Waited until the security guy took a leak, splashed some lighter fluid around, lit a couple of matches, and bingo! In and out like a phantom. No one saw me. Did a good job, if I say so myself . . ."

Al let him go on, bragging about the high quality of his work and the stinginess of his unappreciative employer.

"This Goddard's a shit from way back," said Ray.

"Way back?" Al asked.

"Sure. This isn't the first job I ever did for him. He and I got a history," said Ray, warming to his resentment. "You know what else I did for him?"

"No. What else?" asked Al, acting every bit the confidant, knowing he was hearing something that, if true, would put Charles Goddard away—and keep Caroline from losing Jack. He had never in his whole life known something of value, something that someone else would actually be interested in hearing, something that could make a difference in someone's life. He was all ears.

"I never told anybody about this, but what the hell? I don't care anymore. Not after the way that cheap bastard treated me," said Ray, over a second beer. "I could send him to jail. Maybe even to the gas chamber, if I felt like it." He smiled to himself at the mere thought of the power he held over Charles Goddard.

"So tell me more about this 'history' you two have. What else did you do for Charles Goddard?" Al wanted to know.

"Took care of some business for him. *Family* business—"

said Ray, picking up his third shot and gulping it down. His words were beginning to slur, and he was feeling very confident and full of himself. "And it was a helluva lot more than just torching some store. You want to know what I did?"

"Sure," Al said breezily, his palms sweaty, his throat dry.

Ray leaned toward Al. He had big news to deliver, and he wanted to make sure that his buddy didn't miss a word.

"Here's what I did for that bastard. You know the polo club? Down in Palm Beach? Where rich guys on horses chase after a little ball?"

Al nodded, and sure of his captive audience, Ray Lyons motioned for a third beer. Then he began his story.

Caroline's doorbell rang at eight-thirty on Sunday morning.

"Dad!" she said, surprised to see him at such an early hour and without her mother, who had usually been the one to initiate their visits. He was freshly shaved and his eyes were clear, and as he stood in her foyer, his hands in his jeans pockets, he seemed subdued, almost penitent.

"Honey, I want to apologize. I know I haven't always acted like much of a father," he began, and paused under the weight of what he was about to tell her.

Caroline was stunned by his admission and surprised by his apology. She invited him into the living room, but even before Al Shaw sat down on the couch, he began to talk. He had to tell her the news. And he had to tell her right away.

"I think I can finally do something to help you—"

31

Caroline knew instantly that her father had handed her a bombshell. She didn't even wait until Al Shaw left her condo to move into action. The minute he finished telling her about his encounter with Ray Lyons the evening before—how the groom had been hired by Charles Goddard, not only to burn down her store but to murder Kyle Pringle!—she hurried into the kitchen and, shaking with excitement, dialed Douglas Harding's answering service.

"May I take a message for Mr. Harding?" the operator asked.

"I need to speak with him right away," Caroline said breathlessly, barely able to contain herself. Murder, arson—words she had never used in her life, concepts that barely seemed real to her—churned sickeningly in her mind. Douglas Harding had been right. There *was* "something" in Charles Goddard's past—more than just one "something."

"It's Sunday," the operator pointed out. "Mr. Harding isn't in the office today. I'll have him call you tomorrow."

"This won't wait until tomorrow," Caroline said, doing her best to remain calm. "I need to speak with him today. Now. About my case. It's extremely urgent."

"I see," said the operator. "I'll see if I can reach him—"

"Please!" urged Caroline. Didn't the woman understand that her life depended on it?

"I'll do my best!" exclaimed the woman impatiently.

Caroline hung up, feeling thwarted and frustrated. What if the service couldn't reach Douglas Harding? What if he'd gone out of town? What if he were unavailable for either personal or professional reasons? What good was the information she had if she couldn't tell anyone who had the authority to help her? She paced back and forth in the living room, thinking, her emotions seesawing precipitously between elation and despair. She had to talk to her lawyer, had to reach Douglas Harding!

She stared at the phone, ordering it to ring, insisting that it be Douglas Harding, but the instrument remained obstinately quiet. *Ring,* she commanded. *Ring!* The response was silence.

She was almost, irrationally, on the verge of picking up the telephone and shaking it to life, when, suddenly, she remembered that she didn't need Doug Harding's answering service, after all. She could call him herself! In her excitement she had completely forgotten that she already had his home number. His wife, Gwen, was a client of Romance, Inc., and her home address and telephone number were on the client list Caroline kept on a duplicate diskette at home for safekeeping.

While her father played with Jack in his room, she rushed to the filing cabinet in her bedroom, retrieved the diskette, popped it into her notebook computer, and quickly located Gwen's number. With hands still trembling, she dialed Douglas Harding's home phone number.

"Hello?"

Caroline recognized Gwen Harding's voice.

"Mrs. Harding? This is Caroline Goddard," she said. She realized that her words were rushing out and she took a deep breath, telling herself to slow down. "Is your husband there? I'd never disturb him at home on a Sunday morning, but something has come up about my case. I'm in the possession of some crucial information that could change the outcome of the lawsuit dramatically."

"Oh, oh, just a second," Gwen said quickly, responding to Caroline's tone of urgency. "Doug was rushing out the door, late for his golf game as usual, but let me see if I can catch him."

As Gwen put the phone down and went in search of her husband, Caroline clutched the phone, willing Douglas Harding to be at home, willing him to come to the telephone. She waited, her heart pounding, her mind racing, her hopes soaring, then plunging, then soaring again, as a variety of scenarios played out in her imagination. *If Ray Lyons agrees to talk . . . But what if he refuses? If the police believe him . . . But what if they don't believe him? If Charles is arrested, the judge will . . . But what if he isn't arrested and his lawyer gets him off? Powerful people like Charles Goddard don't go to jail. Powerful people like Charles Goddard do go to jail . . . if they're guilty . . .*

"Yes, Caroline?"

It was Doug Harding! So he hadn't left the house!

"I'm sorry to bother you on a Sunday morning, but—"

"That's all right. Gwen said it was important. Something about new information regarding tomorrow's hearing," he interrupted, eager to hear what had happened, anxious to find out what new developments his client had uncovered.

"It's extremely important," said Caroline, who proceeded to repeat the almost incredible story that Al Shaw had just told her. Word for word. Shocking fact after shocking fact.

When she was finished, Doug Harding was nearly speechless. So the rumors and innuendos his investigator had mentioned were apparently true! Charles Goddard, one of the kings of Wall Street, the public symbol of gentility and respectability, the man who had donated millions of dollars to hospitals and charities and good causes was, according to this story, little more than a common criminal! He was alleged by his client's father to have hired some lowlife to murder his son-in-law and then destroy his former daughter-in-law's business! It was the kind of information that, if provable, would put Charles Goddard in prison and, of course, completely torpedo the Goddard custody suit.

"You're sure about all this?" he asked Caroline.

"Yes, I'm sure," she said. "I repeated to you *exactly* what Ray Lyons told my father just last night."

"And will your father swear to it? Under oath?" asked the lawyer.

"Yes, he will."

"And what about Ray Lyons? Will he tell a court what he told your father?" he asked. And then, before Caroline could even frame a reply, he answered his own question. Of course, Ray Lyons would talk! "Ray Lyons will talk if he's given the right motivation. And I personally am going to see to it that he gets that motivation . . ." he said suddenly, recalling that he had gone to law school with George Hostos, the Port St. Lucie DA. "You just sit tight and wait for me to call you back."

"What are you going to do?" Caroline asked, nearly wild with anticipation and almost giddy at the prospect of finally being able to deal with Charles Goddard from a position of power.

"First of all, I'm going to cancel my golf date. Then I'm going to call the police, and after that, I'm going to call a law school classmate of mine," he said. "I'm going to tell them what you've told me."

"Then what?" asked Caroline.

"Then, I imagine, the police will want to talk to you. And to your father. Will you be available?"

"Any time. We'll stay here all day," said Caroline, feeling a sudden, overwhelming gratitude toward Douglas Harding who had given up his Sunday for her and to Al Shaw, who had come straight to the condo to tell her what he had heard at the Horse Shoe bar the night before. If things turned out as she hoped, if the police believed the story, if they arrested Ray, if they charged Charles . . . *If if if*. . . . She stopped herself. It was too soon to celebrate, too soon to assume her problems were over, too soon to count on the judge to make the right decision.

"Caroline?" said Douglas Harding, his voice penetrating her whirling thoughts. "Are you all right?"

"That depends on what the police think of my father's story," she said, cautioning herself not to get ahead of herself.

By noon two detectives from the Palm Beach Police Department had listened to Al Shaw's account of his Saturday night meeting with Ray Lyons, taken several pages of notes, and asked Caroline and Al to come down to headquarters to give their statements. A few hours later, the police in Port St. Lucie picked up Ray Lyons and booked him on suspicion of murder and arson. George Hostos, the district attorney, introduced himself to Ray, then offered him a cigarette and a plea bargain—a lesser sentence if he would testify against the man George really wanted to nail, a powerful figure whose conviction would *really* make his career: Charles Huntington Goddard.

"It's your choice," the DA told a pale and sweating Ray Lyons. "Jail time or a slap on the wrist."

Ray didn't even have to think twice. He had no reason on earth to while away years in prison just to protect the high and mighty Charles Goddard. After all, he had once asked Goddard to pay extra for his silence—and Goddard had turned him down flat. Maybe if Charles had come up with a few extra bucks, things might have been different. But the way things were, he figured he owed Charles Goddard nothing.

"I can tell you plenty about Charles Goddard," Ray began, inhaling deeply. *"Plenty . . ."*

Ray told the DA everything—dates, times, places, financial arrangements—about his dealings over the years with Charles. He offered the names of corroborating witnesses, guys who knew him from the track and who had a damn good idea of what he'd done to Kyle Pringle's saddle. He even turned over the pair of pants that he'd worn when setting fire to Caroline's store—pants that still bore lighter fluid residue, which he'd spilled in his haste to get his job done and make his escape.

"Charles Goddard is a sleazeball," he told the DA. "All that money and power are just a cover. He doesn't give a damn about anyone or anything. He'd run you over in that Rolls-Royce of his and not even bother to slow down . . ."

At eight-thirty that evening, Charles and Dina Goddard were hosting a dinner party on the flagstone terrace of their Palm Beach estate. The Rittenbachers were there, as were the Lawsons and the Madisons—just the "family," as Dina often referred to her very close, longtime Palm Beach circle. She and Betsy Rittenbacher were sitting at the elegantly appointed, candlelit dinner table, chatting over their husbands' shoulders about the upcoming Hibiscus Charity Ball, when one of the servants appeared on the terrace and approached the table.

"Mr. Goddard?" she said tentatively in a barely audible voice.

Charles, deep in conversation, didn't even hear her. He was holding forth on the subject of the declining value of the U.S. dollar abroad.

"Thank you, Rosalie, we don't need our glasses filled just yet," said Dina, waving the young girl away. Rosalie Scaggs was new to the staff and needed, Dina thought, a good deal more seasoning.

"Begging your pardon, Mrs. Goddard, but it's not about the glasses," Rosalie said timidly, afraid she would lose her job before she'd even worked for the Goddards a month.

"Then what on earth is it?" Dina said sharply.

"It's about Mr. Goddard," said the girl, her lower lip quivering.

Dina rolled her eyes at Betsy Rittenbacher, turned away from her friend, and then tapped her husband on the back.

"Charles, darling," she said, cutting into his discussion. "Rosalie has something she wants to say to you."

Charles looked up, irritated by the interruption.

"Yes, what is it?" he said, reaching for his wineglass and taking a sip of the fruity Beaujolais-Villages that Dina had selected to accompany the rack of lamb.

"Two men . . . are here to . . . see you, Mr. Goddard," Rosalie stammered, growing increasingly uncomfortable with her task.

"Two men? For God's sake, young lady! Use your eyes! I'm in the middle of a dinner party," Charles snapped, then gave Dina a chastising glance. It was she who supervised the staff, after all. Why she had allowed such an inexperienced girl to work a dinner party he couldn't fathom.

"Yes, sir. I know, sir," said Rosalie. "But they said they had to see you anyway. They said it was important."

"I'm sure they did," he scoffed. "A lot of people think they have to see me. Right, Perry?" He looked down the table at Perry Madison, who ran Goddard-Stevens's Palm Beach office and who often called Charles about "emergencies" that weren't. "Tell them I'm tied up. They'll go away," he ordered Rosalie. "And when you've done that, come back and empty my ashtray. These cigar ashes have been sitting here for nearly an hour."

Rosalie looked helplessly at Dina, as if she would somehow come to the rescue. Realizing it was a foolish thought, she took a deep breath and pressed on.

"The men are policemen," she told Charles. "They said . . ." She hesitated, for she knew that once the words were out of her mouth, she would be out of a job. "They said that if you didn't come to the door, they would be forced to come inside the house and get you . . . and that they were sure you wouldn't want to spoil your own party."

Dina's face registered a mixture of alarm, confusion, and embarrassment. Charles sat motionless. He seemed completely stunned. The police? At his front door? Demanding to see him? It was impossible! Wasn't it? *Wasn't* it?

The sweet, balanced flavor of the wine curdled sourly in the back of his throat as the possibilities flashed instantaneously through his mind. Had the police poked their noses into the fire that had burned down Caroline Shaw's store? Had they traced the accident back to him? Had they discovered that it was he who had ordered it burned to the ground? Had Ray done a sloppy job, leaving evidence the police were able to trace? Or had he thrown back one drink too many and shot his mouth off to the wrong person in the wrong place? Had the deeds Charles had done to protect the Goddard name and guarantee its future generations, as his father's father had done before him, finally caught up with him?

"Charles?" Dina asked, her complexion ashen, her eyes wide with fear.

"Everything will be fine," he told her as he rose slowly from the table and smiled weakly at his guests, feigning an air of confidence he didn't feel. "Everything will be just fine," he reiterated, knowing with grave certainty, that for the first time in his life it would not.

Judge William Faraday, who was to have presided over the custody hearing, was contacted on the night of the arrest and informed of the charges against Charles. After staying up to read the transcript of Ray Lyons's confession, implicating Charles in both murder and arson, Judge Faraday summoned Ronald Switzer and Douglas Harding into his chambers the next morning and informed them that he was dismissing the Goddards' custody suit against Caroline.

"Obviously," he said, looking at the two attorneys over his half-glasses, "the boy will remain with his mother."

Doug Harding telephoned Caroline from the courthouse to tell her the good news.

"The judge has thrown out the case," he said jubilantly. "From now on, you and Jack have nothing to worry about."

Caroline screamed with delight at the news, and just as soon as she thanked Douglas Harding for all he had done, she began to call everyone she knew.

"It's over!" she kept repeating. "It's over!"

Truly, she felt as if the weight of the world had been lifted from her shoulders.

Caroline was so happy, so relieved, so overjoyed that Jack would not be taken away from her that at first she couldn't let him out of her sight—not even to attend to her business at Romance, Inc. Gradually, though, she began to recover a sense of normalcy, and their lives carried on as before. She met with her insurance agent, filed police and fire department reports, and received a check for the full replacement value of her flagship store on Worth Avenue. She rehired her architect and contractor and began the rebuilding process.

"Every nail, every board, every lightbulb is going to be exactly the way it was before the fire," she told Francesca as they stood in front of the burnt-out site, watching carpenters, plasterers, and tilemen ply their various trades. "Romance, Inc. will be rebuilt just the way The Breakers was."

"And be better than ever," said Francesca, who had encouraged Caroline to send out announcements explaining that the party had been postponed and giving a new date for what both women were calling the "storewarming."

Brett, Clifford, and Jean-Claude telephoned regularly, wanting to know about the progress of the construction, about Jack, and about their futures with Caroline. Throughout the lawsuit they had been loyal and loving and supportive, each in his own way, and Caroline felt a special affection for them. But it was toward Clifford that she also felt a nagging sense of guilt.

"Clifford, I don't know how to thank you for all you've done for me and Romance, Inc., I really don't," Caroline told him over the telephone in late November.

"For one thing, you can stop being so grateful. For another, you can take back the earrings," he said, his tone heavy with meaning.

"You still have them?" she asked, somewhat surprised. "I would have thought that after the way I treated you, you would have returned them or given them to someone else."

"Given them to someone else? Hardly. I'm in love with you, remember?" he asked, his voice soft with longing.

"Yes, I remember," Caroline said, remembering his words, his caresses. "But, still, I haven't seen you in so long . . ."

"It's not your fault that you couldn't see me," Clifford pointed out. "Your lawyer advised you not to, and you listened to him. I wouldn't have let you risk losing Jack, no matter how badly I wanted to see you."

"Clifford?"

"Yes?"

"Where are the earrings now?" she asked, picturing the gold and diamond earrings with their pristine white pearls and remembering how they had fit the curve of her ear, as if they had been made just for her.

"In the safe in my apartment. Why?"

"I might like to try them on again. Just to see—" said Caroline, feeling suddenly radiant, as she hadn't felt since she was in London. All the anguished months were behind her now. She had Jack, and thanks to Clifford's help with Tamara and Ferdy and his introductions to other investors, she was going to have the money to expand her business.

"What if I told you I've been invited to Palm Beach?" Clifford asked. "And that we've been asked to the same Sunday luncheon?"

"At Tamara's?" Caroline guessed. She and Jack still continued their Sunday ritual with Tamara and Ferdy.

"Exactly. Ferdy wants to discuss his investments, and I suspect that Tamara is up to a bit of matchmaking. She told me you'd be there and that she expected me as well. It was more of an order than an invitation," Clifford laughed.

"Well, I don't suppose we dare interfere with Tamara's plans, should we?" Caroline smiled. Tamara had told her over and over throughout the long months of the lawsuit that Clifford couldn't have been the one who'd betrayed her. The duchess had added that he would make some woman a wonderful husband and that Caroline would be crazy not to grab him. Subtlety had never been Tamara's long suit.

"Under penalty of excommunication at the very least," chuckled Clifford. "But, seriously, Caroline, I'm looking forward to seeing you. Actually, that's an understatement."

"It has been such a long time," said Caroline wistfully.

"Too long," he said, desire obvious in his voice.

Jean-Claude's first phone call to Caroline after the custody case had been dismissed was also full of affection and longing. He was attentive and flattering and almost impossible to resist. Now that she was free of her anxiety over the lawsuit, she told herself, they would be able to explore their feelings—to determine whether there was more to their relationship than a sexual attraction.

"I haven't been able to get you out of my mind," he admitted. "I think about you all the time."

"I've thought about you, too, Jean-Claude. About the way you've been on my side throughout this nightmare with the Goddards. About how supportive and loyal you've been. And about the way you helped change the way I think of myself," she said.

"How you think of yourself?" he asked.

"Yes. You know, you were the first man since James," she explained. "The first man to make me feel like a woman again. When I met you in Pierre's office that afternoon, I felt almost totally out of control—and it was a wonderful, invigorating feeling."

"Then you must feel it again soon, *chérie,*" he said. "When can I see you?"

"I don't know. I can't leave Palm Beach," she said. "I've got a store to rebuild."

"Then I'll come to you," he said. "I'll fly in on Saturday and take you to dinner that night."

She sighed, disappointed that she would have to refuse him.

"I'm so sorry, Jean-Claude, but I can't," she said regretfully. "I'm taking Jack to the Kravis Center. There's a performance of *The Nutcracker,* and I've had the tickets since October."

Jean-Claude was not put off.

"I won't take no for an answer. What about Sunday?" he asked.

"Jack and I were invited to a luncheon at his godmother's house," she explained.

"But I must see you, *chérie.* I must! I will arrive on Saturday, and before the weekend is out we will find a way to be together," he promised.

Caroline was putting Jack to bed when Brett checked in.

"Sweet cakes!" he said when she answered the phone. "How the hell are you?"

"Larry! Darling! It's so good to hear from you," she said.

"Larry? Who the hell is Larry? Some other guy calls you sweet cakes?" Brett demanded.

"A lot of other guys call me sweet cakes," Caroline said with a straight face.

"And you call them darling?" said Brett, sounding outraged.

"Of course." Caroline giggled. Then she decided she had let him suffer enough. "No, I was just playing games with you, Brett. You know, having a little fun? The way you're always telling me I should?"

"Cute, Caroline. Real cute. Now tell me how you're holding up? How's my buddy, Jack, holding up?"

"We're both doing fine, especially considering what we've just been through," she said. "Jack's an amazing little boy. So wise, so knowing. He was so confident and stable throughout the ordeal. He helped me keep from falling apart. And as for me, well . . . I'm just so relieved and happy it's over."

"And I'm happy it's over, too. Because you got Jack the way I always knew you would. And because now I can see you again," said Brett. "So since the coast is clear, I want to reschedule that dinner we never had. What do you say?"

"I don't see why not," Caroline said.

"The baseball season's over, and I've spent a few weeks in Abilene with Patsy, so I'm all yours," Brett said. "Hell, I'll stay down in Florida for the next four months if you want me to. And, boy, do I want you to want me to."

"Oh, really?" She smirked. "That sounded very much like a 'beg,' Mr. Haas. I thought you had this thing about getting me to beg you."

Brett laughed but when he spoke, he sounded chagrined. "I *did* say all that stuff, didn't I?"

"Yup," said Caroline.

"Well, I was a jerk," he admitted. "I'd never met a woman like you, and I didn't know what to do about it. So I acted like a . . . Well, it was my pop who told me to cut the crap. He said to step up to the plate, take my cuts, swing for the fences."

"In English, please," said Caroline.

"My father said I should stop beating around the bush and tell you how I feel about you."

"And how is that?" Caroline asked, egging him on.

"How I feel about you is . . . Well, let's just say that I'm begging you to let me come down to Florida. I could get there Monday. How's that?"

"That's just perfect," said Caroline, thinking that she would somehow fit Jean-Claude in on Saturday, lunch with Clifford on Sunday, and see Brett on Monday. The scheduling was perfect, she thought, marveling at the fact that not one but *three* men wanted to be part of her life. She was in the midst of a marvelous dilemma, and an old saying kept going through her mind: when it rains it pours.

There was another old saying that never even crossed her thoughts. It was the one about how the best-laid plans often go astray. . . .

32

It had rained heavily on the Sunday morning of Tamara's luncheon, but by noon the sky was cloudless and the temperature a tropical eighty degrees, typical for Palm Beach in late November.

"How about wearing those snappy blue shorts your Aunt Tamara bought you?" Caroline suggested as she helped Jack get dressed. "The ones with the white sailboats."

"Do I have to?" asked Jack, looking up at her.

He was getting to be such a big boy with a mind of his own, she thought. She felt a mixture of pride and sadness as she watched him sort through his bureau drawers to find just the right outfit. Pride that he was so well adjusted, despite the upheaval that had nearly destroyed their lives in the past year. Sadness that he was growing up so quickly, that before she knew it, he would be old enough to go out on his own. No, he wasn't a baby anymore, that she knew. He had become a person, a loving young man, earnest and spirited at the same time, a pleasure to be around. He had his father's handsomeness as well as his kind heart. What Jack and James did not share, though, was a love of boats. Jack's passion was clearly baseball.

"No, you don't have to," said Caroline, ruffling his golden hair. "I just thought it would please your godmother, who has been so generous to you. To both of us."

"I was planning to wear my Atlanta Braves workout shorts. The ones Brett got me," Jack explained.

"Not today," said Caroline patiently but firmly. It was one thing for her son to idolize Brett Haas. It was another for him to dress like Brett. "Aunt Tamara has invited us to a very elegant little party. Clifford Hamlin will be there. Remember him, darling?"

Jack nodded. "Is he your boyfriend, Mom?" he asked.

Caroline didn't know how to respond. She was very fond

of Clifford. But then she was very fond of Jean-Claude, too. And, she had to admit, even of Brett. She laughed to herself when she thought of how ironic her predicament was. As a young girl, she had never had a boyfriend, never mind a date. And now here she was juggling three men—men who each, in his own way, touched her heart. She and Jean-Claude hadn't been able to see each other yesterday, after all, despite his offer to rearrange his schedule. Instead, they had agreed that they would get together the next time he was in town. At least she would see Clifford at today's luncheon and Brett sometime on Monday. She knew she couldn't continue to see them all, not for much longer. It wasn't fair to them, and it wasn't what she really wanted, either. What she wanted, she had discovered in recent weeks, was one man, one love, one person she could wake up next to day after day. What she yearned for—and was now ready for, she realized—was what she would have had with James, if he had lived: a partnership that would last "forever and after."

"I don't know how to describe my relationship with Mr. Hamlin," Caroline told Jack. "He's my financial adviser and my very dear friend and—"

"And you love him?" Jack prompted, his expression very serious, very grown-up.

Caroline smiled. "I love *you,* my darling," she said, cupping his chin in her hand. "Now, enough with this chitchat and let's get you dressed. We're supposed to be at your godmother's in fifteen minutes."

Jack nodded and put on his blue shorts with the sailboats in the background. He would do as his mother asked—for now. But the minute he got home—the very second!—he would change into his Atlanta Braves workout shorts and wear *them* for the rest of the day.

When he spotted Caroline and Jack walking out onto the terrace, Clifford Hamlin rose from his chair beside the pool.

"Clifford," Caroline said as she approached him.

His long, thin face softened at the sight of her, and he smiled. It had been months since their trip to London, an eternity since they had been together. But if the stresses of the custody suit had taken their toll on her, he couldn't tell. She looked radiant, her chestnut hair tied back in a ponytail with a satin ribbon, her slim figure dressed in a periwinkle blue linen tunic with matching pants. He wanted her more at that moment than at any time since he'd known her, even as he wondered if the chances of her returning his feelings were remote.

"Hello, Caroline." He kissed her tenderly on the cheek. And then, peering down at her young son, he greeted the boy by extending his hand. "How are you doing, Jack?"

Jack shook Clifford's hand but did not return his smile. "Fine, thanks, Mr. Hamlin," he said politely.

"No need to be so formal. Call me Clifford, okay?"

Jack nodded. "Okay," he said without enthusiasm.

Caroline's heart went out to her son. She guessed he found Clifford a little stiff. So had she, at first. But once Jack got to know him, he would change his mind, she was sure.

"It's wonderful to see you, Clifford," she said, linking her arm in his.

"For me, too," he said softly. "For me, too."

"Oh, thank heavens! You're here!" said the duchess as she bustled onto the terrace, its glass table set with heavy sterling silver and fragile gilt porcelain arranged on pale yellow, hand-embroidered organdy mats with matching napkins. Potted orchids, their terra-cotta pots tied with moss green velvet ribbons, were aligned in the middle of the table and served as centerpieces. Tamara's ruby caftan, trimmed with gold braid, flapped in the light breeze, and her exotic perfume scented the air. "I was afraid you wouldn't come—and after all that food I ordered." She kissed Caroline and hugged Jack to her bosom, nearly crushing him.

"Why would you think we wouldn't come?" asked Caroline, glancing at her watch. "We're only five minutes late."

"Oh. Is that all? Well, you'll have to forgive me," said Tamara, looking more frantic than usual. "I'm really not myself."

"Then who are you?" Jack asked, his eyes wide with curiosity.

They all laughed.

"That's just an expression, darling," Caroline explained. "Your Aunt Tamara meant that she doesn't feel well. That *is* what you meant, isn't it, Tamara?"

"What I meant is that I invited all of you to lunch over a week ago," said the duchess. "And then last night at seven o'clock, the cook up and left!"

"Where did she go?" asked Caroline.

"God knows. She took her things and disappeared," said Tamara, massaging her temples and wincing in psychic pain. "As you well know, Caroline, good help isn't hard to find. It's impossible to find!"

Caroline smiled as she thought back to the revolving door of employees who had worked for Tamara, then quit when they found her temperament too hard to take. She herself had been Tamara's only loyal employee, and even *she* had tried to find work elsewhere when the countess had refused to give her a raise.

"What are you going to do without a cook?" asked Caroline, knowing that the duchess rarely dirtied her hands with anything so mundane as cooking.

"I know what she can do, Mom," Jack piped up. "She can get some of those great frozen pizzas that you always make for us and cook them in her microwave."

"Capital idea," said Ferdy, who had just emerged from the house after his late morning nap. He greeted his guests and then put his arm around his wife's waist.

"Capital idea, my foot, my beloved husband," Tamara said to him. "You haven't eaten a pizza, much less a frozen pizza, in your entire life." Turning to Caroline, she said, "I'm having our luncheon catered by your friend Pierre's place, Café Pavillion. As for future meals, I suppose I'll have to start interviewing cooks. How dreadful."

Clifford laughed. "Come now, Duchess. You're going to enjoy every minute of it," he said affectionately.

"She is at that," Ferdy agreed. "Now, why don't we all sit down and have a cocktail. I'll fetch Soames."

The duke disappeared into the house and returned moments later with his faithful butler, who took everyone's drink orders. Almost everyone's.

"Wait! You forgot about *me,* Soames," said Jack, tugging on the butler's black uniformed sleeve.

"Quite right," said Soames. "What will it be, Master Jack?"

Jack considered the question, then said, "I'd like a C and P, please. No ice."

Caroline looked at him with surprise. "What on earth is a C and P, may I ask?"

"It's a drink that's half Coke, half Pepsi. Brett taught it to me," Jack explained, acting very pleased with himself as Soames went back into the house.

"Brett?" asked Clifford, Tamara, and Ferdy simultaneously.

"A friend of Jack's," Caroline explained.

"Not that football player," said the duchess with disdain.

"Baseball player," Caroline corrected her.

"Brett Haas? The Hall of Fame third baseman for the Braves?" Clifford asked.

"Yup," said Jack proudly, his little chest puffed out. "We're buddies."

"You're lucky," said Clifford. "I've been a fan of his for years, but I've never met him."

Jack suddenly warmed to Clifford. "If you want, I'll tell you all about him," he said, then walked Clifford over to the table and sat down next to him.

Caroline shook her head. Her son never ceased to amaze her.

"Now, dear. Tell us about your progress with the new store," Ferdy said to Caroline, leading her and Tamara to the table. "How's the rebuilding going?"

Caroline was about to answer the duke's question when there was a loud commotion coming from inside the house. Sounds of dishes clattering and angry voices arguing echoed over the tiled patio, and before the duchess could register her dismay, Soames came rushing out, consternation written all over his face.

"There seems to be a slight problem in the kitchen, Your Highness," he said, trying to maintain his oh-so-British stiff upper lip.

"What is it, Soames? Did more staff flee the premises?" Tamara asked with a resigned sigh.

"Not yet, but they're threatening to," he replied. "You see, the gentleman Your Highness employed to cater the luncheon insists on rearranging your entire pantry."

"Why would the fellow do that?" asked Ferdy, who was eager for his cocktail. It was after one o'clock, for goodness sake. Why hadn't Soames brought his Scotch? "He's just a delivery boy, isn't he?"

Soames shook his head. "No, sir. Not this gentleman. He brought two delivery boys with him and then he instructed them to take over for the members of your staff."

"But that's preposterous. Is he demented?" the duchess asked.

"No, Your Highness. He's French," said Soames with distaste.

French? Caroline thought. But the gentleman Soames was describing didn't sound like Pierre Fontaine. Pierre didn't handle the at-home catering department at Café Pavillion. He had someone else oversee it. Besides, he would never barge into a client's home and try to take over the kitchen. Jean-Claude, on the other hand . . .

A smile crept across her face as it occurred to her that barging into a client's home and taking over the kitchen sounded exactly like Jean-Claude. No sooner did the realization sink in than the chef himself appeared on the terrace. He was tall and commanding, his handsome face the center of all eyes. He wore immaculate chef's whites, his name embroidered in canary yellow over the breast pocket of the tunic. With his customary dramatic flourish, he bowed to everyone and then announced himself.

"Bonjour, Mesdames et Monsieurs." He paused for a moment when his eyes lit on Clifford, whom his instincts told him was a potential rival. Nevertheless, his aplomb did not desert him. "I am Jean-Claude Fontaine, and I have come to serve you your lunch."

The duchess clasped her hands to her heart and nearly swooned with shock and delight. This was the Frenchman who had signed copies of his best-selling cookbook at Romance, Inc . . . the talented chef whose restaurant was the talk of Manhattan . . . the handsome bachelor who'd been out with nearly every famous woman in New York! Tamara was incredibly flattered that a man of Jean-Claude's renown would take it upon himself to cater *her* luncheon—personally! And then she realized *why* he was there: to impress Caroline. He had been courting her with luscious meals both in New York and Palm Beach, the duchess knew. Now he was using this luncheon to woo her yet again! It was arrogant and high-handed—and so romantic! But how would Clifford feel about it? He was Caroline's suitor, too. Was there an appropriate way to handle the situation? Tamara had no idea. Neither, she was sure, did Amy Vanderbilt. It was all too exciting, all too romantic—all too, too deliciously fraught!

Caroline got up from the table, walked over to Jean-Claude, and touched his arm. "This was very sweet of you." She smiled. "You didn't have to cater the meal yourself. Not when you only had a couple of days in Palm Beach."

He lowered his eyes to meet hers. "I had to see you, *chérie,*" he said. "You couldn't come to me, so I had to come to you, *n'est-ce pas?*"

She nodded. It had been months since she'd seen him, and he was as handsome and charismatic as ever.

"Jean-Claude, I want you to meet everybody," she said, taking him by the hand, bringing him over to the table, and introducing him to Clifford and the duke and duchess. "And this is Jack," she said, beaming at her son.

"Ah, Jacques," said Jean-Claude with a smile. "Your mother has told me a great deal about you. In fact, I've made you a very special lunch today. Something you are certain to enjoy."

"Oh, boy! Pizza!" Jack exclaimed.

Jean-Claude blanched and looked as if he'd been stabbed in the heart, but then he turned to Caroline and relaxed his expression.

"Your son is a joker, just like you," he said. "Pizza! At a formal luncheon! Hardly! I've made something that was my favorite when I was Jack's age."

"He wasn't joking," Caroline was about to say, when Jean-Claude's two assistants paraded out of the house carrying large gleaming silver trays laden with food. They set the first course in front of each guest, but it was Jean-Claude who personally served Jack, setting the *mouclade à la crème de fenouil* in front of him.

"Especially for you, Jacques," he said, bending down to place the elegant china plate in front of the boy. "When I was a child, I went with my father to the shore in the summers. We would search for *moules,* then bring them home and clean them for *grand-mère* to prepare. This particularly dish, made with leeks, fennel, curry, shallots, and cream, was my very favorite."

"Moules?" Jack asked, wrinkling his nose at the food before him. "What's that?"

"Mussels," Jean-Claude translated with obvious pride.

"Mussels? Yeech . . ." Jack began. He cut himself off when Caroline gave him a cautioning look.

"Everything looks lovely," she said, smiling at Jean-

Claude and thinking that one of her luncheon companions—probably Ferdy, since his appetite was enormous—would eat Jack's *mouclade* as well as his own and that she would feed her son a frozen pizza as soon as they got home.

"I'm still waiting for my drink," Ferdy said, becoming cranky. It was cocktail time, and Soames still hadn't brought his drink—or anyone else's.

"Right away, sir," said Soames, who hurried into the house again and returned later with drinks for everyone.

"My God! This is extraordinary! I still can't get over it!" the duchess cooed, beside herself with joy that the legendary Jean-Claude Fontaine had come to *her* house. To prepare *her* guests' lunch! Wait until her friends found out. Wait until Celeste found out—and Tamara would make sure she did.

"Caroline? Why don't you sit down next to me," Clifford suggested, eager to get her attention away from Jean-Claude. He had so much he wanted to catch up on, so much he wanted to say to her.

"Jean-Claude, do you mind?" Caroline asked, not knowing whether she should let him serve them or continue to talk to him. It was a strange situation in which she now found herself. She had been looking forward to seeing both Clifford *and* Jean-Claude again—but not at the same time!

"Please. Sit," Jean-Claude told her and pulled out her chair for her. "I want you to enjoy the food I have prepared. Now I must go back into the kitchen and finish the entrées. Then I will come out and join you. *D'accord?*"

Caroline answered with a slightly forced smile, trying to picture Jean-Claude and Clifford sitting together at the same table, with her between them.

Jean-Claude disappeared temporarily, and the rest of them ate their first courses—except Jack, who left his untouched and was so bored by the table talk, which centered around Romance, Inc., Ferdy's investments, and Tamara's portfolio, that he excused himself and wandered off by the pool.

At two-thirty, Jean-Claude reappeared. His two assistants followed, presenting a whole grilled salmon with a wild mushroom sauce and souffléed potatoes along with bottles of chilled white Meursault.

"Jack, honey?" Caroline called out to her son, whose legs were dangling over the side of the pool. "Time to come back to the table and eat."

"I'm not hungry, Mom," he said. "Can I just stay here awhile? Until you're done?"

Caroline was about to say no, but Tamara dissuaded her.

"Let him be," she said. "He's not interested in all this grown-up talk. Let him at least get his feet wet. He can change into his bathing suit later."

When Jean-Claude had finished serving the food, he pulled up a chair next to Caroline and joined everybody. Clifford did not look pleased, she noticed, particularly when the Frenchman began to hold court at the table, going on and on about a recent rave review of his restaurant in *Gourmet* magazine.

"I'm quite friendly with the CEO of the media conglomerate that owns *Gourmet,*" Clifford volunteered, his attempt at one-upmanship not lost on Caroline.

"Oh, you mean that man who does nothing but worry about the magazine's profits?" Jean-Claude said.

"Actually, the CEO I'm speaking of is a woman," Clifford said with a faint, self-satisfied sneer.

"Then I stand corrected," said Jean-Claude. "I must admit, I don't pay much attention to those numbers people. My acquaintances tend to be more creative types."

Caroline winced. Jean-Claude was putting down Clifford's financial expertise. For *her* benefit, obviously.

"That's very interesting," Clifford responded. "I've always thought of 'numbers people,' as you call us, as being about as creative as people can be. We're the ones who have to keep coming up with ways to keep you 'creative types' from going broke."

The duchess stole a glance at Ferdy and Caroline. All three of them knew they had become spectators at a verbal tennis match and that the intended trophy was Caroline.

Jean-Claude laughed. "Touché, my friend," he said to Clifford. "Perhaps I must consult you one day. So I don't go broke, I mean." He winked at Caroline. She smiled weakly, flattered, yet suddenly wondering if either of the two men was right for her.

Suddenly, Soames hurried out of the house, a worried look on his face. His starched shirt was looking wilted, and Soames himself was looking frazzled.

"What is it now," said the duke when the butler had reached the table.

"A gentleman insists on joining your party, sir," said Soames breathlessly.

They all turned to look at Jean-Claude, who shrugged.

"Whoever he is, he's not one of my people," he said, as puzzled as the others.

"Did this gentleman give his name, Soames?" Tamara asked.

Poor Soames would have responded, but he was silenced by the man who had wandered out onto the terrace, uninvited.

"The name's Brett Haas. How're y'all doin'?"

Caroline's jaw dropped. Was it possible that Brett had actually had the nerve to crash the duke and duchess's party?

She shook her head in disbelief, but there he was in all his color-blind splendor—this time, wearing shocking pink golf pants, an olive green polo shirt, and pale blue socks!

"What are you doing here?" she asked, as the others at the table were too stunned to speak.

"I came to see *you,* sweet cakes," he said, smiling that cocky smile of his. "I flew down a day early and went straight to your condo. When I rang the bell and you didn't answer, I tried Selma's place. She didn't want to tell me where you were—at first. But you know me, babe. I can sweet-talk a woman into anything. So here I am. You glad to see me?"

"She most certainly is not," the duchess snapped. She wasn't in the habit of having her parties crashed. Jean-Claude's appearance at her home had been enough of a shock, but at least he was a cultured, refined human being. This man was a barbarian!

"Chill out, Duchess. Why don't we let Caroline answer for herself," Brett told Tamara. "What do you say, sweetness? You glad to see me?"

The truth was, Caroline *was* glad to see him, more than she thought possible, and so when he pulled her up from her chair and took her in his arms, she found herself hugging him. And when he tilted her head back and kissed her passionately on the mouth, she kissed him back—in front of everyone! It was a completely spontaneous reaction. She literally couldn't help herself. When she had first seen Clifford and Jean-Claude again after so much time had elapsed, she had been happy, very happy, but also reserved. Something had held her back, and she had assumed it was the public nature of their reunions. So then why had she practically flown into Brett's embrace? Brett Haas, of all people! What did it all mean?

"Brett! Brett! Look at me! I'm over here!"

It was Jack, calling out to his hero from over by the pool. Caroline had never seen that look of ecstasy on his face. It was more than hero worship, she realized. It was genuine affection. Unconditional love.

"Hey, kid! Great to see ya." Brett waved, grinning at Jack, who had stood up and was now tiptoeing around the tiled perimeter of the pool.

"Watch me, Brett! Watch what I can do!" Jack cried as he accelerated his tiptoeing and was now running laps along the rim of the pool.

"Be careful, Jack," Caroline warned. "It's very slippery around the—"

That very instant Jack slipped and fell into the pool. Without a moment's hesitation, Brett rushed over and dove in, tacky clothes and all, and gathered the boy in his arms. They whispered a few words to each other and then, suddenly, both of them disappeared beneath the water!

"Jack! Brett! Oh my God!" Caroline screamed as she and the others ran toward the pool.

"Don't worry, *chérie. I'll* jump in and save them," said Jean-Claude, beginning to lift his chef's tunic over his head.

"No, *I'll* go in," said Clifford, loosening his tie.

"Well, *I'm* not going in," said Tamara, who had never seen the need to learn how to swim. "You go, Ferdy dear."

The duke took a long sip of his Scotch and then began to remove his ascot.

"I'll go in," Caroline shouted, frantic with worry. "Jack is my son and I can't let anything happen to him. And Brett is the man I love and I—"

She stopped midsentence as the others stared at her. The duke and duchess looked as if they might faint, and Clifford and Jean-Claude appeared shaken by her admission. She herself was shocked by the words she had blurted out! When had she realized that it was Brett she loved? At which moment had she felt it with every part of her, known it without a doubt? The moment he stepped onto Tamara's terrace? The moment he dove into the pool to rescue Jack? Or before that? Well before that? Perhaps when she had first laid eyes on him on the airplane. Or when they had danced in the rain. She didn't know and she didn't care. She just wanted his arms around her—as soon as possible.

"Did I hear what I think I heard?"

Caroline spun around in the direction of the voice. It was Brett! And Jack! They had come to the water's surface and were doing somersaults!

"You're both all right!" she cried, kneeling down by the edge of the pool. "You are, aren't you?"

"Boy, Mom. You sure get nervous over nothing." Jack giggled. "I was just doing a trick, pretending to fall into the pool. The kids do it all the time at the condo's pool. Brett knew what I was doing, didn't you, Brett?"

Brett swam over to Caroline and reached for her hand.

"You're dripping water all over me," she said, not knowing if she should drown Brett or kiss him. Whether he had known Jack was kidding or not, he had rushed into the pool either to save her son or join his fun. How could she get angry at him?

"Never mind that," he said, grinning from ear to ear, his hair, like his ghastly outfit, matted to his body. "I want you to repeat what you said before."

"I don't know what you're talking about," Caroline maintained.

"You want me to beg you? Is that it, sweet cakes?" said Brett, a twinkle in his eyes.

She nodded.

"All right. I *beg* you."

There wasn't any doubt in her mind. Not anymore. And there wasn't any reason to hide the truth from him—or from herself.

"I love you, Brett," she said in a low whisper, surprising even herself with the ease and confidence with which she spoke the words.

"Sorry. I didn't catch that," Brett teased. "Could you speak up? I must have gotten water in my ears or something."

Oh! He was incorrigible!

"I said I love you, Brett Haas," she said, loud enough for Tamara's neighbors to hear her.

In response, Brett turned to Jack, who was floating on his back, and said, "Did you hear that, kid? Your mother loves me!"

Jack smiled. "Oh, I already knew that," he said. "I was just waiting for her to admit it."

"You two!" Caroline laughed, her happiness filling her up.

"Now, how about *showing* me how you feel about me?" said Brett, tugging gently on Caroline's hand.

"How about showing *me?"* she countered.

"My pleasure, sweetness." Without missing a beat, Brett pulled her into the pool with him! When she came up out of the water, she squealed with the delight of a child and threw her arms around his neck.

"I love you, princess," he murmured, stroking her wet hair away from her face. "And I always will."

Forever and after, Caroline thought, tears filling her eyes as her son swam over to them. Brett lifted his right arm off her waist, extended it to Jack, inviting him into their circle, and then wrapped them in his strong arms.

"I love you both," he said with a catch in his voice, knowing without a doubt that it was true.

Epilogue

Four and a half weeks after Charles Goddard was indicted for conspiracy to commit murder and arson, Caroline stood at the entrance to what would become, within a few months, the second incarnation of Romance, Inc.'s Worth Avenue store. All the carpenters had left for the day, and she was alone in the quiet of the empty building. The space still smelled faintly of smoke and ashes, but reconstruction had already begun, and Caroline had no trouble envisioning the store the way she had originally intended it to look. The lighting that would make women glow . . . the sheer scrims dancing gently in the stirring air and creating a seductive, hypnotic background . . . the large terra-cotta pots of green plants . . . the soft music and romantic atmosphere.

As she surveyed the vast space, a space larger in square footage than all of 39 Patterson Avenue, Caroline contemplated how far she had come in her short life, how much she had suffered, how much she had learned, how much she had loved.

She thought back to her sad and lonely childhood, to her mother's distance and her father's violence, to her hopes for a new, more honest, more caring relationship with her parents. If it hadn't been for Al Shaw's intervention, for his willingness to share what he knew about Ray Lyons, for his decision to put years of bitterness and resentment behind him and help his daughter in the fight of her life, she wouldn't have Jack. . . .

She thought back to the Sunday at The Breakers when she was a fifteen-year-old with only her dreams to sustain her; to Francesca Palen who, by befriending her and giving her a silk scarf, had introduced her to a world where dreams did come true, where life was full of possibilities, where human beings, like great hotels, could be renewed and restored and become better and more beautiful than ever. . . .

She thought back to her job at L'Elegance, to the demanding, unpredictable but nevertheless delightful Tamara Brandt, without whom there would have been no place to learn, no way to find out about herself and her abilities, no avenue to experience, no Romance, Inc. Tamara had been aghast at Caroline's admission that she was in love with Brett Haas, the ruffian! But when the duchess realized how happy Brett made Caroline *and* Jack, she could hardly complain about the man. "Perhaps, if we send him to Ferdy's tailor," she had suggested one afternoon when Brett had showed up at Romance, Inc. wearing a green and magenta shirt. . . .

She thought back to James, her precious, precious James, the man who had given her the confidence to follow her dreams the way he had intended to follow his. He was the first person to really care about her, the first to believe in her. He had taught her that love wasn't only for storybooks and fantasies, had shown her that she could love and be loved, had changed her life and given her Jack, the living embodiment of that love. . . .

She thought back to Jean-Claude Fontaine, the dashing, often temperamental, tremendously talented Jean-Claude, who had pulled her out of her widowhood and into the land of the living by the sheer force of his charm. She did not love him—not in the way she loved Brett—but he had stirred a part of her that she had let die along with James. He had made her feel sexy, feminine, desirable, desired, and she would treasure their friendship always, particularly now that he intended to take over his father's restaurant and would be spending more time in Palm Beach. "Some things are not meant to be," he had said when it was clear that he and Caroline would not have a romantic future together. "But we must never say never, eh, *chérie?*" . . .

She thought back to Clifford Hamlin, her rock, her supporter, her adviser, the brilliant man who had literally saved her professional life and nearly risked his own in the process. He had been devastated that she had chosen to forge a lasting relationship with Brett and not with him, but, a gentleman to the core, he had given her his blessing. "I'd be lying if I said I'm pleased with the outcome of this contest," he had told her. "But I can't say I lost. Not really. I've *gained* something as a result of loving you, Caroline. I've gained the capacity for love. I used to think that work was my life. Now I know that there's more, I *want* more. For that, I'll always be grateful." "And I to you," Caroline had said, embracing him, knowing that while they would not be lovers after all, they would always be close business associates and dear, dear friends. . . .

She thought back to Brett Haas, a man who approached life as if it were a wonderful adventure; who treated each day as if it were his last; who made her feel lighthearted, carefree, joyous, and compensated for her childhood, where laughter was rare and happiness even rarer. She loved Brett with total abandon, her heart soaring whenever she even thought of him. He worshipped her, admired her, cherished her. And he adored her son as if Jack had been his own. She couldn't wait to meet Patsy, who would be arriving in Florida in mid-December, in time for the four of them to spend the Christmas holiday together. They would be a family, the kind of family Caroline had yearned for her entire life, four people who would stand by each other and take care of each other and love each other unconditionally . . . forever and after.

Yes, Caroline nodded as she crossed the threshold of the shop. Just as I am rebuilding the store, I have rebuilt my life. And this time, I will be stronger, sturdier, better able to withstand whatever may come, whatever the future may bring.

She turned the key in the door and locked up for the night.

Whatever the future may bring, she smiled, as she stepped out onto a nearly deserted Worth Avenue, into the brilliantly setting sun. . . .

Win a fabulous three-night getaway at The Breakers® Hotel in Palm Beach!

(Official Entry Form)

Name ______________________________

Address ______________________________

City/State ____________________ **Zip** __________

Daytime phone ______________________________

SEND ENTRIES TO:

POCKET BOOKS
"Win A Three-Night Getaway
at The Breakers®" Contest
Marketing Dept. — 13th floor
1230 Avenue of the Americas
New York, NY 10020

See next page for full contest details
and official rules

1186 (1of2)

Official Rules

1. No purchase necessary. To enter, submit the completed Official Entry Form (no copies allowed) or send your name, address, and daytime phone number on a 3" x 5" card to the Pocket Books "Win a three-night getaway at The Breakers®" Contest, Marketing Dept., 13th floor, 1230 Ave. of the Americas, New York, NY 10020, along with a 50 word or less essay stating your favorite romantic getaway. For Canadian residents submit your entry to: Distican "Win a three-night getaway at The Breakers®" Contest, Attn: Line Robbins, 35 Fulton Way, Richmond Hill, Ontario L4B 2N4. All entries must be original and the sole property of the entrant. All entries must be received by June 15, 1996. Pocket Books is not responsible for lost, late or misdirected mail. Each essay can only be entered once. Enter as often as you wish, but one entry per envelope.

2. Essays will be judged on the basis of originality (50%) and creativity (50%). Decisions of the judge(s) are final.

3. One entry per person. Entrants must be residents of the U.S. or Canada. Void P.R. and wherever else prohibited by law. Employees of Viacom, Inc., its suppliers, affiliates, agencies, participating retailers and their families are not eligible. All entries must be original and must not have been previously published or have won any awards.

4. Prize: Four days and three night stay at The Breakers® Hotel in Palm Beach, Florida for winner and guest. Includes round-trip coach airfare from major airport nearest winner, ground transportation to and from airport to Breakers® Hotel, 3 nights accommodations (double occupancy), and breakfast and dinner daily. Approximate retail value $2,000 U.S. Certain blackout dates apply and prize is subject to availability. Prize is not transferable and may not be substituted. Prize will be awarded provided qualified entries are received..

5. All federal, state and local taxes are the responsibility of the winner. Winner will be notified by mail and will be required to execute and return an Affidavit of Eligibility and release within 15 days of notification or an alternate winner will be selected.

6. If winner is Canadian resident, s/he must correctly answer a skill-based question administered by mail. Any litigation regarding the conduct and awarding of prizes may be submitted to the Regie des Loteries et Courses du Quebec.

7. Winner grants Pocket Books the right to use his/her name, likeness and entry for any advertising, promotion and publicity purposes without further compensation to or permission from the entrants.

8. For name of the winner, available after June 15, 1996, send a stamped self-addressed envelope to Prize Winner, Pocket Books "Win a three-night getaway to The Breakers®", Marketing Dept., 13th floor, 1230 Ave. of the Americas, New York, NY 10020. For a copy of the Official Rules, send a stamped self-addressed envelope to Official Rules, Pocket Books "Win a three-night getaway to The Breakers®", Marketing Dept., 13th floor, 1230 Ave. of the Americas, New York, NY 10020.

1186 (2of2)